A TANGLED WEB

"Why can't you just let me disappear?" Dulcie demanded.

"While you're my wife you're my responsibility. You must pretend to be my wife for your own good. You're too valuable to too many bad people, alone and unprotected. Do you understand?"

Crispin hardly heard his own words. All he could see was those wonderful eyes, awash with tears, and that sweet plump mouth so near to his. He traced the tear track with gentle wonder as she stared up at him, breathless. Then he lowered his head and brushed her lips with his. He meant to comfort her. Or reassure her, or himself, that she was really so fresh and lovely. But he was shocked by the electricity that coursed through him at her light, tentative touch. And so, against all reason, he had to seek whatever else he could from the warm sweet mouth beneath his. . . .

The Wedding

Edith Layton

POCKET BOOKS

New York   London   Toronto   Sydney   Tokyo   Singapore

This book is a work of fiction. Names, characters, places and incidents are products of the author's imagination or are used fictitiously. Any resemblance to actual events or locales or persons, living or dead, is entirely coincidental.

An *Original* Publication of POCKET BOOKS

POCKET BOOKS, a division of Simon & Schuster Inc.
1230 Avenue of the Americas, New York, NY 10020

ISBN: 0-671-88300-3

First Pocket Books printing May 1995

10 9 8 7 6 5 4 3 2 1

POCKET and colophon are registered trademarks of Simon & Schuster Inc.

Cover art by Danilo Ducak

Printed in the U.S.A.

CHAPTER

1

London, 1753

He thought he'd never laugh again. But when he looked up from the cobbles as he walked the gray streets of the city, he saw the man in front of him lose his hair—all at once.

There was nothing unusual about the fellow's fine curled gray bagwig, but Crispin's uninterested gaze suddenly sharpened when the wig began to waver on the man's head. As he watched, fascinated, he saw it slew a little to one side, droop to the other, and then all at once, as if realizing its ability to fly, stretch, rise on end, and then soar straight up into the gray sky of London Town. The gentleman, now as bald as a newborn, clapped his hands over his bare skull and screeched, "Thief! Thief!"—which showed he was a Londoner, for this had obviously happened to him before. While he shouted, his wig continued to rise like a slightly soiled dove into the grimy heavens. Laughter rose in Crispin's throat, shocking him into actually seeing the world around him again.

He glanced up just in time to see the wig thief silhouetted against the gray London sky as the boy bolted from his hiding place beside a chimneypot. Crispin watched the slight lad as he leaped onto the next rooftop, still carrying the fishing rod and line that he had used to snag his prize, and clutching the stolen wig tightly to his narrow chest as though he were a shepherd and it, a tender lambkin.

"Ho! There 'e is, the villain!" a fishmonger shouted, pointing. The men and women on the street looked up and saw the thief. They began running in pursuit, the shadow of the boy dancing his escape above them.

Crispin followed, laughing. It was a ridiculous thing to be doing, but the boy was nimble and clearly knew his rooftop passage well, and thief or not, he looked so merry and carefree that Crispin was entirely on his side. He followed anyway, because the hunt was on, the chase was up, and as long as he was running he couldn't brood about his fate.

An ill-assorted mob was soon lumbering down the street with him, staring upward and running onward. Costermongers, shopkeepers, ragmen, servant girls, and matrons all bobbed down the street as if swept along by some unseen current in the wake of the leaping, laughing lad so high above them. Crispin's long legs made such great strides that he soon led the pack. And just as soon he found that wasn't enough for him. He wanted to run freer and farther. He wanted to shrug off his stiff brocade coat, rip open his constricting vest, kick off his shoes, and fly down the dirty streets the way he'd run along the sweet hillsides and meadows as a boy. But he was a man now, and this was London. If he was fool enough to discard any garment in this neighborhood, it would be pounced on, stolen, and sold twice over before he could catch his breath.

He didn't mind losing his breath if it kept him from thinking of anything except the blood beating in his veins as he ran. He saw the boy turn and caper along a rooftop that led down a narrow alley, and he followed, with the mob tagging along behind him.

He was almost at the end of his endurance, with the crowd far behind, to judge from the echoes of their cries, when he lost sight of the boy. He stopped, his breath sawing in his chest, and stared upward. He saw chimneypots and clouds and an occasional wheeling gull . . . but no sign of the boy or the wig. The boy might have dropped down on the rooftop to hide and wait the mob out, but judging from the merry dance he'd led them, Crispin guessed that the imp had taken a leap in a different direction. While Crispin bent, hands on knees, recovering his breath, the mob thundered past him, continuing its pursuit. Before long he was left alone except for the echoes of their angry cries. Or so he thought.

He straightened at last, his breathing again normal. His blood cooled and his spirits plummeted. Once more he found himself alone with the real world and all his woes. He sighed. At least this was a loss in a good cause. Even though he had enjoyed the chase, he wished the little thief well; he realized that the theft of a man's wig would likely have cost the boy his head if he'd been caught. This way at least the wig would serve two masters; it would cover a new head, and the price for it would fill the lad's stomach.

Crispin smiled at the thought, buttoned his vest, pulled up his crumpled hose, straightened his coat, and began to retrace his steps—until he saw a movement. It was only a slight shifting of shape seen through the corner of his eye as he passed an alley. But he had been a real hunter, and a good one, once upon a time, when he'd had time for leisure and the pleasures of real sport. He stopped, patting his pockets as though checking to see if he'd lost anything out of them. He glanced around as he did. There was no one else in sight. In this crowded slum, that was rare enough to be miraculous. Everyone else was in full cry after the thief. Crispin quickly stepped into the alley.

The stench in the narrow alley was overwhelming. Most things that would have been garbage in a better district weren't thrown away here; like the inhabitants of the slum itself, anything that had an ounce of life left in it was used for something. Only real garbage, waste and debris too rank and worn to be of use to anything but mold and rats, lay in piles at the base of the buildings. But Crispin had seen a part of one of the piles move—a small brown tattered sleeve of it.

"You might as well come out," he remarked casually. "That mess you're hiding under will kill you faster than the mob will."

He spoke to the air, and got no answer.

"If I'd wanted to turn you in, I would have called them down on you by now, wouldn't I?" he asked impatiently. "Your arm is showing," he added helpfully, when he still got no answer, "and I refuse to so much as touch that vile muck you've buried yourself in."

"Right," a thin voice finally answered. "Yeah, too right. I don't blame you neither, sir. I'd be out of it like a shot myself if I could," the voice from the garbage said weakly.

Crispin braced himself and bent to the task before him. He ignored what he saw, the way he wished he could ignore what he smelled, and managed to remove much of the garbage, grimacing at what he might find there aside from the thief. But the eyes he suddenly found himself staring into were as desperate and terrified as any cornered rat's. They were indigo and hard and assessing beneath their panic. They were too old to belong to the thin boy Crispin had unearthed. He recognized at least one emotion in those eyes, and wished he hadn't.

"I wouldn't run if I were you," Crispin said quietly. "There might be worse than me at the alley's end."

"Naw. Right. Couldn't bolt," the boy said with bitterness, dropping the thick stick he'd raised. "Done my leg, I did, with that fall."

"Broken?" Crispin asked, reaching toward the thin leg beneath the filthy trousers.

"Think so," the boy said, wincing as Crispin prodded with gentle hands. "I can wiggle my toes, leastwise."

"Ah, well, if it is broken, at least it's a clean break," Crispin murmured, sitting back on his haunches and staring

4

at the boy. "But now what's to do, I wonder?" he muttered to himself.

"To do?" the boy asked in astonishment, "God, take the wig, it's yours fair 'n' square. Bring a pretty penny, it will, too," he said wistfully, looking down at the wig he still clutched to his chest. "Only don't rat on me, sir, and I'll make it up to you. I will, I promise. Willie Grab pays his debts, he does, you can be sure."

Despite himself, Crispin grinned again. The gray curls he saw protruding from the top of the urchin's shirt made unlikely chest hair.

"I don't want the wig, boy," he said, then stopped. He heard other voices coming near. He stood swiftly, positioning himself so his shadow fell over the boy. Crispin was tall and lean, but he was all muscle, so he cast a formidable shadow. He planted his feet apart, put his hands on his hips, and stared down the long alley.

A group of the boy's pursuers paused at the mouth of the alley and saw Crispin standing there. They hesitated.

Crispin glowered at them. He was dressed like a gentleman, yet with his breadth of shoulder and length of leg, he didn't look like the sort of man anyone would want to meet in an alley. And he looked angry—very angry. But not at them, it seemed.

"Ho!" a burly man finally called to him. "Have you found the villain, sir?"

"No, but I saw her run through here and then simply vanish!" Crispin said indignantly.

"*Her?*" one of them shouted. "Who the devil is *she*, sir?"

"Why, the wretch who robbed me," Crispin said. "She took my kisses and said she was taking me to her room, but she only brought me here, and then she vanished—with my purse! I looked away for only a moment. . . . I can't find a sign of her. Have you seen her? A pretty little piece, about sixteen, I'd say: a prime bit, all golden curls and with eyes as blue as a summer sky. She was wearing red, and her hat had a red feather in it, too," he added hopefully.

"If you looked away while doing yer trousers up again, then I'd say it were a fair cop, and more power to her," the man said, and the group with him laughed.

"I say!" Crispin said with a show of anger. "There's no call for mockery, fellow! Anyway, she took my whole purse, and she certainly wasn't worth it!"

They guffawed and, still laughing, left him standing in the alley.

"We'll wait until dark, I think," Crispin said to the boy.

"You wouldn't want to be here at dark, sir," the boy said, struggling up from the garbage again. "Naw. Just get me a crutch I can hobble on, and I'll be gone."

"Certainly, to the gallows," Crispin said in annoyance. "There are a hundred people out there looking for you, boy."

"Naw, there's a hunnerd lookin' for a *thief,* sir. Not for me. Get me a crutch and you'll see. There's a little shop two streets from here," the boy said with desperation, "two streets to the right. It ain't far, honest. It says Gentle's over the door. Anyways, even if it don't, everybody knows it. Just ask for old Watt. He'll have a walking stick, cheap. You don't have to put a penny down. Just ask for a crutch—an old one, mind—and say it's for me, Willie Grab, and he'll give it to you quick. He knows I'm as good as my word. Bring it to me, if you please, sir, and I'll be fine. I will, you'll see. I'll make it worth your while. I'll make it up to you, I promise."

He wasn't sure why he did it, but Crispin nodded. He left the alley and made his way to the shop the boy had told him about. He found it quickly. The sign above the door read "Gentle's," but more likely it had once read "Gentlemen's . . ." *something,* in its long distant past. The window was too dirty to see clearly into the shop, so Crispin opened the door and entered.

"May I help you, sir?" an old and dusty male voice said from somewhere behind the dingy counter.

"Ah, Willie Grab asked that I get him an old crutch. He'd said you'd have one, and that he'd make it up to you,"

Crispin said, so fascinated by the way he was actually doing what the boy asked that he failed to be surprised by how quickly his words produced a result.

A crutch slid over the counter. It was scarred and warped, and its cross brace was reinforced by a grimy rag wound over it, but it looked as though it could still bear weight.

"Thank you. I'm sure Willie will be pleased," Crispin said as he inspected the crutch.

"Tell young Will it's tallied. But the less said, the better," the old voice said, and when he heard no other sound, Crispin was sure he had been left alone.

He made his way back to the alley.

"Ah, that's the ticket!" the boy cried when he saw the stick. He struggled upright, wincing with pain, but he grinned when Crispin helped him place the stick under his arm.

"Now, then," the boy said in a brisk businesslike fashion, "my mug's too famous to be seen. I'll have to dirty it before I take a step further."

Crispin would have sworn there wasn't room for any more dirt on that thin, pinched face, but a few handfuls of earth from the alley soon obscured most of it, except for a wide, cocky grin.

"I'm a new man, guv'nor," the boy said. "Sure you don't want the wig? It's a prime one."

"No," Crispin said, bemused.

"Well, then, thanks and thanks again. Now I'll be off, and I'll be owing you."

"Wait!" Crispin said, because he didn't want that bright smile to vanish forever. Standing, the boy seemed smaller, and even the bulk of the stolen wig inside his shirt couldn't conceal the fact that he was rail thin. The way he rested on his stick showed he was in pain, and he seemed more vulnerable than ever. "I'll go with you," Crispin decided.

"'Fraid I'll do you out of your share?" Willie said, with a world-weary smile. "Never mind. I'll be glad of the company. Yeah, it'll suit fine, be icing on the disguise. Only call me

Dick or Tom if you talk to me out there, sir. Yeah, that's a good one: Tom."

They left the alley and went down the street together. The boy held up his injured leg and hopped along on his other foot. He grimaced and panted, and soon there were tear tracks on his intent face. But when Crispin offered to help him, he snatched his arm back. He teetered on his crutch and hissed, "Stay away! Leave me be! I'm a cripple, get it?"

He grimaced in exasperation when he saw Crispin's face. He lowered his voice to a whisper and explained. "Now, how's a crip going to pinch a wig and run with it, eh? And over the rooftops, too? Sure, that would be a treat to see. Not too likely, right? So leave me gimp, sir, and I'll be as safe as houses. Try and help me and everyone will notice. A gent helping a beggar boy? Now, that would be a sight, wouldn't it? Everyone would stare, and some might put two and two together. But a beggar trailing after a fine gent? Why, that's natural, ain't it? Makes me near invisible, see?"

Crispin was silent in the face of such shrewdness. He didn't like the way the boy was hopping painfully down the street, but he didn't see any way around it. It wasn't until they'd gone on for a while and the walls of the Fleet prison were in sight that the boy's discomfort seemed to vanish. He grinned widely, spun once around on his crutch, then rested his back against the gray wall of the prison.

"There we are," the boy said, sighing with satisfaction. "You done me a huge favor, and I'm owing you. Now, how can I make it up to you?" He looked at his rescuer as though seeing him for the first time.

He saw a tall, well-proportioned man with wide shoulders, a trim torso, and long shapely legs that had more than a gentleman's share of muscle to them. The gent wore his hair clubbed back in a queue, but it didn't look out of fashion, because his hair was thick and so light a brown as to be pale silver in the sunlight. The face was a gentleman's: free of the poor man's scars and blemishes, with skin as clear and smooth as only good and regular meals could produce. He was a handsome fellow, Willie thought, with a fine well-cut mouth, a straight, thin nose, and a determined chin. His eyes were large and deep blue, framed by long, starry black lashes a lass might envy. But despite the pretty features, there was nothing feminine about that face. "Elegant" was the word that came into Willie's crafty mind and stayed there, turning keys, opening doors to other possibilities.

He eyed Crispin carefully. His clothes were good, the shirt of fine linen and the vest, coat, and britches of excellent cut and quality. But they weren't new, and although clean, they weren't fresh from the press. Willie knew to a pence how much a man had in his pockets by the cut of the coat those pockets were in. This fellow, he thought shrewdly, had come down in the world, maybe only recently, but down, definitely. In fact, the gent's handkerchief would probably be worth more than his purse right now.

"Say," he said suddenly, "hold on. I think I know a way I can make it up to you right away. I think I really do."

Crispin smiled. "Not necessary, lad. How much farther have we got to go? You need to see a sawbones right away and get some good wood on that leg."

"I live here," Willie said with a shrug, "and we got more quacks inside than in a duck pond on a May morning. Some of them owe me, too. I know one who'll put my leg together faster than I snapped it, and mend it straight as an arrow, if he's not gut-drunk yet. Yeah. It ain't noon yet," he said, squinting up at the sky, "so I'll be fine with him. But I think I know of a job of work for you, guv'nor, one that will pay good, too. Afore you turn your nose up," he added quickly, seeing a slow grin begin on the gent's handsome face, "let me tell you it pays good and there ain't no work to it, and no danger in it neither."

"Then why is the position free?" Crispin asked.

"'Cause you got to know somebody to get it," Willie said, puffing out his thin chest. "An' you do—*me*. Come on. I'll tell you whilst we walk."

He picked up his crutch and hopped along as Crispin followed, intrigued. He needed money, Lord knew that, and it was only a sign of how much he needed it that the boy's sharp eyes had discovered it in spite of his best efforts. As they passed the first entry to the prison, some ruffians who had been lounging against a doorway there accosted Crispin.

"Hey, sir, need a girl?" one asked, while another added eagerly, "Pretty. Young and clean . . . No? Well, then, old and dirty? How about—"

"How 'bout puttin' a sock in it, Yert?" Willie said with disgust. "The gent's with me."

"Oho! It's a skinny lad 'e wants, is it?"

Before Crispin could move, Willie did. He grabbed the ruffian by his grimy neck stock and pulled so hard the fellow's surprised eyes were dragged down to a level with his. "Somethin' the matter with your ears, Yert?" Willie snarled. "Maybe you need a bit of hemp nice and tight around your neck to clear them. This gent's with me, I said."

The man swallowed as hard as he could with his throat still locked in that rough grasp. "Beggin' yer pardon, sir," he managed to say to Crispin, and then said it louder. Willie released him, and the man smiled sheepishly, ran a filthy finger around his neck, and said, "Only foolin', Willie lad, only a jest."

"Not funny," Willie said, and hopped on toward the next gate. Crispin followed, smiling and shaking his head, wonderfully diverted.

As they walked, they were approached by several other men who were eager to offer Crispin the services of women, matchmakers, fortune-tellers, attorneys, and doctors, until a word from Willie sent them away.

"There seem to be several thriving businesses around here," Crispin remarked. "Which are you engaged in?

"All," Willie said simply as he hopped through an entryway.

A guard standing there began to speak, but a nod from

Willie made him grin. He touched a finger to his forehead in mock salute and, after a glance at Crispin, waved him on, too. Crispin followed Willie into the vast confines of the Fleet prison. He noticed the signs that adorned all the walls inside, advertising everything from the lawyers and doctors he'd been offered, to all sorts of tradesmen and women.

"And these enterprises are run from the prison?" Crispin asked incredulously.

"You ain't from Lunnon, then. Thought so," Willie muttered, before he answered, "Sure. Why not? Just 'cause a chap's body is in jail don't mean he leaves his wits outside, does it? If a fellow can mend a boot or another man, why should he just sit on his hands while he serves his time at the king's pleasure?"

Speechless, Crispin nodded. The jail in his district at home wasn't seen as a career opportunity for prisoners. But he was far, far from home now. And the practice did make sense. The only flaw in this system was that crime was meant to be punished, not made profitable for the criminal. But as he went farther into the deep recesses of the Fleet prison, he saw that with so many prisoners in London, the rules for crime and punishment would be as different from what he was used to as everything else was these days for him. He looked around in wonder. He'd seen the canals of Venice and the cathedrals in Rome; he'd crossed the Alps and tasted the pleasures of Paris, but he'd never seen a place like this. The prison seemed to go on forever. There were at least as many people within the gates as on the streets outside. It was a city in itself.

The ancient, tilted buildings were a jumbled mass of old and dirty gray, dusty stone; they looked dismal and sorry but the pavements and courtyards surrounding them were teeming with vibrant life.

There were vendors selling their wares from push carts and baskets, crying out the price and condition of everything from fish to flowers. People shouted their orders from high barred windows and threw down coins to pay for them. With a nod and a wink, the items were wrapped and handed to boys who raced upstairs with them. There were cleaning women armed with brushes and mops hurrying to their jobs, barbers and bloodletters hastening about their business with their trays and cutlery. People were strolling as well as running, dressed as fine as fivepence or as poor as beggars. The place overflowed with life, and Crispin couldn't tell visitor from prisoner.

A long covered table gave off the scent of fresh-baked bread and pies to tease his nose. As they passed it, Willie flipped up a corner of the cloth, filched a bun for himself and tossed one to Crispin with a wink.

"Here! You young villain," a buxom woman shouted, as she came rushing from the building to box his ears. "Oh, Willie," she said fondly when she saw him, "you'll like them. They're all over currents." She lowered her floury hands, spread her apron, and curtsied to Crispin, saying, "Sir." Then she looked up at him with a frank invitation to more than her honeybuns in her sparkling eyes.

Crispin was accustomed to being stared at by women, and he was not particularly interested in the baker's overblown charms. Still, he bowed to her as though she were a lady. She put her hand to her heart and sighed as he walked on.

"She can bake as good as she looks, but I wouldn't go near her" Willie commented through a mouthful of sweet bun. "She done her man in with a cleaver. The judge thought she was as sweet as her apple pies, so she didn't have to walk on air. But she ain't walking out of here for a while, neither, that's certain."

"Thank you for the hint," Crispin said dryly. He hadn't been so well entertained in years. Certainly not in weeks, he thought. But Willie didn't give him time to think more.

"Here we are," Willie said, and disappeared inside a small dark doorway.

Crispin followed, ducking his head as he did. Now he

could tell he was in a prison. The room he followed Willie into was dark and dank, and the small high windows were barred. The furnishings, however, were lavish, though mismatched and outlandish. A silken couch was pushed up to a wall where satin draperies hung over the barred windows. Several delicate chairs were grouped around a magnificent mahogany desk, which dominated the room. When his eyes adjusted to the murky light, Crispin saw a middle-aged man sitting behind the huge desk. He wore a fine bagwig and his coat was made of an excellent slubbed silk, but the cuffs of his shirt were not clean, and though he'd recently shaved, it was clear that he would never shave his blue cheeks entirely clean. He was as pale as milk, and his thin mouth wore a smile that never showed in his light, calculating eyes. Crispin grew wary. Shake hands with that one, he thought, and count my fingers after.

"Why, Willie my lad, who is this fine gentleman you've brought to see me?" the man asked genially, looking up. "May I help you, sir?"

"He's just that, Harry. A fine gent," Willie said before Crispin could speak. "He helped me out of a tight spot. See, I broke a stem, on a wignapping lay," Willie said, gesturing to his leg, and then proudly produced the wig from beneath his shirt. "Took it off a Mr. Wigsby with a pole and a hook. Rum flash, ain't it?" he asked proudly. "I swiped it clean, and was on the fly across the rooftops when I missed a step and came down like thunder. But this here gent didn't peach on me when he found me. And he helped me here. So afore I go see the leech, I thought I'd bring him to see you as a favor to him—and to you. See, I thought he'd be able to do a good spot of work for you. You know," Willie prompted when the man didn't speak. "The trouble you been having with John Finch and all. Come on, Harry. Use your eyes. Did you ever see a finer groom?"

"Perhaps not," the man he'd called Harry said thoughtfully. "Perhaps not."

"I'm afraid Willie didn't understand," Crispin said quickly. "I merely came along to see him safely home. I'm not looking for a position. I've never worked as a groom," he added, startled at the thought, wondering how much his appearance had deteriorated in the weeks since his fortunes had changed.

"I never doubted it," the man said, "which is why, perhaps, you'd make such an excellent one. Yes. So you would. Good work, Willie. No, sir, you don't look like a groom to me, either. But you do look like a fine groom. Ha, ha," he said with an artificial laugh. "You're not from London Town, are you?" he said when the harsh laughter stopped. "Well, there's sense in what I said, I assure you. At least, *here* there is. Ah, you run along now, Willie lad, and I'll have a word or two with your gent . . . Mr.—ah?" he asked delicately.

"West, Crispin West," Crispin said truthfully. He was honest enough to give his name, if not all of it, and certainly not his title. That, he thought, would be not only unnecessary but mad as well.

"Mr. West . . ." Harry began, but frowned as Willie said, "No, thanks, Harry, I'll stay and see what's what, I think."

"But your leg," Harry said, shaking his head. "Do you think it wise?"

"It's broke now," Willie said. "That won't change for a while, so what's the hurry? I'm staying, Harry," he added in a harder voice, and the man gave him a glinting look, then shrugged and turned to Crispin.

"My name is Harry Meech," he said smoothly, "and the lad's right: I might have work for you. You're a gentleman, Mr. West. Anyone can see that. But if you don't mind my saying so, it occurs to me that you might be interested in a job of work?"

Crispin could almost feel the one lone coin in his pocket cry out an answer before he could. The sweet bun Willie had filched had been his breakfast and his luncheon, and might be his dinner as well. This was a terrible man, no doubt, in a terrible place. But a job of work would mean that Crispin wouldn't have to smile and pretend he'd just eaten when he called on his friends tonight. The pretending was getting harder every day.

"I might," Crispin admitted, settling himself in the chair Harry Meech indicated and hoping that the pinch of hunger in his gut hadn't made him wear more than a politely interested smile.

"Ah, well," Harry said. "Let me explain it clearly, then. I am in need of a groom. Not for my horses," he said, holding up one hand, "but for a bride. For several of them, in point of fact."

Crispin got up from his chair. "I do not think," he said through clenched teeth, "that this is a very funny jest."

"So it is not," Harry said gravely. "It is mortal truth. Stay, please, and hear me out. I run several rigs here, Mr. West. I don't live here, though. I only work here."

"He *used* to live here," Willie put in.

Harry frowned again. "Well, that was then," he went on, with a stiff little smile. "I'm wiser now, and in no hurry to live here again, if you get my meaning, Mr. West. So all that I do, I do with circumspection," he said proudly. "One of my enterprises is the bridegroom lay—that is to say," he added when he saw one of Crispin's thin finely arched brows rise in inquiry, "I provide bridegrooms for females who need them. For purposes of debt, Mr. West. I don't *procure* men for women."

"Only women for men," Willie muttered, and earned another hard glance from Harry, before he went on, "I *certainly* wouldn't ask you to involve yourself in anything like procurement, Mr. West. No, all I need is a fine-looking, well-spoken gentleman to marry women who find themselves in ruinous debt."

He saw total incomprehension on Crispin's face, and sighed. He got up from behind his desk and paced in front of it before he swung around and confronted Crispin. "If a female discovers herself up to her ears in debt, what becomes of her? I ask you, sir."

"I imagine she must find a way to pay," Crispin said.

"Yes. Or else she ends up in prison until she can pay, which is difficult to do from here. Ah, the poor dears. They end up selling themselves or, worse, they never leave this prison. So what can they do? Why, marry, of course. Marry. Then their husband becomes responsible for their debts. Ah, but what if the poor dears can't find a man willing to take on their debts, much less their hand in marriage? Why, then there's nothing to do but come here and stay forever, or until they earn enough to pay whatever they owe. It's tragic. Which is why I see myself as their benefactor. What I do is provide husbands for these poor wretched creatures."

Willie groaned, but when Harry glowered at him he stared down at his leg, as if it was that which had pained him.

"Yes, well, I can see that's it's a problem," Crispin said, rising, "Come along, Willie, let's get you to that doctor. I have no money, Mr. Meech, and so I'm afraid I can't help you. And there's no way I wish to marry now."

"Don't be such a thick head," Willie snapped. "Listen to the man. Do you think I'd haul you here to grab your gold? Really!" he said with disgust.

"Inelegant but correct," Harry said. "I don't need your money, Mr. West, just your hand—and for a quarter of an hour, not a lifetime—and your name, whatever name you wish to use, because," he said before Crispin could say anything, "it will change on each wedding certificate you sign. You see? It's a practical solution to a cruel problem. We supply men to wed all of these dear creatures. I have three or four bridegrooms presently working for me.

"Here," he said, holding up a finger, "look. The bride. I introduce her to her groom." He held up another finger. "She pays a fee, the vicar pronounces them man and wife." He smiled and crossed his fingers. "He documents the glad event on a wedding certificate—carefully dated the day *before* her debts were incurred, of course. What's in a date?" he asked jovially. "You're a man of the world, sir. I put it to you: is it better to clap a poor lass in prison for years, or for life, because of a debt, or simply to move a few days or weeks about on a bit of paper and thus free her to earn an honest livelihood? It is a sensible solution to a senseless law, is it not?"

He nodded at Crispin's thoughtful expression. "Exactly," Harry said and went on. "Then her groom signs the marriage register as, say, Mr. Black. And then they part," he said, moving the two fingers apart again. "Forever. The bride gives her wedding certificate to her debtors. They search high and low for Mr. Black, but he is nowhere to be found, because he does not exist. So the debt is discharged and the bride goes free, as does the groom. Everyone is happy except the debtors, and my sympathy, I assure you, is not with them. Neat, is it not?"

Crispin thought for a moment. "No one notices that it is a false name?" he finally asked.

"No one ever bothers to say anything about it. There is only me, the false groom, and the poor beset bride. And the vicar of course, but he is nicely paid and addled to boot. Come, now, Mr. West, it's a common enough practice. Think about it. How do any of us know any fellow's true name? Why, no offense meant, but you might not be Mr. West after all. You might be Mr. Black or even Lord West, for all I know," Harry said and, seeing Crispin's sudden start, added quickly, "as I might not be Harry Meech for that matter."

"Might not?" Willie muttered, gazing innocently at the ceiling.

"How is anyone to know?" Harry continued. "And who is to care? I assure you, Mr. West, no one cares. I have men who have married a dozen females and who are still free bachelors in every sense of the word. It is an easy job, a good living, Mr. West, a choice position."

"Then why do you need me?" Crispin asked.

"Because, sir, females are fussy, even the worst of them—women who slop hogs for a living as well as ladies born. If I present them with a low and badly spoken gent, they'll turn up their noses and go to a competitor. Oh, yes, this is a competitive business. So my bridegrooms are well spoken and good-looking, the sort a female can put her trust in. Such men are difficult to find around here. My grooms inspire trust, Mr. West, and frankly, so do you."

"Yeah. Silky Frankie is as handsome as he can stare," Willie agreed, "and John Finch used to be one of the best pimps in town afore he got on the bottle."

Harry scowled at him, but Crispin laughed. Willie's comment was what he'd needed. A good bucket of cold water on a scheme that had momentarily looked much too warm and tempting to him.

"I am afraid this is not for me, Mr. Meech," Crispin said with genuine regret.

"Ah, well, at least, Mr. West, say 'not yet,'" Harry said.

Crispin chuckled and nodded his agreement.

"A glass of wine, then, to show good feelings all 'round!" Harry shouted to someone unseen. When there was no reply he made a great show of annoyance, begged Crispin to wait only a moment, and left him and Willie alone in the room.

"Too bad," Willie sighed. "You'd do, and it's a rum lay. Harry's no better than he should be, but he's got a good thing here. And he *is* having trouble with John Finch these days. . . . Well, then, sir, what are you going to do?"

"Is need so visible, then?" Crispin asked, amused.

"It's never *in*visible," Willie said seriously. "So what are you going to do?" he persisted.

"Why, I suppose I'll just go on with what I've been doing," Crispin said, smiling sadly and speaking the absolute truth. "I'll wait for my ship to come in."

Harry finally came back with a bottle and glasses and poured out three drinks. Crispin was going to protest when he saw the brimming glass that Harry handed to Willie, but then he thought of the boy's broken leg and was silent. He remained silent when he saw how neatly Willie downed it and smacked his lips afterward.

"Well, then, Mr. West, let us get young Willie here to the sawbones, shall we?" Harry finally said, and led them from the room.

They walked together, but once out in the entryway, Harry turned to the left as Willie swung to the right. Crispin stopped, wondering which of them to follow. Willie hopped on for a few steps more and then, seeing he was alone, looked back. When he saw where Harry was standing, waiting for him, he grinned brightly, struck the side of his head with his hand, and said, "Oi! What was I thinkin' of? Right. Let's go, Harry," and returned to him.

They entered the room next to Harry's. It, too, was strangely furnished with elegant mismatched chairs and couches, but it was also occupied by several mismatched people. And it seemed to be a scene from Bedlam rather than the Fleet prison.

There was no doctor there, but there *was* a minister. He was old, and his wig was so crooked that the fine, straggly white hair beneath it formed a halo all around his long, seamed face. The vicar was beaming at a couple standing before him, and he seemed to be holding on to his Bible for support as he frequently listed from side to side. As he did so, he hummed tunelessly to himself. Two big grinning oafs in rough clothes stood on either side of him, completing the strange bridal party.

It was the unhappy couple, however, who caught and held Crispin's attention. The groom was a tall, well-dressed man who was obviously completely besotted—and not only by love.

"Now come, m'dear," the groom said in slurred accents. "Gimme a kiss before signing. I vow I've never seen a prettier minx, have you?" he asked the grinning louts. "What a pretty piece for poor old Frankie. I tell you what!" he said with gusto as he leaned forward to try to gather the shrinking bride into his arms. "I think this one will be a real one for me. I think you are my destiny, love," he said ardently. "We shall suit exactly, my little bride. God in heaven, did you ever see such eyes? The exact color of the . . . of the nectar in my glass. Where is my glass?" he demanded, releasing his bride to look down at his hands as though he might discover a glass in one of them if he looked hard enough.

Crispin couldn't stop looking at her.

She was neatly if not fashionably dressed in a blue gown trimmed with fine old lace. And she was unexpectedly lovely. He had a fleeting impression of a trim, curved figure and fine regular features set in a very white face. She wore no wig, only the masses of her own honey-colored hair, and her huge eyes were indeed the golden brown of fine whiskey. But it was the tears in them that he noticed immediately, and the absolute terror he saw reflected in them moved him.

"I cannot," she whispered to the vicar. "No, no, I will not. Please, forget my request; I will not wed this man, not even in a counterfeit wedding."

"Oh, what's the matter, lovey?" the groom crooned. "Getting cold feet? No matter. I will warm them," he promised as she shrank from him.

Crispin turned to Harry, who was beaming at the wedding party. "I see," he said resignedly. "The bride is a debtor, I take it?"

Harry's grin widened.

"And the groom is the troublesome Mr. Finch, no doubt?"

Willie whistled. "There ain't no flies on you," he said in admiration.

"And of course there is no one else to wed her?" Crispin asked.

"Why, no, not today, and I believe she said the bailiffs are coming tomorrow," Harry answered with pleasure.

"I'll marry her. I have no other honorable choice, do I?" Crispin said with a long sigh. "But just this one, Mr. Meech."

"Of course, of course," Harry said happily.

"And what name shall I give the vicar—aside from Fool?" Crispin asked wearily.

"What you will, Mr. West, whatever you will, sir," Harry said, as he signaled his men to remove John Finch and bring Crispin forward to meet his bride.

CHAPTER

2

She would not cry. Crying would make her absolutely defenseless and rob her of her breath and her dignity. And she needed both now. She called on her pride and all of her wisdom as she searched for a neat, sensible solution to her problem, and then she closed her eyes and prayed that when she opened them again she'd be gone from this awful place and that none of this would ever have happened.

"Mistress?" she heard a man's voice say. "Mistress Dulcie? I think we have found a solution to your problem."

Only death or an angel from heaven could solve her problems now, she thought. But she pushed back the terrible weight of the tears behind her eyes, swallowed down the leaden ones rising from her throat, and said as clearly as she could, "Yes?"

"Mr. Finch was obviously indisposed. I'm shocked and terribly sorry," Harry Meech said, as though he'd no idea of how drunk Finch had been when he'd ordered his men to drag him out from under a table at the inn.

"I believe we have an acceptable substitute at hand. Mistress Dulcie Blessing, it is my pleasure to introduce . . ." He cleared his throat and stared at Crispin.

"Ah . . . Mr. Black," Crispin said, as he looked down in fascination at the young woman before him.

"Mr. Black," Harry repeated with a grin. "It will be his pleasure to act as your groom this day, my dear."

"My *great* pleasure," Crispin said in a soft voice. He wondered what this beautiful young woman had done to come to such a terrible pass.

It was more than her beauty that intrigued him, although her eyes were fine and her mouth was soft and tempting. It was that she was so unusual and unexpected in this place. She was clean, for one thing. Her neck was free not only of jewelry but also of the dirt he often saw on the necks of ladies of high fashion as well as those of low birth. Her skin was fine and clear, and her hair shone even in the dim light. She was slender and small; the top of her beautiful head came just to his chin. And she was vulnerable. He didn't know what it was about her that made him think this. Perhaps it was her trembling hands or her downcast eyes. Whatever it was, she seemed to need him. He might not be able to help himself, but he was determined to help her, if he could.

"Mistress Dulcie?" he said softly. "Don't be afraid. I'll go through this charade with you, and then I'll trouble you no more. Is that all right? Is it what you want?"

She raised her eyes to his. She had no idea how this perfect gentleman could have appeared to replace the lout who had terrified her, unless he was actually the answer to her prayer. She knew better than that, but there was no other way to account for his presence. He was tall and fine-featured, the face of the angel she had requested. She stared at his long eyelashes until she became aware of the quick understanding in his azure eyes, and then she caught her breath and looked away from his face. She couldn't imagine why such a man had to earn his bread by pretending to wed strange females, an occupation without honor. She had to avail herself of his services, so she had no right to judge him, but for someone of his stature to have sunk to such deception! She had no choice, but he . . . ?

And yet, and yet . . . he seemed to be capable of taking on all her problems and fears, as well as her enormous burden of debt. She knew it was a fantasy, but she was glad to give him her hand, if only for that moment. She would pretend it was for all time. She nodded, and gave him her hand.

"Thank you," she said.

"Proceed," Crispin told the vicar.

"Dearly beloved," the old man began.

When the service was ended, Crispin clasped the bride's hand warmly before letting it go so that he could sign the register. Only then did he tear his gaze from her and carefully examine the paper the minister thrust at him. Her name was entered as Mistress Dulcie Dawn Blessing, but there was none listed for him for him to sign his alias over.

A glint of intelligence appeared in the old vicar's mad eyes.

"No name. You gave me no name, sir. Shall I register you as Mr. No-Name, then, sir? Or as Lord No-Name, perhaps?" He tittered.

"It's Black, Mr. Black, Mr. . . . Ebon Black," Crispin said, and turned to see his false bride blush at his foolish play on words.

"Ebon Black," the minister said with a high-pitched laugh as he scrawled on the paper.

Dulcie signed and then passed the paper to Crispin.

"Thank you," she told him in her throaty voice. "You can't know how your kindness has helped me today. It was a hard thing to do," she said, ducking her head. "I almost didn't come here, but I had no choice. I'll try to live my life so I'll never have a reason to regret what I did today. I don't want to remember anything about it except your part in it. I'll always remember you with gratitude, sir. Thank you."

"I wish I could have done more," he said gently, and meant it. If he'd still had his fortune, he could have done so much more for her. Now he could offer her nothing. But he saw fear spring into her eyes again and realized she wondered what "more" he meant.

"My part in this is over, I assure you," he said. "I only meant that I would wish my part in this profited you more than for just this hour."

"It has," she said with relief. "Oh, believe me, it has. I felt like a cheat and a criminal until you came along. You make it seem . . . better. Thank you."

"The paper," the minister whined, pushing it at him for him to sign.

"If you can't write, make your sign. Harry here will swear it was you," Willie said. "It don't matter what you put down. Frankie Silk's sign is the ace of spades, so that won't do, but any other old mark will. Mine's a windmill," he added helpfully.

"I can write," Crispin said distractedly still staring at the bride's face. Barely looking, he scrawled his own initials on the paper.

"A toast to the happy couple," Harry said.

"No, thank you," Dulcie said. "I must get back to my father. I have a dozen things to do."

She took a leather bag from her pocket and gave it to Harry. He shook it once, listened to the coins jingle, then smiled and handed her a copy of her marriage lines. She took it, dropped a swift curtsy, and after one last swift glance back at Crispin, went quickly out the door.

Harry rummaged in the little bag, brought out a heavy coin, and handed it to Crispin. "For you," he said, as Willie's eyes widened.

"The pay won't always be so grand, but, since it's your maiden voyage, so to speak, take it." Harry said with a shrug.

"I'm not sure you should be so generous," Crispin commented, looking at the coin he was turning around and around in his long fingers. "I don't know if I'll ever be back."

"Oh, well, life's a gamble, isn't it? And I'm a gambler. I think we'll meet again," Harry said, chuckling.

"I doubt it," Crispin said, and hoped to God he was right. He turned to Willie. "We ought to get that leg taken care of," he told the boy. Use this to pay the doctor." He handed Willie the coin, though he felt the pain of loss down to his toes as he did so. He saw Willie hesitate and added, "You found me the job of work, and it only took a moment. That leg needs mending. I have two good ones to go out and find other employment with."

The boy's thin cheeks grew red. "Ah, well, see," he muttered, "I ain't so sure it's broke, after all. See, I figured you wouldn't be as quick to turn in a kid with a broken leg." He handed back the coin and said decisively, "Keep it. You don't owe me nothing anyways. Saved my neck, didn't you?"

"Well, since it refuses to leave me, I'll keep it for a reminder—for good luck" Crispin said with a sad smile. He dropped the coin into his pocket. "Thank you, gentlemen," he said, sweeping them a bow, "for a most educational and enlightening morning. Good day."

When he was gone, Willie sighed. "Nice gent," he said wistfully. "Hope I see him again."

"Oh, we will. Never doubt it," Harry said. "It's like the cat who found the cream—now he knows where the money is, he'll be back. Now, then," he said, turning to the minister, who was staring into space, "let's see that register, and we'll settle up with you. Is it a bottle or a coin you'll have for your services today?"

The rheumy old eyes focused on Harry, and the lines on the old man's face shifted as he smiled beatifically. "Ah, but I have already been rewarded," he said in a cracked voice. "I have realized my fondest, dearest dream. My dearest, fondest dream. Ah, yes, I have. Have you ever seen such a bride as the one I gave to that dear boy?"

"A bottle, I guess," Harry said in disgust. "See to it," he commanded one of the oafs who had witnessed the wedding.

Harry wandered over to the old man's desk and glanced down at the bridal register. And then stood stock still, reading it again. And then over again.

It was over! It was done! Dulcie took the worn stone steps two at a time as she raced upstairs to tell her father. She would ordinarily have climbed the long stairway slowly, sunk in sorrow as she passed cells on the lower floors which were warmer in winter and cooler in summer. Her father couldn't afford such luxury, but at least he had a private room to call his own. If she hadn't gone through with the plan, he would soon have been moved into a cell with dozens of common criminals. But she'd actually done the incredible thing, the vile, awful thing: she'd married and not married. And yes, it was a lie, but no one would be hurt by it, and she was free! She felt as if a heavy weight had been lifted from her heart. Joy gave her the extra energy to fly up the last of the steps.

She threw open the door to her father's room and was about to shout the glad news when she saw that he had company. She closed her mouth.

"Dulcie!" her father said happily. "See who has come to visit us!"

"I see," she said quietly.

"Well? Do we behold a blushing bride? Come, child, did you do it?" Jerome Snode said eagerly.

Dulcie despised Jerome, who lived in the next cell and was full of schemes. Her father said there was no harm in him, and perhaps he was right, but she thought he was full of mischief. He was the one who had arranged her false marriage. She thought he was a coward and a braggart, and she didn't trust him, but it was so good to see her father smile again that she almost forgot her misgivings.

That was her father's and her own fatal flaw, she remembered sadly. They forgot too much too often. Her father never remembered how many of his schemes had failed when he heard about a new one, and when he smiled, Dulcie always forgot how angry she was with him. That had to be a trait she had inherited from her father, because her mother certainly didn't suffer from a soft heart. She'd left them both years ago. Dulcie's mother might be treated like a lackey by her sister, and it *was* true that her sister took too much pleasure in reminding her of her folly in marrying Philip in the first place, but at least she ate regularly, dressed nicely, slept well at night, and didn't go in fear of the bailiffs.

But, Dulcie reminded herself, she didn't take after her father in everything. She couldn't tell a lie without blushing, for one thing. Her father said he never lied, and in a way, it was true. He always believed so firmly in whatever scheme he was running that he actually convinced himself that he was telling the truth. He had really believed in that ratty treasure map he'd brought home that time, the one that had led him to raise money to hunt for buried treasure. The one that had made them pack in the night and leave Bristol double-quick, before their investors found out the captain of the ship they'd hired had floated out to sea on all the whiskey he'd bought with their money.

Her father also believed in the silver polish he'd invested in and sold—a preparation made of bat dung, spider silk, and caustic acid that had eaten through silver, their earnings, and their friendships with investors. He'd believed in those and in all of the other schemes, which had failed so utterly that he had finally landed here in debtor's prison for life, or until he could talk his way out. Or talk his daughter into taking on his debts and then marrying a stranger so he could be free.

Father and daughter weren't much alike in other ways, either. Philip Blessing made friends easily, while his daughter was deeply distrustful of strangers—perhaps because of the way they'd had to keep moving to escape the violence with which his former friends always wound up threatening them.

Dulcie didn't look like him, either. He had gray eyes and had once had fair hair. Now he carried a little paunch on his slight frame, and most of the hair had left his small, well-shaped head. He was glib and well-spoken, and his eyes twinkled. He could sell anything to anyone. The problem was that his merchandise was like the jewels from a bad fairy, for the visions they bought always turned to tears.

"Yes. It's done. I married," Dulcie said curtly, handing her father the certificate their last coins had bought them. He snatched it up, and Jerome peered over his shoulder at it.

Two heads bent low over the marriage certificate. Then two pairs of eyes stared up at her.

"This is a joke?" her father asked.

"No. Everything went the way Harry Meech said it would, except that the bridegroom he arranged for me was drunk, so he got another. A gentleman, Papa," she said softly, her eyes begging him to believe what she scarcely did, "a real gentleman, I think. Not that it matters," she added with a sigh for her own foolishness.

"Oh, but it might," Jerome said with too much pleasure. "Oh, indeed, it might."

First, he went back to the docks. It was a stupid thing to do, and Crispin knew it, but like a man who has lost his watch and keeps patting his pocket expecting to find it there, he couldn't stop returning to the docks. And then there was the matter of money. He had none, and had to think of a way to get some so he could leave London. The docks were as good a place as any to think. He had spent weeks there doing just that while he waited for his ships.

They still had not come in. One look down the wharfs told him that. Two of his berths were still empty, and the third now held a vessel called the *Relentless,* not one of the ships he wanted to see.

"Ho! My lord!" a rough man called to him. "Sorry, but she just limped in," he said, indicating the *Relentless.* "We give 'er the space, seein' as 'ow there's been no sight nor sound . . ."

"No word?" Crispin asked, but knew the answer before he saw the man's averted eyes.

"None," the man said gently. "The cap'n of the *Relentless* come that route and said as to 'ow it couldn't been otherwise. 'Twas a turrible time, yer lordship, 'twas somethin' turrible to 'ear tell."

It was a bright and windy day, and as Crispin stood on the wharf and inhaled the sea air, he avoided the eyes of the other who waited there. People who hoped for miracles: boys who dreamed of growing old enough to leave the land; sailors who had grown old or who had lost limbs or eyes but whose souls still rode the high seas; men who had lost everything but their souls to the mighty sea. Like him, he thought, staring out at the horizon.

It had made such good sense. There was no flaw in his reasoning. Even now he knew he had done the right thing.

Along with his title he had inherited something terrible. Not the usual sort of noble ghost but something as frightening and twice as destructive: debt. His grandfather, the fifth Viscount West, had lost the family fortune in the South Sea bubble. His father had repaired some of their fortune, but the family still had nowhere near enough to keep their land. Without the land, the fortune would soon vanish again.

The South Sea bubble had been a swindle, and his grandfather a rash gambler. His own father had been overcautious because of that. Crispin couldn't afford to be either rash or cautious. When he inherited the troubled estate, he asked questions, read books, consulted experts. Money bought money, if a man invested it wisely, and foreign investment was a good idea. New lands were opening; tobacco, spices, sugar, and cotton were in demand. Nothing he could do in England could earn him such profits, so this wasn't a gamble so much as an investment.

He'd gone to school with rich and noble boys whose families owned plantations in the New World. Satisfied with their huge established fortunes, those boys, now grown men, were content to live on the proceeds from their holdings in the New World, and so with lazy, well-fed goodwill they offered Crispin a chance to dabble in commerce for them. Crispin didn't deceive himself. He knew this would be a onetime venture. He would make more money than his investors would, and when they realized that, they would probably decide to cut him out. Rich men were lazy, but not foolish. But by then he would have invested his share in his own plantations and more ships.

Crispin had raised enough money to finance three ships. He'd picked the finest captains and let them fit their ships with true and tried crews. He'd forged contracts abroad and at home and accepted some financing from his oldest friends. But most of the money was his—the last of it. It had seemed like a foolproof scheme.

But he had forgotten about the hand of God.

An Atlantic storm had struck, a fierce wind of the kind born in the tropics in that latitude, a full month after the season for such storms had passed. The tempest had raged through the islands and colonies he'd traded with, and still, the growers had gotten their harvest in and on his ships before the storm hit. Everything had gone as he'd planned.

But then his ships had been lost: captains, crew, and cargo.

One of the vessels had been seen fleeing before the wind; another was said to have foundered near the first. The last ship had not been seen since it had left safe harbor. There had been no further sign of them. Crispin had asked every captain, every sailor, if he had news of his ships, but no one ever did. They were gone, along with his future. He grieved for the loss of life, and accepted that one death had been his own. This marked the end of the life he had known, for now he would have to sell his birthright, if he could break the entail, and certainly everything else he owned, in order to pay his debts.

His hopes were gone, Crispin thought, staring out at the wide sea, gone in one mad gamble. And until now he had not been a gambler, as Harry Meech had been. Thinking of that made him remember the one heavy coin in his pocket. He stared down at it, tempted to fling it in the sea. But the sea had taken enough from him. He would keep the coin, he decided, dropping it back into his pocket, as a reminder of how low a man could sink.

He would not borrow any more money from his friends. They had been feeding him for weeks, deftly and discreetly. He had let them, thinking he would make it up to them when his ships came in, but now he knew they never would. He had to eat tonight, though, and he would need to pay his fare back home.

He shrugged out of his fine jacket and rolled up his shirtsleeves. The crew of the *Relentless* would need help unloading.

"Hey! Captain!" he called from the dock. "Can you use another man?"

The captain squinted down at him. "Not afraid to get your clothes dirty, my fine fellow?" he called jovially, thinking Crispin a drunken gent or one out for a lark.

"More afraid of starving, I think," Crispin called back.

"Then aye, lend a hand or a back!" the captain called, and winked to his first mate, determined to give the pretty fellow the dirtiest work and see how long he was willing to keep up the jest.

"Thanks," cried Crispin, as he hurried up the gangplank.

"Soak 'em in brine," said the sailor who had been working beside Crispin, staring at Crispin's hands. "Luckily there's a bit o' that about. I been served meat patties looked healthier than your hands," he said with a low whistle as he took a better look. "You must've been ashore a while, laddie."

"So I have," Crispin said, gazing at his torn hands.

"Aye, it's whiskey or salt water they'll be needing, for sure, to stop the bleeding," the sailor said wisely, "and brine's cheaper this season."

Crispin nodded and, after bracing himself, plunged his

hands into a bucket of salt water. He closed his eyes until he could hear again over the roaring in his ears, and when the cold water had blessedly numbed his hands, he withdrew them. The salt had stopped the bleeding, but he doubted that he could get his gloves on again. He shrugged, and remembered the handkerchief in his pocket.

"Would you mind doing the honors?" he asked the sailor, as he gingerly withdrew his handkerchief.

The man whistled at the quality of the linen handkerchief, and Crispin realized he must have filthied his shirt and trousers so much no one could tell that they had been made for a gentleman.

"Right- or left-handed?" the sailor asked.

"Clever fellow. Right," Crispin said, then watched as one blistered, oozing hand was securely wrapped. He thrust the other in his pocket, and straightened as much as his aching back would permit. His shoulders, however, were beyond aching. He'd worked all afternoon unloading cargo, but he hadn't earned much. Still, three more days of work and he might be able to afford an outside seat on the coach home. Unfortunately he would have to spend some for food and lodging. He couldn't return to his friends' fine London rooms for dinner, for they would see him, and know the truth. Better to spend a few of his hard-earned coins for dinner near the wharves.

Pride had a high price, he mused, tucking his jacket under his arm before he walked on, but it was one he would gladly pay. Disgrace, he reckoned, would be costlier, at least for him.

The old man looked into his glass and sighed with pleasure.

"A fine day's work. I have done a good day's work," he repeated with contentment. He sat by himself near the hearth and congratulated himself. Since no one at the inn ever listened to him, no one would hear him now. He was certainly mad, and not even amusingly so. He didn't endanger or offend anyone enough to be taken away and locked up, nor had he any relatives to worry about his besmirching the family name. He always seemed to have at least a coin in his pocket, so he was ignored, except when he called for more drink. Business was business, and the old man was a sponge. He might have been half sane without the gin, some thought, when anyone bothered to think of him at all.

He was dazed with age, and some strange process aside from the gin muddled his mind further. At times, like mist rising from the ground, his brain was swept clear of confusion, and everything became stunningly, heartbreakingly clear. And then, just as suddenly, it was all gone from him again. That was why he drank, if anyone cared. No one did.

"He told me his name," he said to the glass, because he was both drunk and clear at the moment, and the only thing that would listen to him was the gin, "as if he had to! I knew him when . . . when," he murmured, the tears starting to course down his seamed cheeks, "when he was a babe. I knew his name at the baptismal font! I gave him his name! As if I didn't remember him!"

He sat still for a moment, remembering with the cruel clarity that had come to him the minute he'd laid eyes on the young bridegroom that afternoon. He remembered when he had known the viscount; he had been the respected vicar in his village. He had watched the babe grow to boy and then to youth, in those days of his own glory, when his parishioners had praised him, his wife had loved him, the bishop had promised advancement, and the world had been constantly clear to him. Before the mists and the drink and the slow progression to disgrace, dishonor, loss of livelihood and family, and finally memory itself. The road that had led him to this place in London.

In those long gone days, when he had worn another face, the face of youth and dignity, he had known the viscount as well as he'd known him today, whatever false name the boy had given him. And so he had written down his true name quickly, before confusion could snatch it away from him again.

In that stunning moment of clarity, he'd been happy for the young lord, and pleased and proud to unite him with such a beautiful bride. He had said the service and written everything down in a firm hand, as in the old days. When he was done, the young lord had absently scrawled his initials. He had done so quickly and thoughtlessly, no doubt anxious to get to his beautiful young bride. But he had signed his own initials.

"Married them, oh, such a handsome couple. A beautiful couple," he told a passing serving wench.

She was a kind girl and paused to hear him out, because there were tears on his old face.

"Married the dish and the spoon, the cow and the moon, the lord and his lady together," the old man said, because the mists were closing in again.

"Aye, you did, I'm sure you did, Grandfather," she said, and patted his hand before she bustled back to the kitchen.

"I did," he whispered. "I married the seventh Viscount West, Crispin George Thomas Knightly, of Darnley Hall, to Mistress Dulcie Dawn Blessing. Before God and man, if there is nothing else I know, I know that it is so. Before man and God, it is."

CHAPTER

3

Crispin waited for her in the salon. His linen was fresh, his coat pressed, his wounded hands had healed enough for him to cover them with fine soft kid gloves. He was clean shaven, and his hair was pulled back in a neat queue. He would enjoy his wardrobe and the services of his valet while he still had them. That wouldn't be for long, for he meant to give the servants notice, but he had a more important notice to give first.

He had arrived home late the night before. It was only early morning now, but he had to see her. Of all the things he had to do now, this was the first, the most important, and the most painful, but he had to do it before the rumors began. It would not be easy, but if he could no longer give her his love, he could at least leave her with consideration.

He breathed in deeply as she glided through the doorway. Her every movement was so graceful that she seemed to float toward him.

"Crispin!" she breathed, and came straight into his embrace.

She was dressed in creamy, delicate lace. But none of it so exquisite as the fine lady who wore it. Blond, with large blue eyes and a straight nose over a small plump mouth, of small stature, with a slender, graceful figure, she was justly an acclaimed beauty. Her gown showed off her tiny waist, and the fashionable cut of it forced her small, plump breasts upward, crowding them together, like roses bunched in a sweet bouquet, their swelling tops exposed to his gaze. Once, in a garden at midnight, he'd bent his head and pressed his lips to that breast and felt that flawless petal-soft skin against his heated cheek before he'd drawn back, dizzy with desire. That one fleeting touch had nearly broken his control—and control was absolutely necessary with the lady who had promised to be his bride. She was to have been his forever, and he had known that what they would have was too valuable for him to sully with clumsy, premature desire.

Her physical beauty was in keeping with every other thing about her. It was rare to find beauty, charm, and high birth all in one lovely woman. She was witty, high-spirited, and always charming. He'd had many women, but his desire for her was so intertwined with his desire to make her his in every way that his lust transcended anything he'd felt before. That one moment of privileged intimacy with her had meant more to him than an hour in any brothel he'd ever patronized.

She put her cheek to his, and he smelled jasmine as he stood for a moment breathing in her scent. His hands went to her tiny waist before he remembered that he no longer had the right to hold her. He dropped his hands and kissed her cheek and then her mouth—lightly, because he was desperate to have one last taste of her. Then, trembling slightly from the effort of withholding so much, he stepped back.

She arched one thin brow.

"You call that a kiss? Gone an entire month, and returned with not so much as a real kiss for me? Tell me how I've offended you, my dear," she teased, suspecting a jest.

"*I* have offended," he said quickly, because he had to say the thing straight out or never say it at all. "I no longer have the right to kiss you, love. I've lost all my money, Charlotte, every last bit of silver. I'm searching my pockets for copper now. The ships were lost at sea—all of them," he said bluntly as she stared at him in astonishment, "with everything I owned and begged and borrowed aboard them. No fault of mine, or theirs. A great storm, heavy seas, and so I'm rolled up, love. I have my teeth and my hair and my whole skin, so the saintly would say I shouldn't complain. But I have nothing else. I've lost all I own, and so I've lost you as well." He concentrated on keeping his voice to its usual calm irony, and almost succeeded. He wore a small grimace as he added, "I'm sorry. You can't know how sorry."

"Oh, Crispin," she said, staring into his eyes in disbelief, her own eyes as blue and stormy as the sea. "Oh, Crispin," she sighed, with dawning comprehension. "Truly?"

He nodded. She stared a moment longer and then turned in a flurry of her skirts and paced to the windows, where she stood, looking out blindly. In a moment she turned back to him, shock and pity gone. It was what he had expected, and yet his heart sank when he saw it.

"Oh, my," she said on a long sigh. "Oh, my, oh, my, oh, my. Oh, blast. I'm sorry. I'm so sorry. I had so looked forward to our future together. We would have been so good for each other, wouldn't we?"

He couldn't answer. His hands were fists at his sides, and though he felt like hitting something, he suddenly felt drained, too weak and tired to raise a finger. He had only enough strength to control his face and voice.

"Is there no hope?" she asked.

"None, for at least the next decade, I should think," he said. "I'll work to advance myself, but I'll likely be starting with less than your footman. At least if he saved his wages, and didn't send them to sea."

She placed her hand on his. "What's done is done. But wait! Would a loan from my papa be of help?"

"Perhaps," he said, pained to see the dawning hope in her eyes, but eager to put it out, because it was not based on reality, "a sizable loan might take three or four years off my projected term of recovery. But I can't even promise that, not really. No, the truth is that I'm sunk as surely as my ships are. I'll have to strip the estate, sell off everything that's not entailed, and then look for an investment. I get to keep my title, of course," he said with a crooked smile, "and my education. But that's all."

"Oh, lord," she sighed. And then straightened her slender shoulders. "Then there's nothing for it?" she asked.

"Nothing I can see," he said lightly, hoping beyond foolish hope that she would offer to wait for him. He knew he couldn't accept the offer, but he longed to hear it. It would warm his long exile.

"Ah, well. So be it. What's the sense in pining?" she murmured, before she said in more normal tones, "So. How do we go about this?"

"Very simply," he said with forced calm, his lips white. "You put a notice in the *Times*. That's all. If friends ask, or even foes, tell them the truth."

"Oh, no, Crispin. How can I tell them the truth?"

"Don't fret, you won't be telling tales. Everyone will know anyway. I had mortgaged the London house to the rooftop, so that will be gone when the next payment comes due. I can't sell Darnley Hall, because of the entail, but I'm here to close it up, make it a rest home for spiders until I come about—or my heir does. That's what I've come home to do. So don't worry about being tactful or saving face," he said with a gentle smile, though his eyes still devoured her. "The world will know soon enough."

"It's not a matter of saving *your* face, Crispin; it's trying to save mine from blushes. My dear, just think!" she said with a rueful look at his puzzlement. "Won't I look like a monster saying: 'Oh, yes, it's been called off. I dropped Crispin the moment I heard he lost his fortune'? It will look bad, my dear. You must see that."

He watched as she paced the room. She was right, of course. She knew the proper thing to do—as he would have, if he'd still had his wits about him. But they seemed to have vanished with his fortune. Lady Charlotte Barrington, as clever as she was beautiful, was not a fool for love.

She had been born and bred to wealth and privilege, and the moment Crispin had lost his money he had lost her as well, and he knew it. He couldn't picture her in rented rooms with him, stirring a pot of soup. The notion was obscene. She was a fine lady who couldn't begin to imagine the world he must now enter. Charlotte wouldn't believe how he had earned the few coins in his pocket now, and if he had told her, she would have been appalled. Poverty didn't exist for such a rare and beautiful creature. It was first her father's and then her husband's duty to see that the thought of it never intruded upon her. A poor man should have no place in her life.

The only time a lady might even notice a man without money was after long years of marriage to a gentleman of fortune. That was when she might find a handsome footman or groom interesting company in the night. But otherwise, a man without funds was not a man to her. Crispin couldn't blame her for that any more than he could blame the sun for rising. It was the nature of things. But that didn't stop the pain.

"Say, then, that when I lost my fortune I called off the engagement and refused to let you make the sacrifice of staying with me," he said.

"Oh, pooh, and who will believe that?"

"Why, but it is so," he said softly.

"Well, of course. You're a gentleman. I know that. But it's what they'll say about my letting you do it that's the problem."

He desperately wanted this interview to be over and done with so that he could remember how they used to flirt and joke together, how she constantly watched his face for his approval. "Say, then," he said with sudden inspiration, "that I told you I was leaving the country and wouldn't take you with me."

"Why, that should suffice," she said thoughtfully. "Yes, that will do it, even if you don't leave. Thank you, Crispin. But," she said staring at him for a long moment, regret clear in her eyes, "are you entirely sure, my dear? Because I . . . I wasn't fibbing when I said I set my sights on you when I first saw you. Remember? Years ago, that afternoon party, at the Stantons'?"

"With you not out yet, but with all the airs of a great lady. I knew you would be a handful," he said, laughing, remembering. Then his eyes grew bleak and all the laughter was gone as he said, "I'm sorry, but I'm very certain."

"Is there anything I can do to help?" she asked. "Do you—do you have enough funds to get by until the sale? I have some money from my allowance and . . ."

He had never seen the self-assured Lady Charlotte blush. "No," he said, before he saw more than he wanted to see, "but thank you. And good-bye."

He turned and blindly sought the door. But before he reached it he heard her wail, "Oh, Crispin!" He turned to find her in his arms, her lips seeking his. She'd never kissed him with such fire. Her embraces were always like her chatter, full of charm and teasing. But now she clung to him and kissed him as a woman might. Her mouth was warm and clinging. He answered her kiss with his whole heart, even though he knew he should not. He had been cold and lost for so long that he kept promising himself another minute until all thought fled his mind.

She was the one reluctantly who ended the kiss. When she drew away, she was shaking, but she was smiling and her eyes were filled with wisdom. She touched his lips with one finger and smiled a tremulous smile.

"So handsome," she whispered. "Such a mouth. Someday we will be together," she said fervently, "and in not so long a time, not really. You'll see, Crispin. You and I are fated, you know. Everyone said what a fine couple we'd make, and still we shall. Someday when I've done my duty and fulfilled my vows, we'll be together, I promise."

He blinked. "Do you mean to poison your new husband, love?"

She gave him a tearful, trembling smile, but it was the new wisdom in her eyes that bothered him. "Silly—no. I mean that I intend to live my own life someday, come what may."

"You mean, someday when you've married someone else and had his children, and are free to play?" he asked, beginning to understand, and not liking what he was hearing.

He didn't know why her words should disturb him so much. Such affairs were commonplace, but he had never thought of such behavior in terms of himself or anyone he really loved. Infidelity was a thing he'd always expected would come *after* marriage, and in the way of such things, like old age and death, he supposed it was something he thought would never happen to him.

"Of course," she said. "Oh, but it won't be long. Not really. I'm only nineteen. It could be"—she closed her eyes and calculated, then opened them, and excitement shone in their blue depths—"in as little as ten years. It sounds like a lifetime, and I suppose in some ways it is, but I'll still be young. And so will you—at least relatively so. And if I accept Prendergast," she said with sudden inspiration, "perhaps even in three years, because he's a widower who already has his heirs, you know, and so should only require one babe of me. Oh, famous!" she said, her eyes glowing.

"And if you had married me," he asked, cocking his head as he gazed at her, "would you have taken someone else as your lover after, say, ten years?"

"Oh, who can say?" she said impatiently. "Likely, I suppose. That's how long it takes for the bloom to wear off the rose, isn't it? Why, just look at my own mama and papa. It happens. *C'est la vie.*" She shrugged.

"Not with my parents," he said quietly.

"Ah, but they had financial problems, did they not? And lived in the countryside. Oh, what a face! You could curdle milk! Don't tell me you're a moralist, Crispin, for I shan't believe it," she cried gaily. "I know of several opera dancers who will deny it, you know. And Lady Walton and Lady Stanton and . . . Oh, I'll spare your blushes. But I know," she said, making the wise little face that had always made him laugh.

He didn't smile.

"Come. Really," she said with a hint of annoyance. "You didn't ask for my fidelity when you proposed marriage, did you?"

"I did not think to," he admitted.

"And rightly so, not wishing to ask me for a promise you'd no intention of keeping yourself. Really, Crispin," she said, stamping her foot in vexation. "Are we bourgeois little shopkeepers or Bible pounders or the like? No. I know the way of the *ton* and of the gentlemen in it. What are we to do when you fine gents start eyeing the chambermaids?" she asked flirtatiously. She took a step away from him and pointed her fan at him in mock accusation.

"We females can expect passion from you for a fivemonth, then restlessness while we poor creatures breed. Then you men dandle a tot or two on your knee and stifle a yawn in our beds not long after. That's the way of it. Then one day we go to the opera and see you already there with an interesting companion, or plans for one, after. The next time, we sit in our box with an attentive companion of our own, and you sit in the orchestra with your choice for the evening. You've seen it a dozen times. It doesn't even require speaking of. Very civilized and satisfying, I understand. I look the other way, and so then do you. Sauce for the goose, my dear.

"We cannot wed," she said firmly, snapping her fan closed, all teasing gone from her voice, "but we will have each other, when we can, when *I* can—you first, and you only, for so long as you wish. That I do promise you." She laid her hand on his heart. "I must go to my husband a virgin. He must be sure my first child is his. After that I can and will make my own life. Oh, please smile, Crispin. At least come kiss me. What more can I offer you?" she asked sadly.

"I don't know," he said.

He knew she spoke the truth. And she *had* promised him whatever love she could offer in the future. He could ask no more of her. Indeed, he knew he ought to be grateful, but he wasn't. He couldn't think of pleasure ten years in the future, and he was not inclined to contemplate leftovers. Not when he wondered how he would be able to eat in ten days. Not when he thought of how she would have to pass the next years in her lawful husband's bed.

"Good-bye, my love," he said, and didn't kiss her or let her embrace him. He knew he had no right.

"You're sure you want me to take them, Crispin?" Andrew Moffit said anxiously, eyeing the horses standing in the paddock before them. "They're very fine animals."

"So they are," Crispin said, "and believe me I'm grateful that my horses aren't included in the entail. They, my carriages, and a collection of tin soldiers I found in the attics are about the only things that aren't," he mused as his old friend and neighbor looked at him and swallowed hard.

"What about Wrede?" Andrew said. "He's your oldest friend, and rolling in gold. Wouldn't he want them?"

The earl of Wrede wouldn't want them. But he'd buy them out of kindness to his friend, Crispin thought, even though Wrede had given enough already.

"No," Crispin said with amusement he didn't feel, "Wrede's stable is well stocked with horses, believe me. As are those of my other friends."

"You could get a fortune for them in London," his neighbor persisted, though he couldn't take his gaze from the horses.

"Not quite a fortune," Crispin said dryly, and then laughed, "Oh, take them, man. You've coveted them forever, and fine as they are, still you've given me a price so near to charity, I almost refused it. Almost—but not quite. Go on, Drew, I mean it," he said gently. "They're sound beasts, and I know you'll treat them well. I'd be grateful if you'd take the dogs too. They'll eat too much, and they won't contribute much to the hunt but noise, but the staff I've left here are on pensions, and I don't want them doing without so that those foolish hounds can be fed."

His servants knew of his love for the dogs, and his old butler had offered to keep the hounds. Crispin chuckled with genuine humor. "Can you see old Mansfield fighting for a soupbone with Sounder? You keep them, Drew."

"Of course I'll take them, and glad to do so," Drew said at once. "I only wish you'd let me do more. But, Crispin, if you've sold the carriages, and I'm taking your horses, how will you get to London?"

"There are coaches for hire, you know," Crispin said gently. His friend looked at him in horror, and he laughed. He didn't mention that he intended to buy an outside seat on the mail, not because gents did that sometimes for sport but because it was the cheapest way to ride.

He soon found out why it was so cheap, and why every coachman he'd ever seen had a nose as red as the side lanterns of his coach on foggy nights. Nothing but raw rum staved off the chill of a damp windy night, and certainly nothing else was strong enough to keep a man hanging on to his precarious perch high atop a rocking coach as it bumped and rattled along the long road to London. Crispin had never known how many ruts the roads had, or how ridiculously easy it was for frozen fingers to lose their grip after a few hours aloft. After only a few dark, cold hours sitting atop the coach, a man grew weary. Incredibly enough, in all his frigid misery, Crispin even grew sleepy—at least sleepy enough to forget that the only thing between him and the road he was being jounced over was eight feet of air.

So, too, must exhausted sailors droop in their high seats in the masts and come to imagine the billowing sea below as a comforting pillow, he thought the first time the rhythm of the road lulled him to careless drowsiness. But the thought of the turbulent, treacherous sea woke him to bitter reality. That, and another offer of rum and the singing of his fellow sufferers high atop the coach.

None sang so loud, however, as the handsome young gent with the starry eyes. Everyone agreed that it was peculiar how a fellow with such a fine voice insisted on singing sea chanties as if they were dirges, how his rendition of that usually rousing ditty, "I Saw Three Ships A-Sailing, Oh!" was so filled with grief and mournfulness that it reduced even the heartiest lads among them to easy tears.

"I've found rooms!" Dulcie announced as soon as she entered her father's cell and regained enough breath to speak. "Only two, but then, there are only two of us, aren't there?" She giggled, ignoring the ever-visiting Jerome Snode, not caring if she sounded foolish. She'd come to pack up her papa's things and to take them, and him, back to those two blessed rooms with her at last.

"They're not much," she admitted as she dropped the huge carpetbag she'd wrestled up the long stairs, "but at least they're nowhere near here. You can't see the Fleet from the windows even if you stick your head out. And we'll be on the fourth floor. It's high, I know," she said hastily, "but at least it's not beneath the roof. The landlady said there are public cookstoves not three doors down the street—two of them. Just think! No more bought meals for you, my dear sir. *I* shall do the cooking!"

She'd do the washing on the banks of the Thames if she had to, and smile about it. Because her father was free, and if she could take him from here and help him find a decent job of work, there might be a chance for them yet. They'd try here, and if not here, then there. She'd heard of lands across the sea where penniless people went. Places where strong men and women could make new lives for themselves. Disgruntled Puritans had gone there, and adventurers were going there too. And paupers. It was true that many such places were filled with savages and strange beasts, but accounts she'd read said some of those places were very like England itself had been a few hundred years ago. That might appeal to her father. He was very proud of their ancestors, after all.

The Blessings weren't of the nobility, but Papa always bragged that his ancestors had been here to fight William the Conqueror when he came. The fact that they had lost didn't matter. They were here first. Her father also claimed that he had a distant cousin who was remotely related to a baron. Papa's own father had been a landowner, but soon after Dulcie was born, Philip had lost the farm and acreage in an ill-fated complexion cream scheme that hadn't removed pimples so much as it had removed complexions.

But her papa could read and write and had an education that almost equipped him for a great many things. He was such a persuasive speaker that she was sure he could acquire a job as a clerk or a salesman, if he would only apply himself—and stay far from evil companions. She glared at Jerome Snode.

Jerome was a medium-sized man in his twenties or thirties or forties. He had straight brown hair and small features on his smooth face. He looked like half the men in any crowd. He was so instantly forgettable, in fact, that if he'd any grace at all he would have been a wonderful pickpocket. His hands were his only distinguishing feature —almost all palm, very broad, and short-fingered. His hands and his smile were the most noticeable things about him, Dulcie thought. And they were both unexpected and unpleasant. Jerome, too, was in jail for debt. He claimed it was all a misunderstanding, which would be righted when he received certain letters from home. Privately Dulcie thought he meant to say it would be righted when he found the right victim far from home.

She was as relieved that her father was free now as she was that he had no money to lose. She knew that her father admired Jerome, and she suspected Jerome dealt in disreputable schemes. At least her father truly believed each of his schemes would be the salvation of mankind; she knew Jerome was only after his own comfort—and her father's gratitude.

It was Jerome who had arranged for her to take on her father's creditors and transfer his debts to her name. He was the one who set up interviews with their creditors and produced false papers to show them that she would soon be gainfully employed and capable of paying off the debts. When the only position she could find was in a millinery shop, and that at such staggeringly poor wages that she estimated she might be able to pay off the debts in a century or two, he was the one who had proposed the false wedding. And arranged it. The fact that he could so easily pick false documents out of the air and devise such schemes spoke volumes to her. But not to her father.

She wished Jerome would say or do one thing to verify her belief that he had villainous designs on her, just so her father could see it. But although Jerome's bland blue eyes often watched her with unnerving concentration, he was never anything but polite to her. He never made a lecherous move, but he never ceased to watch her, either. She feared him more than the men belowstairs who howled like the brutes they were when she hurried past their cells. At least her father knew what they were, and would protect her, and himself, from them.

"Well, then, this is good-bye, dear friend," her father told Jerome, putting out his hand for Jerome to take in his own broad one.

"Only for now, dear fellow," Jerome said smoothly. "I shall soon be calling upon you for tea, my friend."

Dulcie repressed a snort and hurriedly placed her father's neatly folded clothes to her bag.

"And upon our dear viscountess as well," Jerome added, with a side look to Dulcie.

Her father laughed at Dulcie's puzzled expression. "Guess what, my dear? It transpires that the gentleman who 'wed' you was a gentleman indeed. Jerome vows he was no less than a viscount."

Dulcie's hands stilled on a coat she held. That would explain his gentility, his soft, cultured, comforting voice that still calmed her broken dreams in the night. But, she thought, getting on with her packing, it meant nothing to her.

"Poor fellow," her father continued.

"Poor indeed, to have to stoop to such employment," she said harshly.

"Still, to be a noblewoman . . ." Jerome persisted.

"And still to be impoverished? What use is a title when there's not a cent in it? A man can't eat honors and titles. Noblemen have to eat as well as we poor common folk do."

"Ah, yes, too true," Jerome said, flashing one of those smiles she detested. "But a viscountess," he persisted. "Something could be made of that, surely."

"By his mother, or perhaps his wife. Not by me," she said as she packed the last of her father's few garments. "Although what gain there is in a title with no money for *anyone,* I cannot say."

"Ah, well, just a thought, because neither can I, try as I might," Jerome muttered.

"My poor Dulcie," her father jested, "to be wed to a nobleman and still to be penniless."

"And still to be free, Papa," she reminded him. "Don't forget that."

Jerome smiled in such an oily way that she hoped her father saw it. She almost wished she really had married the hapless viscount, impoverished or not, for even though she was getting her father back, she still felt very much alone.

Crispin relished his last nights in his town house almost as much as he had his first ones. Taking up residence in the house was the first thing he'd done to establish his independence when he was a young man, down from university, a decade past, a lifetime since. He had prowled the rooms, surveying his realm, wrapped in his silken nightrobes, as full of himself as any Eastern potentate. He hadn't seen the amused look his father had worn, only his friends' envious ones.

The house, although small, was in a good section of town. Its size would keep it from fetching a lavish sum on the market, but it would be a bargain for the moneylenders because he had defaulted on the mortgage. Its furnishings weren't rich, but when he had bought them, just out of the university, he had thought them elegant. Now they were little better than interesting firewood. They'd be worth more, of course, he'd been assured, if they were sold at auction from the residence itself, with the owner in the background to embarrass the buyers come to see how far down his fortunes had brought him. He decided to sell them anonymously. His humiliation was too dear a price, and anyway, he thought with bitter humor, it wouldn't bring him *that* much extra.

It had taken three days to assess the worth of it all. All but the items in the attics. That was taking a whole night for he knew that once he'd tallied the worth of every last box and trunk he'd have no more excuses to stay and would have to be off and about his new life, with not enough left of his old one to keep in a trunk. He could now carry his whole life, his whole worth, in his pockets.

Nothing, he thought with bitter humor, as he sorted through the last trunk, nothing but books and letters, sketches and prints, certificates of merit for literature and mathematics, little gilt medals for endurance at sports. Souvenirs and geegaws, oddments signifying triumphs and efforts—the flotsam and jetsam of a fellow's life, irreplaceable and as personal as his own thumbprint. And none of it worth a penny to anyone else.

He had neither parent nor sibling, neither wife nor lover, who cared for the trunkloads of history he'd unearthed.

Lord, he thought, wiping his hands together to make sticky strings of the old spiderwebs that clung to them, how vain he'd been to save such stuff. How much he was learning, he thought, as he took up the lamp and made his way back down the long stairs again. It seemed that vanity was just another privilege of wealth, for while the vanity of kings and pharaohs was priceless, the vanity of a man who had lost his fortune was simply foolishness.

There was no longer any possibility of staying on. He had nothing left and would have to take to the sea, as his fortune had done, and hope for a better fate. There were lands overseas where a man might start with nothing—lands where men went because they had nothing but their own two hands. Men like him. He'd traded there when he had money. Now he would trade his own strong back for money. He'd go, no matter how much he dreaded it—and he did dread it—but, he thought, weary beyond mere headache and pain, he'd be leaving so much behind, even though he owned so little.

For all his sorrow, Crispin slept very well that night. There was nothing he could do to help himself now. It was done.

"Come in, Mr. Phipps," Crispin said, nodding to the man who stood in the doorway to his dining room. "Have some ale or some beefsteak . . . no? Kippers, then? Jellies? Pudding? Toast or scones? The condemned man eats a hearty breakfast, you see. I thought my fortune could extend to one last feast. And my staff has one last day to show me how much they'll be missed. Come, join me. Don't fret. All is in hand. I've done all you said. Look at the table. There's more than breakfast laid out here. Here are the keys. Here, the papers. Inventories, permissions, and bills of sale, readied and waiting for your approval. I can't think of anything else."

He frowned. The good Mr. Phipps, solicitor and conscientious counselor, was shifting from foot to foot, looking most peculiar. His somber face was very red, and his usually immaculate wig was all pushed to one side, as though the wind or mischievous fingers had gotten into it.

"What is it now?" Crispin said wearily, putting down his fork, feeling the food in his throat turn to cold ash. "A debt I'd forgotten? Is every cent to go, then? It doesn't seem possible. What have I overlooked? A rightful pension or a ridiculous claim? I tell you I believe I've covered it all. All my creditors are known to you. Out with it, sir!"

"Your ships," Mr. Phipps croaked in a high unnatural voice.

"My ships are in Neptune's comforting arms, I know," Crispin said, turning back to his plate.

Mr. Phipps sputtered.

Crispin looked up again. "What? Not so? Don't tell me they were taken by pirates, have attacked England, and now the world is at war with me? That seems to be the only indignity I've not suffered, so why not?"

"No, no," Mr. Phipps squeaked, and his face grew redder, something very like a mad titter escaping from his prim mouth before he managed to squeal, "They've come in, my lord! Your ships have come in!"

"My ships," Crispin said, his face grown white, "have come in?"

Mr. Phipps nodded until his wig slipped over his streaming eyes. "With everything on board. All safe! All is well! All is returned! They were damaged in the storm but they finally limped into harbor. They waited out the weather and made repairs from each other's stores. Then they sailed back together, under assumed flags, because they feared piracy. But they're back, my lord!" Mr. Phipps shouted. "They're back!"

Crispin stared at him for a long silent moment. Mr. Phipps kept bobbing his head up and down, smiling joyously.

Crispin nodded, and then looked at a little silver teapot that sat, still steaming, next to his cup. He raised it and carefully poured some tea onto the back of his hand. He yelped.

"So it really is true!" Crispin said in astonishment, dabbing at his hand. "I am awake, after all."

CHAPTER

4

"**P**ut it here," Crispin told the men pausing in the hallway with his new settee balanced between them.

They placed it under the bow window in the sitting room. He came close and studied it while they held their ragged breath. The mahogany wood glowed, the pale pink embroidery on its fabric was the innocent color of unborn pearls. Little saffron-colored flowers bloomed everywhere on it, while tiny Chinese men, all worked in silver thread, bowed over them. It was in perfect condition, and perfectly useless to him. But it wasn't there to be sat on. It was there for him to be congratulated upon.

He couldn't remember ever being happier. It was like being warm after being frozen. It was like breathing freely after a bad cold. It was like eating after being hungry. Everything was new again, every commonplace occurrence became an event, every common privilege was an honor. He was rich again—richer than before, and with every prospect of getting richer still.

He and the three ships' captains had celebrated first. He'd run to them on the docks as if they were his long lost lovers returned. In a sense they were. He'd embraced them and then rewarded them and their crewmen. Then they'd gone off to a quayside inn to settle in for some more serious celebrating. Even Captain Yates, newly wed and frantically eager to return to his home in Rye and to his wife's arms, was willing to tarry, to raise a few dozen toasts to celebrate the success of the enterprise. And to tell and retell all the stories of bravery, cleverness, and endurance that had snatched the three ships back from the sea.

Captain Yates left after a day or two—Crispin would never be sure exactly which day it was. All he knew was that when the party ended, a week had vanished somewhere in a joyous mix of rum and song and story and some very exhilarating dancing. The tavern wenches had tired easily; otherwise he would never have known what a remarkable dancer old Captain Froud was—although having a partner with such a long beard had been disconcerting at first. When the party was at last over and the last surviving tar had been swept up from the tavern floor, he hadn't even minded the headache that had come with the first sober dawn. It was extraordinary how gold could cure a headache—and whatever else ailed a man.

Now he was buying things.

"I say!" his friend Wrede said after being let into Crispin's parlor.

"I should hope so," Crispin commented as he watched his friend stare at the room in astonishment.

New gold silks, fresh from ships' lockers, were stretched taut on the walls, enveloping the two men in the reflected glow of their rich color. Rich satin draperies at the windows were drawn back to let the sunlight, fractured by new Brussels lace curtains, shine down on thick Persian carpets of peach and gold.

He'd bought elegant new furniture, too—oak from the Caucasus, teak and mahogany from India, sandalwood from the East, even some good stout English oak; forests across the world had contributed to his new tables, bookcases, and chairs. There were antique statues, porcelain figurines, and vases of fresh flowers on every tabletop. The newly acquired paintings on the walls were bright enough to insist on being seen as well, although they were certainly old enough to know better.

"I take this to mean," his visitor said, after he'd surveyed the entire room, "that you won't be needing my invitations to dinner anymore."

"I'll always need your invitations, Wrede," Crispin said, "but no, not the way I needed them last month. Then I was hungry. You knew it. You asked me to dinner so many times that I began to think you couldn't look at an oyster or a roast without thinking of me."

"But you only accepted a few times," Drummond Haye, earl of Wrede, said gently.

"A few dozen," Crispin corrected him.

"But not very often lately."

"Offended, are you?" Crispin asked with amusement, eyeing his tall, lanky, long-jawed friend. Crispin had known Wrede since their school days. The earl never showed any emotion unless it was forcibly wrested from him, but Crispin had never known any man to have more humanity and compassion.

"Offended? Possibly," the earl said, "at the thought that one's friend only wished to share his"—he waved a languid hand at the room—*"munificence* with him."

"Well, I couldn't share my poverty, you know." Crispin laughed.

"No, I don't know," the earl said. "Actually, I thought sharing was the nature of the thing when one lost one's fortune and one's friend offered to help. But what do I know?" he asked, his voice becoming bored.

"I couldn't let you go on helping me forever," Crispin said seriously.

"Why not?" the earl asked, equally serious.

There was a moment of silence before Crispin laughed again. "You know?" he said, "I can't think of a reason why not now. Because now that I have everything again, it seems foolish, even ridiculous, to have starved when my best friend offered to share his dinner with me. But then? Oh, then it made perfect sense. I never wanted to hurt your feelings so much as I was desperate to spare my own."

"You're excused, though it's nonsense," the earl replied with a shrug. Then, suddenly grave, he added, "But next time you lose everything you own, remember that you don't need friends to share this sort of excess. Anyone will do for that. Friends expect to be needed, you know."

"I'll remember," Crispin said, "but what's this 'next time'? I had to invest everything this time; otherwise the profit wouldn't have made any difference. Next time, if there is a next time, even if I lose, I won't lose all. I'll never risk everything again. Especially since it wasn't only *my* money."

"It was a pittance, and hard enough getting you to accept that," the earl muttered.

Crispin shook his head. "It wasn't and you know it. Anyway, it doesn't matter now. I've got a bank check here for you, Wrede. Every cent is paid back. That's why I asked you here today."

"Really? How disappointing. Thank you, I'll take it, and be off before I disturb you further," the earl said haughtily.

"You know that's not what I meant."

"Do I?"

"Well, you should; you've known me long enough. Look, Wrede, I'm sorry," Crispin said, because his friend did look very affronted and had begun to put on his gloves again. "I just never knew how to take charity as gracefully as you gave it."

"I know," the earl said comfortably. "I just enjoyed watching some of that conceit disappearing."

"Conceit?" Crispin asked in surprise.

"Oh. Then not permitting me to sit down until I admired all this blinding gilt is the latest fashion?"

"Was I that bad?" Crispin laughed. "I suppose so. Good God, Wrede, I don't know why you stay friends with me."

"Well," the languid earl sighed, "you see, it isn't at all the fashion for noblemen to actually keep jesters anymore . . ."

"Wait! Would my friend care for some sherry? Speak now or forever hold your peace."

"Your friend would dearly love to sit down and drink in peace—that is," Wrede said, "if there is a place to sit amid all this opulence."

"If your lordship would please to place yourself in this chair," Crispin said, laughing as he hauled out a chair, "we will drink in peace."

"And so," the earl said, sitting back before the fire after dinner was done, "all is restored. What are you going to do now—or rather, first?"

"What won't I do!" Crispin had discarded his coat and waistcoat and stood in his shirtsleeves before the fire. "Ride in my carriage, go to the theater—all of it without wondering if I shall end up sweeping the streets free of dung for the lords and ladies. Did you know that a man can't just pick up a broom and go to it?" he asked suddenly. "No, there's no such thing as free enterprise in the streets of London. Each man has his own corner and, I suppose, his own allotment of horse dung to sweep for the day. I know this because I nearly had my head removed the one time I tried to work another man's patch . . . oh, all right, I'll stop. You're puffing up like a bladder in outrage. But I did have to do some odd things in order to survive. Some I don't even want to discuss."

Crispin stared into the fire. "The work didn't kill me, though. It taught me a valuable lesson about survival. I hated being poor, but I didn't mind the work involved in getting rich—only the time it would take. I reckoned it would only take me ninety years to put everything back to normal. God bless those captains. The only pity is that I'll probably forget it all and take my pleasure for granted again someday. Someday soon, from the look of things," he added with a little smile.

"I see. You're busily buying furniture, carpets, and wallpaper. Whatever happened to wine, women, and song?"

"I've been drinking enough to float my ships home these past few days. I don't want such a memorable time in my life to become a blur. And I never understood why song was included. You can sing all you want without paying, and if you're good enough, someone will pay you. I wasn't good enough, unfortunately," he added with a smile, because he couldn't seem to stop smiling these days. "As for women . . . there were one or two at that tavern, I think . . . unless Captain Froud was even more talented than I thought. Anyway the day I have to buy a woman is the day I'll give them up. No. I'll stick to furniture and wallpaper, thank you, and leave the wine, women, and song to poorer men. Oh, God, Wrede—it's so good to be back!"

"What joy. You must feel like our late King Charles, returned from exile in triumph."

"Exactly like old Charles. All has been restored—except for a fine pair of horses. I bought back the dogs and most of the horses, but taking that pair from young Andrew Moffit would have killed him." He paused and then said seriously, "Nothing will ever be exactly the way I left it."

"Ah," Wrede said softly, "yes, I know. I noted we did not drink to the health of the lovely Charlotte. So it's to be old Prendergast for her, after all. I would have thought that with your fortune restored . . ."

"You thought right," Crispin said. He braced his hands on the mantel and hung his head between his arms so that his friend could not see his expression. "I mean to have her still," Crispin said softly. When his friend didn't answer, he chuckled. "Very quiet is our sanguine earl, isn't he? Why should you be surprised? I loved Charlotte."

"And you said she loved you," Wrede mused. "Odd, then, how quickly your engagement was terminated. It seemed to sink from sight even as your ships did."

"But she chose me before that, when she had richer men to choose from, didn't she? So she left me when my money did. I never expected otherwise. God, man, can you see Charlotte darning hose and plucking chickens?" Crispin eyed his friend.

"I would hate to see *anyone* darning hose and plucking chickens," the earl commented, "and there might have been richer men, but few of them were as young, eligible, and handsome as you. Don't protest, Crispin. Humility is not one of your strong points. But gossip has it that Charlotte will wed Prendergast now. And he's twenty-five years her senior, with a parcel of unlovely kiddies left over from his first wife, to boot."

"Exactly," Crispin said bleakly, all humor gone from his voice. He spoke carefully, the spacing of his words allowing them many meanings. "She chose him because she felt he would want less of her than I would. She thought she'd be able to earn her freedom faster—and earn her chance for a relationship with me faster too."

Wrede gave a long, low, tuneless whistle and then said guardedly, "But now you have your fortune. And so the shoe is on the other foot. If marriage is a thing one enters with an eye to earning one's freedom . . . Is that what you want, Crispin?"

"It's what men of our rank get, my friend, when we get any choice at all. You know that."

"No, actually, I don't. My parents were unfashionably devoted to each other, as were yours, if I recall. I harbor dreams of a similar match."

"That's why your dreams and mine are still safe at harbor. We're nearing thirty," Crispin reminded him.

"What does that matter?" the earl asked. "I expect faithfulness in marriage. I don't want to count shoes under my bed each night before I retire, and I'm too lazy to go seeking someone else after I settle on a wife. It's only economical. Now I pass out trinkets to ladies for the pleasure of their company, but if you give a wife a bauble, it stays in the family. Sloth and economy. The idea appeals to me."

"Then why are you still single?"

"I said the *idea* appeals to me," Wrede explained. Crispin's cough might have been born a laugh, but he covered it as the earl added, "But that is me. As for you . . . so you'll have her, after all?"

"Yes," Crispin said, and now there was definitely a smile in his voice. "I swear I'm not a monster of vanity, but I find I'm only human, after all. I would have refused even if she had begged me to continue our engagement, though I must say, I would like to have had the chance to try to change her mind."

There was unholy glee in Crispin's eyes as he added, "I've been thinking about holding a ball here, with flowers and footmen to attend footmen and what all—the whole lot, the most spectacular ball of the season, to announce my return to good fortune. I'll invite Prendergast, too, and his whelps, if need be. And my lady Charlotte. Then maybe, just maybe, I shall propose marriage to her again."

"Maybe?" Wrede said with interest.

"All right . . . after an hour or two. But I'll give her time to worry about it first. Not enough to make her frown too long, mind you. I don't want a wife with wrinkles. And after our marriage—well, I've been thinking about that, too. I wonder if she'll find many lovers after she's had the eight children I think I'm going to require of her."

"I see, you're marrying her for revenge?" his friend said dryly.

"I'm marrying her because I want her. I want everything —*everything*—back the way it was. *Just* the way it was. That will stop my nightmares."

"A restoration ball," Wrede said thoughtfully. "Lovely theme."

"Yes. So it is. I hadn't thought of it that way. What a good idea. You're a genius," Crispin said.

"Of course," Wrede said, and they nodded to each other. Then two of society's most eligible bachelors got down to the task of planning an engagement ball with all the enthusiasm and delight of any matchmaking matrons in the land.

Crispin took a deep breath and strolled into the flower-decked ballroom to greet his guests. This evening was of prime importance to him, and he wanted everything to be beyond perfect. And so it was. Everything from the linen on his tables to the clothing on his back was impeccably correct. He'd spent enough money to ensure it.

"Prendergast is a model of unmanly grace, isn't he?" the earl of Wrede murmured as he joined Crispin and saw the older man his friend was staring fixedly at. "Those three kiddies of his are said to be his image. I suppose there's no accounting for some tastes. Charlotte Barrington seems to be thrilled to be his chosen lady this evening, doesn't she?"

"Is she? I wonder," Crispin said cheerfully, before he left his friend and walked directly to Lady Charlotte, where she stood with Hugh Prendergast. She wore a gown of apricot silk with pink roses embroidered on its panniers. It was tight at the waist and bare nearly to there, too. Crispin's eyes widened when he saw how much flesh she was displaying, until he remembered that she was on the arm of Hugh Prendergast. When Charlotte saw Crispin and then his rueful half smile, she smiled for the first time since she'd entered his house. But that smile faded as he walked to her—and past her—without a nod, to bow over pretty young Cissie Rule's little hand, asking her to partner him in the first dance.

Crispin stood up with a different beauty for every dance. He never chose Charlotte, nor did he exchange a word with her, but he never stopped watching her. She danced with a variety of partners too, but she looked as though she might weep during the first dance. She was more sullen than sad during the second and third. She laughed too much and tossed her head too often during the fourth. But by the sixth dance she looked as if she was about to kill someone—her escort, her host, or maybe even herself.

"I shall propose at dinner," Crispin confided happily to the earl. And then—seeing the murderous look the lady flashed him before she gave off a long trill of artificial laughter at something someone said, he added, with laughter in his own voice, "I don't think Charlotte can take much more of my teasing, and though I admit I've enjoyed this little jest, the time for games is over. I will have her before this night is out," he vowed, flashing a wolfish smile that made his friend wonder just how much of the lady he would have before he asked for her hand.

Crispin, finally bowing to his fate, began to make his way toward the beautiful little blond woman who was so pointedly trying not to notice his approach.

A footman intercepted him halfway there. The man was flustered and apologetic and so warm with embarrassment that Crispin could smell the damp heated wool of his livery even above the mingled aromas of many perfumes, hot melted candle wax, wine and beer, banked flowers, and sweat. It was a very successful ball, and the air was stifling and redolent of human pleasure. But the scent of the footman's agitation was acrid.

"My—my lord," the footman stammered, "there are persons to see you in the house."

"There are a great many of them," Crispin said calmly, only half listening as he watched Charlotte pretending not to see him.

"Stroud said I was to fetch you," the footman persisted.

"Now? He couldn't have meant now," Crispin said, astonished at the footman's presumption as well as his anxiety, wondering if he'd gotten into the wine cellar.

"Right now. Immediately," the footman said unhappily.

Crispin knew that his butler, Stroud, would never interrupt the master at his ball for something trivial. He would, however, send a footman to fetch him for a matter of life and death. Crispin wondered what it could be that couldn't wait. He flashed a look to his friend Wrede, and nodded to the footman. By the time he'd left the ballroom, the earl was at his side.

"I've no family to die at a moment's notice—everyone who matters to me is either dead or here. I can't imagine what Stroud thinks is important enough to disturb me now," Crispin muttered as he strode into the hallway.

"Perhaps it's only a murder—the cook doing away with a scullery maid or some such," Wrede said comfortingly. "Last year Bigelow's rout was interrupted when one of the footmen stabbed a downstairs maid in a jealous rage. Quite made the night, you know."

"They're in the salon, my lord," the footman said worriedly, and flung open the door to the salon as Crispin arrived there.

A number of people were waiting in the salon, and they all fell still when the two tall elegantly dressed noblemen appeared in the doorway.

"My lord," Crispin's lawyer said the moment he saw him, "forgive me, but this is a matter that cannot wait." He hesitated, and then, as he saw Crispin's eyes widen, he gave words to what Crispin had just seen and couldn't believe, "Your wife and her parent demand to be seen."

"My wife?" Crispin said no more. He let stillness fill the room as he gazed at her, so everyone else could also fully take in how ridiculous it was.

She wore a gown made of some shiny brown stuff that didn't suit the chair, the room, or the house she was in. Her eyes, those strange whiskey-colored eyes he remembered so well, were wide with fear. And rightly so, Crispin thought murderously. He wanted to kill her.

He'd been trained to be a gentleman before she was out of the nursery, however, so he only cleared his throat and forced a smile on his ashen face. "I see. Charming. What sort of a joke is this?" he asked with just the right sort of amused anticipation, as though he really thought it was a jest.

"No joke, my lord," Mr. Phipps, his lawyer, said immediately, his voice quivering with indignation. "The woman states she is your wife, and she has produced papers to verify the union," he added, with a look to his employer that was as good as a plea for him to deny it so he could throw the baggage out.

Crispin extended one long hand, and the lawyer placed the paper in it. A smooth-faced, fattish young man made as if to snatch the paper back, but was stopped by a touch from another man who appeared from the shadows—Harry Meech, Crispin thought, his eyes narrowing. Very interesting.

He gazed at the paper. It was just as he remembered it. He sighed and handed it to Wrede, who studied it closely through his quizzing glass.

"Yes, I remember this," Crispin said, his voice filled with all the disgust he felt. "I told you I had to turn my hand to all sorts of work, Wrede," he explained. "This was one of those . . . odd employments." Pointing to Harry Meech, he said, "He is a fellow who operates out of the Fleet prison. He provides false bridegrooms for debtors, among other things. This girl," he said, indicating Dulcie and noting how much paler she grew before he turned away from her, "was such a one. For a fee, I went through a charade of marriage with her to free her from her debts. And that was an end to it. Or so I thought. Or so they promised me. Obviously they've heard of my recent change of fortune and have come here to see how much money they can extort from me."

Crispin passed a hand over his eyes and said wearily. "Pay them, Mr. Phipps. Nuisance value. And do so before they demand something more. Pay them, promise them payment, or call the footmen to toss them out. Anything to get them out of my sight."

Harry Meech spoke up sweetly. "Ah, but that won't suffice, my lord."

Crispin cocked one eyebrow, and Harry took a quick step back.

"Mr. Phipps?" Crispin said with emphasis.

"He's right," Mr. Phipps said with difficulty, as Crispin stared at him. "The papers are in order. I don't know how they did it, my lord. But they *have* done it. According to these papers, this woman is your wife. Your legal wife."

CHAPTER

5

~~~

This was even worse than Dulcie had thought it would be. It had taken days for Jerome and her father to wear her down, and she'd finally come with them only because she couldn't bear not knowing what was happening. She'd told herself it might be worse if she wasn't there, but now she knew that couldn't be true—nothing could be worse. She didn't belong in this house, and she couldn't bear the look in his eyes. It was more terrible than any name he could have called her. She shivered.

"I didn't want to come here," she blurted suddenly, before Harry or Jerome could stop her. "I didn't credit the marriage, either. I don't want to be married to you."

She knew the viscount had recognized her immediately. She'd seen it in the widening of his eyes. But he had ignored her until she spoke. Now she wished she had kept silent.

"Oh. Yes. Of course. You don't want riches. You don't want a title," Crispin said sarcastically, glancing down at her. "I see. Certainly."

"Believe me," she said, shamed because of the way he looked at her but also determined to make him believe her.

Her expression must have touched him, because his tight mouth softened into the beautiful lines she remembered—but only for a moment.

"Then why are you here?" he asked. "Why didn't you just tear the damned paper up? Then there would have been no marriage, because I assure you, I have never thought of it—or you—since that day."

"They had the paper," she whispered weakly, averting her eyes because the look in his was so chilling.

"Of course," he said, dismissing her. He looked at his lawyer and demanded, "How did they know my name?"

"The vicar recognized you," Mr. Phipps said.

"The vicar? But he was an old madman," Crispin said.

"Now, now, my lord. You'll hurt poor old Dr. Featherstone's feelings," Harry Meech cautioned him jovially.

"Featherstone?" Crispin said, startled. "Hiram Featherstone? But he was minister in my parish—a hundred years ago, or so it seems. I remember him from when I was a boy. He must be dead this age. That old man in the Fleet? No, it couldn't be. Featherstone was a brilliant man."

"Oh, still is. Now and again. When's the moon's shining right. Here, Doctor," Harry said, turning to a rumpled figure slumped in a chair so near the fire that the man's boots were steaming, "the viscount wants to chat. Here!" he shouted. "Are we in tonight? We never know, with the dear doctor," he explained merrily. "Sometimes he's with us in body, and sometimes in spirit, but then, he's usually deep in spirits, isn't he? We kept him to two bottles tonight, so maybe you'll be in luck, my lord. Hey, old man," he shouted, shaking the vicar's shoulder. "Here's the viscount to see you."

"The prince will see me, too," the old man said, waking.

"Yeah, doubtless. But first a word with the viscount, eh?" Harry said.

"We could, of course, have the old man examined," Mr. Phipps said with sudden hope. "If he's a madman, then he has no right to wear the cloth. The marriage could be invalidated."

"Viscount? Viscount West?" the old man gasped. He struggled to his feet and, brushing Harry aside, limped toward Crispin. He gazed hard at him, then his seamed face wrinkled into a smile. "Why, see? It is no other. Crispin George Thomas Knightly, of Darnley Hall. Oh, my boy," he said, his old eyes filling with easy tears, "how good to see you again. And how is your lovely bride? I remember your wedding day so well. How honored I was that you chose me to officiate. Just weeks past, wasn't it?

"They told me another name," he said wisely, touching a shaking finger to the side of his nose, "but this time the voices couldn't deceive me. No, I knew it was you, and so I wrote down your name. And so it was, and so it is. So good to see you again. Such a lovely ceremony. Pure and simple. No fuss, nothing elaborate . . . Not like old Squire Moffit, who released a flock of doves, eh? Remember that wedding, lad? You were but a boy—all of eight, weren't you? And so worried about the doves getting overheated in their baskets that you let them out before time, on the green. What a wedding! But no one scolded you. Think what a mess they would have made in the nave. All the village was there. Oh, those were glorious days, were they not? Before the darkness came. Before the mists . . ."

"You'll never prove him dotty," Harry told Mr. Phipps confidently. "He's only half in the bag half of the time. That's better than most members of Parliament."

"I remember," Crispin assured the old man gently, taking his trembling hand in his. "Yes, sir, I do remember."

Crispin, Mr. Phipps, and the earl stood in a huddle by the door while all of the others, except Dulcie, fell upon the tray of refreshments Crispin had called for.

"I suppose that you believe, as I do, that the certificate is valid enough for them to make considerable trouble," the earl said to Mr. Phipps.

"Agreed," Mr. Phipps said nervously.

"Is there no way out of this?" Crispin asked, his fists on his hips, his eyes furious.

"Immediately? Short of murder, I think not. Time. I need time," Mr. Phipps said.

"Time? How long? An hour? Two? Mr. Phipps, I don't *have* time," Crispin said through clenched teeth. "There's a lady in the other room tonight. A young woman to whom I have given my heart. Tonight I was going to ask for her hand. What can I do right *now?*"

"I—I don't know quite what we can do now, my lord," Mr. Phipps said.

"Then think harder, man," Crispin said angrily. "How long do you expect me to wait until you can free me of this girl who claims to be my wife?"

"There's no cause to shout at me," Mr. Phipps said boldly. "*I* did not marry her, my lord." Then he stopped, aghast at what he'd said.

Crispin laid a gentle hand on the lawyer's shoulder. "No," he said with a sigh, "you didn't, did you? I did, damn my eyes. All right. What are my options?"

"How much money do they want?" the earl asked.

"Yes," Crispin said eagerly, his spirits rising. "Trust you, Wrede, to get to the heart of it. I was thinking of idiotic things like honor and responsibility—you saw to the crux of it. Of course. How much, Phipps?"

"They haven't said. But I wouldn't advise offering a lump sum in the heat of the moment," Mr. Phipps said cautiously. "It would be sure to cost much more than careful dealing with them over the weeks would. That way we can whittle down their demands with threats and pressures. None of them are anxious to have their background held up to the light, I am sure."

"I haven't got weeks," Crispin said, thinking of Charlotte dancing in Prendergast's arms even as he stood in the salon fighting for his freedom. "I barely have hours. I can't afford to risk having people discover my monumental stupidity.

This must end now. We'll bargain, if you think we have to, but we must do so now, and the marriage papers must be in the fire before we leave this room."

They waited until their unwanted guests had their hands and mouths full, and then Crispin sauntered over to them and broached the subject.

"Well, gentlemen," he said, forcing himself to speak in a friendly tone, "time's a-wasting. You picked an unfortunate night to visit. My other guests must be wondering what happened to me, and so we'll have to cut the negotiations short—shorter than my lawyer would have wished." He nodded to Harry Meech, whose mouth was full of bread and roast pigeon.

"So, then, let's have done with it," Crispin said. "Tell me the sum you want, and we'll discuss it. Then, if we are all agreed, you will hand me the papers, I'll hand you the sum—and farewell."

"Well, my lord," Harry said thickly, because he hadn't been able to swallow all that was in his mouth but wanted to be the first to speak anyway. "Shoun't we say, 'ow much is your freedom worth?"

"It's all relative, isn't it?" Crispin said with a cold smile. "There's freedom and there's freedom. The cost of buying you out of Newgate or the Fleet prison, after you'd been put there for attempted blackmail of a lord of the realm, and the cost of a nobleman's being rid of a foolish mistake are two entirely different things, aren't they?"

"Ah, too sadly true, my lord, too true," Harry said smoothly, his voice finally clear of crumbs. "The cost of a poor man's life and a nobleman's leisure *are* two different things. But even a high court would put a high price on the cost of a poor but decent girl's virtue and a nobleman's false promises, would they?"

"Decent girl?" Crispin said on a harsh laugh, "I'm not so certain of that. Come, Harry, state your price and let's be done with it." Crispin heard Dulcie's soft intake of breath, but he refused to look her way.

Harry frowned as the smooth-faced man he'd introduced as Jerome Snode whispered in his ear, while the smaller man who apparently was the girl's father put down his plate and rose from his chair.

"Here, now, sir!" Philip Blessing said, his voice trembling with outrage. "I can't believe I've heard right. My daughter is as much a victim as you are, my lord. She entered into the union in good faith and now finds herself reviled? Shame."

"Good faith?" Crispin shouted, ignoring the warning hand his friend Wrede laid on his arm. "Shame? She entered into a false marriage to free herself of debt and finds herself really married to a lord of the realm. If she wants to act in good faith she only has to remove herself from this charade of a marriage."

"If she removes herself from the marriage," Jerome Snode pointed out, "she goes back to prison for debt."

"Tell me the amount of the debt, and it will be paid," Crispin said in cold fury. "Then add what you will, within reason, and we can be done with this nonsense." He turned his back on the company so they wouldn't see the sheer murder in his eyes.

"The old man registered the marriage," Jerome said.

"And marriage registers have never been altered, I suppose," Crispin said dryly.

"Not without adequate recompense," Jerome said.

"Ah, we come to it at last," Crispin said with bitter satisfaction.

"What are you talking about?" Philip Blessing asked. "My daughter is legally wed to this man. 'What God has joined together let no man put asunder.' Bad enough my poor child had to attempt a mockery of a marriage in order to free me of my folly. Worse, if she should now be told to attempt another deception in the eyes of God. I will not have it. She cannot call down eternal damnation, as well as the possibility of criminal prosecution, upon her poor, innocent head. No, no. I won't have it."

"What? What in God's name are you rattling on about?" Harry Meech cried.

"Philip, my friend," Jerome Snode said in dismay. "What are you saying?"

"I'm saying she is married to the viscount, and married she will stay. I am a foolish man, gentlemen, a weak man and an incautious one. But that is my life. I will not let my daughter ruin hers." Philip Blessing planted his feet far apart and stood stalwart before them.

They all stared back at him. The other men had never heard him speak that way. But Dulcie had. She could have wept. Somewhere between their poor flat and this sumptuous house, her father had changed his mind—or rather made it up, for she recognized that tone of voice. He was selling, and so, of course he believed in his product, and she knew nothing would change his mind. But she had to try.

"Father," she said hoarsely, "I don't *want* to be married to the viscount. I don't know him. I want to be free. We have a nice life now, or at least a chance for one. It's wrong to take money from him, but I think we'll have to take enough to clear your debts, because your creditors will want payment when they find out that the marriage was a false one."

She glanced up at Crispin. "We paid good money for the certificate, and I entered the marriage in good faith—even though it wasn't the good faith you mean," she told him. "Still, my father should not have to go back to jail just because you were stupid enough to sign with your initials," she finished with a watery sniffle.

Crispin was tempted, against all reason, to smile. The night had taken on an air of unreality. She *did* look adorable in her confusion. He was surprised by how well he remembered her. Even her plain clothes couldn't conceal her fresh beauty, and her reasoning was just skewed enough to appeal to him. Whatever her faults, she had the same desire he did: to be free. For that, he might be able to forgive her.

"Daughter," Philip Blessing said sadly, "to think I would

live to hear you speak such blasphemy. You are a good God-fearing girl. You married this man for the wrong reason, but you are married, and that is that."

Dulcie shuddered. "Father, please listen . . ." she pleaded.

"What kind of double-dealing is this?" Harry Meech thundered.

"Philip, are you mad?" Jerome shouted.

"Mr. Blessing," Phipps called, "what are you saying?"

"Be still!" the earl of Wrede commanded.

"My children," old Dr. Featherstone proclaimed over the babble of raised voices. "Peace! Peace, I beg of you!"

"My lord? Do you need our help?" a new voice intruded fearfully, as the door slowly cracked open.

Three nervous footmen stood in the hall peering into the room over the butler's shoulder. Behind them a cluster of lavishly dressed guests stood on tiptoe, trying to see what was causing the ruckus in the viscount's salon, and why he'd been gone so long. Crispin saw one beautiful fascinated face he knew too well peeking through the knot of servants. Charlotte was fanning herself furiously, but watching avidly. So was Prendergast, who stood at her side along with a dozen others. Before he had a chance to close the door, Philip Blessing saw them all and spoke up.

"My lord! Are you going to keep your marriage a secret?" he asked, his voice loud, clear, and distinct enough so that his words echoed in the absolute silence that fell after they were spoken.

"Now you've done it!" Harry growled, as the first murmurs of "Marriage!" were heard in the hall and began spreading beyond to the rest of the company.

"It's not too late, my lord," Jerome cried, "a mis-saying, that's all."

"It's far too late for bargaining. I have the marriage papers," Philip Blessing said implacably, patting his pocket and then resting his hand on his heart. "You'll thank me for this one day," he murmured to Dulcie. Then he smiled at his new son-in-law. "Aren't you going to introduce your new lady wife to your guests, my son?" he asked him.

Crispin closed his eyes. When he opened them again they were bleak. He looked into the hallway and directly into Charlotte's disbelieving eyes. His misery was replaced with white-hot rage.

"So be it," he said with awful clarity. Then he grasped Dulcie by the wrist, pulled her to her feet, and dragged her toward the door.

"My ladies, my lords," he said through gritted teeth, "you must have guessed there was a special reason for tonight's festivities. I ask your felicitations. Behold! My bride. We were married recently, quietly because of a death in her family."

And as the guests gaped and whispered, he added, for Dulcie's ears only, "Yes—a death, of her common sense and her sense of fairness and her peace of mind. You will regret this night's work, my dear.

"Come and meet your guests, darling. I know they will excuse your clothes, understanding how far you've traveled today," he said. Then he pulled her out of the salon and into the midst of his gala ball.

Dulcie wanted to run, but he kept his hand hard on her wrist. She'd argued in vain against coming here, imagining the many things that might happen—from being bodily thrown from the viscount's elegant town house to being laughed to shame. But never this! Although he only held her wrist in his tight clasp, it was worse than being beaten. His contempt was far more cruel than the rude laughter she had been worried about. The brittle smiles his guests wore as they stared at her were even more painful than outright scorn would have been. She'd thought Harry's ugly plan would not succeed, and she'd been right. But she never guessed how badly things would turn out.

He dragged her into the crowded ballroom, and his guests

circled about, eyeing her. They were perfumed and powdered, adorned with the snowy hair of angels, and so covered with gems, satin, silk, and brocade that they did not seem to be people at all, but rather the fantastic creatures she saw sometimes alighting from carriages, or riding past on her street. Their painted faces were shocked and dismayed. At first they thought it was a jest, and their eyes were alight with cruel humor, but they soon began to realize that there was no joke.

Dulcie tried to keep her back straight and her face blank, but she was unable to conceal the terror in her eyes or the rapid beating of her heart. She was afraid she might faint, but was too frightened to lose consciousness among them. Crispin led her through the ranks of his guests, introducing her to all of them as music played on. She didn't hear their names and was only able to nod, because she didn't trust her legs to curtsy. She had worn her best clothes tonight so that the viscount wouldn't think her entirely impoverished. She'd put on her brown taffeta dress and wore her hair piled high, with her best silver pins in it. These people stared at her unpowdered hair and narrow skirts and the simple cameo she wore at her neck on a plain ribbon, and they acted as if she were being led through their midst naked.

Crispin continued the introductions until the faces became a blur to her. Only when they entered a small dim room off the cavernous ballroom and shut the door did he ease his grip on her arm. She looked around wildly, seeking escape, but the tall windows were closed and curtained, and she could see no other way out except back through the throng of guests in the ballroom. She couldn't bear to face them again, but she didn't see any other path to freedom. She paused to gather her courage.

"Do you think this wise?" a tall bony man asked the viscount in an intense voice.

"Do you think I had a choice?" the viscount answered with savage intensity. "What was I to do, Wrede? Deny it there and then? Her damned father had the marriage certificate in hand and was dying to show it off to everyone. That would have been a pretty picture, with me denying all, and that old man waving the papers in their faces. Was I supposed to wrestle him to the floor before he could produce them? No. There was no way I could avoid it. I had no choice but to accept the girl and to put as good a face on the situation as I could."

"Yes, well, I see your point," the tall man said. When he saw the viscount's grip again tighten on Dulcie's wrist, he continued, "But the way you're going on, there'll be even more talk. If that's possible. Come, Crispin, it looks bad. She's dressed like a servant and you're treating her like a truant."

"What am I to do with her, then?" the viscount asked with sudden weariness, releasing her hand. "She's my wife—for the time being, at least. In God's name, what am I to do with her?"

"Let me go," Dulcie said quickly, "please. I don't want to be your wife. I don't belong here. Let me go home, please."

"Yes, home. Wherever that is," Crispin said dryly, "so your father and Harry Meech and their charming friends can sue me for abandonment and Lord knows what else. Once you're out of my sight, God knows what they'll do."

She tried to step away from him, but he moved with lightning speed and captured her hand in his again.

"This is wonderful," the earl of Wrede swore. "If you're going to beat her, for God's sake take her elsewhere, man."

"That's not such a bad idea," Crispin said wearily, and tightening his clasp, he led her out of the room. They went up a long stair and then down another endless hallway. She stumbled, but went willingly, for at least they were moving away from the crowd of people. When they came to a door, he opened it and pushed her inside.

"You stay put," he growled, and pulled the door shut hard behind him, leaving her alone in the room.

"There," Crispin said, dusting off his hands and looking at Wrede, "the bride is in her chamber. What in hell do we do now?"

"We go back to the ball and tell everyone she has an aching head. We say it's because of all the excitement, and make light of it, and circulate among the guests, telling the same story you invented: married in a private ceremony because of a death in the family, more to be made known later and blah, blah, blah. Then we escort Harry Meech and company from the premises. But we keep her father. He's the key to this whole mess—if there is one."

"Pray there is," Crispin said savagely, "for my sake and for hers."

Crispin eyed the man thoughtfully as he poured a brandy for him. He wondered if the fellow was really the girl's father. There was nothing similar about their face or eyes. The girl was remarkably lovely, but the supposed father was completely unremarkable. It didn't matter. The man claimed to be the father, was acknowledged to be, and held the marriage papers, and so had Crispin in the palm of his hand. Although the situation infuriated him, he couldn't afford to show his anger. It was ironic that now that he finally had his fortune back, the one thing he couldn't afford was anger.

"It's a lucky thing you decided to stay with us this evening, sir," he commented pleasantly as he handed the snifter of brandy to Philip Blessing, "Your friends seemed very displeased with you."

"My acquaintances," Philip corrected him as he accepted the brandy.

"Ah, yes. But they might argue that point with you, among others. It took four footman and a promise of the watch to get them away from you and out of here. So, then, sir," Crispin said, as he took a chair by the fire, "what are we going to do now?" he asked.

Philip, he noticed, was now cautiously eyeing the earl of

Wrede, who sat nearby, listening closely. "The earl is an old friend of mine."

"Well, my lord, what shall I say?" the older man said, sitting back and crossing his ankles, "I don't chose to be an interfering in-law."

"No," Crispin said with barely controlled anger, "just an insistent one."

"No, just a man with the facts. Number one: you are married; that is a fact, like it or not. Number two: you have married my daughter, another fact. She resembles her mother," Philip added with a little smile, "in case you were wondering. Those are the facts. Nothing can be done to change them. But now I've a question for you. What are the ways out of marriage?

"There are only two," Philip answered before Crispin could speak. "Death and divorce. Both are hard solutions. And divorce is difficult, costly, and unmentionable in polite society. I should know, gentlemen. My wife and I have lived apart for years. She might want to wed again—I know that I would love to, but neither of us wants to die. People only die for love, you know, not for lack of it. We don't have enough money to sue for a divorce, nor would it do either of us much good. A divorced woman is a woman shamed, and there is my family name to think of. Those of us who have no titles also have good names, you know. My family is a very old one. You may be able to trace your ancestors to Normandy, my lords, but mine go back to the mists of time."

"Your daughter is charming and very beautiful," Crispin said impatiently, "and your family may be a proud one, but I don't want to be part of it. To put it plainer: I didn't mean to marry her. I did her a favor. Now I want to know what favor I can do you in order to undo this unfortunate marriage."

"I see," Philip Blessing said, considering Crispin carefully. "Do you favor death or divorce?"

"Neither," Crispin snapped, rising and pacing the room.

"Nothing so dire. I was thinking more of the simple movement of a few papers. The loss of some, and a sheet taken from a marriage register. That should do it."

"No," Philip said calmly, "I think not. Number one, that would leave us open to blackmail from my acquaintances. And, number two, it would sully my daughter's name forever. People will find out. After all, you introduced her as your wife tonight."

"She doesn't know those people, and she'll never see them again," Crispin said in agitation as he swung around to confront the older man. "I'll give you money, Blessing. A lot of it. You can take her to France or to the Colonies. You'll be free to go wherever you want. She'll be rich, and you'll both be much happier without me, believe me."

"Are you implying that you'll do her an injury if I don't take her away?" Philip asked quietly, watching the lean, broad-shouldered viscount closely as he paced the room.

The earl began to speak, but Crispin waved him to silence. "No," he answered wearily. "I know what I should answer, Wrede. But lies, even well-meaning ones, have gotten me into enough trouble. No, I won't do her harm. I'm not that sort of man. But can't you see reason, Mr. Blessing? I want out of this marriage because I wish to wed another."

"Yes, yes, I understand. I heard the other guests talking. And I saw the lady. Very lovely she is, too. But I also heard that you were free and at loose ends when you met my daughter and I've also heard that your lady gave you up when your fortune ran out."

"That, sir, is no concern of yours," Crispin said in a deadly voice.

"My dear sir," the earl put in quickly, seeing the murderous rage in Crispin's eyes, "while it is true that my friend must purchase a wife in either case, he prefers to purchase one of his own choosing."

"So I see," Philip Blessing said, nodding and staring at Crispin as though he saw many other things besides, "but as I said, there's nothing I can do about it now."

"At least," the earl pressed him, "say 'tonight' instead of 'now.'"

"Very well," Philip said, "'tonight.' But, please, gentlemen, I am rather weary. I'm no longer young, and with all the recent excitement . . . I'm afraid I must bid you good night. It's a long walk back to my lodgings."

"Longer than you think if you leave now," Crispin said. "London is not safe at night, and I'm willing to bet that your 'acquaintances' are lurking in some alley between here and your lodgings, eagerly awaiting your return. Be my guest tonight, sir. I think you'll be more comfortable with me than with them."

"Yes. Likely. Thank you," Philip answered thoughtfully, and finished his drink as Crispin summoned a footman to show him to his bed.

It was long after the man had gone when Crispin finally spoke again. He stood at the hearth and gazed into the leaping flames. His face was set in lines of wretchedness such as Wrede had never seen, and only the flickering light gave it any illusion of expression.

"What am I to do?" Crispin said at last. "When I had nothing, I had everything and didn't know it, because I was free. Now I have everything but my freedom. Oh, God, Wrede, what can I do?"

"Wait until morning," his friend urged him. "Things always look better in the light."

"Imprisonment will look better?" Crispin murmured, and then said with a pained smile. "I suppose you are right. There is nothing left to do tonight."

When Dulcie tried the door of the room in which she was closeted, she was relieved to find it locked. She had no idea whose room it was. It seemed too ornate to be his, but then, the men in his world dressed better than the women in hers, so she could not be sure. There were rich rugs and glossy tabletops, and everything seemed to be wrapped in silk or edged with pearls. The room was warm and sweet-smelling, and the flames of the fireplace were reflected in the mantel of dappled pink marble.

In fact, the furniture was so beautiful she was afraid to sit down anywhere. Dulcie took one look at the high bed that dominated the room and backed away from it. It was very inviting with its plump coverlets and pillows, its silken canopy and gorgeous curtains, but she didn't dare approach it. Why had he locked her in this room? She doubted it was so that he could come back and ravish her. Kill her, possibly. It was clear that he found the idea of being married to her distasteful, and she guessed it would be even worse if he came back to find her in that magnificent bed, as if she were waiting for him. She sank into a chair by the fire and hung her head in her hands, suddenly realizing that she didn't know things could possibly be worse.

Later on, she heard noises in the night, and woke from her troubled sleep in the chair. Nothing moved in her room but the last logs crumbling in the dying fire. She listened closely, trying to pick up any other sounds in the velvety night. She thought she heard men's voices, low and busy, coming from the hall outside her room, but the walls were too thick for her to hear more than the steady rumbling of deep voices. Then there was nothing again except the frightened beating of her heart.

She settled down in the chair again, her cheek snuggled against the brocade back. He was not coming in. No one was coming in. She might be held here forever, alone and in the dark. Somehow, exhausted as she was, that seemed the best solution she could imagine. And so she slept.

CHAPTER

6

She woke to find two round-eyed maids and a grim-faced housekeeper staring at her.

"There's soap and water in the dressing room," the housekeeper said as soon as she saw Dulcie's eyes flutter open. "Towels and perfumes as well. We've brought chocolate, tea and coffee, biscuits, toasts, and jellies for you. They are here on the table. More substantial fare awaits you downstairs in the dining room, if you wish it. I shall freshen your dress for you if you'll remove it."

Dulcie shook her head dumbly. She would have nothing to wear if she took off her dress.

The housekeeper's mouth thinned further. "Very well. The viscount will see you in his study at noon. It lacks an hour to that . . . my lady," she added, as though the words had been pulled out of her mouth with tongs. She shepherded the maids to the door and left Dulcie alone again.

Dulcie was awed by the magnificence of the water closet in a corner of her dressing room and spent some time inspecting a cleverly fashioned skirted chair that concealed the chamber pot. The porcelain from which it was made was of better quality than the dishes she usually ate from. There was a huge hip bath, and a counter laden with soaps and powders as well.

It was only when she splashed deliciously scented warm water over her face that she really woke up. She immediately blushed, remembering the look on the maids' and housekeeper's faces as they'd gaped at her—as if she had to be told first off that there was soap and water available! Then Dulcie stiffened, remembering that she'd been told to go downstairs if she wanted a heartier breakfast. Which meant she wasn't a prisoner anymore. And whatever else awaited her downstairs in this house, one thing was sure: there would be a door to the outside world. And escape.

She straightened her dress as best she could, and put her hair up with as many of her silver pins as she could find in and around the chair she'd slept in. Dulcie gave one last hungry glance at the tray of biscuits and toast, and hurried to the door. She hadn't eaten since early the day before, but she remembered that mice got trapped if they stayed to nibble. At the last minute, however, she snatched up a particularly golden piece of toast to eat later, when she was finally on her way home. Then, silently, she cracked open the door, looked both ways to see that no one was there, and ventured into the hall and down the long stair.

The stair led to the great hall and to the front door. Dulcie sighed with relief. She would find her father, and together they would seek a way out of this. He had said that he wanted her to stay "married" to the viscount, but she was sure that idea had only come to him while they'd sat waiting in that beautifully furnished study, for she had seen the way her father's gaze wandered around the room, pricing and estimating, and then, at the last, the way he'd watched her. Her father, she knew, had decided she belonged here, just as surely as she knew she didn't. The viscount was as wonderfully handsome as his house, and just as far beyond her station.

Dulcie was glad the viscount had regained his fortune, and had been from the moment they'd found out, long before they'd come here. Money being lost or found anywhere had a way of making itself known to Jerome and his awful friend Harry Meech.

But that was the viscount's good luck. Not hers. None of this was for her, and her father had to know that. Clean morning light would clear his mind further, and if it didn't, no matter—she would never come back here. She went straight to the front door and found someone stepping in front of it before she could touch the knob.

"My lady, the dining room is this way," the butler said.

"Ah, but—" she started to say, but he looked all the way down his long nose at her, silencing her. She thought she might reach past him and race out the door anyway, but then she saw his expression and what he was looking at. He was staring at her hand. She'd forgotten that she still held a piece of toast with one bite missing.

"This way," he said again, and she no longer had the nerve to disagree. So, clutching the toast in front of her like a nosegay, she followed, with only one last plaintive glance at the door.

The viscount was sitting at a long table, but he rose the moment she entered the dining room. It was the first time she had seen him in true light. They'd met in a murky room that first time, and he'd glowed like an angel then. Last night the light had been dim in his study, and the ballroom had glowed with a thousand candles that gave off an aura of golden light that would flatter anyone. Today he stood in a shaft of light from the window and the sight of him forced the breath from her.

He wore a blue coat over a pale blue waistcoat. It complemented his wide, bright, clear blue eyes, which were enhanced by long lashes and dark brows. His skin was clear, his hair shining and clean. Tall and straight and strong, refined and elegant, he was altogether the most handsome male she'd ever been so close to in her life. She was so stuck by his presence that she felt as though he'd hit her.

Then she saw the expression in those amazing eyes, and knew that he wished he could do just that.

"Mistress Blessing," he said, and she let out her breath. He wasn't acknowledging their bizarre marriage for a minute, and though she was glad of that, she also felt curiously insulted.

"My lord," she said, remaining aloof but curtsying low, to show him that she, too, had manners.

He held out a chair for her. She hesitated, and then swept across the room to be seated. She moved with such exaggerated grace she was afraid she'd trip and spoil it. He stared at the piece of toast she still held as she took her seat.

"Are you going to eat that?" he asked, amused in spite of himself.

"Of course," she said, her head still held high. And then realizing how foolish she must look trying to act the grand lady while clutching a piece of toast, spoiled it all by giggling.

It was hard for him to imagine a shy, deceitful creature who giggled. Wrede had been right, Crispin thought with rising hope: daylight was taking the sting from it. This girl was no monster. She was only young, and she had a greedy father. The problem suddenly seemed soluble. They might free themselves of it, after all. He smiled down at her.

"It is a delicious-looking piece of toast," he said. "But wouldn't you like to try something else as well? Eggs or beefsteak? Kidneys? Porridge? Pudding? Some roast? Fish?"

She'd never seen so much food so early in the day, so she only nodded.

"Some of each?" he asked, his brows rising as he signaled to a footman.

"No, no," she managed to say, watching the chafing dishes the footman was opening for her inspection, "just some buttered rolls. Oh, and one of those buns and some honey, yes, thank you, and some of those jellies, and a cup of tea," she said on a sigh, hunger getting the better of shyness. "Tea would be lovely."

Most high-born women he knew ate only lightly before noon. Only women of the lower classes were fond of beefsteaks and ale at that hour. This lovely creature was different, Crispin thought, noting that her eyes were the same color as the tea in her cup. No, he thought a second later, they were the color of the honey she was spreading on her toast. She ate with delicacy but also with enthusiasm.

Her enjoyment of food didn't seem to have done her neat figure any harm. Her dress was badly wrinkled and cut too high over her breasts to be fashionable, but its drab color and inferior material couldn't hide high a superior female form, with full breasts and a neat waistline. She was a lovely creature, and very much aware of him as a man. He hadn't missed her reaction to him. That was the kind of thing a man never mistook.

She would make an excellent mistress, Crispin mused, not for the first time. But then he remembered he was planning to marry Charlotte and he was determined to stay in his own marriage bed. And so, with a sigh, he put even the idea of a mistress away.

Simply offering this girl the post of mistress might have influenced her enough to give up her claim to be his wife, but he didn't have that choice. Fortunately he had something else to offer, something a woman from debtors' prison couldn't refuse: money.

He waited until she took a second cup of tea. "You slept well?" he asked, looking for a neutral topic to open negotiations.

"Oh. Yes. Thank you," she said, blushing slightly, because he had spoken just as she was debating whether or not to try to lick a drop of honey off her forefinger, and his sudden attention had caught her with her finger halfway to her lips.

She licked her lips instead and hid her hand in her napkin. Now her fingers would be sticky, but at least he wouldn't catch her lapse in manners.

He smiled, because he had seen her dilemma, and said, "Good. I'm glad things could be arranged at such short notice. We hadn't been planning on overnight guests last night, you see."

She looked stricken.

He was encouraged.

"To be quite blunt," he added gently, "your visit came as quite a shock to me. Last night, you see, was meant to be my betrothal ball, not a celebration of my marriage."

She grew pale, so he dared to go on. "I'd planned to marry this woman for weeks—years, actually," he said, watching her. He paused, and decided not to mention Charlotte's hopes and dreams. Although this pretty little thing might feel sympathy for him, women seldom felt any for the competition. "Now," he said sadly, "I don't know if she'll even speak to me again. She thinks you and I are married, but we're not, you know. I think you know that very well. And so, Miss Blessing, I ask you, what am I to do?"

She swallowed hard. "My lord," she said in a tiny voice, her topaz eyes so honest looking in their confused sorrow that he felt encouraged, "I wish I knew. As I told you last night, I don't want to be married to you. Really."

His eyes grew hard, but he kept smiling and kept his voice even. "Well, then, why did you come here last night with a vicar and papers and thugs to back you up? Let's be honest, Miss Blessing. I asked you, and ask again: what do you want me to do? I have money and influence, and I can be dangerous, but I'd rather be generous. If we can reach an agreement here and now, we can be done with this matter simply and smoothly. I'm sure if we come to terms, your father will have no choice but to accept our decision."

"We have no choice!" she blurted.

"Now look you, Mistress Blessing," he snapped, his patience at an end, "I'll beat you in this. You know that as well as I do. I have influence and power; you've only got false papers, an old madman, bad companions, and a disreputable past. Can you see the magistrate's face when you confess that you married a stranger in order to leave debtors' prison? No one in London will believe you're a poor innocent after that. It's a trick no matter how you dress it up, and everyone will see it!"

"Yes, and they'll see how noble it was for you to marry me in order to earn a few coins!" she snapped back, so stung by his harsh words that she forgot her fear of him. "I may have behaved badly in order to stay out of prison, but I think anyone would understand that. But no one was trying to lock you or your father up for years! All you were after was the money. At least I was trying to preserve my father's honor!"

"Honor?" he shouted. "Is that what you call it? I'd think there's a simpler word for something that can be bought and sold so often."

"*I* sold nothing, my lord," Dulcie shot back. "*You're* the one who was paid on the spot!"

"Oh, good morning, my children," a voice said from the doorway.

Crispin and Dulcie stared at the giant who appeared before them. The earl of Wrede paused in the doorway. Dressed impeccably, Wrede dwarfed the butler, who had shown him in, and dominated the room.

"See? I told you, Stroud," the earl told the butler. "I knew the happy couple wouldn't mind my interrupting their wedding breakfast. Marriage is an odd thing, is it not? Sometimes wedded bliss sounds like domestic strife. But what do we old bachelors know? I'll have a cup of coffee and a few of those rolls and some pastries. Thank you, yes, perfect," he said as he took a seat between Dulcie and Crispin.

"I thought I'd come to terms with the girl," Crispin explained to Wrede with some bitterness as soon as the door closed behind the servants, "but see how that turned out."

"How? You looked like most married couples I've known," the earl commented as he picked up a roll, "which is why I'm still single."

"I offered her money and she threw the offer in my face," Crispin said angrily.

"You offered me an insult," Dulcie said, so angry that she failed to be intimidated by the awesome earl. "I don't want your money. Can't you see that? Can't you make him see that?" she appealed to the earl, who stopped buttering his roll to stare at her. "I don't want to be married to him. I've told him and told him, but he doesn't listen. He locked me in a room last night when I tried to explain. Truly I don't want this marriage any more than you do," she told Crispin slowly and distinctly.

Knowing that he would not do her an injury in front of his friend, she went on talking while she could. "Coming here wasn't my idea. Harry Meech and Jerome Snode got hold of my father and filled him with dreams . . . Well, all right, they talked about money," she grudgingly admitted. "They said you should be made to pay for tricking me into a real marriage. Father's very protective of me, really he is," she insisted. "But sometimes he forgets about me when he gets caught up in his schemes. At any rate, they said you had come into a fortune and ought to be made to pay for tying me up in marriage. They said you might go ahead and marry again anyway, thinking I was nothing, but that *I* couldn't marry because I was a virtuous girl. Which I am!" she added defiantly.

"I objected to their plan," she continued. "I wanted the marriage annulled. I didn't think it was right to make you give us money, because I didn't think you actually knew we were getting married any more than I did. *Really* getting married, I mean. They said you had designs on me. I knew that couldn't be true," she said with simple conviction. "But my father believed it. So I came along with them, thinking that when I got here I could make them see reason, or that they'd see the truth simply by coming here and talking to you. I didn't know my father would change his mind and decide to let me stay married to you! Never, never, never, I swear it," she said fervently.

"You are very handsome," she said, lowering her lashes in her embarrassment, "but I don't belong here. I know that as well as you do. Not because I'm not a lady," she said, her eyes snapping open, "but because I do not go where I am not asked." She raised her small nose. "Our marriage was a mistake. You really were arrogant, you know, writing your true initials down like that. That's just another reason why I don't want to be married to you. I'm not a fool, or a saint. Money is lovely, but you have far more of it than I need or can imagine. And your looks don't matter either, because I don't like you very much."

Crispin blinked as she continued quickly, "So if it's all the same to you, I would like to talk about getting out of this. But if you offer me money or insult me again, I'll stay married to you! See if I don't."

This was so clearly a threat that Crispin found himself beginning to believe her.

"So what do you suggest we do?" the earl asked pleasantly.

"Why, I don't know," she said in surprise. "I thought you did. I mean, you were willing to offer me money to go away, so I assumed you had a plan. I should think we could just do the same thing, only without giving me the money."

Both men sat still. The earl gazed at his plate with interest. Crispin looked at her in silence.

"You didn't mean that I should just go away, so you could marry in peace!" she said with a gasp. "How could I leave it at that? I'd never be at peace, nor would I be able to marry. I do want to marry someday. It may be fine for noblemen to commit bigamy, but I assure you, to the people I associate with, it is not. Or, at least," she added, irresistibly honest, as usual, "to the people I hope to be associating with, it is not."

"It is not precisely 'fine' for people of our rank, either, I assure you," the earl said with a little smile, staring at Dulcie in fascination.

She was tousled and badly dressed, but the immaculate earl was looking beyond that. Dulcie Blessing's odd topaz eyes gleamed with intelligence, her honey-colored hair shone in the sunlight, her complexion was smooth, her mouth sweet and full of promise. The earl was tall and bony, with an angular face that even his best friend would never call more than pleasant. Still Wrede was acknowledged to be an excellent judge of women, and he clearly found this girl to be as interesting and diverting as his friend's predicament was.

"What did you expect me to do?" Dulcie asked in exasperation. "Was I supposed to simply disappear after you paid me? I'm not a papist, so I can't go to a nunnery. Did you expect me to simply vanish off the face of the earth?" she asked. Then all the light left her face. Her hand flew to her lips and she looked at them with widened eyes, as the worst possibility came to her.

But since her expression was as transparent as her horror was, both men knew exactly what had occurred to her the moment it did.

"No. I wasn't thinking of murder," Crispin said in annoyance.

"Yes, you were," she breathed.

"Last night I was thinking of stuffing you in a trash heap, but I didn't do that, did I?" he retorted. "I don't do everything I think of. Do you? Yes, I was furious with you, but no, I do not go around killing people who make me angry. Murder is definitely not in my plans. I suppose I did expect you to simply vanish, but if the marriage papers vanished, too, what would it matter if you really vanished or only disappeared from my life?"

"Oh," she said, but she was pale and very subdued, and looked at him distrustfully.

Suddenly it was very important to Crispin that she believe

him. "If I wanted to do away with you, I wouldn't discuss it in front of Wrede, would I?" he asked.

"He's your friend; he'd hardly care," she said.

"Of course I would care! Never fear, I won't let him murder you, my dear," Wrede said helpfully, smiling at her so warmly she couldn't help but give him a shy smile in return.

"Look you, Wrede," he said when this friend looked at him with a quizzical half smile, "we've no time for conversation. What are we going to do? She seems sincere about renouncing this travesty of a marriage, but her father has the marriage papers." He turned suddenly to Dulcie. "Mistress Blessing, do you think you can make your father change his mind?"

"Last night I'd have said no," Dulcie said thoughtfully, "because when he gets an idea in his head he's like a runaway horse. He won't listen until he's run ragged and can't run anymore. But now a day has gone by. Perhaps I can make him see that I don't intend to go along with his plan, no matter what. If he sees that I am in earnest, he might change his mind. He's not a bad man, only an impulsive one. He's kind and good, and wants what's best for me. Perhaps I can make him see that the best thing for me would be to be free. But even if he gives up the papers, what can we do about the marriage register and the minister and"—she ducked her head shyly—"all those people last night?"

"I can take care of the register and the minister," Crispin said. "As for those people last night, I agree that's unfortunate. But let that be my worry. After all, you won't ever have to see them again."

"Yes," Wrede said, "the viscount can simply explain that it was all a jest—to tease a certain lady. Don't look so dismayed, child, our set does enjoy such jests."

It was so true that Crispin winced.

"Very well," Dulcie said, rising from the table. "I'll just go home and find Father."

"You don't have to go so far. He's here," Crispin said, "I

93

persuaded him to stay the night. I didn't want him running into Harry Meech and his friends in the dark."

"Bad enough to see them in the light," Dulcie agreed nervously.

"Don't worry about anything," Crispin said. "I'll cover your debts. It isn't fair that you should be jailed for my mistake. Then I'll see if I can find you and your father a home far from London and Harry Meech's crew. I'll get the register from poor old Dr. Featherstone and have him write down what we said, not what he imagined. That's only fair, too. Then I'll find him safer harbor than the Fleet. Now you go talk to your father, and we'll have the whole thing settled before long.

"You'll be staying here until I can find you lodging elsewhere," Crispin added.

"I must go to my father," Dulcie said again.

"Ask Stroud to have a footman take you to his room," Crispin said. He followed her into the hall, and watched her as she went up the long stairway.

"I thought you would be intent on getting your own lady back," the earl commented from his side.

"I am," Crispin said absently, still staring after Dulcie. "But this little thing—she's so young and inexperienced. She has no money, no connections, and no friends of any influence at all."

"Indeed," the earl said dryly. He seemed vastly amused.

As they stood in the hallway waiting for Dulcie and her father to return, they heard the door knocker sound. Stroud opened the door, and Crispin heard a familiar voice. His butler turned to look at him. Crispin froze, then silently nodded his head, as the earl whistled low. The front door was opened wide to admit visitors, come to congratulate him on his wedding.

It was raining, so the two sedan chairs outside were carried directly into the hall so that their lady passengers wouldn't get wet as they got out of them. Crispin had only enough wits left to signal Stroud to pay the sedan men, as the two ladies stepped from their chairs. But he had eyes for only one of them.

She removed her cloak to reveal a magnificent gown of brocaded yellow silk with a tight bodice and wide skirt. It was much too elegant for a morning call, but he had never seen her look lovelier. Lady Charlotte's hair was dressed high, as it had been the night before, and was still fully powdered. Only now there were artificial butterflies in the elaborate curls instead of the fresh flowers she'd worn to the ball. Charlotte stared at him and then, without a word, came into his arms. He held her close, before he remembered he had no right to hold her at all.

"Crispin," she said when he released her, and she stepped back to stare up into his face, her eyes bright with emotion, "I didn't sleep at all last night. I didn't know if I should come this morning. Auntie, here, said I should not. But here I am. I had to speak with you. At first I never wanted to see you again. Then I thought I must, if only to say that it was a cruel jest. A cruel, cruel jest. One that I doubtless deserved. But you? Dear boy, no matter how I suffered, you will pay the higher price. To be married to such as that—because of me. To think that you shackled yourself to that creature only to spite me!" she said in wonder. "It's an honor, I suppose, but one I could have done without."

"Are you congratulating Crispin or yourself?" the earl asked sweetly.

"Oh, Wrede," she said as sweetly, "I should have expected to see you here. After all, what else have you to do?"

"I would not have missed this for anything," Wrede assured her so merrily that her smile grew cold and she looked to Crispin again.

"My dear," she sighed, gazing at Crispin from behind the fan that she'd produced, "it was a coup, I'll admit. And for that I do congratulate you. You quite astonished my ene-mies, and you startled me. To marry so soon to show that my rejection meant nothing to you! What a retaliation—it was stunning! Everyone's talking about it. But to trade one night of blissful revenge for a lifetime of unhappiness? A high price for such a little triumph, surely. I'm not at all sure that even Prendergast will be so modern as to allow me to meet with a man who has married so far beneath himself." Her voice held great sympathy, but her eyes blazed. The fan fluttered wildly as she went on, "Rumor has it that she's a commoner with neither money nor reputation to sweeten the pot!"

He'd expected anger, but Charlotte's spiteful attack took Crispin by surprise—until he realized it was typical of Charlotte. Although he'd regretted having to cause her unhappiness, he had honestly never expected her to dissolve into tears. Crying wasn't her style, and Charlotte's style was what he admired most about her. She was as bright and hard as a diamond, and he'd thought himself just the man to appreciate such a gem. Trust Charlotte to give back as good as she got. She might bleed to death from a broken heart, but no one would know it but her pillow. She had a tongue that could cleave like a dagger. No wonder she was society's darling. He would never have been bored with her.

He smiled. "Things may not be what they seem," he said.

Hope sprang to her eyes. "Really?" she asked, her fan slowing to a pulse beat. "A jest within a jest? I see. If so, dear Crispin, how vexed our friends will be with you. They like to watch someone being deceived, but they detest being deceived themselves. I wonder if they'll forgive you for such a joke. I wonder if *I* will," she mused.

"I didn't say it was a joke," Crispin said, suddenly serious. "I only said things may not be what they seem. Charlotte," he said, his handsome face grave. "I can't say more now. I have no right to ask this of you either, but I will anyway. Please wait at least a little while."

She studied his face, and then with a great sigh of pleasure, she returned to his embrace. He would set things right. She would make him pay for this one day, she supposed, because she was not accustomed to being treated badly, but not now. Not until this danger of losing him had passed.

He held her tight, bending to rest his cheek against hers. But it was like resting his head against a stuccoed wall. Her stiffly pomaded and powdered hair scratched his cheek. It had looked exquisite last night, but now it felt like a hard shell atop her head. When he felt Charlotte stiffen and then saw her staring beyond his shoulder with wide eyes, he was glad of a chance to step away from her.

Until he saw what she'd been staring at.

Dulcie Blessing stood on the stairway, white-faced and frightened.

"My lord," she said, and paused, looking at Charlotte.

"Oh, you must not hesitate to speak in front of me," Charlotte said quickly, her gaze traveling up and down Dulcie's slender form, noting her cheap, wrinkled gown and her simply dressed hair. "We met last night, but allow me to reintroduce myself. I'm one Crispin's dearest friends. So dear to him, in fact, that I was going to marry him. Why, the only secret he had from me, it seems, was you. Isn't that so, Crispin my dear?" she asked, her voice sweet but her eyes hard as they slewed to Crispin.

Dulcie spoke before Crispin could. "My lord," she said again, "my father is gone. Vanished. He left only this." A paper trembled in her hand as she held it out to Crispin.

Before Crispin's hopes could rise, he saw that it wasn't the marriage paper, but only a note.

"He left a message for you. And one for me. He says—he says he's not coming back," Dulcie whispered, unbelieving, "for my sake. And he's taken the papers with him to protect them—from you and me and Harry, forever."

CHAPTER
7

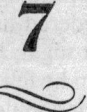

"Charlotte was almost as hard to get rid of as Harry Meech and company," Crispin muttered as he propped his lean frame against the wall near the front door and began to read the letter in his hand.

He couldn't wait to see what Philip Blessing had written in his letter and didn't notice the footmen's stares. After he'd read the note twice, he put out one hand to Dulcie.

"Let me read yours," he commanded. And then looked up from his letter, his eyes hard, when he didn't find another letter in his hand.

Dulcie's chin went up. "No," she said boldly. But he noticed that her defiant chin was trembling.

"I want to read that letter," he said.

She shook her head, backed up, and put her letter behind her back. She look so like a child that he found it hard not to laugh, exasperated as he was.

"It's private," she said warily.

"You're my wife, aren't you?" he asked. "Isn't that what this is all about? So until you're no longer my wife, you have to act like you are. And a wife has no private property, remember? Her husband is her lord, master, and receiver of her letters. Now—the letter, if you please!"

"I don't please," she said, "and that's just another reason I don't want to be married to you."

"Nor I to you. But if you want to change things, you'll have to let me know what's going on, won't you?" he asked, irritatingly aware of the fact that Wrede was still lounging nearby, grinning.

"Well, I suppose," she said hesitantly, handing it over to him.

A moment later he looked up, with an expression of disgust. "It's practically identical to mine," he said. "Full of apologies and telling me nothing I need to know. All I know is that your father has vanished, the way I asked you to do."

He slid the letters into one of his wide pockets and stalked off to speak with Stroud. The butler and the footmen held a hurried conference. One ran off to the kitchens, and when he returned they consulted some more. Crispin nodded and dismissed them.

"At dawn," Crispin reported, "your father left this house wrapped in a cloak, quiet as a mouse. Or a rat. A scullery maid saw him creep out though the kitchens. He was said to have been 'ever so nice,'" Crispin told Dulcie and the earl mockingly, before he stalked off to his study. They followed. When they got into the room, Crispin was standing with his head down, his arms braced on his desk.

"Any idea where he went?" he asked the air.

"No. He could be anywhere," Dulcie said sadly. "We traveled all our lives. He has friends—well, people he knows—everywhere in England."

"Could you be a little more specific?" Crispin asked through gritted teeth.

"London, of course. But Kent and Sussex and Hampshire too. Oh, and we spent some time in Leeds and in Dover, Chester, Bath, and York. And once we went to Scotland. I don't think we ever went to Wales though," she said, considering it.

"Did you tell him you wanted to stay?" Crispin asked, straightening and glaring at her.

"Oh, certainly," she said sarcastically. "Last night I lay on the floor and whispered it under the door. When could I have?"

"I don't know," he said quietly. "You tell me."

"I would tell you if I could," she cried. "He left *me,* not you. He's *my* father, not yours. I want to find him even more than you do. But you don't believe that," she spat. "Oh, no. To you I'm vile and terrible, and something to stare at like a . . . rat, as you say. Well, I'll trouble you no more," she said, and without another word she turned and ran upstairs. But both men heard her crying as she went.

"Don't say it," Crispin said wearily, putting up one hand. "I was very hard on her. Agreed. But she and her father have been hard on me. What you forget is that women can weep at the drop of a handkerchief, so their tears mean nothing. What does mean something is that she bears my name, damn her."

"She seemed very upset," the earl commented.

"So she seemed," Crispin agreed. "But what does *that* mean? I wish I knew. Will she leave? I doubt it, Wrede. Where would she go?"

That was exactly what Dulcie herself was wondering. But go I shall, she thought defiantly, as she glanced around the sumptuous room where she had spent the night. Nothing of her was in the room but her body. And that, she vowed, wouldn't be there for long.

It was one thing to be locked in a room after a harrowing night, but it was broad daylight now. Her father had gone from this terrible place. She hoped it was because he really did think it was the best thing for her. It wasn't, but it would be easier to bear if she could convince herself that he'd really thought it was. She'd be better off elsewhere. But where?

For a start, she thought, dashing her hand across her eyes to dry them, she'd need her things, such as they were. Her clothes and her books . . . She didn't have that many belongings, she realized sadly. She'd always had to travel light, and had collected few mementos. Only those things that would fit in one carpetbag and her pockets. But, she reminded herself sternly, those few things at least were hers.

She would go get them. She would wait an hour or two, until the viscount and his friend forgot about her and then quietly slip away. Her room overlooked the front of the house, and she stayed at the window, waiting for darkness, or enough courage to leave, whichever came first. When she saw the viscount and the earl go outside and saunter down the street together, she knew her moment had come, whether she was ready or not. Her cape had been brought up from downstairs sometime during breakfast, and it was the sole garment hanging in her wardrobe. No wonder the servants had looked at her so strangely. She threw it over her shoulders. There was a thin rain falling, and her cloak was threadbare, but that didn't matter. Nothing mattered, except being able to leave.

There was a footman at the door when she approached it.

"My lady," he said unhappily. He glanced over her head, his apparent distress the signal to another footman to fetch Mr. Stroud.

"Can I help you, my lady?" the butler asked from behind Dulcie, as the footman blocked her exit. Dulcie thought he asked it as though he knew he couldn't.

"No, not at all," she said, wishing she knew his name so she could have the better of him. "I'm only going out for a while."

"Very good. Winston, accompany the lady," Stroud commanded the footman. Winston nodded, straightened his coat, and opened the door.

"No," Dulcie said firmly, "I do not wish to have an escort."

"It is unheard of for a lady to go out without being accompanied by a footman," Stroud said with scant patience.

"Exactly," Dulcie said, sweeping out the door as though she were wearing ermine, "And I, as you certainly have been informed, am not a lady."

She was down the street before the butler could move. She turned the corner, running so fast he would have had to send Mercury after her to catch her. She pulled her cloak's hood over her head and then hid in a doorway, just to be sure they hadn't followed.

When she ventured out again the rain had resolved itself into a cold, sullen mizzle that seeped into her clothes, shoes, and bones. She was alone, however, and Dulcie felt rejuvenated. She headed for her lodgings, and didn't slow her pace. She hurried past the taverns, clubs, and shops in the viscount's part of town with her head down, in the admittedly foolish hope that if she didn't see them, the viscount and his minions wouldn't see her.

She only dared to look up again when she heard familiar raucous music. She knew the voices of the street vendors in her own part of town, and as she walked, she found herself relaxing. She smiled as she listened to women singing the virtues of their flowers, fruits, oysters, and eggs, and heard the rough counterpoint of men bawling about their fish and vegetables, firewood and meat. Their cries were loud and discordant, but the sound was truly music to her ears. She felt as if they were serenading her, welcoming her home.

She shuddered as she sidestepped a rabbit seller whose long poles were strung with skinned and trussed little bodies, hung head down, and she was making her way down the alley to her door when her luck ran out.

"Why, viscountess," Harry Meech said with great satisfaction as she was forced to stop short in front of a hulking brute who had stepped directly in front of her, a smirking giant she dimly recognized from her nightmare of a wedding party. "How good to see you again.

"If you will come this way, my lady," Meech said as he saw her eyes darting about, looking for a way around him and the two bruisers who accompanied him.

"Your father's not at home. We checked. And since your husband's not with you, either, I offer you my escort. After all, we wouldn't want anything to happen to you, would we? This is a very dangerous city for a young, beautiful noblewoman traveling alone," he warned her, offering his arm.

"No," she said, and was as shocked as he was by her answer. But if she could be rude to a viscount, she reasoned, trying to hold back her panic, she could be just as bold with a common swindler. She swallowed hard and spoke before she could think better of it. "No," she said again, "I do not want your escort."

A nobleman had ignored her rudeness, but Harry Meech didn't. He grabbed her arm. "Too bad, because you're having it and more, my lady. You're most definitely coming with me, like it or not."

"I don't see why," she said. "My father is a pauper, the viscount doesn't want me, and I don't want him. I've left him. So you can't hold me for ransom. Well, you could, but it wouldn't do you any good. The viscount would be only too glad to have you do away with me, or dismember me, or whatever," she said, shivering, "so there's no profit it in for you."

"But you *are* still his viscountess, whether you like it or not," Harry said with a smile. "All sorts of interesting things can be done to or with a woman who bears his name. Whether or not he likes you, I do believe he values the name you now bear. So you're worth a great deal to him, my lady. And to us, too."

"I can't see how," Dulcie said, thinking she might be able to argue her way out of this predicament, though the coldness in Harry's smile and her own stomach was arguing that she could not.

"Oh, but I can," Harry said. "For example, your employment in a brothel might do it. You're a lovely girl; many men would like to lie with you, I'm sure. But no matter what you looked like, many would find it amusing to bed the Viscountess West for a few coins. It would be great sport for a certain kind of gentleman. Lovely gossip in their clubs, too. I think the viscount would mind that, don't you?"

"I told you," she persisted, though her knees felt weak, "he doesn't care what happens to me."

"Doubtless," Harry said impatiently, "but the name you have now—he cares very much for that, doesn't he? There are other things," he said, when he saw how quiet and pale she became as she thought about it, "even worse things. I won't discuss them now. Or ever—if you come along with me. After all, I've every confidence he'll pay up to get you back. I'm not a cruel man. So why should I bother your pretty head with all the unpleasant possibilities he's going to be presented with? Just come along, my lady, won't you?"

Dulcie planted her sopping shoes firmly on the muddy street, as though she hoped they'd take root there. "No," she said. "No, I won't. I won't."

Never, she thought. They would have to pick her up and carry her, and she would scream louder than the fishmongers, and kick and pinch and bite, and they'd have to knock her silly to get her to go with them. But at least that way she'd be unconscious, and so wouldn't feel as terrible as she did now. Her bravery wasn't much, but it was the only thing she could do to assert herself. She braced herself.

"Oh, you will," Harry promised.

"No, she won't," another voice said from behind her.

Dulcie spun around. She had thought that he looked like an angel the first time she saw him. Now he looked like an avenging angel. The viscount had drawn his sword, and his eyes glowed with blue fire. She wanted to applaud, but was happy enough to have her wrist wrenched hard as he grabbed her and pulled her to his side. Then Crispin thrust her behind him, and she was never so happy to be cast off. The earl of Wrede, who was standing beside her, she noted absently, was smiling.

"Don't worry, my dear," Wrede said loud enough for everyone to hear in the tense silence, "your husband is a brilliant swordsman."

"No matter," Harry said from the side of his mouth to his two men, who stood hesitant. "One swordsman, brilliant or not, can't do much against three men."

"Two men," Crispin corrected him, taking advantage of the moment of hesitation to toss his sword to his other hand. He used his free hand to throw a hard punch to one burly man's considerable stomach. When the man bent over double, Crispin slammed the hilt of his sword against his chin so hard they could all hear the man's teeth click together before he crashed to the cobbles.

"No, sorry, make that one man," Crispin said through his own tightly clenched teeth, as he placed the point of his sword at the other ruffian's throat. As the man stood, irresolute, Crispin stamped hard on the toe of his boot. He yelped, and Crispin said, "So sorry," and landed a hard punch on his chin, then landed another and sent him sprawling.

"Ah, alone at last, Harry," Crispin said with a snarl, advancing on Harry Meech. *"Now* I get a chance to show off my brilliant swordsmanship," he said with a feral grin.

"I think not," Harry cried, and turned and ran, with considerable speed for a man of his age. He had disappeared into the shadows by the time Crispin sheathed his sword.

"Now," Crispin said, advancing on Dulcie with no less threat than he'd shown the men groaning at his feet, "I'd like to know what you thought you were doing?"

"Getting rid of myself," she said, her lips trembling because of the terrible look in his eyes, which was not glad or welcoming or comforting. "Vanishing. Or trying to. The way you said you wanted me to do. But I don't know how to throw myself away, although I tried. Surely you must see that I tried."

Then she began to cry, and so she didn't see the look in his eyes. Although it was still not welcoming or glad, it would have pleased her.

"She's in her room, sleeping, or pretending to," Crispin said wearily to Wrede, as he nursed his snifter of brandy.

He didn't mention that he'd gone to Dulcie's room when she hadn't appeared for dinner, and when he received no answer to his repeated taps on her door, he had opened it anyway and found her sound asleep, curled up in a chair, as though she found even his bed loathsome. He'd stared at her for a moment, noting how her face was slightly flushed with sleep, as a child's might be. He'd seen, too, the steady rise and fall of breasts that proved she was no child. She was still wearing that dreadful gown of hers. But she'd let her hair down, and it fell in soft, shining curls to her shoulders.

He was fascinated. Her hair was silky. He'd been drawn to it, and couldn't resist feeling it first with the tips of his fingers and then, bemused, with the back of his hand. She'd stirred beneath that light touch, as though her soft flesh had felt his caress. He'd snatched his hand away and left, quickly and quietly.

Now he looked at the hand that had stroked that cool silken fire, until he saw Wrede watching him quizzically. Then he turned his hand over and gazed at his cut and bruised knuckles. "I'm becoming too much the London gentleman," he commented. "A few blows and my hands turn to forcemeat. I should have skewered Harry and his friends instead of crushing my knuckles on them."

"You behaved very badly," Wrede said, as he rose from his chair.

"Don't I know it. I was way off form," Crispin agreed. "It took too much effort. It wouldn't have happened if I'd more practice."

"That's not what I'm talking about," Wrede replied. "She's only a young girl. You were beastly to her. If I had such a pretty little thing in my care, I wouldn't thunder at her and make sour faces."

"You don't have her," Crispin said bluntly, the firelight showing a strange glitter in his eyes.

"Oh. So you want her, do you?" the earl asked, lifting an eyebrow.

"No, I do not. And you know it," Crispin answered edgily, "but Harry Meech was right about one thing: for so long as she bears my name, I will protect her. Good God, Wrede, seriously—just think of the hold she has on me! Until I straighten this mess out, I have to be her chaperon as well as her bodyguard."

"Flight, capture, violence, then laughter and tears," Wrede said with relish. "Discussion at my clubs can't touch this sort of stuff. Even my brilliant friends' efforts to amuse pale in comparison. Why, your company these days is better than the theater. It's only too bad I can't invite my other friends along."

"I'm glad you're enjoying yourself," Crispin said sourly, "because I'm not."

"Don't bother to see me out," said the earl, heading for the door, "I've an engagement this evening or I'd stay. I wonder what will be dished up when she eventually comes down for dinner? I haven't been so amused in years. Thank you, Crispin."

"Wrede," Crispin said as he turned his empty goblet around and around in his long fingers, "thank you for helping."

"But you never gave me the chance."

"Knowing I was not alone was helpful."

"My dear friend, you had an army behind you. Two footman who followed her from the house, another lurking at the father's lodgings, and that odd little boy who kept peeping out at us from various places after we left the tavern when your footman came running to tell you she'd escaped. At first I thought there were three or four young boys along the route, but they all had the same filthy, furtive, and very intelligent countenance. Was he with us or against us, by the way?"

"I don't know," Crispin said, with the first real smile he'd worn all afternoon, "but knowing Willie Grab—both, I think."

Then, as though the words had reminded him, he put a finger to his lips and rose quickly from his chair. While his friend watched, puzzled, he stalked to the partly open window and threw it all the way open suddenly.

"You might as well show yourself, Willie," he called out. "I felt the draft when I came in but didn't understand it until now. There's no other reason for this window to be open on a such a dank night, not even just the crack you lifted it so you could hear. So give over. There's someone I'd like you to meet. A gentleman. Don't worry, it's not anyone from Bow Street. You know which gentleman I mean—the tall one you've seen with me all day."

"Oh, him!" a merry voice said, and a grimy face appeared at the window. Then a knee, and then all of the thin boy who scrambled into the room through the opened window. He wore threadbare hose and baggy breeches, and his coat was ill-fitting enough to conceal anything he chose to stow in its many pockets. But his grin was wide and congenial, as though he were welcoming the two fine gentlemen to his rooms, instead of having just clambered in their window.

"Willie Grab, may I present the earl of Wrede?" Crispin said. "Wrede, this horrible youth is the author of my difficulties. He's the one who recommended me as a groom to Harry Meech in the first place."

"As a favor, my lord," Willie reminded him, gazing around the room in fascination.

"Yes," Crispin mused, putting a hand in his pocket and withdrawing a coin. He watched its dulcet golden glow in the firelight, and smiled. "It seemed like a favor at the time. Now, of course, it's a millstone, isn't it? Leave off counting the merchandise, Willie. You'll never get a piece of it outside this door without a fight," he commented idly. "Why were you following me today?" he asked suddenly, without looking up.

The boy was too quick for such tricks and answered just as idly, without removing his roving gaze from the room as he took inventory of it. "Keeping an eye out for you, my lord."

But then, as though he felt the icy force of Crispin's continued stare, he turned to him and protested, "Honest. I was. I knew our Harry was up to no good. Been lurking, he has. He and his bully boys. Lurking all about the place, watching for her, or you. Very narked, is our Harry. There's money about, and he can't get his hands on it. It makes him wild."

"But it's not his money," the earl said, fascinated.

"In *his* head it is," Willie explained, throwing a bright look at the earl's splendidly clad figure, "'cause, see, he was the one brought the girl to the lord, as he sees it. So if she's in the gravy now, he wants a spoonful too—any way he can get it. Leave it to Harry to think up ways. He looked for old man Blessing everywhere, but he's run for it. If you get Bow Street looking for the old man, remember that some of the Bow Street crowd owe Harry a favor or two too. Just thought I'd pass that on."

"Kind of you," Crispin said. "Is that why you were following me today? Out of kindness? And if so, then why didn't you come speak to me, instead of scarpering off each time I saw you?"

"I didn't have to tell you nothing when I saw you today 'cause you were already on the right scent," Willie said. "I was just making sure of it."

"Or were you following Harry's orders?" Crispin went on pensively. "And if so, I wonder why you let me see you at all. When you don't want to be seen, you're invisible." Crispin began to smile at the thought, but remembered someone who had just tried to vanish. It wiped the grin from his face. His voice was chill when he asked, "You're full of mysteries, aren't you? How much will it cost me to discover them? And how much will Harry pay you to tell him about this conversation? You'll be a rich lad soon, won't you, Willie?"

"Nah. Nobody gets rich working for Harry," Willie said

with regret. Then he drew himself up, looked Crispin in the eye, and said clearly, "Listen, my lord. I work for Harry sometimes, but I think for myself all the time. There's things I'll do and things I won't—not for no money. Harry asked me to keep an eye on you. I done it. You don't need to pay me a thing. That's my coin, my lord, if you remember. You offered it to me once. I gave it back, but I remember it. Just look on it like I'm protecting my investment. You watch out for yourself, my lord. And the pretty lady. Harry's hungry, and when he's hungry, he puts rats to shame."

He grinned at his own cleverness, and then, after a mockery of a bow, he put one hand on the sill and vaulted out through the window.

"Don't bother looking," Crispin said, as the earl hurried to the window and looked out. "He's either a mile away or so close by that he could pluck off your wig before you could blink."

The earl straightened, but not before both men thought they heard a giggle—or perhaps it was a branch, stirred by night breezes, scratching against a pane of glass.

"I claim a friendship with the Fielding brothers," the earl said after a moment's thought. "Henry's a good man. But gone from the country at the moment, alas. He's off to write somewhere else, leaving London's crime and criminals to his brother, Sir John. A good man, too, he's the magistrate now. Would you like me to ask him to have Bow Street look into Harry Meech and the missing father?"

"No, no need," Crispin said. "Anyway, don't forget, my actions were as criminal as anyone's in this. I entered a mock marriage for purposes of deception, as well as for money, you know."

"Ah, but you're an aristocrat, and so much can be forgiven—and forgotten," the earl reminded him.

"Didn't you hear the boy? Bow Street may be useful and the runners good at their work, but not if Harry can reach them. And don't forget, the girl is as guilty as I am. She'll be in trouble if the marriage is annulled as quickly as I hope it can be."

"Oh! So you *do* care what happens to her? Ecod, man!" the earl said in mock astonishment. "She was the one who got you into this difficulty."

"Not so," Crispin reproved him. "*I* was the one who got me into this difficulty," he added with a rueful laugh.

"This is a bad business. You bought yourself more trouble than I suspected when you took a bride," the earl said, looking at his friend with concern.

"No," Crispin corrected him, "I bought myself more trouble than I knew when I let them buy me as a groom. Don't worry," he said when he saw his usually cynical friend so apprehensive. "I'll be careful. With luck, I'll be rid of my 'wife' before long. Then, my money restored, my unwanted wife gone, I'll be able to live the normal, safe, boring life of a proper aristocrat."

"No need to be insulting," the earl said huffily. But Crispin noted his eyes, usually so amused, were still deeply troubled when he left.

Crispin stayed in his library, sipping brandy and staring into the fire for a long while. He was not as surprised as his butler was when he was eventually told that he had another visitor waiting to see him.

"It is very late, my lord, and so I told him" Stroud said, nervously fingering the buttons on his hastily donned coat. "We forcibly ejected this same fellow the other day. But he said it was a matter of life and death this time. He said he had news it was to your advantage to hear. He insists on speaking with you. I reasoned it was better to tell you of this imposition now than to have him accost you on the street tomorrow. The footmen searched him, and he carries no killing weapons."

"He carries only threats and plots," Crispin said wearily, "but they're better heard than imagined. You acted rightly. Don't fret. Let him in."

"Hello, Harry," Crispin said without looking up, when the man was shown into the room. "Have you found my beloved father-in-law?"

"Regrettably, my lord, no," Harry said, standing where the butler had left him, hat in his hands.

Crispin turned his head slightly to eye his visitor. "You didn't come at this hour to try to convince my lady 'wife' to leave her bed and follow you, and I'm too big to carry off—as you found out this afternoon. So, what is it? Have you come to challenge me to a duel? . . . I didn't think so. It must be something important, for you to risk coming to see me after what you tried today."

"I'm only trying to be helpful," Harry said.

"You? Here at this hour, to be helpful? Do tell," Crispin said, and looked back into the fire. When Harry said nothing, Crispin cocked an eyebrow. "I forget my manners. Have a seat, Harry, and tell me what's on your mind, before morning comes, please."

Harry perched on the edge of a chair opposite his host. The room was lit only by the fire's inconstant light. But no trace of the amusement he'd heard in the viscount's voice could be seen in his stern, handsome face.

"You, my lord, have a problem," Harry said, "and you blame me for it. But I had no way of knowing who you really were when you married the girl. Even if I had, you hadn't a penny to bless yourself with when we met, so it wouldn't have mattered. When things turned out the way they did," Harry said, shrugging, "I tried to take some advantage of it, true. But you can't really blame me for that, my lord. Oh, maybe if you were a man of God, like our poor addled Featherstone, you could. But you're a man of the world.

"Myself, I'm but a poor man," Harry went on, "with no prospects except those I can invent for myself. You're a nobleman, with a full purse. Your life stretches ahead of you like a pleasant prospect, but mine is an unhappy dream. The good Lord may have given us the same number of years in our cups, but I have to wake each morning and find a way to eat in order to get to the next day to see out my life. Sometimes the ways I discover are not lawful or moral, but they see me through and so I have no choice but to use them. Blame me or our society? I wonder, my lord."

"Touching sentiments. I won't dispute them," Crispin said dryly. "They need you in the House of Commons, Harry, not at my fireside. Get on with it."

"So you mustn't blame me if my plans sometimes run counter to yours," Harry said.

"I mustn't? But I do," Crispin said. "When I found myself without money, I damned near broke my back earning some. You try to earn it from other people's backbreaking work. We'll never agree there. But you didn't come here to talk philosophy. My patience is wearing thin, Harry. You wanted to see me tonight. Why?"

"All right," Harry said, "here it is plainly. You have a wife you don't want. I can't find her father, and I can't get my hands on her. So there's no profit there for me. I take what I can, where I can and when I can. There's still a way for me—and for you, too—to profit in this. You're a man of the world, my lord. Think on. We can work something out, surely."

The library was still except for the licking of the fire on the grate.

"I want to be quite sure I understand you correctly," Crispin finally said quietly.

"There's nothing to it. Just let her leave. And look the other way. You won't ever have to see her again, I promise you that," Harry said nervously.

"Ah," Crispin said, "and of course, you wouldn't then come to me for more money for the rest of my life?"

"How could I?" Harry asked. "A murderer asking a nobleman for money for such a foul deed? Even *I* could never do that. Who would believe me? I'd swing before I could hint it. You have connections, I don't. I've no title, no property, no stake in the realm at all. That's why I would ask a substantial sum for doing the deed. It would be quick," he went on when he heard no answer, "and as painless as these things can go, too, I assure you. Little fear and less pain—that's the way to snuff a lady. Then you'd be completely free and who would know—or care? The father's gone, and of no account anyway. She'll have no mourners; no one will miss her. It's so simple, my lord. Expensive, I grant you. But simplicity itself."

Crispin stood in one lithe movement. "Harry, leave now," he said so quietly Harry didn't understand him at first. But then he heard the tone and saw the look in Crispin's blazing eyes. They were the brilliant blue that burns in the heart of fire. "Leave before I make matters worse for me and for you. Never come back. If I ever see you again, it will be the last time you see anything. That I promise you."

Harry rose and began backing out of the room, never taking his eyes off Crispin, as though the viscount's cold words were a hot wind from hell itself.

When he'd gone, Crispin turned and gazed, unseeing, into the fire again. His teeth were clenched, his shoulders tight with anger. He was still furious, but mostly at himself now. He realized there had been a time, when all of this had first begun, when he had wished she had never existed. He had wanted her to vanish. She'd seen it and had damn near ruined herself trying to accommodate him. He flinched at the memory.

He turned from his thoughts abruptly. The remembrance was painful, but she was his responsibility now, for good or evil. And he took his responsibilities seriously.

CHAPTER
8

Dulcie avoided her husband by taking breakfast in her room. She couldn't have any of the lovely porridges and puddings they served downstairs, she thought with regret, but it was a fair trade because she avoided the eyes of the servants. She didn't try her door to see if she was a prisoner after the maids left her breakfast either, because she didn't know what to do if she wasn't. She had no desire to meet up with Harry Meech, and less to meet the viscount's eyes if she dared escape his house again.

She didn't remain idle in her room, though; she made herself very busy all morning. She rinsed out her underthings, and then she waited for them to dry. She also washed her hair, and sat by the fire until the dampness was out of it. Then she heard a tapping at her door.

"His lordship wishes to see you now," the housekeeper announced, "in his study."

Dulcie inclined her head in what she hoped was a stately nod, and followed the stiff-backed woman down the long stairway.

He was waiting for her in his study. He motioned her to a seat near his desk as soon as the housekeeper left the room.

She sat, lowering her eyes, observing him from beneath her lashes until she saw he wasn't looking at her. He stood beside his desk, staring out the window at a courtyard bathed in the watery sunlight of the early spring day. His dress was immaculate, and she was sure that she had never seen such a handsome man. Or a colder one. When he turned his head to find her watching him, she dropped her gaze in sudden confusion, fretfully smoothing the skirt of her dull brown gown. She did not want him to see what was in her eyes, and because of this, she missed the look of regret in his.

"There are certain things that have to be taken care of," he said, without preamble. "You need clothes, for one thing."

"Good morning to you too, my lord," she said, her quick temper chasing away her fear.

"Oh, is it a good morning?" he asked sweetly. "You treated me to such a lovely night last night. I really enjoy chasing through the streets of London, searching for a woman I don't dare name to passersby. Wouldn't that have sounded wonderful? 'Excuse me, sir, have you seen my wife, the viscountess? No, I have no idea where she's gone, but she's wearing an ugly brown gown and is running for her life. From whom? Oh, from me, of course,'" he said, and glowered at her.

She was helpless against his attractiveness, but she knew how to defend herself against his anger.

"Oh, really?" she flared up. "Whose fault is that? You asked me to disappear. And this gown did very well for me before I came here. Besides, I have nothing else here to wear. I was going to get my clothes last night, as a matter of fact."

"Your clothes, and a fine lesson in reality from your friend Harry Meech," Crispin said. He saw her grow pale as she remembered Harry's threat. "You have to stay here with me until we decide what to do next. That's all there is to it. Forget whatever you left at your lodgings. We'll have to get you new clothes, anyway. You're a viscountess now. *My* viscountess. People will talk if they see my household staff dressed better than my wife."

"But I'm not *really* your wife, and people are already talking. Why shouldn't they? Who ever heard of a nobleman marrying a commoner on the sly and dragging her out by force to present her at a ball he's supposedly giving to pick another lady for his wife? Your friends are probably not talking about anything else," she said, rising to her feet, shaking just to think of what people must be saying about her. "So what does it matter what I wear? I could wear a queen's clothes and they'd still talk."

"Yes. But their tone would be different," he said more softly, hating the way she was shaking. "It would be interested chitchat, not vicious gossip. They'll speak more kindly of you if you're well dressed," he said more gently, seeing the tears start in her eyes, making them even more dazzling.

"Mistress Blessing," he said softly, coming closer as she averted her head and fought back the treacherous tears, "this marriage is a mockery, but we have to make the best of it until we can dissolve it. After that, I'll find a clever way to explain my part in it. You can explain away anything if you have money and position," he said with a little smile. "Then I'll give you enough money so you can disappear in comfort this time. Why, this marriage may be the making of you.

"But," he went on, "you have to behave like a viscountess as long as you are one. That means wearing new clothes."

"Why can't you just let me disappear?" she demanded. But to her chagrin, it came out sounding more like a plea.

"Because," he said as he touched a fingertip to a tear that had escaped her vigilance, "while you're my wife you're my responsibility. You must pretend to be my wife for your own good now. You're too valuable to too many bad people, alone and unprotected. Do you understand?"

He hardly heard his own words. All he could see was those wonderful eyes, awash with tears, and that sweet plump mouth so near to his. He traced the tear track with gentle wonder as she stared up at him, breathless. Then he lowered his head and brushed her lips with his. He meant to comfort her. Or reassure her, but she was so fresh and lovely. He was shocked by the electricity that coursed through him at that light, tentative touch. And so, against all reason, he sought the warmth of her sweet mouth.

Dulcie could only gasp in wonder at the delicious feel of his lips. She'd never felt anything like it. She'd been curious enough to have given a boy a kiss once, and then had to give him a slap for the kiss he'd tried to steal immediately afterward. But that had been nothing like this. This kiss was so sweet. His mouth was cool, then warm, then fiery. She gasped and he moved closer, taking advantage of her slight submission.

What had begun as a light pressure against her lips became an altogether different sensation throughout her body, a pleasure that was new to Dulcie but only too well known to Crispin. The kiss became deep and urgent as they both sought more. The thickness of her gown and petticoats encased her body from the waist down, but still she felt his body hard against hers, and she needed every bit of his strength to remain standing, seeking what his mouth offered her. He held her face like a cup from which he must drink his fill, both his hands in her silken hair, stroking it across the satin of her skin, everywhere smooth to his touch.

It was only when his tongue touched hers, hot and strange and intrusive, showing her that this feeling came from someone else, someone who was invading her, that Dulcie came back to herself with a thump, as if she'd fallen a long way back to earth. This was a kiss that had turned serious. More serious than Dulcie had ever gotten. More serious than a girl like Dulcie could afford to get.

She pushed him away, her eyes wild with anger at him and herself.

"Ah!" she cried, shaken, "I see, indeed! Pretend to be your wife indeed! Wear new clothes and take them off to get into your bed, no doubt! Oh, I'm impressed. What a fine tale. And all the time you'll be telling me that people will talk more kindly about me. Well, I can't be bought, my lord, with a gown or with kind words."

"That kiss," Crispin said as he stepped back and stared down at her with eyes hard as gemstones, "was a mistake."

"Oh, certainly," she said. "And how many more are you planning? Let me go."

"It won't happen again," Crispin said, as angry at her as he was at himself. It had been a strange moment of inconvenient desire that he should never have allowed to happen. He could not afford to let a temporary desire ruin his whole future. If he took her to his bed, she would become his wife in truth—a high price to pay for a moment of pleasure.

Unwilling to look at him, she stared out the window, seeing no way to escape him. She didn't know what to say in defense of herself. She was spared the embarrassment of trying.

"Good morning," the earl of Wrede said as he strolled into the room, "We did have a luncheon appointment, didn't we?" he asked, looking with interest from Crispin to Dulcie. "Am I interupting something? Why I believe I am. Would you like me to leave?"

"Wrede," Crispin said threateningly.

"Well, then, I have an idea," Wrede said, as they both looked at him glumly. "Let me take Mistress Dulcie to get her new clothes. She bears a noble name now; she can't cause more gossip by wearing threadbare garments. My presence will quell gossip, and the clothes will silence it further."

Crispin glanced at Dulcie and grinned. She thought he looked triumphant, and her eyes blazed.

"What say you, Crispin? Do we get the girl new gowns?" the earl asked.

"Have I no say in this? Don't you consider me at all?" Dulcie blurted out. "I may be poor, I may have no title, but I am a person."

"You do have a title," the earl reminded her, "and at the moment you are not poor, either. But you are dressed abominably."

"No! Not abominably," Crispin said quickly, seeing the hurt spring to her eyes. "Just not extravagantly. And so not correctly, for a viscountess."

Dulcie looked up at him. "Thank you," she whispered.

Crispin smiled at her, a clear unshadowed smile. She had to look away from those smiling lips because she remembered how that mouth had felt against hers and when she did, she grew warm and embarrassed. Her rising color made him remember, too, and his eyes grew bright.

He laughed when he saw how adorably confused she looked, but spared her feelings by pretending he still thought her reluctant to be properly gowned. "Be guided by Wrede in this, please," he told her gently. "He knows what a lady should look like and, having three sisters, has much more patience than I have with such matters."

"She'll need new gowns, caps, and wigs," Wrede said comfortably, "which are now becoming fashionable for the ladies. It's the latest craze. We'll go to Monsieur Pamplemousse."

"No," Dulcie said, "I mean to say: no, please. I don't like to wear anything heavy on my head. It gives me headaches."

"Because you've *tons* of your own hair, child," Wrede said. "Crop it and a wig will fit like a glove and feel very good, I assure you."

"No," Dulcie and Crispin said in unison.

"Ladies first," Crispin said, and waited for her to speak.

"Well, I just don't want to wear a wig. I won't do it," she said mulishly, because she was very much afraid she'd be wearing one by nightfall, "and that's that."

"That's decided then," Crispin said quickly. "No wigs. But Wrede will accompany you and help you choose a whole new wardrobe. All right?"

Dulcie nodding, looking at him with gratitude. Crispin

smiled at her. Wrede watched with a raised eyebrow as he saw the warmth of that smile.

Dulcie was due at luncheon, but was afraid to get dressed —or, rather, terrified to wear her new clothes. They belonged behind glass, surely, she thought, staring into her wardrobe. They were hastily altered leftovers from a canceled trousseau. Much more had been ordered, but Wrede insisted she have some things to wear immediately. She didn't know why he'd bothered to order more. What she had now took her breath away.

A gown of peach satin with gold brocade to shame an emperor. A blue gown with embroidery so fine she'd rather hang it on her bed than her body, and a green silk gown with silk panniers embellished with citrines and seed pearls. And a gown of sunset yellow silk. She had clothes of such rare subtlety that it seemed to her to be immoral to wear them.

A person, Dulcie thought glumly, could never feel comfortable in one of those magnificent gowns. At least this person wouldn't, she thought sadly. Not for the first time she wondered how long she would stay in this house, for surely, beautifully gowned or not, she didn't belong here.

She let Annie, her maid, help her into the new blue gown. It was fashionably cut, with a hooped petticoat. The dressmaker said it was casual enough for daytime, although Dulcie thought it would suit an evening at a palace. The silk felt wonderful against her skin, and she wondered how she could ever stop stealing little strokes at it once she was downstairs. What if she spilled something on it? How could she ever replace such a dress? But she stopped worrying about its cost when she glanced in the mirror and saw the amount of breast the dress exposed. It was very low in front, and her new corset, though it was more comfortable than the coarse one she'd had, pushed her breasts up and out in a shocking manner. It made them seem to be trying to peek up out of her gown.

"I can't wear this," she muttered.

"Ooo, but you look lovely, my lady, truly you do," her maid said.

"Well, but . . ." Dulcie began to dither. Then she remembered she'd only earned the maid's respect by being distant and decisive—she'd been copying the earl's manner for the past week, since she'd been living in the house. It had worked. The household staff might not think any better of her, but they acted as though they did. And that, she supposed sadly, was all that really mattered. It was true the servants were just as respectful of Crispin, who was much more casual with them. But she couldn't deal with, much less copy, his air of cool command.

She couldn't deal with him at all, she thought, nibbling her lower lip. Not since that kiss. All two hundred kisses— the real one and all the others she'd imagined since. That was the only way she could have gotten them, because she'd seldom seen him since that day. Wrede shopped with her and then left her, but she hadn't even seen her husband. He dined elsewhere, was gone before she was up, and returned home after she went to her room. Marriage, Dulcie thought, might not be bad if it was lived this way. She was still lonely and friendless, but at least no longer frightened—except when she found herself longing to meet up with her distant husband again.

Dulcie glanced in the mirror and squared her shoulders. When she saw the effect that had on her bodice, all her breath came out again. Having decided to use her new fan to cover her breasts, she snapped it open, squared her shoulders again, and went down to luncheon in her new gown.

"Voilà! Behold!" Wrede said triumphantly when she appeared in the salon.

Dulcie glanced worriedly at Crispin. He had no expression at all on his handsome face as he stared at her.

"Very nice," Crispin finally said, circling Dulcie, looking at her from her carefully arranged curls to her satin shod feet. "Quite lovely."

Dulcie didn't know what to say, so she curtsied instead, and saw his eyes widen as she dipped down. That was when she decided that the bodice of her gown was perfect, after all. When she rose from her curtsy, her cheeks were as bright as her eyes.

"You look wonderful. That dress suits our needs perfectly," Crispin told her. "We've gotten a stack of invitations since I announced the marriage. We'll ignore them, for we will need some time to sort things out. Meanwhile, however, we can't keep you caged up like a mad mother-in-law in the tower. You have to go out sometime, and we have to be seen together, or there'll be more talk."

"But when it's over . . . ?" she whispered.

"When it's over, it will be over, and you'll be gone from my circle and well rid of them. But I have to live in my world, Dulcie."

It was the first time she'd ever heard him say her name, and it caused her heart to contract. She had to concentrate very hard on whatever else it was that he was saying.

"Look you, Dulcie," he went on, "I can't become famous for having married a recluse or a monster of some kind. Not even once upon a time, in my foolish youth," he said, watching her face to read her reaction to his words there. "I showed you to them. It was a mistake, but now I have to make good on it. A divorce will be bad enough, but a mysterious hidden wife would be a mark I'd never be able to erase. Secrecy breeds suspicion and horror stories. I know these people. They'll put three humps on your back and give you a tail if we don't take you out for a public viewing soon. They saw you only briefly, when you were terrified and badly dressed. This time you'll still be terrified, but very well dressed."

When she didn't smile, he went on, "You won't have to get to know them intimately. That would only make it harder when you leave."

"I don't want to know them intimately!" Dulcie protested.

"Good. Because you won't go to teas and women's socials either. But I do have to show you off, if only for a little while. You must see that. Then I can say you're a victim to headaches, or whatever other fashionable ailment you like. After that, all we'll have to do is produce you for occasions of state until you're free to go about your own life again."

His clear eyes searched her face, and she nodded. She did see his reasoning, although she wished she didn't. He offered her his arm so they could go in to luncheon. As they walked to the dining room, he told Wrede, "I thought we'd go to several house parties this Saturday night."

"Good thinking," Wrede said, "I suggest the Rivingtons' and the Dumonts', certainly. Rivington made his money recently, and so he has no airs. The Dumonts are social climbers and can't afford to offend anyone. And the Wildes', too, of course. He married a miller's daughter, but he has so much money they're accepted almost everywhere."

It wasn't what Dulcie wanted, but she could see the necessity of it. She even began to enjoy the idea. She didn't know what was going to happen to her anyway, and so far each new thing she'd dreaded had turned out very nicely. Crispin himself, for example. He'd frightened her near to death the night of the ball, and now he only frightened and confused her with longings she shouldn't have. And even Wrede was treating her well. The luxury of being a viscountess was no small thing either. Perhaps moving in exalted circles would turn out to be a dizzying pleasure, she thought with her natural resiliency. But first she had to prove she could manage it.

She managed luncheon very well. As the men discussed which invitations to accept and which to ignore, she had the time to take great care with her meal. Not a speck of the oysters, baked fish, roast beef, or jugged fowl went anywhere but into her mouth. Her gown was spared the soup, the sauces, and the wine as well. Her fear of stains made her eat sparingly, as did her tight new corset. Still, she got through the entire meal without mishap and was proud of herself.

But when a footman brought Crispin a note as coffee was being poured, a bite of buttery fritter went slithering down her chin to her chest.

She dabbed, blotted, and sponged, and hoped they thought her distress was because of the spill. But that was the least of her worries now. She had recognized the note. Such letters had been arriving with regularity. She saw them on the table near the front door each day when she went out, each evening when she came in. All were for him. She'd come to know that handwriting, that parchment paper, but most of all, she knew the pungent aroma of jasmine emanating from it. The lady must bathe her whole house in it, Dulcie thought bitterly, as she scrubbed the butter deeper into her silken gown.

Crispin finished scanning the note. "Excuse me," he said. He put his napkin down, rose, and quickly left the table and the room.

"Perhaps," Wrede said carefully, avoiding Dulcie's eye, "there's a fire."

"Charlotte, what are you doing here? Why must you see me now?" Crispin asked when he saw her waiting for him in his study.

"Fie! What a greeting," Charlotte said. She plied her fan and flounced across the room to him, her swaying skirts eloquent testimony to her irritation. "I had to see you, my dear," she said, her fan now rigid and furled as she clenched it tight, "whatever the cost to my reputation."

"Oh. Well, I can't see the cost," Crispin said, relaxing, "since I saw both your maid and your poor old auntie in the sitting room as I passed it just now. I think there were a few footmen belonging to you in the hall, too. It's not likely that even such a bad man as I could get up to much serious defiling with your army camped in my house, is it?"

She snapped the fan against her palm. "I'm not supposed to be alone with you."

He walked to the door and began to open it. She called,

"No!" and when he turned to look at her, she said, more quietly, "No. You're right. My reputation is safe—for the moment. It's the future I'm worried about. That's why I've come here. Crispin," she said, all artifice gone from her expression, even her fan hanging from her wrist, forgotten, "you won't call on me, so I have come to you."

"How would it look for a newly married man to be seen visiting your house alone?" he asked bitterly.

"Yes, just so," she said, "but you haven't even answered my letters."

"I had nothing to answer yet," he said.

"That's why I'm here now," she said. "It's been ten days since we heard you were married. You told me all might not be what it seemed. I've waited to see what it was. I don't care to look a fool. Or to be one. Even Prendergast can be put off for only so long. What's going to happen? To put it plainly, sir: have I a reason to wait longer?"

She was dressed all in yellow today, like the spring sunshine spilling through the window behind her. She wore a crushed yellow velvet gown with blond silk panniers studded with tiny rosebuds worked in gold thread. Her hair was lightly powdered, and a pert little yellow hat sat tilted atop it. It suited her blond loveliness. Such colors wouldn't do for Dulcie he mused, she needed warmer hues. He blinked, realizing he was thinking about Dulcie instead of being struck by Charlotte's beauty. Even being a mock husband was changing him.

That thought made him know what he had to say. "I couldn't ask you to wait," he said sadly, "even if I wanted to. It would be wrong of me. I have no right to you," he said, taking her little gloved hand in his. "I can't even tell you the how and why of it, because that would be unfair to someone else."

Her blue eyes searched his, and he knew he owed her more. "Charlotte," he went on, choosing his words carefully, searching his own heart and his mind, trying to walk the thin line between honor and desire. "I'll admit that I hoped to revive our engagement when I restored my fortune. But I can't do that now. Here is truth: I am married. You know what that means," he said, and saw her eyes flicker. "Yes," he said. "Legally wed. And so although you said you might consider me after you'd produced an heir for your legal husband, I'm sorry but I can't say the same to you. It's not my way—or yours, is it? When the shoe is on the other foot, that is."

"It's entirely different for women," she said, her nostrils flaring.

"No," he said quietly, "it isn't—not really."

"I see," she said. "Revenge, is it?" She spun around, prepared to march away from him.

"No," he said, keeping hold of her hand so she couldn't leave. "You don't see. I did understand your decision. I regretted it, but I wouldn't let you make a sacrifice, remember?"

She fell still, remembering how she hadn't tried to make any sacrifice. Still, they had been engaged and so his was the greater fault. She might have ended the engagement, but he was the one who had married. Her decision might have seemed cold-blooded, but she'd had no other choice. His actions seemed deliberate and cold-hearted.

"Charlotte, let me tell you what I can," he said despairingly. "I didn't enter into this marriage for any of the usual reasons. All I can say is that if it's at all possible, I'll renounce it. As will my wife. She has no fault in this, but it's a tangle, believe me. We're investigating all possibilities now, all possible ways out. It might be accomplished, but it may be later rather than sooner. Or it may never happen. I just can't say. I can't ask you to wait, either. I won't do that to you."

"Don't you want me to wait for you?" she asked.

"Charlotte," he sighed, "don't ask me to say what you know I shouldn't."

"Ah, 'shouldn't,'" she said wisely, "is far better than 'can't.'"

"Think what you will," he said, "only please don't discuss this with anyone. I'm not thin-skinned, but I hope you'll keep this to yourself. I owe you an explanation, but I owe nothing to anyone else. And I don't want Dulcie to be the subject of cruel gossip."

"*Dulcie,* is it?" Charlotte said angrily, "and you don't want her to be the subject of cruel gossip? My dear, do you want to walk on water too? The poor thing is shot through already. I daresay there's no rumor foul or bizarre enough not to have been whispered by now. *Everyone* is talking about her."

"I was afraid of that," he said. "I plan to introduce her soon, take her around, so people can see for themselves that she's just an innocent girl."

"An *innocent* girl?" Charlotte asked, her eyes wide.

"It's true," he said in exasperation. "I do intend to take her out in society to put an end to the gossip."

"*Where* is your *head,* my dear?" Charlotte asked.

"I don't mean to make her a sensation," he said, "only to show the world she is not one. Secrets are poisonous. If I keep her a secret, the gossip will grow. If I show her to the world and she seems unexceptionable, they'll grow bored with us."

It was true, and Charlotte knew it. The girl was a pauper, but she was lovely. Put her in fashionable clothes and she would be acceptable, too. If it was all a mistake, as he claimed, then it would seem less so the longer she stayed at his side. But Charlotte couldn't admit any of this, even to herself. It was ridiculous for her to fear another female, so instead, she laughed.

"Take her into society to kill the gossip?" she asked. "Why not pour oil on the fire while you are at it? My dear, they'll tear her apart. If you take her to the opera, even the singers will fall silent to gape at her and whisper. Everyone —*everyone*—thinks she's an adventuress of the lowest sort. If you adored her, if it were a case of wild passion, it might be different. Scandalous, of course, but different. Everyone understands passion, although they decry it. But your face on the night of your ball, Crispin! We wondered if you'd slay her before the evening was out!

"You're a nobleman; she's an obscure commoner. Everyone believes she has trapped you by some foul means. Everyone knows Wrede has been taking her to dressmakers and milliners, spending your fortune on fine feathers for her. We put that down to her avarice. But now you say that you plan to show her off! You are mistaken if you think that finery will stem the tide of gossip. Only time will do that. Maybe in a dozen years or so, people will stop talking, but until then you'd best keep her locked up here, for her own good. It hardly matters to me," she said, although it did. Locked up wasn't half of what she wanted for the girl who claimed to be Crispin's wife. Charlotte would have liked to see the wench at the bottom of the Thames. But if there was one thing Charlotte knew, it was men. If she attacked the girl, no matter how richly she deserved it, Crispin would feel obligated to defend her.

Charlotte sighed. "Were I in her place, I could fend off the jests, but I doubt she can," she said, "And as for us, I *will* wait, Crispin. But not forever."

She gazed at him. Tall, strong, and intelligent, he was beyond handsome; he was elegant. Charlotte was accustomed to getting whatever she wanted. It was inconceivable that she would not this time too. When Crispin had nothing, she'd been willing to let him go because he had become something she didn't want anymore. But now he had everything again, and she *would* have him as husband. She never doubted it for a moment, despite this bizarre situation. She suspected that he'd been trying to make her jealous and had somehow been caught in a trap of his own devising. He was doubtless suffering now, but he had shocked and insulted her, and there was nothing wrong with a little retaliation.

She stood on tiptoe and pressed a light kiss on his lean cheek. "Do as you will, my dear. I can survive it. But,

Crispin," she said, turning to look at him as she put her hand on the doorknob, "I don't know if *we* can."

She sailed out into the hall and out the door, her skirt bouncing lightly with her steps, leaving him staring after her.

Crispin paused outside the dining room where Dulcie sat in her new gown. She looked bewitching in it, but had been so unsure of herself he hadn't known whether to grin or frown when he saw her bobble her curtsy. Damned if the girl didn't always catch him between laughing and yelling. And damned if that was what he'd expected of his wife.

He sighed. His wife. He still couldn't believe it. The woman he had thought to marry had just flounced out of his house to meet another man who might become her husband while Crispin's wife sat in his dining room still frantically blotting the front of her new dress.

She looked up at him with hope and fear as he entered the dining room. He thought he'd never seen anyone so apprehensive.

Wrede merely sat watching the two of them with hooded eyes.

"The weather is clearing," Crispin said, as he took his seat. "It's been a while since I've been home. Forget about Saturday night and London Society. We're going to the countryside. We leave for Darnley Hall tomorrow."

CHAPTER
9

A dense man-made fog lay over the room, so thick it was hard to distinguish faces in the gloom, but no one seemed to care. Indeed, many of the men in the room were contributing to it as they puffed their pipes. The smell of tobacco combined with that of beer, male bodies, and clothing that was too elegant to clean very often or very well. And yet the earl of Wrede paused as he entered the coffeehouse, elevated his long nose, took in a deep breath, and sighed.

"Just smell that brew! Arabian beans, if I'm not mistaken. Jessup makes the finest coffee in London," Wrede declared.

"This is the best seat in the best coffeehouse in town these days," he told Crispin as they sat at a small table. "You can hear what will be said in the House of Lords before the poor secretaries can write up speeches for their masters to mouth. This is where it's really happening, politically, of course. In an hour we'll be off to a tavern that has the latest literary gossip. Then we'll go to a coffeehouse where I vow the latest news of court is already old hat. Then tonight: two assemblies, a choice of dinners, and a grand ball. How can you think of leaving London?" he asked, gazing at his friend with curious pity.

"I might want to breathe," Crispin commented.

"Country air smells like manure and dirt," Wrede said with a sniff.

"And this?" Crispin asked, his eyes tilted in suppressed laughter.

"Aroma of civilized man," Wrede answered and then said, more seriously, "I understand why you think you have to leave, and perhaps you're right, not to protect her from the gossips, but to protect the lady who bears your name from villains like Harry Meech, and to protect yourself from what might happen to that name if she runs away. That I do see. But your clubs—won't you miss them?"

"No," Crispin said. "It's strange—when I thought I couldn't afford them anymore, I missed them terribly, but now that I can pay for my dues and dinner, I have no desire to visit them."

"No, really, Crispin. How can you? London has so many clubs and wonderful coffeehouses—Macklin's, the Turk's Head, Bedford's—why go on? There are over a thousand. If a man has the money, he owes it to himself to join a club. I like the one Dashwood started: the Dilettanti. Some of our best minds meet there. And the Beef Steak Society and White's, of course, and a dozen or two more for you to choose from.

"A man has to unwind somewhere," Wrede went on, ignoring Crispin's boredom with the subject. "Why, I hear there are even clubs in the wilds of the countryside. They say there's a gentlemen's club in Buckinghamshire with many influential members. Women are provided, and they come in the guise of nuns or some such. There's talk of orgies in abandoned abbeys, caves, haystacks, and other rural locales. A vigorous man like you might find it amusing," he jested.

"No, thank you," Crispin said sourly. "I'll take my women without any disguise, and in private. And as for clubs, I suppose I'd find them more pleasant if I could forget that when I didn't have the money for them, I didn't have the camaraderie of the men in them, either."

"You'll forget," the earl said comfortably. "I promise you."

"I wonder if I should," Crispin mused.

"But now, my friend," Wrede said happily, "I'll treat you to a time in London such as you've seldom had, so you'll have a reason to hurry home from exile."

"I don't think so," Crispin said. "I have to be up early tomorrow, and I don't want to start out with a pounding head."

"Marriage has made you very dull," Wrede complained. "I'd thought it was the monotony of the marriage bed, but that isn't the case here, is it?"

"That's something we won't talk about, Wrede," Crispin said coldly.

"Oh, beg pardon. I hadn't realized marriage made you so prim. I'm surprised. You *have* changed."

"Wrede," Crispin said in a warning tone.

His friend grew still, and inclined his noble head in thought. "Very well, very interesting," was all he said.

"I'll share a cup or two with you now, visit some of your friendly clubs, have dinner, and then go home," Crispin said.

"I don't like this change in you, my friend," Wrede said, looking at him oddly.

It was difficult for Crispin to know if Wrede was serious or not, for no sooner had the earl said this than he started joking again.

They dined with friends of Wrede's, and the lively conversation and good food did make Crispin sorry when it was time to leave. But he had things to do before the night was done.

"I just don't understand why you still insist on leaving for the country," Wrede said in annoyance as they left the tavern. He paused to signal to one of the many linkboys standing in the street offering burning tarry torches to guide rich folk through the dark streets of London. A ragged boy came running with a spitting, flaring torch. He walked ahead of the two gentlemen and held his torch high to make a ragged circle of leaping light for them to walk in.

As they walked on, Crispin said, "I like the country, remember? And it is the safest place for Dulcie. I don't think she'll try to run away again; she's impetuous, but not a fool; Harry Meech and his cronies want her badly, and she knows it. And then there's Lady Charlotte to contend with. She can pop in my door anytime when I'm here in London. She's so mad at me she might forget that the harm she does may hurt us both someday—if I'm successful in ending this charade of a marriage. Stowing my 'bride' in the countryside makes sense. It won't be so bad. It's springtime. I know that means nothing to you except horseracing on the Mall, watching the chimney sweeps parade on May Day, and watching outdoor cockfights again. But spring is a good time in the countryside."

"I take it you mean to install the girl among the daisies and then come speedily back?"

"Maybe. Maybe not," Crispin said. "I've arranged to be notified immediately if her father is found, and believe me, I have men looking for him. But so does Harry Meech, doesn't he, Willie?"

The linkboy's torch dipped for a second, and even the earl's shoulders jerked in surprise.

"Aye, well, he still has the smell of money in his nose," the linkboy said with grudging admiration, turning to show his sooty face split by a sheepish grin, "and he don't give up so easy. How'd you know it was me?"

"You haven't changed your face, Willie," Crispin said. "All I wonder about is how you got the torch? Did you pay for it with knuckles or coins?"

"I got friends," Willie said proudly, and added, "and they know I got knuckles. I got to hand it to you, my lord. Most gents don't look servants in the face, never mind linkboys. They're invisible."

"So they are. What made you look?" Wrede asked his friend curiously.

Crispin smiled. "I'd be a fool not to. Try spending some time in those amusing lower depths, Wrede, instead of just observing them for sport. You might learn a lot."

"No, thank you," the earl said, but he said it thoughtfully.

"Are you working for Harry tonight, Willie?" Crispin asked casually.

"The boy would be a fool to tell you if he was!" Wrede snapped.

"He's no fool, and I think he'll tell me. Right, Willie?"

"Right. I'm working for Harry, and I'm not," Willie said, shrugging his thin shoulders. "He wants to know what you're doing. So do I. I can always use a few pence. But there's some things I won't sell. Harry knows that. He's got others watching you right now, likely. He knows you're planning to go out to the country."

"So I suppose he'd pay, and heavily, to have someone in his hire there?" Crispin asked.

"Dead right," Willie said, "so when you get there, I'd watch out for a new maid or footman coming into the house if I was you, I would."

"Good idea. But if I had, say, a new boy to ride in my carriage with me, or a likely lad to work around the house or stables, a boy who knew what was up and could be watching for what might come . . . that would be better, wouldn't it?" Crispin mused.

"Right," Willie agreed. "You want me to look sharp for someone for you?"

"I'd prefer to look no further," Crispin said, staring at the tattered boy and his spitting torch.

"Ah. Yeah, right. Makes sense," Willie said slowly, "but I dunno. I ain't never been to the country, and I ain't sure I'd like it any more than the earl here does."

"Oh, well, but gold has a way of making any prospect brighter, doesn't it? I'd pay well, and promptly," Crispin said, holding out a gloved hand in which two big gold pieces shone in the flaring torchlight. "And often," he added.

"Done, then," Willie said, and the coins disappeared.

"Best get my things together. I'll be in your back door at dawn, my lord." And with a nod and a wink, boy and torch disappeared almost as fast as the coins had.

"Was that wise? Have you hired yourself an ally or an enemy?" Wrede asked.

"Oh, an ally, if it suits him, and I don't know why it shouldn't," Crispin said. "And don't think I hired him. I believe he signed on."

When they reached his doorstep, Crispin paused, his smile clear to see in the light of the lantern that hung by his door. "Care to come in for some brandy to take the chill off the night?"

"No, thank you, I've buckets to consume before the sun rises. I'll go now and wish you well. But, Crispin, I've a thing to say." Wrede laid his hand on his friend's arm. There was unusual gravity in his voice as well as in his long face. "I may jest," he said, "but I'm aware this is a damnable situation you've gotten yourself into. To be forced into a lifelong liaison with a woman from the streets, simply because of a misapprehension, is more than wrong, it's barbaric."

"She's not a woman from the streets," Crispin said abruptly, all the warmth gone from his voice.

"No, she's your lady now, but not forever, we hope. So what I want to say is: don't give in to her, Crispin, not while there's a chance you can be rid of her."

"Wrede," Crispin laughed, "she's charming, yes, but no siren."

"Whatever she is, she's not what you wanted, is she? That's the point," Wrede said, seeing his friend's suddenly arrested expression. "I want to warn you to wait on *everything*. You've put up with a lot from me these last days, as well as over the years. Just remember, Crispin, I'm not without influence. I know many men in many high places. You're not alone. I'll be doing what I can for you here in London. We'll free you of this monstrous marriage, my word on it."

"Don't promise what God can't. But thank you for your offer."

"Then you'll allow me to be your deputy in this, when I can, where I can?" Wrede asked.

"I can't see why not. But do be discreet. I don't want everyone in London to know the details of this marriage."

"Not a problem," Wrede assured him. "I'll have it taken care of, just wait and see. Meanwhile it's of utmost importance that you resist her. It's lonely out there in the woods, and she'll begin to look very good to you."

"Good night," Crispin said abruptly, "and thank you, old friend. I'll do what I must, you do what you can, and we'll see what happens. No man can ask more of his friend, or of his fate."

Crispin watched the earl disappear into the night and then entered his house, patted a sleepy footman on the shoulder, and told him to go to bed. He didn't seek his own bed, however, for although it was late and he'd passed an interesting evening, he was edgy and restless. He thought of his bed, then thought of who was sleeping down the hall from it, and turned and strolled to his library. There was nothing like a twice-read book to make a man bored enough to slip off to sleep.

She was curled up in a chair by the fire fast asleep, with a forgotten book on her lap. He stepped softly and stopped when he stood over her. It made him feel strangely guilty to watch her as she slept, but he seldom got a chance to see her when she was unprotected by her wit and bristly pride. She was so very pretty, he thought, watching her. He discovered it wasn't only the sparkle of her personality that gave her face beauty; she had it in plenty in the delicate structure of her very bones. Flushed and rumpled, she looked more than desirable. She looked so vulnerable he almost felt like waking her, taking her in his arms, and apologizing to her for leaving her alone this evening, for planning to leave her alone for the rest of her life.

What was he to do with her? he wondered. She was a

stranger, foisted on him by a doting father. It was hard to believe the worst of her. Still, he thought, his head cocked to one side as he considered her, how could he believe the best of her? How could someone who seemed so sweet and innocent be found entering into a false marriage in the Fleet prison, of all places? And yet how could he doubt his own senses? Whatever she was, he resolved, he would have to be very careful during the next weeks: careful of her—and of himself.

He eyed the sleeping girl with caution. "Dulcie?" he whispered softly.

Her eyelids flickered open; her eyes focused. She started and leaped to her feet.

"I—I didn't know . . . Was I asleep?" she stammered. "I only meant to read for a moment. I meant no trespass. I hope you don't mind," she said, backing away from him, clutching the book in front of her. Her hair was tousled and her cheeks flushed. She looked wholly adorable, and he felt like a monster because she was so afraid of him.

"Of course I don't mind," he said. "I only wondered why you weren't in bed."

Her eyes flew open wider.

"Not that I looked," he said, and then ran his hand through his hair in exasperation. "I mean, it's obvious you are here, isn't it?"

She nodded and swallowed hard. He could see her smooth throat moving. He wanted to comfort her, but didn't dare.

"It's very late," he said. "I was out with Wrede, saying good-bye to London for a while." A thought occurred to him. "How thoughtless of me! Was there anyone you wanted to say good-bye to?"

She shook her head, "Only my father."

"Yes, so would I," he said in clipped tones.

He loomed over her, as immaculate as he had been when he'd left this evening. He had come in from the night with the soft breath of springtime on his coat, and the mingled aroma of his cologne and the lingering scent of tobacco on his hair and skin. She felt dowdy and frowsy and stale compared to him. She wondered what she was doing here with this fine gentleman. It all seemed unreal in the depth of this night. So unreal that she found herself longing for him to take her in his arms and tell her everything would be all right. She knew that wouldn't happen, but she couldn't help what she wanted. She stared up at him, and everything she thought was clear in her eyes.

It was a moment before he spoke. "I think you should go to bed," he said abruptly, staring into her eyes.

"Yes, I will." She backed up a step because of the cold tone of his voice. "Good night," she said, and fled, leaving him to sink into the chair and curse himself and his unruly desires.

Dulcie sat in the carriage in solitary splendor. It was such an unfamiliar situation, and she felt so pampered and privileged that she hardly felt a pang of worry as the coach rolled away from the viscount's town house. The seats were plump and soft and smelled of fine new leather. There was a rug on her lap, a hot brick at her feet, and even little vases of fresh daffodils fixed beside each window. She was off to a house in the country, away from London and its terrors and pleasures. She had been promised that she would be told if her father returned, so there was nothing for her to worry about, really. Except that she was off to the wilds with a perfect stranger who was legally her lord and master for the rest of her life. A man who was everything she could desire in a man and nothing she deserved, and they both knew it.

She refused to cry. Instead, she stared out the window and watched London slipping away from her. She was excited, in spite of herself. She was young and on the move, and anything might happen. Crispin rode outside, along with the armed footmen he had brought with him because travel wasn't safe, as he explained. And because he couldn't bear to sit enclosed in a carriage with her, she guessed. He looked very fine, she thought wistfully. Distance shielded her from those astonishing eyes of his, so she could gaze at him to her heart's content whenever he rode up alongside the carriage.

She had three gold coins and some silver in her purse, and she constantly fingered them, the way a nun might count her rosary beads. Those coins were her only hope of salvation. If things became unbearable, at least she had the price of escape in her pocket. She might be a viscountess now, but her purse had more weight than her title, no matter what Harry Meech thought.

They stopped for luncheon in a wayside inn, and Crispin showed her into a private parlor redolent of stew and roast meat. She sniffed appreciatively as he helped her take off her fine new cloak.

"I should have thought to have a maid accompany you," he remarked, and she lowered her head, thinking he was annoyed because she hadn't had the sense to take off her own coat. "But I sent her on ahead with the baggage, so everything would be ready for you when we reach the hall."

He seated her at the table and told the innkeeper to bring her a hot luncheon, whatever was fresh and best.

"I'll eat on the run. I've got to be sure the men have everything in readiness," he told Dulcie. "We'll be crossing the heath," he explained. "There have been some highwaymen active there. I don't think they'll trouble us, there are too many of us. Still, we have to be ready for any possibility. Enjoy your luncheon," he said, and was gone.

The serving girl brought hot pigeon pie, roast beef, fowl, savories and meat pies, a selection of cheeses and fruits, and mince tarts. But Dulcie couldn't enjoy eating alone, and the fear of encountering highwaymen made her lose her appetite. Her purse was, after all, her only insurance in this new world she was being taken to. She was served country cider. It was strong and winy, and she frowned after she tasted it. It didn't taste as good as the kind she usually had, but she soon discovered it made her feel warm and pleasant, and so she downed the whole hearty glass of it—then another. She wasn't afraid of anything by the time Crispin appeared to help her back into the coach. Not even him.

"I'll ride this part of the way with you," he said, after he helped her up the step into the carriage.

She was pleased by that, but also a little hurt that he hadn't asked to ride with her; he'd only *told* her he was going to. Of course, she realized, he had every right to do whatever he wanted. Then she thought of all the other things he had a perfect right to do, and blushed. Good heavens, she thought a little muzzily, she really didn't know him at all.

She waited until he was seated beside her in the carriage before she decided to get better acquainted.

"My name," she said slowly and distinctly, "is Dulcie Dawn Blessing. It may have been Blessingham in the past, but Father said someone changed it. 'Snipped off our little piggy tail,' as he put it. Anyway," she went on, trying to ignore Crispin's wide, brilliantly blue, and fascinated stare, "I am twenty years old, and will be one and twenty in the summertime. July the first, actually. I've lived all my life in England. I can speak a little French, though. Very little," she said sadly, "having never traveled much farther than Scotland. My father taught me French. Actually, one of his lady friends did. But I haven't seen her in ages. Neither has he, but you mustn't think he's a bad man because he used to see her. He was very discreet. My mother has lived in Lincolnshire with her sister since I was eight, you see. That's why I can't sew very well, I imagine. But since Father and I were often on our own, I can cook, if I have to, and my cooking is quite good . . . if you're very hungry," she added, and tried not to giggle. What she'd said had sounded good in her mind, but silly when she'd said it aloud. Everything seemed very silly to her now.

He smiled at her and said kindly, "The ale at the inn was fresh and good, wasn't it?"

"Oh, no. I mean, I don't know. I don't drink ale. I had the cider instead. It was very good—fermented," she told him.

"Really?" he asked. "I wouldn't have guessed."

She continued to gaze at him expectantly.

"My turn?" he asked. "All right," he said, leaning back against the squabs and stretching out his legs. "My name is Crispin George Thomas Knightly, Viscount West. I've seven and twenty years to my credit—or discredit. I'll have one more this autumn. October the eleventh. My parents are gone, several years now. No brothers or sisters surviving. Now, what else? Yes. Let's see: I've been on the grand tour and visited France, Italy, Belgium, Spain, Portugal, and some of the Germanies. Egypt, and Greece too, of course. I speak French, German, Spanish, and Italian. And I can read Latin. Why are you crying?"

"You're s-so accomplished," she said, biting her lip as tears coursed down her face. "How you must detest being married to me!"

He took out a handkerchief and touched it to her cheek, and she managed to stop crying as he blotted her tears. Then he offered her his handkerchief, but she only shook her head in horrified denial and sniveled, although more quietly. It seemed rude to use his handkerchief for her nose. He insisted, however, and she honked in it in as ladylike a manner as she could manage. But she glanced down and saw how fine it was, and began to cry again to think she'd used it at all. She told him why, and he started laughing, which made it worse. So he took her in his arms and held her and told her she should try to sleep. Which was absurd, she thought, considering it was only early afternoon.

When she opened her eyes again it was dusk. Her cheek lay against a hard surface. She was about to raise her head when she felt the steady comforting beat beneath the woolen coat her head was resting on, and realized who she was with, and where she was. And that she was, incredibly enough, lying against the viscount's warm and breathing chest. She lay still, enjoying the warmth, the comfort, the fresh clean scent of his linen, the spicy smell of his cologne, his soap, himself. It was a small, secret, stolen pleasure, and she reveled in it. It was almost like being home; it was almost like being loved.

"We're almost there," he whispered against the top of her head, and she started, wondering how he'd known she was awake. "Your breathing," he said in answer to her unspoken question, and she heard the smile in his voice, "it changed. You have the faintest suggestion of a snore." He chuckled. "Like a mouse's, no more than that, I promise you. It may just have been your drunken stupor."

She struggled to sit upright, and he released her instantly. She blinked and scrubbed her eyes with her fists. Then she sat bolt upright, and her hands flew to her hair as it tumbled about her shoulders. He'd taken the pins out while she'd slept. He held them out to her on his outstretched palm. She chose them one by one, thrusting them into her hair quickly so she wouldn't have to keep noting how large and shapely a hand he had. Or how he kept staring at her tumbled hair.

"Feeling better?" he asked when she was done.

"Yes," she said, and couldn't say more, she was so flustered.

"We won't reach the hall until well after nightfall," he said, sitting back and pretending not to watch her anymore.

She'd been warm and curved and perfumed as she'd lain in his lap, and he'd refrained from touching her only because he was a gentleman and she was obviously sodden. And, he admitted, he didn't know if he'd have been able to stop touching her once he started. Her silken hair, he'd discovered, was scented with vinegar and flowers. A most unlikely combination. It stirred him even as it amused him. Vinegar and flowers, he thought, bemused. Very like the girl herself.

"You'll like the hall," he said, for something to take his mind off the pale oval of her face and those great amber eyes watching him in the dusky light. "It was built in Henry Tudor's time and is old-fashioned, I suppose, but comfortable. And very beautiful. Or was. I need to do some work on it—buy back paintings, rugs, statuary. I couldn't sell the flowers from the gardens when I needed money, thank God. Or the wallpaper. And I left beds in the bedrooms," he said. He realized he was babbling, because he was trying so hard to forget that she was no longer drunk and that they were alone, and she was so warm and he was cold now without her.

"It's very beautiful," he said, leaning close, breathing in her scent again, "Lovely," he whispered as he drew her back into his arms. But this time, for his own comfort.

Her mouth was newly awakened and tender beneath his. She was just as warm and curved as he'd remembered, but now her hands went to his shoulders as he pressed closer, and she held him tight. His tongue traced her lips as his hands traced her body, and he felt as well as heard her catch her breath at his touch.

And then she was gone—halfway across the carriage from him and spitting like a cat.

"Save your breath," he said with bored amusement he didn't feel. "I know: you're not that kind of girl. Spare me, please. But I'll remind you," he said as he tapped his walking stick on the roof to signal the coach to stop, "that you are my wife, this is my carriage, that is my gown you're wearing, and before you start raging at me, that was my kiss you were enjoying. Very much. I'll ride the rest of the way," he said as the coach stopped and the driver looked in to see what he wanted.

Dulcie watched him as he swung out of the carriage, and then up on to his horse again, leaving them both to wonder what would happen when there was no horse nearby for him to leap on.

CHAPTER
10

This kissing business had to stop. Absolutely, Dulcie told herself fiercely as they rode through the night. Crispin stayed outside, though the night was pitch, lit only by lanterns on either side of the coach. He obviously didn't want to come in, though it must have been like riding through ink out there. What must he think of her? If it was anything like what she thought of herself, she was in terrible trouble. She'd never had such a problem before. This was a fine time to start having it, she thought with a groan. Was she an utter fool as well as an unlucky one? She was at the man's mercy, for heaven's sake, a poor girl with only her virtue as her dowry.

Well, not really, she reminded herself. She had her hidden coins and could leave if things got really bad.

Someday she hoped to really marry, and her husband would expect her to be pure. He had a right to expect that. He could toss her out if she was not. A ruined girl of her expectations was fit only for selling what she had rashly given away. Chastity was her only dowry. She'd heard that all her life, and had seen it to be true over the years as she'd been dragged across the kingdom with her father. The vulgar saying was that once a girl had experienced carnal love, she couldn't do without. She'd never believed that. Until she met Crispin. And that was only kisses! she thought miserably.

She wasn't afraid of passion—only of tasting it beforetime. She'd been raised properly, but she had lived among the lower classes, and among people who spoke frankly about life. So she knew a lot about what she'd never experienced. It struck her as an improbable act, with little reward for the women involved except for children or, in some cases, money. Men, however, thought it was wonderful, and she supposed, generously, that for them it was. For some women, too, she hoped, remembering ribald comments of older women she'd overheard.

But she'd had little experience of men. Decent men did not get serious with wastrel's daughters, and she'd had nothing to do with less than decent ones. With gentlemen, she'd had no experience at all. Her new husband had every advantage over her: money, title, position, and experience. And the opportunity to make love with whomever he chose, whenever the whim moved him. It seemed it moved him often.

She was certain that he wasn't the sort to try to overpower her. He hadn't yet had to, she thought bitterly. What was the matter with her? He already thought her the lowest creature, however kind he was to her.

She had to leave as soon as possible. She wished things could be different, but wishes were nothing, as she knew too well. She had to get through these next days or weeks with her dignity and her virtue, intact. It wasn't his wiles, but his face, voice, and manner that were a threat.

No more kisses! If she was as firm with herself as she intended to be with him, she thought she could get by. Until . . . until when? That question made her even more unhappy, and so she was melancholy when the carriage finally came to a halt. The clouds were breaking up in a freshening wind, and she saw Darnley Hall for the first time in a sudden flash of bright moonlight. She took in a breath, and wasn't sure she ever let it out again.

Crispin had said he had a house in the countryside. Dulcie had expected a rambling cottage, or maybe a fine house on a hill overlooking the village green. Not a castle—or something very much like one—all by itself in a park with gardens and drives. Myriad windows glittered with candlelight. A wide double door opened on a vast hall filled with servants, who had lined up before a great stairway to greet their lord and his new lady—a lady who was afraid to venture inside and who couldn't catch her breath. A firm arm on her shoulders led her in, and she breathed, she supposed later, only because she'd no choice in that matter, either.

She nodded to the servants' curtsies and bows, and was glad to see her maid from London waiting for her in the bedroom to which Crispin led her. It was furnished in pink and gold, and in spite of what he'd said in the coach, she could find nothing lacking in it. She washed, put on a night shift, and tumbled into a feather bed made up with fresh sheets, and thought she was in heaven. After all those hours in the coach it was wonderful to stretch out on something that wasn't moving. And despite her fears, she was left alone. But, tired as she was, she was a long time falling asleep, because her pillow wasn't warm and breathing and was not scented with shaving soap and spice.

It was cruel to leave the girl alone, Crispin thought as he rode back from seeing one of his tenants. After all, she was a child of the city. What could she find to do with herself here? He had an estate to oversee, old acquaintances to drop in on. Then there was the village itself. He could always stop for a chat and a pint of ale—or cider, he thought, smiling at the memory of Dulcie's inadvertent intoxication. Leaving her by herself might even be considered a form of punishment, since they'd only arrived at the hall the day before. He decided to take her into the village that very morning. He spurred his horse homeward. She'd be grateful, of course, but he was only being kind, as he would to any lonely, confused young person, he told himself sternly.

It was hard to share a house with her, for she was impossible to ignore. It was a big house, but not so big that he didn't know exactly where she was every minute. The scent of her always lingered in the room where she'd been, and he seemed to know just when to turn his head to catch a glimpse of her as she walked by. Finding her in a room he entered was like meeting a friend after a long absence. Her face lit up at the sight of him, and then, just as suddenly, dimmed as she struggled with her embarrassment. So he couldn't ignore her, he told himself; it wasn't right.

He hadn't lived with a woman for years. His mother had been gone for many years, and he'd had no sisters. He liked women, although he'd never liked any enough to marry, except Charlotte. She had been his goal in life. Yet, curiously, he found it hard to grieve about losing her while he was so occupied with his present problem. Thoughts of Dulcie seemed to overshadow everything else these days. That was only natural; this false wife of his was a problem to be solved—that and nothing more, he told himself sternly. And yet there was also this queer protectiveness he felt toward the girl . . .

He remembered Wrede's warnings and resolved to keep the thought of Charlotte bright in his memory. And he would have, if thoughts of Dulcie hadn't kept intruding. It was really too bad that she was all alone in a strange place today, he reminded himself.

This was a time to be gotten through with the least pain for all concerned. But there was no reason it couldn't be a pleasant time, was there? That, he told himself, and only that, was the reason for the sudden surge of pleasure he felt as he hurried home to spend the day with Dulcie.

* * *

"I thought we'd ride into the village today," he said.

"I thought you didn't want anyone to see me," she said.

He looked at her; he hadn't been able to stop doing that since he'd found her strolling in the garden. She wore a white gown sprinkled with violets, its belled skirt adorned with lavender panniers. A matching violet ribbon was threaded through her curls. She looked as fresh and lovely as the country morning, and he felt perversely proud of her.

"I must show you to the people I know here, which is everyone, I suppose," he said. "There'll be rumors, otherwise. You're my wife, for however long that may be. They'll talk unless they see you. They'll talk anyway, but don't worry, people are much kinder here than in London."

"I wasn't worried," she lied, "because I never heard what they said in London, did I? And I guess that if you keep me here in the house until I can leave, I'll never hear what people say here, either. You're the only one who'll know what they say."

If her chin got any higher, her little nose would be tilted at the sky, he thought with a pang of tenderness. "True," he said. "So shall we go?"

"Now?" she asked, her voice breaking in a squeak of surprise.

"Why not? We've got a rare sunny morning. Do you ride?"

She looked down at her shoes. Only ladies knew how to ride. She liked horses, but all she'd ever done with one was feed it a carrot. "No," she murmured, shamefaced.

"It doesn't matter. We'll take a light carriage. You'll enjoy it, I think. The sun's taking the chill off the morning, so you'll only need a bonnet for your hair, and a light cloak. Can you leave now?"

She nodded, so touched by the simple courtesy of his asking when he knew she didn't have anything else to do, and by his caring about what she wore for her comfort, that she couldn't speak. She hurried up to her room, caught up a cloak, plopped a bonnet on her head, and raced downstairs again before her maid could come running to help her. She ran light-footed to the door and out onto the grounds, smiling and as radiant as the sun above her.

Until she saw who stood in back of the two-horse open carriage. He wore clean new livery and had a clean face, but his smirk was unmistakable. She stopped and looked up at Crispin in astonishment.

"Do you know who that is?" she whispered fiercely.

"The one and only Willie Grab," Crispin answered with a grin.

"But . . . if you know," she said, confused, "what's he doing here?"

"The boy's the right weight for the balance we need, and he does need to learn a trade. I hired him on in London, and he rode here with the servants; you just didn't see him."

"Being a deadweight seems right enough for him," she muttered. "He's two-faced and crafty. I wouldn't trust him. You brought him here? Bad enough he spies on us. Do you have to pay him to do it?"

"He says he spies for me too now," Crispin told her gently.

"Oh, wonderful," she said.

She was about to say more on the subject, but she bit her lip. There was nothing for her to do but pick up her head, take Crispin's hand, and enter the carriage.

The ride sent her spirits soaring. Springtime made the roadside so beautiful that Dulcie couldn't do anything but exclaim over it. Crispin knew the name of every flower and shrub on his estate. She learned that the banks of purple blossoms thick as cabbage heads that lined the drive were exotic imported rhododendrons, and the stretches of what looked like flames leaping near them were azaleas he'd also imported from the Continent.

"Horticulture is a gentleman's avocation now." He smiled when her eyes widened at his knowledge. "It's not enough to compete with horses and houses anymore. Capability Brown is in such demand for designing gentlemen's gardens that he was too expensive for me when I began this, but now . . . Oh, I won't become 'a son of Flora,' as so many budding horticulturalists are doing. Going to meetings to wage real wars of roses isn't my style. But it's interesting. The world's opening; we have to move with it."

"You may know about exotic flowers, but we common folk," she said with mock haughtiness, "are the experts on common beauty. There, look—next to the hedgerows—daisies and violets . . . and primroses!"

There was nothing common about the way delight lit up her expressive face, he thought, although he only said, with a grin, "Yes, so it is: *Bellis perennis, Viola adorata,* and *Primula vulgari.* You're right."

She laughed as hard as he'd wanted her to, but stopped abruptly when the carriage rolled into the village. Then she became nervous, silent and withdrawn. He missed her joyous mood almost as much as she did.

She was polite and shy with everyone he introduced her to, but the farmers, merchants, and local folk found her demeanor just right. Not a bit high in the instep, but not pushy either, and just distant enough to be a true lady, they decided. News of her arrival spread quickly, and anyone who was able came down to the tavern to see the new viscountess. Even though they'd all been expecting Lady Charlotte, a famous beauty, to be their lord's wife, they weren't disappointed with his bride. Pretty, prettily behaved, and fresh as springtime. No wonder the viscount was so taken with her, they agreed.

But Dulcie didn't know how the villagers felt about her, even if Crispin guessed it. He didn't know whether to be pleased about their reaction or not. They'll feel bad when she is gone, he thought, watching her smile a shy greeting to two village matrons. But he knew it would be worse if they'd never seen her at all. He decided he wouldn't say the marriage had been invalid when it was over, after all. Or tell anyone that he'd been divorced when she was gone. He could always say she died, he decided, as another local woman curtsied low to his beautiful new wife.

After Dulcie was done stammering shy answers to polite questions and turned a flushed and worried face to his, he offered her his arm. "Luncheon?" he asked.

"Oh. Certainly," she said, her spirits sinking. They'd only just got to the village. If he was taking her home again so soon it meant she'd embarrassed him as much as she had herself. If that was possible. She'd tried to act like a lady, but had obviously failed. She took a deep breath that sounded dangerously like a sob, and took his arm. So be it. She had tried.

But instead of walking her to the carriage, he led her up the main street, on toward the green, then past the little cemetery to the very top of the hill, where an ancient church stood tall and rough-shouldered, dominating the scene. Dulcie picked her way across soft early grass pied with little flat daisies to a courtyard overlooking the bright river that rushed past the town.

"The monks thought like warriors in the early days," Crispin commented as she gazed around, "and so both castles and monasteries were built on the highest hills. Whether they did it to protect themselves or to be closer to God, only they knew. This used to be a monastery, but there wasn't much protection for them, after all. Good King Henry decided the monks had to go, and they did. Stones from here were used to build my own home. Only the church remains. There are cellars here with rooms of stone where the monks slept and ate and wrote and prayed. I played there as a boy. We'll lunch here. I think the monks won't mind. They enjoyed a good bottle of wine too, you know."

She was so bemused she couldn't speak until she saw Willie and the coachmen spreading a long cloth on the ground. Then she stared at Crispin, and he grinned at her.

"The ground is warm from the sun, and the cloth is thick. If I give you my hand, do you think you can sit down? Your skirts will give you added protection from the damp, I think," he said, holding his hand out to her.

She'd never tried to sit on the ground in one of her grand new gowns, but she'd spent hours on the floor at her father's feet as a girl. She gave him a bright smile, took his hand, sank to the ground—and bobbed right up again, like a cork on a millpond. Her face flamed for as she had tried to sit, her skirt had begun to tilt, and she'd had a sudden horrified picture of herself with her skirt, hoop, and petticoat up around her ears. She stood up again as fast as she could.

A quick glimpse of a shapely leg was considered very provocative. Legs were much more erotic than breasts, after all. Breasts were commonly on display—on the half shell, as Dulcie had heard it put—all the time. Fine ladies and fast women knew how to show pretty little glimpses of their legs. But Dulcie was neither, and although she privately thought her legs were fine, she still thought a girl's underpinnings were her own concern, unless she was looking for trouble. And Dulcie certainly had enough of that already.

Crispin hid his grin and cocked an eyebrow at her, waiting for her to be seated. It took a while. She held her skirt down, and finally discovered that if she crossed her ankles and balanced weight, she could lower herself like a bell without mishap. She finally managed to sit gracefully, as she thought a lady would, and when she was settled, her narrowed gaze made Willie put his hands in his pockets and whistle and caused the coachmen to turn around and survey the view. Crispin was beside himself with mirth, and only smiled politely so he wouldn't end up being pushed down the hill. She looked capable of doing it.

"Ah, we have fowl and ham, bread and cheese, butter and relish and some meat pasties, too. I think we won't starve," Crispin said with pleasure as he peeked into the basket the coachman handed him.

"You men can go off to the tavern; they've got a good fresh brew today," he told the coachmen and Willie. But he saw how Willie was eyeing the basket and said, on the spur of the moment, "No. You, lad, have had too much of that kind of refreshment in your young life, I think. Stay and share luncheon with us, if you please."

Dulcie was going to say something about that, but the look on Willie's young-old face stopped her.

"You mean it?" Willie asked, his face twisting, as uncertain of kindness as he was of a kick, and trying hard not to show it.

"Of course," Crispin said. "I never say a thing I don't mean."

"Lor'!" Willie said, clearly as surprised at that thought as he was at having the lord of the manor ask him to tea.

"Well, not often," Crispin added, and Willie laughed, and so, then, did Dulcie. But she too felt as confused as Willie did. Crispin's asking Willie to dine with them was so odd, endearing, and unexpected that it twisted in her heart and almost hurt.

Willie hunkered down nearby, as though unwilling to take Crispin too much at his word. That, too, made Dulcie feel both good and bad, but the way Willie fell on the food Crispin offered him soon made her glad that he sat a little way apart from them. That was the way it went during her odd luncheon: she felt both good and bad about all of it.

She'd been afraid of being alone with Crispin, but what he'd done had won her over faster than the soft, sweet talk she feared he would have tried if they'd been alone. She gazed at him, sitting at his ease, one booted foot drawn up as he ate, and she wished he'd wolf his food down, or smack his lips and disgust her in some way. But even the way he licked his fingers made her stomach warmer than the wine he'd poured for her.

"You look like a new-blown flower fallen on the grass," he said, turning to look at her.

She would have been pleased, if the meaning of "fallen flower" hadn't worried her.

"Don't you think so, Willie?" Crispin asked, puzzled by the play of pleasure, followed by dismay, on her face.

"Oh, yeah. Look lovely, you do, my lady, and that's solemn truth. I saw a pincushion once, all satin and lace; it looked like you do now," Willie said.

"Yes. Very apt. Soft, yet prickly, just like a pincushion," Crispin agreed. He ignored the murderous look she shot him. "Well, then, lad," he said, "now that you've done the pretty, let's get down to business. Anything odd going on that I ought to know about? . . . Oh, you can talk in front of the lady. It's her concern as well as mine."

"Going on?" Willie said thoughtfully. "Aye, well, your youngest dairy maid's going to be producing like your cows if you don't get that randy new groom away from her, and soon. She'll calve by Christmas day, the way she's going. And your butler here is a sight more friendly than that fellow in London, but that may be because he likes your wine cellar so much. And your housekeeper . . ."

"I mean," Crispin said with admirable steadiness, "about Harry Meech and company. Any new faces or odd business I should know about?"

"Oh, that. Nah. Nothing yet," Willie said.

"Well, let me know if you see anything here or on the estate—anything that is to do with Harry, that is," Crispin added quickly. "So tell me, do you like it here in the countryside?"

"No. Sorry, my lord, but I do not. Food's good, and the company's better'n' I expected, but the quiet's near killing me. Nothing but wind in the trees and listening to stars fall at night." His thin body shivered. "No hearing the watch calling the hour, no horses in the streets, no sounds of folks coming and going, having a good time or fighting and screaming and living all around you. How can you sleep?" he asked with genuine curiosity.

"It's a trick we learn," Crispin said and grinned at Dulcie. But she wasn't smiling, because the quiet of the countryside frightened her a little, too.

"But I'll stick it," Willie said, "long as you need me. The money's good, and I can use the rest, I guess."

"Won't anybody in London miss you?" Dulcie asked. With all his cleverness, she knew that Willie, seen this close, and this cleaned, was ten years old at most—perhaps only nine. It was hard to say. He was thin and small, his fine-boned face was pinched, and there was a world of wisdom in his watchful eyes.

"Miss me? Maybe the runners will," Willie gave a sour laugh. "And Harry might, but nobody else, nah. I got no folks no more. I had some baby brothers and sisters, but they died when they was tykes. I had a big brother, too, but I lost him a few years back."

"Oh, I'm sorry," Dulcie said. "He was ill too?"

"Yeah. Rope fever," Willie said, his shrug so slight that only one small shoulder moved. He pulled up some grass as he spoke, his plate of food forgotten. "He was hanged for pinching wipes—stealing handkerchiefs, to you. He was older'n me, but not so fast. See, he was getting bigger, and slowing down. I told him and I told him, but he wouldn't listen. Truth to tell, he wasn't that bright, didn't know the ropes, poor mutt, though he figured he knew better'n me, being older 'n' all, and taking care of me for so long, or trying to, y'see." Willie's voice became softer and his enunciation more careless as he went on, shredding the grass as he spoke. "So they got him for being on the nab, and they hanged him high. At Tyburn Hill, it was. I watched, 'cause it weren't right to let him go alone. He didn't see me, actually, 'cause he had a bag over his head. They dropped him, and he kicked a little, and then he was gone. God. It's queer. Sweating and praying in the morning, talking sixteen to the dozen, scared and shaking—and gone off the face of the world by night, like he'd never been here. He was a good sort, but too slow for the handkerchief game no more, don't you see?"

"How old was he?" Crispin asked gently.

"Old enough to know better, that's what gets me," Willie said in a growly voice. "He was ten."

"Oh," said Crispin and Dulcie together, and then looked

at each other. That was all they could do, but they found much comfort in each other's eyes. Boys were hanged if they were villains; that was life. But suddenly they both knew, as they never had before, that life was short and capricious.

"As to the rest of it, my lord," Willie said, breaking the silence and bringing Crispin's thoughts back, "I'll be staying on here till this affair is all settled. But I been thinking it might be nice to learn a trade while I'm here. I like horses, and never seen none so fine as the ones you got. Think I could help out in the stables and learn a thing or two about driving, maybe?"

"If my head groom doesn't mind—and I doubt he does, the way you two seem to get on—I don't see why I should. Does this mean you'll be asking for double wages?" Crispin asked.

"Why, now, I never thought of that!" Willie said, laughing so hugely at the joke that Crispin and Dulcie had to join him, and laughing louder because they were so relieved to be doing it.

By the time they finished their luncheon and strolled back to the village, the sun was lowering in the sky. They rode home in silence, although the flowers still blew in the light breeze, and more had opened during the warm spring day.

Evening came lavender and fragrant, but Dulcie felt restless and ill at ease as night drew in. Rain was slashing against the windows by the time they had dinner, and she shivered even though she had changed to a simple wool gown. Crispin noticed and invited her to take some brandy with him after dinner. He led her to a small salon whose outer walls were protected by shrubbery and ivy, and even the chill fingers of the most insinuating drafts couldn't find their way through the thick draperies he drew over the tall windows. A fire roared in the hearth, and the golden brandy was warm in her throat, but Dulcie still couldn't fight the chill in her hands and heart. The room was rich and cozy, but it was new to her, and not hers, and suddenly she realized how far from home she was tonight.

"The day was too fine to last," Crispin commented as he turned from the windows to see her staring into the fire, "as was your happiness, wasn't it?"

"I know that such things as hangings happen," she said wretchedly, knowing she didn't have to explain what she was talking about, although they hadn't spoken of it for hours. "Who doesn't? In London I saw the crowds going to the hangings every week. And though I never wanted to go with them, I understand many people have a wonderful time there. They sell pasties and lemonade, and broadsheets with the history and last words of the condemned, so everyone in the crowd will know who's going to be hanged. It doesn't seem like death that way, does it?"

"Oh, yes, it does," Crispin said quietly. "I went to a hanging once upon a time, when I was younger and thought I'd live forever. It didn't amuse me; it only made me want to get drunk. Maybe that's why so many people go. Or it might be that people appreciate life more when they see how easily it can be taken. Even the most meager life must seem brighter when the alternative is shown to them. But why do those who have everything enjoy seeing the death of those who have nothing? I don't know. But there are those who wouldn't miss the spectacle for the world. Maybe they feel safer, thinking that their rights are being protected. They're not, though. They could hang half of London—and sometimes I think they are doing precisely that—but it only makes the surviving villains more clever. Look, it's life. You can't change it, so try to forget it."

"How can I forget?" she said miserably. "I never knew a hanged person before."

"You didn't know Willie's brother, either," he said, sitting beside her. He took her hand in his, and was shocked at how icy it was. "You don't even know what his name was."

"But I did know him, in a way. And so did you. He was like Willie, only slower, and sadder, wasn't he? Oh, dear," she murmured to herself, shaking her head. "It's not as if I don't have enough trouble of my own. Now I must grieve for a boy I never knew."

"Maybe that's why you're so disturbed," he said thoughtfully, though the chill of the story of the dead boy was still in his heart, too. The pall of the hangman seemed to lie over them both, so Crispin avoided thinking about it by concentrating on how to console her.

"Dulcie, I know this situation—your being here with me, our being married though we are strangers to each other—isn't easy for you. I'll admit that at first I thought this whole thing was your idea. Now I know it was not. Your love for your father got you into this. And his love for you is keeping you here. It doesn't matter anymore who's at fault. We'll just have to make the best of it. Right?

"Now," he said, putting his arm around her, moving nearer to share the warmth of his body and his voice, "what shall we do? I know that the uncertainty of your future bothers you, as well it might, and probably brought on this blue mood."

She allowed him to draw her close, because she was melancholy and needed human company to keep Willie's cold nameless brother at bay.

"Well," he went on, "worry no more. Most of our tasks are already done. I had to introduce you to the people of the town and countryside. All you have to do now is wait it out with me. When we find your father, or when my lawyers find a hole in the fabric of this monstrous lie of a marriage, we'll both be free. Don't worry about that, either; I'll see you're well provided for. You entered into this pretense for money, and you won't be penalized for that. I won't let you go penniless. Be still. It's what I want to do. All right," he said, laughing at how stiff she'd grown. He gave her shoulder a gentle shake. "We'll argue about money later, when the time comes."

He read her thoughts in her sigh and in the way the tension left her shoulders. He stared into her worried eyes. "Relax and be comfortable. We don't have to fight," he said, bending his head to breathe in the scent of her perfume at her neck. "We can be friends, can't we?"

"I suppose," she said, lowering her gaze to her fingers, which were fidgeting in her lap.

"Oh, such enthusiasm." He chuckled, and she could feel his laughter reverberating in his hard chest. "Of course we can be friends."

He saw the uncertainty in her whiskey-colored eyes, but he also saw the quickening of her breathing, the way her breast moved. He clasped both of her hands in one warm hand. She heaved a little broken sigh at how that solid clasp comforted her. Then he leaned closer and touched her hair.

"Oh, Dulcie," he breathed, hardly knowing what he was saying because of the warmth of her, because of the pleasure of being alive and having a soft, curved body so close to his on such an empty night. "Such a cold night, such a sad old world out there, isn't it? Why can't we be friends?"

She honestly didn't know why. A whining wind drove rain against the windowpanes and whistled down the chimney, causing the fire to complain. She remembered all the misery in that cold world out there, just as he said. And he was near and warm and real and so very alive in a world filled with cold, uncertainty, and death.

His eyes were tender; his well-shaped mouth held a sweet half smile as he gazed at her lips. She could only stare at that beautiful mouth and wonder what she should say. It felt right and natural when he lowered his head to taste her lips.

And even more natural when he drew her closer as she sighed against his mouth. His hands sifted through her hair, skimmed over her throat to touch her breast as his mouth sought more than she knew she had to give.

He opened her lips and slipped little tastes of his tongue inside them so that it was gone before she could protest the strangeness of it, and back as she began to yearn for more. He lowered her on the settee, kissing her cheek, her neck, the white skin that covered her rapidly beating heart. He lowered the tight bodice of her gown to bare the soft pink tip of one breast, and sighed with pleasure at the sight and what it promised as it puckered to a deep rosebud. He fulfilled the promise by bringing his hand to it, to warm the tingling cusp of it, and then his mouth to it, to warm himself even more.

"Crispin," she said, in an agony of want and fear, squirming against the terrible pleasure and wrongness of it. He was warm, and smelled of soap and cedar and spicy liquors. His mouth was firm as the body he pressed close to hers, and yet it was gentle. As was his body, although she could feel the driving urgency in it. She realized they'd set something profound in motion, but his kisses, his caresses, and this wonderful newfound intimacy between them almost made her forget it.

"Oh, Dulcie," he groaned, covering her breast with his palm, allowing his mouth the pleasure of hers again.

But the pleasure was so intense they both had to stop and catch their breath before proceeding. In that instant, they both woke to reality.

She was horrified at herself and shrank away from him. He was no less appalled at himself. He drew back slowly, closing his eyes so he could see reason, because she was half out of her gown and her face showed she was still dazed with desire. He was half out of his mind with frustrated desire himself. He had to force himself to remember his circumstances.

"Dulcie," he said slowly, trying to steady his voice, "that wasn't a very good idea."

"You think it was *my* idea?" she asked, shocked, her hands covering her breasts.

"Damn and blast," he said in agitation, rising and pacing away from her, "I don't know. It doesn't matter. It was a mistake, that's all."

"I wasn't the one who started it," she said, lowering her head, her face flaming. She wanted to accuse him of trying to seduce her but was too aware of how earnestly she'd cooperated. That was what made her blurt, "I suppose you think the worst of me again?"

He saw her downcast face. "No, but . . . oh, Lord, look Dulcie," he sighed, "I wasn't thinking. I grant you weren't, too, right?"

"You *grant?*" she squeaked. "You think I was trying to entice you?"

"You *do* entice me, that's the problem," he said bitterly, "but I didn't say you tried to. I don't think the worse of you for it, either. I mistrusted you at first, true, but am I never going to live it down? It was only natural, I'd have been a fool if I didn't at least wonder about why you married me so fast, not to mention why your father insisted the marriage was valid. After all, there are a dozens of other reasons why a woman might have to marry a stranger quickly, and some are very unpleasant."

"I wanted only to help my father," she said, her chin trembling.

"I know that," he said, seeing her distress, and trying to explain himself. "But there might have been other reasons, that's the point. A rich girl might do such a thing too, if she found herself suddenly needing a husband. She might need one because of her condition, for example. That's common enough . . . not that every girl in that condition has misbehaved," he said quickly when he saw her horrified expression. "Not that I thought you had. Why, you didn't even know how to kiss until . . . ." He ran his hand through his hair. "But there are times when a girl may have been forced . . . Oh, Lord," he said miserably, "I'm not explaining this well, am I?"

She rose with awful calm, her face ashen. Her warm refuge from the cold world had turned into the heat of unseemly desire and then to disgrace, in very short order. She didn't know what to do with desire or disgrace; she only knew she had to strike back.

"Well, then, am I an adventuress?" she asked shakily. "Or merely with child?"

"I didn't mean that, I never meant that. I was just trying to explain how I felt before I knew you," he said, starting toward her. He stopped, realizing he couldn't trust himself to take her into his arms as he yearned to do. Not when she looked so vulnerable and he knew he was no less so.

"And now you believe me to be a saint? Of course, that's why you kissed me just now. Well, I'm going to bed. And you may go to the devil, sir!" she cried, and fled the room before she could ruin the effect by bursting into tears.

"Why bother? I'm already there," he told the empty room when she'd gone, and then hung his aching head in his hands.

CHAPTER
11

"Do you want anything else, my lady?" a footman asked.

He couldn't hear Dulcie's soft answer, but Crispin allowed himself a dour smile at what it could have been.

Yes, would you lie down on the floor so I might walk on you? If she'd said that, he thought resentfully, the servants would probably have done so happily—any of the servants in or outside the hall. They doted on her. She hadn't spoken to her lord husband for three days—three entire days, morning till dusk—and yet they fawned over her. He hadn't even seen her, except for stolen glimpses, in all that time. She breakfasted in her room, went to bed early, and managed to avoid him during the hours in between.

He didn't know where she lunched or when she dined, for he had studiously avoided doing either at the hall since their kiss three nights ago. He was sure she wouldn't have come down to eat if he had been there, yet none of his servants seemed to notice his absence. Whenever he heard her voice, he also heard how the servants leaped to attention for her and attended her with gentle voices and little sighs. They saved their reproachful glances and thin-lipped looks for him, as though he were a monster.

She was a penniless girl from Fleet prison, with no name except the one he'd given her, and no fashion except for the clothes he'd paid to put on her back. And yet they all clearly adored her. But then, they weren't Londoners, nor were they enlightened.

Only a few generations back, Crispin recalled sourly, the lord of the manor would have kept company with his household staff, even to eating and sleeping in the great hall with them, like a tumble of pups before the hearth. He could actually have picked a wife from their ranks in those days, if the king didn't order up one for him as part of some grand political scheme. The lord reigned, and his rule was absolute. But there'd been few real tyrants in the countryside since the day some lower lordlings got King John to swallow his pride and sign a charter limiting his power over them.

What held for the king of all England served for every lord as well. Unlike his French counterparts, an English lord did not own his serfs' souls as well as their bodies. Since there was no droit du seigneur, he had no feudal rights to bed a virgin serf on her wedding night. In fact, he had no absolute authority at all, Crispin thought moodily. The lord built his keep with the help of his men-at-arms, and with them he protected his serfs, and that was the way of his world—in theory. Let him neglect them or his duty to them, however, and he'd find no food in his larder, no serfs in his fields, and no life in his body before long. A charge of murder needed witnesses to support it, and there were always more agreeable, ambitious lords to be found. An agreeable lord was one who knew his people and who, in his way, catered to them.

They were very egalitarian in those days. Just because one man held a higher station in life didn't mean another couldn't speak his mind. And this was the countryside, where nothing changed more slowly than people's minds.

So woe betide a viscount they thought was treating his young bride badly.

Crispin's bath was cold in the morning, but not so cold as his breakfast or his butler's smile, and none of that was as cool as the looks he got from his grooms whenever he escaped to the stables. All because of a girl who'd come into his house under false pretenses and might never leave.

He knew he should fly to London, but he couldn't—not with the way his household staff catered to her. Who knew what she might do while he was gone? And yet he couldn't bear to look at her, because when he did, he felt not only incredible desire for her but a tenderness as well, and he didn't know how to cope with these feelings.

But he wasn't going to hide from her anymore, either. Three days was long enough.

She was sitting in a window seat in the yellow salon when he strolled in. He didn't look at her after that first brief encompassing glance, but he knew she'd stopped reading to look up at him. He felt her attention to the tip of each hair on his head, and he could feel the loss of warmth when she quickly averted her gaze. It was ridiculous, but it was true. She affected him in a way no other woman had, and that wasn't the least of the reasons why he was so frustrated now.

"Madam wife," he said coolly as he looked out a window, "how have you been? More to the point, *where* have you been?"

"Here," she said in a small voice. "Where else should I be?"

"Where indeed? Maybe I should have asked where you were hiding? I've been here too, and I haven't seen you."

"Yes, you have," she said with quiet dignity. "I know you have, because I've seen you—the other afternoon when I passed your study, yesterday when you passed the dining room while I was having luncheon, last night, when you came in and walked right by me, and, oh, a dozen other times, I think. I've just been ignoring you the way you ignore me. But it's getting foolish now. If I can't go to London and you can't bear to look at me here, what am I to do? I'd be out of this marriage in a moment if I could. I . . ." she said, her voice breaking so that he turned to look at her. "I should think you'd know that by now."

She was pale, he noted with sudden alarm. She wore a vivid pink gown, but it served only to make the flush in her cheeks seem hectic against the pallor of her skin. Her eyes were dim. It seemed to him that she was in pain, if only because of the rigid way she held herself, one arm around her waist, the other fisted on her book.

"I'm not a mind reader," he said gruffly. "Look, Dulcie, there's no reason to cry," he said, and would have come to sit by her if she hadn't waved him off so fiercely. Her lovely eyes filled with tears. But they were tears of anger as well as sorrow, and though she was crying, she was obviously trying to stop. Her chin trembled, her mouth looked fragile, her eyes were streaming. He felt terrible—both guilty and outraged that she made him feel that way, and helpless, because he didn't know what to do except to hand her his handkerchief.

"Please go away," she said in a muffled voice after she accepted his handkerchief and hid her face in it.

"Not until you tell me what's the matter."

Her reply was to lift her head and stare at him in disbelief.

"I mean," he said uncomfortably, "aside from the usual."

"The usual?" she asked, her eyes getting wild and her voice heating up to a fine fury. That pleased him. The little he knew of her was enough to assure him that once she got mad at him the treacherous tears would stop. He could face anything but her weeping.

"The *usual?*" she cried. "Do you mean the fact that I'm married to a stranger who seems unable to stand the sight of me, who has carried me off to nowhere, and who keeps kissing me and apologizing for it, and making me so confused that all I can do is cry? Is *that* what you mean?"

"Well . . . yes," he said, with a smile.

And then she didn't know what to do. She could face his scorn more easily than his smile. Or at least, she thought, seeing how that tender smile transformed his hard face and warmed his eyes, she could avoid his anger and stoke her own while she did so. But there was nothing she could do but respond to his smile and damn herself for a fool.

"What have I done now to make you cry?" he asked gently. "Or, let me rephrase that, what have I done lately? Aside from avoiding you as cleverly as you've avoided me, that is."

"Well, nothing," she admitted grudgingly. "Nothing new. I just feel low, and not at all well. It's—it's only . . . all of it, you see. That, and . . . you know." She turned her head away.

"No," he said, sitting beside her and taking her hand, "I don't."

"It's nothing," she said in a fierce whisper, caught between anger and embarrassment.

He was fascinated by the way her emotions showed in the slow flush that crept up her neck and flooded her smooth white skin with ruddy color. Then he became bemused by the silkiness of the tiny ringlets that weren't long enough to be caught up with the rest of her hair at the nape of her neck. He wondered how they'd feel against his lips.

"Please tell me," he said absently.

It was an outspoken age, and she was not a retiring girl, but she had little experience with men, and less with gentlemen. And while it was daring, even exciting, to talk about *some* things, *other* things were simply embarrassing. Her confused mortification was so acute she felt pressure building in her head and her ears actually seemed to be ringing.

"You know," she finally said in a grieved whisper, her head turned aside. "I don't feel right physically, but I do in my mind because at least there's one less accusation you can make now."

He was completely lost. *"What* do I know?" he asked carefully, enunciating each word in case she was the one who hadn't understood.

"About . . . about my monthly cycle," she said in a sudden rush, to get the thing said and done. "That's what," she added defiantly, looking straight at him. "So now there's no reason for you to suggest I married you for that reason."

"Oh. That!" he said, remembering his muddled words and almost blushing himself. However young and innocent she seemed, he realized he'd trusted a relative stranger far more than a prudent man should have done. It wasn't like him, but then, he hardly recognized himself when he was with her.

"I never suggested that you were with child," he reminded her. "I merely mentioned it. I'm sorry if you thought I was accusing you. Poor girl, are you in much pain?" he asked, remembering how some women suffered at their monthly time. "Can I get you anything?"

All of it was there, clear to see on his face: his sympathy, his amusement, and his relief.

"Yes. You can go away!" she snarled. "Go find a nice dark dungeon for me. I'm sure you have one here. Just leave me," she said miserably. Life was unfair; man and nature made it so. She was poor and female, and she hated to hate him, and besides, her heart as well as her stomach hurt now.

He took her hand and placed a light kiss in the center of her palm. "I'm sorry," he said, holding her hand, which lay tense and rigid in his own. "I really am, about everything that has happened. But it's been difficult for me too, you know. When I lost all my money, I lost all chance to live the kind of life I wanted. I met you in a prison, through the best efforts of a little thief and a big one. I went through what I thought was a mock marriage, to save you. Not for the money . . . No. Really, see?" he asked, slipping two long fingers into an inner waistcoat pocket and extracting a gold coin.

"I never spent it; it became a good-luck piece." He gave a cough of a laugh before he slipped the coin back into his pocket. "Yes, even so, a good luck piece. Because my ships did come in—I regained my fortune and my position. And then, on the eve of my greatest triumph, I found myself truly wedded to a girl I didn't know. But one I've come to care for.

I'm as confused as you are, Dulcie. Think hard now, put yourself in my place. What should I have done? What should I do?"

"Murder me?" she asked in a little voice.

"Well, no, I don't think that's necessary," he said with a smile. "Maybe I wanted to at first, but what was I to think when you first showed up? Look, Dulcie, let's begin anew. I know I proposed a truce with you before and it came to nothing. But we've come a way since. Who knows how much further we'll have to go? This isn't about the clothes you should wear or what society might think. This must be for us.

"We're in this for however long. Let's come to some kind of terms with it or we'll tear each other and ourselves apart. I'll concede that you are blameless and not scheming for anything but your own freedom. You must forgive me my anger and suspicion. All right?"

She considered this. He hadn't mentioned what they would do about the kissing part, and she hadn't been able to stop thinking about that. But she didn't want to bring it up or he'd know she was thinking about it. She'd been deeply lonesome. It had been terrible being so lonely when she knew he was in the house, seeing glimpses of his wide back always turned to her as she crept past whatever room he was in. She was used to her own company. Her father had often left her alone, and they'd moved too often for her to make any fast friends. But there was always someone she could talk to: a landlady, sympathetic neighbors, even the vendors she bought their meals from. Now she was utterly alone in a household full of servants she didn't know how to approach. She didn't know if she even had the right to approach them.

Hard as all that had been, it was far worse to be living in the same house with a man she was beginning to admire, and not even being able to chat about the weather with him. His abandonment of her was more hurtful than she could have imagined. There was danger in knowing him, but the promise of friendship was a strong lure.

"All right," she said, sniffing away the last of her tears, "but what then?"

"Then," he said and she saw a sad, lost look in the depths of his eyes before they warmed as he turned them to her. "Then, we'll see. At least let us be friends until then, shall we?"

She nodded.

"So then," he said, more confidently. "Laudanum for the pain of your present condition?"

Only hemlock would cure that, she thought, but knew he was only speaking of her monthly pain, and said, "No, I don't like being drugged and stupid. It will pass. A warm brick will ease it if some hot tea doesn't."

"And company," he said, decisively. "Mine. Company warms the heart. I think we can be friends. Yes?"

"Yes," she said, and sighed, because that was one of the nicest things he'd ever said to her.

They took tea. He sent for a hot brick for her and, ignoring her blushes, had it wrapped in flannel before he ordered her to hold it in her lap as they sat and talked. It eased her pain almost as much as his light conversation did. He told her he had seen the wonders of the ancient and modern worlds. He had acquaintances around the world, and he related merry stories about them. But she questioned him with such interest that he found himself telling fewer stories and talking more about himself.

She'd awakened to many mornings in new places, too. In her case, it was because she'd been dragged off in the night and carried in secrecy to some new place that her father's creditors didn't know about. But now she found herself laughing with Crispin as she told him about the Fabulous Youth Elixir, the Excellent Silver Tarnish Preventive, and the Miraculous Hair Restoring Paste—all of which worked the same way, which was to say, not at all.

They discovered they'd read many of the same books, and she envied him his hard-won skills in Latin and Greek, but not his skill with horses and the hunt, because she was a city girl. When he argued that she enjoyed flowers and trees, she had to admit that there was something to the countryside— but not much. He claimed she was exactly like his friend, the earl of Wrede. She recoiled with such horror that he laughed. He imitated Wrede's distinctive drawl, and she upset her teacup. They had such a lovely afternoon that they never noticed the time passing until the lengthening shadows told them it was dinnertime.

This alarmed Dulcie and bemused Crispin so much that they were both almost glad it was time to go upstairs and dress for dinner.

As she did, Dulcie remembered the afternoon and found herself tingling, though he'd never done more than touch her hand. Then she became frightened. She comforted herself by thinking that he wouldn't want to touch a woman in her present condition. And refused to think an hour beyond the coming night.

Dinner was wonderful. The soup was spicy, the fish fresh, the capon juicy, the duck lean, the mutton truly springtime's, the beef tender, and the wines rich and fruity. By the time the desserts were brought out, they could only pick off bits to savor, exclaim over and tempt each other with. They laughed as much as they swallowed, and ate every bite that was presented to them. It was a lover's dinner, but they each for their own reasons pretended it was just a friendly feast.

Full, and merry, they retired to the small salon and sat beside a mumbling fire. It was dark, but it wasn't late, and they had an evening in front of them.

"Cards? Chess? Dice? Or perhaps you'd like to play at something other than a game?" he asked. "There's a fine harpsichord in the music room."

"I don't play," she said sadly, knowing that a lady should.

"At anything?" he asked, with a half smile.

"Well, cards," she admitted, "but I don't play often because I'm a very bad loser."

"Ah, so am I, so let's have a game and see who can hold his temper better. Two games in one, much more interesting."

They played by fire and candlelight. The challenge of keeping their tempers even when they were losing made the game more comical than serious, and twice as delightful. She was a terrible player who was, however, capable of spurts of brilliance; he was a good player who was always surprised by her occasional clever ploys. They laughed so hard they sometimes dropped their cards.

Often they stopped laughing and playing, to talk, to listen.

"My mother was a demon player," Dulcie said.

The wistfulness in her voice made him hold his hand and look at her. "Do you miss her?" he asked, genuinely curious as to why Dulcie hadn't mentioned her before. Now that he thought about it, it was odd that a girl wouldn't tell her mother of her marriage, whether it was a mock one or not. Odder still that she hadn't applied to her for help.

"No—no more than always, that is," Dulcie said simply. "She left when I was a little girl. I've seen her since, but it was always clear that she didn't regret going. It's not that she doesn't like me," she added quickly, as though daring him to contradict her, "because she says she does, and she never forgets my birthday. She sends me lovely things every year. And she loves to gossip with me about the royal family and about the people she knows. We visit every year, and she writes to me regularly, every few months. She likes to shop with me, too, whenever we meet," she went on a little less confidently. "It's just that some women are not cut out to be parents. I know that some people would disagree, but so it is."

He was trying to decide what to say when she added, "And *your* mother, do you miss her?"

How could he miss a dim, fond memory with more than passing regret? She'd been a gentle woman who always appeared in his memory in the same blue gown. She had played the harpsichord and loved roses, but whether he knew that from his father's stories or for himself, he didn't know. But suddenly Dulcie's words and this warm, gentle night by the fireside conjured up another vision—a long forgotten one, of firelight and laughter, of sitting by the hearth with a roasting apple on a stick while a laughing woman in blue silk cautioned him to watch his fingers. There'd been a laughing girl with him then, too, and another boy or two. He'd been the youngest.

He remembered how he'd looked down—had his hands really been so small and plump and ineffectual then?—to find his apple splattered on the hearth. He remembered how his tears had been washed away and how he'd been presented with a new apple on a stick. The memory was there because it had been a hard, tangy fresh apple, and he remembered the despair he felt, wondering if he'd ever be able to hold it over the flames long enough to make it sweet and soft and fragrant.

Nothing had ever been that sweet again. The other boys were gone, and the laughing little girl, and the laughing mother. Only the little boy remained, and he too had all but disappeared. Until tonight.

"Yes," he said, surprising himself, "I miss my mother very much."

He and Dulcie played for walnuts, they played for grapes, they played for the fun of sitting up and talking without her having to worry about him looking at her lips, and then acting on the look that sprang to his eyes, without him worrying about her trying to lure him to her bed. Tonight was unique; tonight they could appreciate each other without fear of compromising themselves. And so they did.

When at last they had to admit the night was done, he took a brace of candles and walked her to her room. He stood with her by her door, hesitant for the first time, denying how much he didn't want to go.

"How do you feel now?" he asked. "Any more pain? Are

you sure you don't want some medication? Another hot brick?"

"No, no," she said. "I'm fine, really, much better already. I'll feel better every day, I assure you. It never lasts long."

"Then good night, Dulcie. Sleep well and be well, my dear."

When she saw him look down to her mouth, she wasn't afraid to offer him her lips in a kiss of peace, for the night had created between them a certain understanding.

His kiss was light and gentle but no less thrilling for that. It was filled with warmth and friendship as well as delight. His arm came around her, and she yielded and leaned against him, savoring the hard warmth of his mouth and body. She felt comforted and cherished; it almost felt as if they were really married, she thought as she kissed him freely and without fear.

And it was almost as if he had read her mind when he spoke again.

"Ah, Dulcie, if you were only really, truly mine," he whispered against her hair, "I'd hold you close, your bare skin to mine, your cold little bottom tucked into my lap, my hand on your aching stomach, Dulcie, I promise you."

Then he released her, as shocked and surprised by what he'd said as she was.

He bowed abruptly and left her, after one long last look—left her to dream of what could be, and he to lay awake longer than he liked, thinking of what could not be, and what might have been.

"Red and pink and gold! And white!" Dulcie cried. "Every color they come in! If I had a rose garden here," she said, indicating the newly leafed bushes they were strolling past, "that's what I'd plant."

"Just what I thought. So I did just that," he said.

She gave him a brilliant smile and walked on, pleased at the way her deeply belled skirt swung over the crushed-shell walk, noting with satisfaction the expensive lace that trimmed her bodice and her sleeves. Today she looked, and almost felt as if she belonged here.

Crispin looked handsome in his dark breeches and white shirt. She thought they both looked like a picture of rural contentment, and almost believed it.

The place awed her. She had seldom seen parks that were so big, and few that were so carefully kept. She couldn't stop thinking that she wasn't just a visitor here; by the law of the land, she owned all of this with him. It was too huge a concept to hold in, and the words escaped her as she thought them. "How does it feel to own all this?" she wondered, because she knew that she really didn't—and never would. "How must it feel to own so much!"

"If you're born with wealth, it feels normal. Too normal, I think," he answered slowly. "It doesn't feel unusual—until you lose it. Then you feel as if half your heart's been torn out, as if you're left with nothing but yourself, which seems like very little after you've had so much. It's not just the land, you see," he went on, voicing just what he was thinking. "It's the history. Knowing that your grandfather planted that tree and your great-grandfather planted that other one. It's as though your history is written in the earth itself, and you're only another one in the line. So you feel as if you belong here as much as that great white oak over there does. And you feel just as disrupted when you're uprooted."

This time she didn't say what she thought: that she felt like a weed in his glorious gardens. She knew very well that she didn't belong here the way he did. She'd never owned anything of any real importance, and had lost everything— except her heart. And even that was now in jeopardy. But she still had her pride, she thought, unconsciously raising her chin, and that she must keep.

He saw the wistful sorrow on her lovely face and paused, appalled at his thoughtlessness, realizing how much he had and how little she possessed—beyond grace and beauty and a quick mind, of course. So he determined to entertain her.

He took her hand and changed the subject, making light conversation as he led her down his winding paths.

He showed her his world with such charm and grace that she almost began to believe he really welcomed her to it. He strolled at her side, commenting on everything they saw, as delightful a companion as she could have wished, with not one unkind, or too fond, word to trouble her. She didn't know how how long that would last, but didn't let that bother her now. She was sure she could handle anything that happened on this soft, misty spring morning. It might be that his sensuality came only with the candlelight. She would face that tonight.

". . . but I think we should concentrate on present pleasures," he commented, and she almost tripped, wondering if he could read her mind. But then he went on, "These roses won't bloom for a month. Till then, you shall wear one of these." And he plucked a sprig of lilacs and tucked it in her hair.

"Oh, but you said they'd wilt if they were taken," she protested, touching her hand to her hair.

"The best pleasures are fleeting," he answered gruffly, and lowered his head to breathe in the scent of the lilac. And then had only to turn his head an inch to find her parted lips.

Her hand faltered in the air, and then found his hair instead of her own. Her other hand went around his waist. His mouth felt so warm that she realized she hadn't known how chill the morning was. And he found such sweetness in her kiss that he forgot all his resolutions. He'd been caught off guard. All he could think of was the moment, and the softness of her lips and the sweet yielding of her body against his.

"Heavens!" a familiar voice called. "Should I return? But I only just got here!" The earl of Wrede waved his walking stick to get their attention. They sprang apart like guilty children surprised.

"Good morning, your ladyship," Wrede said, his cool, bright glance on Dulcie, crimson in her confusion.

Crispin kept his arm around Dulcie and felt her tense, ready to bolt. He pulled her up close to his side, as she looked up at him. He gazed at his friend impassively, his smile less than welcoming. But that might have been because his composure was absolute again. She'd grown used to a warmer expression in his eyes. Now they seemed only to reflect the light.

"Wrede," he said calmly, "what brings you to the countryside? I thought you said it was fit only for flowers."

"Of which you have a multitude," Wrede said, "but even so, I found myself concerned for you, dear friend, and decided to have a look for myself." He looked at Dulcie as he spoke to Crispin, and she felt uneasy.

"Am I not welcome?" he asked sweetly.

"You're always welcome in my house," Crispin said.

"Even on your honeymoon? Oh, yes, I'd forgot, there wasn't to be one, was there?" he asked with patent falseness. "I've news for you," he said before Crispin could say the hard thing obviously on his lips. "News I know you're eager to hear."

"About Dulcie's father?" Crispin asked quickly.

"Alas. No. Mr. Blessing is vanished, hide and hair," the earl said, shrugging as he looked back to Crispin. "I even paid a visit to Harry Meech with a pocketful of gold, which he slavered over—to no avail. He'd sell his granny for a fourth of it if he could find a buyer for her, but he couldn't earn a groat from me because he can't find Mr. Blessing, either. No, I'm sorry to say I've no news of him. But I've word of someone else you'd like to hear about.

"I come on a mission from a dear friend of yours. Who *specifically* begs to be remembered to you. Lady Charlotte sends her love, Crispin," the earl said, staring down at Dulcie now with a look that made her back up a step, "and asks not to be forgotten. It appears that, consoling as they are, your constant letters are not enough for her anymore."

There was a second of silence, as the earl smiled at Dulcie, and Crispin drew in a quick breath. Dulcie spoke before he could. "I'll leave you two to talk," she said.

She spun away from Crispin and marched down the path back to the house, her skirt swaying to the beat of her rapid steps. The shells snapped and crunched beneath her feet and she hoped she made enough noise so that they wouldn't hear her crying.

When she'd gone from sight, Crispin turned on the earl and demanded, "Was that necessary?"

"It seemed to me that I had interrupted a true honeymoon. I thought someone should remind you of reality. Has she bewitched you? I saw where your mouth and your hands were, but where is your head, my boy? Have you made this a true marriage? I wish you'd told me, and spared me the horrors of having to seek out Harry Meech in his rathole."

"No, it is not a true marriage," Crispin said through tight lips.

"You relieve my mind."

Crispin ran a hand through his hair, his face was anguished when he spoke. "Ah, Wrede, I tell you, it's a coil. Am I married? Yes. Am I wed to her? No. But it's not her fault. Should I become her husband? Do I have a choice at all?" He laughed bitterly. "I don't know. Was ever a man in such a strange position?"

"I have made some discreet inquiries regarding your situation," Wrede said seriously. "There may be a solution yet. It is agreed that Fleet marriages are a vile practice, causing havoc financially and morally. It's the financial aspect that concerns the government most, of course. Something is going to be done about the situation there, and perhaps be done for you, too. It may take time, but don't give up."

"But do I want to keep fighting? Or do I want to give up. I wonder?" Crispin asked.

"I think you've been in the countryside too long," Wrede said in alarm.

"Once you were Dulcie's champion. Now you seem to be her enemy. What has changed your opinion?" Crispin asked, gazing at his friend with a clear, unwavering gaze.

"Circumstance," the earl said. "My judgment was a victim of circumstance too. When I first saw Dulcie in London she seemed young and frightened, honestly out-raged at her father's contentions. The situation looked temporary then; she appeared as eager as you to end the farce. Now I've had time to think. So, obviously, has she. I don't want to see you cheated, even by yourself, but most especially not by some young woman. Things have changed. Dulcie's father has bolted. She's been left on your doorstep, and seems inclined to stay there, permanently."

Crispin stood very still and glared, blue fire in his eyes. "I suggest you remember that Dulcie is my lady, and until she is not, you are to give her the courtesy due her as my wife!"

He closed his eyes and sighed. When he looked at Wrede again, there was weary sorrow, not fury, in his eyes. "I'm sorry, old friend," he said, laying a hand on the earl's now rigid shoulder. "I know you mean well. But you can't know . . . Look, Wrede, I have no proof she's anything but what she says. And I believe her."

"Because you are alone with her here in the back end of nowhere!" Wrede exclaimed in alarm.

"Because I have begun to know her," Crispin replied softly. He patted his friend's shoulder. "Don't worry . . . Now, do you want to rest after your trip down from civilization? Or would you care to come with me? I've tenants to see this afternoon."

"Work?" Wrede said with a shudder. "Whatever you call it, that *is* work, is it not? No, thank you. I think I'll stroll for a while and then rest up for dinner. You *are* feeding me, aren't you?"

"Of course, and well, too. I'll leave you now," Crispin said. He started to walk on, then turned and said with as much apology as determination, "Please don't speak with Dulcie until I return. We've had enough tears for one day. All right?"

"Oh. Certainly," Wrede said. "Your wish is my command." He swept Crispin a low bow. But his long face was set in worried lines as he watched his friend walk away.

CHAPTER

12

The earl of Wrede spent the rest of the morning acquainting himself with Crispin's estate. He saw that his valet was comfortable in his rooms. He exchanged pleasantries with the housekeeper and butler, taking care to be sure he was nowhere near the lady of the house. He visited the kitchens to beg a glass of lemonade and left with a pastry, a tart, and a wedge of cheese wrapped in a cloth. He took that outside, and after a few minutes spent joking with a pair of milk-maids near the dairy, he strolled down to the stables and passed some time talking horseflesh with the grooms.

Then he took his parcel of delicacies, entered the box-wood maze, and without a misplaced step, went straight to the center of it. There was a bench in a clearing in its secret heart. Sighing with contentment, he dusted off the bench with his handkerchief, spread his coattails, and sat down, crossing his long legs. He raised his face to the sun and closed his eyes. Then, although he appeared to be complete-ly alone, he spoke.

"Skulking is hard work, I'd think. I've a lovely luncheon with me. Cook even put in some pickled onions. Would you care to join me?"

There was only intermittent birdsong for answer. He sighed theatrically. "Oh, come," he said wearily. "I don't mind your continuing to hover, but once I begin to dine, the sound of your secret slavering will distress me Come out, come out, wherever you are," he said in bored accents. "I suspect you're behind the hedge on my right. Am I correct?"

He heard a rustling sound and opened his eyes to see Willie Grab, looking chagrined, standing near him.

"How'd you know?" Willie asked in disgust.

"If my friend the viscount can do it, then so can I. But I believe he had the more difficult task," the earl answered.

"It's the leaves," Willie said with considerable grievance. "They *crackle*. There's stones and stuff. How's a fellow supposed to be sly here in the woods?"

"Just so," the earl said calmly, "and your giggling at me in the rose garden didn't help your cause much, either."

There was a sudden silence that the earl appreciated hugely.

"The next question, of course, is *why?*" the earl said. "Oh, not why you found me so amusing; I cannot hope to plumb the infant mind, nor do I wish to. I would, however, like to know what you hoped to gain by observing me in secret." Wrede was suddenly serious, his eyes alert and cold. "Did the viscount ask you to? Or was it Harry Meech? Or some other employer of yours? How many masters do you presently serve, by the by?"

"Two," Willie said promptly. "Harry and the viscount. But you knowed that. I was keeping my eye on you for both of them . . . and 'cause there ain't much else to do around here." He looked as disgruntled as he sounded. "I never seen such a place. The house is grand, like a palace. But why build it here, I'd like to know? There's nobody to see it and nothing to do in it, or outside it. It's for the birds and bees, and that's flat *all*. If I was a vegetable, I could see it. But people should stay where they belong. In London.

"It's spring," he went on. However bored the earl pretended to be, he was giving Willie his complete attention, despite his half-closed eyes. "Now, back home in London there's so much to do it's a shame to sleep," Willie said. "There's always someone selling things, and twice as many to buy—everything from milk to muffins, fish to fruit, and all in the street. You can buy your dinner and eat your breakfast without going two steps from your bed."

He sighed. "The Fleet Street market's got anything a body could want, too. If that ain't enough, there's Bartholomew's Fair and Southwark Fair, the May Fair—Lor', I can't think of them all! With food and games, music and dancing. That's for us. The gentry don't care for the pushing and drinking, noise and carrying-on, so they got gardens: Ranelagh and Vauxhall and the like, to visit and sport in."

"Yes," the earl agreed, "so they can do their own pushing and drinking, noise-making and carrying-on. But I perceive your point, and agree, utterly."

"Yeah. There's always fun in town," Willie went on in dreamy reverie. "Rivermen going up and down the water, cursing and singing, with the barges all decked out for spring. There's carriages and horses, carts and sedan chairs in the streets. And fun? There's puppet shows, and the quacks with their medicine shows—all free, unless you're a fool. It's like living at a fair year-round. And frolics— footman races, sedan chair races, cockfights, and watching the poor scrubs sitting in the pillory with egg and worse on their faces, waiting to get out." He chuckled at some fond remembrance.

"Yes, lovely public sports, and don't forget the jolly hangings," the earl said, but paused when he saw Willie's smile vanish and his face close hard on something like pain.

"Yeah," Willie said gruffly, "them, too." He kicked at a pebble. When he looked up again, his voice was scornful. "But here? The kitchen maids here, they tell me they got *fairies* at the foot of the garden. They're supposed to dance in the moonlight. The maids really believe that swill! They even leave out a plate of milk for them sometimes. But they never seen one. You know why? 'Cause, they say, if you look hard at the fairies they disappear! You know why?" he asked the fascinated earl. "'cause, the poor lasses ain't got nothing else to do but dream up little green men, that's why. If they was in London, they'd be cured of that soon enough I can tell you."

"Yes, and infected with something else promptly too, no doubt," the earl said. "But we are agreed: London is far superior to the countryside. So, then, that being the case, my boy, why are you still here? Are you being paid handsomely enough to make such deprivation worth your while?"

As Willie thought about his answer, the earl could see some of the calculations on his face. It was a young face, lean and sunburned, harder at times than most adult faces the earl had seen. But sometimes, when a happy thought occurred to him or when he was caught off guard, Willie, for all his wisdom and bravado, was just a boy of nine or ten—only Willie and his Maker knew the count of his days. And only those two, the earl suspected, cared. He was a child from the alleys of London, where there were almost as many orphaned children as rats. But the rats at least had mothers to succor them for longer than the street urchin did.

There were thousands of such boys in London, but few of them, the earl thought, were as clever and calculating as Willie Grab. The fact that he'd survived to this day was astonishing enough. The further fact that he had remained free was proof of his shrewdness. He was not an apprentice or a chimney sweep or a brothel boy or even a lower servant forced to live out his days in the basement of a fine house, nor was he in prison or in the workhouse or subsisting on garbage in a back alley. He was alive and thriving and had reached the age of eight or ten without selling his body in bondage or losing his soul. Yet.

"They pay me good," Willie finally said. "The viscount pays better, but I been working for Harry longer. I could stay in London, but I'm staying on here 'cause this is kind of like a story now. I want to see how it comes out. Anyway, the work is easy, and I'm learning a trade," he said, puffing out his thin chest. "I might be a coachman someday. Maybe not," he said, interpreting the earl's silence as laughter at his presumption, "but it's a useful thing to learn, anyhow. A man can't know enough trades, you know."

"Do I?" the earl asked quizzically. "I don't think so. I only know one. Being an earl is not a difficult thing to learn. It requires only breathing in and then breathing out—repeatedly. Sometimes, I'll grant, it's a tiresome job, often a fruitless one. But it's the only one I know. And it pays well.

"Be that as it may," he continued quickly, astonished to see something like pity in the boy's hard blue eyes, when he had only been jesting—or thought he had been, "I have a proposition for you, one that pays well. Would you like to have three employers instead of only two? I, too, would like to know the end of this story, and I can't think of anyone better than you to keep me informed. All I want to know is what Harry wants to know."

"Well," Willie said, considering, "that could be arranged, my lord, but there's a thing I got to tell you before I take a penny: I may have three masters now, but I always got one—myself—and I do what suits that one best—first and always."

The earl considered Willie from opaque eyes. "You've discovered the secret of successful men, God help you," he finally said, unfurling himself to stand towering over the boy. "Very well," he said. "Consider yourself in my employ."

"Done!" Willie said, not backing a step away from the gentleman who loomed over him, "but I got to see some gold afore I do that, my lord." He braced himself for a blow, and tensed to run.

The earl paused, and then laughed. "You'll end up ruling all England," he said, opening his purse, "and that may be the best thing for this kingdom."

And Willie, for once, wasn't sure if he was hearing a jest or not.

* * *

She looked every inch a fine lady, the earl of Wrede thought as Dulcie took her seat at the table. Her skirts were spread out like a fan, twice as wide from side to side as from front to back. The gown was cut low, the neck embellished with lace and furbelows. It was slouched in back in the popular bagged shape, but her lissome figure couldn't be disguised by that. Her skin was clear, her features fine. Her topaz eyes were alert, showing her to be clever as well as alluring, and she had the most plump, kissable mouth he'd seen in a long while. In all, he thought, eyeing her, she was an enticing woman, and thus a formidable enemy.

Wrede had no doubt that she was that. She'd landed on Crispin's doorstep in London, and now seemed to be here to stay. In London Crispin had been ready to wring her neck, but now he looked as though he yearned to kiss it. But Crispin had worked long and hard to rebuild his fortune, and the earl couldn't bear to see an adventuress sharing it with him through no choice of his own. Crispin was no fool, but he was kind. He was also deeply sensual. A homeless waif with such a face and form, and with his name, and sharing his house—she'd share his bed in no time, and then his fortune.

Well, not if his friend had anything to say about it. It wasn't fair that she had so easily achieved her goal of trapping a man into an indecent legal marriage.

"You look very lovely, my dear viscountess," the earl said, and Dulcie turned to him, her face aglow with happiness.

She'd been so afraid of his reaction to her. When she'd last seen him in London, he'd been charming to her. The next time she'd seen him she was locked in Crispin's arms and so thrilled with what she'd found there that she wouldn't have heard the earl if he'd come down the garden path blowing a trumpet. He hadn't been very charming then. She wondered if he was as appalled at her reckless submission to Crispin's kiss as she herself had been. But now he was complimenting her, and when she dared look at him she saw his admiration.

"Thank you," she said, breathlessly.

"Astonishing what money can do, is it not?" the earl said lazily.

Crispin's eyes blazed, and he clenched his fists. Wrede was too clever to be so tactless. Crispin had often found his sly cruelty amusing in the past, but now it was like skewering a baby rabbit, for Dulcie's hurt was clear to see. It was worse when she lifted her chin and smiled as though she thought it was nothing but a pleasantry. Her courage hurt Crispin even more than the insult to her did.

"It's astonishing if you're considering only gowns," Crispin drawled, "but the lady in them remains constantly beautiful."

Dulcie shot him a look of surprised gratitude. Crispin was delighted to see a relieved smile light up her face again.

Wrede's eyes narrowed. "And she sets a tolerable table," he said, gazing at the dishes before him. "Not the usual mutton, but creamed soups, fresh produce, and tender spring meats. I'm in for a treat. Did you direct the kitchens to produce this, viscountess?"

Dulcie scarcely knew how to find the kitchens, much less assert herself enough to order up anything for dinner, and she was sure the earl knew it.

"She doesn't know your jaded appetites," Crispin snapped before Dulcie could stammer an answer, "but I do. So I instructed the cook as to your care and feeding, my friend," he said in a less than friendly way.

Wrede saw the look Crispin bent upon Dulcie, and her shy answering smile. It seemed that his every cruelty drew the two closer. He managed a smile himself and decided to retreat for the time being.

Dinner went well after that. Wrede was a wonderful storyteller, and Crispin knew how to encourage him. Dulcie was too wary of Wrede now to try, although he was completely charming again, as though he'd never been anything else to her. By the time they groaned at the size of the desserts being brought out, Dulcie had forgotten to be afraid of the earl.

"No solitary gentlemen's brandy for us tonight," Wrede said as Dulcie rose. He stood as well. "Please allow an old bachelor the pleasure of a lady's company instead. Shall we?" he asked, crooking an arm and offering it to her.

She gave him an honest smile of pleasure and let him lead her to the salon, thinking he must be regretting his earlier cruelty.

"May I offer you some brandy?" Wrede asked, once they had reached the salon.

"Dulcie doesn't indulge," Crispin said. He crossed the room and perched on the edge of the settee on which Dulcie sat. He put his hand on her shoulder. Without thinking, she raised her own to cover it and hold it there. "She doesn't indulge in anything but cider, that is," he added, with a smile down at her, as he squeezed her shoulder comfortingly.

"I see," Wrede said, his voice troubled, because he'd seen too much.

"Gads! Look at the time!" Crispin said with an exaggerated yawn.

"It's an infant of an evening!" Wrede protested. "We've started out on the town at this hour in London."

"It's the country air," Crispin said with determination. "I'm to bed. Do you want to stay here?" he asked Dulcie, who was looking from one to the other of them as they argued.

"Oh, no, no," she said, hopping to her feet. "I'm so tired I can hardly think straight, or I'd have said so immediately. I can't imagine what made me so stupid with weariness—the food, the fire . . ."

"The company," Wrede said in annoyance. "Don't worry, I *quite* understand. No, no, don't fret about me. I'm not tired, but I scarcely wish to impose myself on such sleepyheads. No, you go off to bed. I'll just go to my room and write a novel or two during what's left of the night," he said. He bowed and, with barely concealed bad temper, left for his room. Crispin didn't notice. He was watching Dulcie with a thoughtful expression. When he rose, it was with a new determination in his eyes.

He had seen and felt enough, and he was tired of defending her, and himself. He was a grown man with control to equal his desires, but his desires were paramount tonight. Wrede was here, but even he seemed alien, misplaced. London and everything and everyone in it seemed a long way off. Dulcie was here. He couldn't stop wanting her just because it wasn't wise to want her.

Crispin saw Dulcie up the long stair, holding a brace of candles to light their way down the hall to her room. It was an eerie reprise of the other night he'd accompanied her to her room, and once again he stopped with her at her door and waited expectantly.

"May I come in?" he asked.

She stared at him in disbelief. She couldn't gauge his expression in the dancing light, but his gleaming gaze was intent.

"Why?" she asked, hardly believing he would just come straight out and ask to share her bed.

"To do this," he said, and dipped his head and kissed her lips, which had parted in surprise. He didn't touch her in any other way. "And this," he breathed when he drew back to see her stunned expression, before he used his free arm to clasp her closer.

"I have to put these candles down," he muttered against her neck after releasing her mouth long enough to speak, "because any more of this and I'll forget them. You're too pretty to go up in flames like a moth," he whispered as he brushed tiny kisses down her throat. "I want you to catch fire for me and only me."

"No," she said distractedly, as shivers coursed up and down her body. "No," she said again in a tremulous voice when she heard herself. And "No!" she said at last, pushing him away.

"Why not?" he asked gently, as he put the candles down. He caught her hands in his and held them apart, looking down at her searchingly. "You can't deny you want me. You know I want you. I can't—won't—fight you, or myself, anymore. Ah, Dulcie, I've done with the battle. You win. Or shall I say, 'we win'? We're adults, and this is needless suffering. Why go to our separate lonely beds? We're such good companions in the daylight, let us try to find pleasure with each other tonight."

"Pleasure is not enough," she said, closing her eyes to the look in his, wanting to believe what she had to say.

"Good God, Dulcie, what is there to lose?"

"What would I lose?" she whispered fiercely, opening her eyes to reality. "Your respect. My respect for myself. My future too. If we can end this, someday I will marry."

"And so?" he asked impatiently. "Your husband will know you were married once before, won't he? Whether he does or not, it makes no difference. I won't do anything to let him know it if you don't want me to. Please let me hold you, let me show you," he said with tenderness and desire, his voice low and urgent. "I can touch you to delight, and let your touch help me to find mine. Hands, lips, oh, so many ways. You're a virgin now, and you'll still be a virgin for him then, but we can share great pleasure anyway, you'll see."

It was everything she wanted, and nothing she wanted. She trembled with confusion. She wanted his approval, his touch, and his kisses, but she was greedy; she wanted more, too. She'd never known the pleasure he promised, and she didn't doubt he could give it to her. But she realized he would give her nothing more.

She liked him better than any man she'd ever known except her father, and she certainly trusted Crispin more. She admired him, and desired him as she'd desired no other man she'd ever met or seen. But he offered her only pleasure, though he had to know how much more she needed. The hurt of that cleansed her of all desire, leaving her empty and cold.

"I see," she said, nodding. "A **knowing** virgin. Is that what you'd make me? Because I sold **my name** in marriage once, you think I'll sell anything?"

"Dulcie, Dulcie," he said, releasing her hand so he could cup her cheek and tilt her head up. "I'm only asking you to take comfort from me. It's a simple, delightful thing. Kisses, caresses, touching, stroking—it's lovely. Your body next to mine all through a long and lonely night. We'll play, and nothing more. I'll take nothing from you, and only bring you pleasure. What is wrong with that?"

It sounded so simple, so exciting and pleasurable, so companionable, that she almost succumbed—until she remembered the name that had riveted his attention and struck her to the heart tonight.

"Tell me," she said in a firm voice. "If your lady, the beautiful and clever Lady Charlotte . . ." He stiffened at that name, and she went on quickly, before she could be hurt more deeply by the way he reacted. "If Wrede or some other man came to her and said, 'Crispin is married now, so would you dally with me until he's free? All we'll do is share great pleasure, and he'll never know, I promise.' Tell me: would you mind if she agreed, as you are asking me to do?"

She saw the truth in his eyes and in the way he remained still.

"Yes," she said, even as he did.

Their words hung in the silence of the hall. Her hurt was so enormous that she didn't know whether to run from him and his house or run into his arms so she could pretend it wasn't true. She swayed where she stood.

"But it's different. Charlotte already knows me," he said a little desperately. "You have no one else . . ." He stopped as he heard what he'd said, and winced.

"That's so," she said slowly, realizing she had no one but him in her mind now, and perhaps forever. "But I have me," she said, struggling to hold back tears. "I'm not a prig or a saint, and I won't pretend to be. But I won't make love with you, though you leave me a virgin seven times over. Maybe it's because I want you to think I'm as good as your lady. And maybe," she said, raising her chin, "it's because I am."

Or maybe, she thought, it's because I'm afraid I won't care what you think, once I'm lost in your arms.

"Good night," she said, and managed to get into her room before she began crying.

He stood there for a long moment before he went to his own room. He was tense and edgy as he readied himself for his lonely bed. He'd forgotten all caution, but he wasn't so much alarmed as furious with himself. He should have been grateful for his narrow escape, but he wasn't. She had wanted him as much as he'd wanted her; there was no disguising that. Her body had grown as hot as her mouth. She'd kissed him with abandon and clung to him between kisses, her breath sawing as unevenly as his. They ignited each other; she'd never denied that. And yet she'd said no.

He looked at his bed and thought of all the nights he'd passed awake there since he'd met her. Then he paced the night away, thinking and remembering, and realizing that he needed and wanted her more than he had ever needed anyone or anything.

Dulcie missed her father very much that night. She tried not to think of him, because it hurt so much. She knew he'd left London for her sake, but it seemed to her that the people she loved were always leaving her. Two people had done that: her mother and her father. And fortunately she knew how to deal with being alone. She'd had practice sleeping in strange places and being afraid of the morning to come. So she crept into bed and burrowed into her pillow and told herself a wonderful familiar story she'd made up, about another time and place, where good girls got the happiness they deserved. Then she lost herself in sleep. She had no trouble doing that because she'd had experience with loneliness and desire, and wanting things she knew she could never have.

Wrede went to sleep early and effortlessly, and he slept dreamlessly. His mind was made up; he knew exactly what he had to do. He needed to rest so he could ride like a fury back to London at first light and set his plan in motion before time ran out. His friend was in danger and didn't know it. And only Wrede could save him.

CHAPTER

13

The man appeared in the doorway and stood gaping at her. Dulcie was startled but not frightened. It would be hard to be afraid of such a young, innocent-looking man, especially with dozens of servants standing nearby. He had a tanned, round, blunt-featured face and was only a little taller than she, and stocky. His clothes marked him as a country gentleman. His long coat and breeches were dun brown and rumpled, his linen dusty, and his sturdy boots covered with mud. He wore nothing but his own sandy hair beneath his hat. That—and a fascinated stare.

"Andrew," Crispin said, as he came into the hall. "Good morning to you. Oh, I see you've met my wife."

"Agh," the man said, whipping off his hat, turning it in his hands, and blushing beneath his tan.

"We haven't met," Dulcie said, glad of that, if only because it gave her a chance to speak to Crispin. They hadn't spoken since the night before. They'd been neatly avoiding each other all morning since the earl had left.

Andrew said something else that was strangled by his collar or by the acute embarrassment he seemed to be experiencing. Dulcie hoped he wasn't flustered because he'd been told something terrible about her. After last night she was prepared for anything.

"Dulcie my dear," Crispin said with no hint of irony, "may I present our near neighbor and my good friend, Andrew Moffit? He's Squire Moffit's son, a bruising rider and a fine judge of cattle. Andrew, my wife, Dulcie, the Viscountess West."

Dulcinea, Dulcie thought sadly. Now, that would have been a proper name to go with "Viscountess West." Or Demeter, or something else long and full of syllables would have been much more fitting than plain Dulcie. But plain Dulcie was who she was and if the red-faced man presently trying to choke out something coherent didn't like it, he could—he could not like it, she concluded realistically, as she dipped a little curtsy.

Crispin came to her side and put one arm around her waist. She worried whether she'd blundered—if she wasn't supposed to give a man of lesser rank a curtsy. When Crispin spoke, she was so relieved that she leaned into him instead of holding herself up haughtily, as she'd planned to do when she saw him again.

"She has lovely teeth, true, but she doesn't bite," Crispin said, his lips quirking. "Truly, Drew, she's probably as afraid of you as you are of her. She's from London and probably never met a country gentleman before."

"She's beautiful!" Andrew blurted, then looked confused, as though someone else had said that. He pounded the side of his head in vexation. "Never meant to say that. Meant it, but know it's not the thing to say. Ecod! I'm turned about. First I hear you've wed, come straight to offer felicitations and an invitation; the parents are mad to see her. But then I see her and lose my wits! She's beautiful, Crispin. Just beautiful."

"She also speaks," Crispin said, "Or does she, I wonder?" he asked more seriously, looking down at her.

His eyes were light blue, as clear as sparkling water in the morning light, but she could see traces of a sleepless night in the faint shadows beneath them. She could also see regret there, and a tenuous smile, offered to her like an apology.

"Sometimes she speaks," she said, looking up at him, "when there's someone to listen."

He nodded. "If someone says he will, in future, will you believe him, I wonder?"

"If he means it," she said, lost in his warm gaze.

"He does," Crispin said, taking her hand and pressing a light kiss to it. "So he vows."

"Ah . . . huh!" Andrew said, or coughed, growing red again at the look on the faces of the two people before him, who seemed to have completely forgotten him. "Came at the wrong time. Rushed my fences. Ought to have given you more time alone. Mother said so, and I, like a fool, didn't listen."

Crispin laughed and turned to him, but didn't release Dulcie's hand. "I don't want to say your mother was wrong, but she wasn't right. You're welcome here, Drew, anytime."

"Well, then, truth is I also came to give you back your horses, Crispin. I never felt right about buying them in the first place."

"Oh. You think I cheated you?" Crispin asked.

"No, no," Andrew said, horrified, "the opposite, I assure you. The plain fact is that those nags are too good for me. I coveted them and felt like the cock of the walk when I got them. But it's no good wanting something that doesn't suit you. Fine London goods is what those horses are. When I take them to town or market, it's like casting pearls before swine. Oh, the men all gather 'round the team, and they touch them, feel them, sound them, and nod their heads, but they don't know the quality of what they're seeing. They're as wasted on me as"—his eyes slewed to Dulcie, and he colored again—"as any other beautiful thing I see and want, and know is not meant for such as I."

Dulcie turned pink with pleasure when she realized what he meant. Imagine him thinking her such a fine lady that she'd be wasted on him! It wasn't true, and not fair to him, but she was glad he'd said it. It was the loveliest compliment she could imagine, and she needed it badly this morning.

"No man deserves loveliness," Crispin said quietly. "It's a thing he must earn. And you, Drew," he went on in a lighter tone, "definitely deserve such horses. If you insist, I'll buy them back. But I've already replaced them. I think you should keep them if you appreciate them. The point of quality is that it gives pleasure wherever it is. It's not important what others think. It's what you want and love that matters." And as if those words had made him think again, he stopped talking to Drew and looked down at Dulcie, gazing deep into her eyes.

"Right. Well. Aha! Then," Drew said in a welter of words as he backed toward the door. "I'll just be off, then. Thank you kindly for the advice, Crispin. Delightful meeting you, lady, and we'll meet again. Good-bye," he said, clapped on his hat, and escaped out the front door.

Crispin and Dulcie didn't notice.

They went out and strolled in the gardens together, without speaking or, when they spoke, without paying mind to what they said. A sudden shower chased them indoors, but they hadn't noticed the rain for so long that they were both sopping wet when they got back to the house. After they changed their clothes, they met by accident in the hall outside their rooms and smiling with pleasure at their chance meeting, went down to the salon together.

Dulcie was afraid to believe in their harmony. It was wondrous, but not tranquil. She only had to meet his eyes and see the look in them and all her serenity was gone. It was a delicious sort of nervousness she felt, however; he actually seemed to like her now. He treated her like a friend, not just a potential lover. She refused to ruin the moment by worrying about what might happen, for joy wasn't such a common thing for her that she could jeopardize it by studying it too closely.

He was as bemused as she was. It wasn't Andrew's outright adoration that had made him see how rare she was—that was only confirmation. It was the way she'd borne up under what must have been unbearable tension. It was the way she effaced herself, yet never lost her pride. It was the way she appreciated his humor, enjoyed the same things he did, and made him feel, for the first time he could remember, that someone shared his least emotion with him.

They were looking at a book together in his study when they got word of another visitor.

"He's here!" Willie panted in excitement, as he clambered in a tall window. He'd been running, a look of wild elation made his blue eyes sparkle.

"My father?" Dulcie cried, and stood up, hands clasped together. She was both happy and terrified, for now she would have to do the right thing and give Crispin up, and she felt that it might kill her to do that.

"Him? Nah," Willie said, as he bent double, catching his breath.

"You have a fear of doors?" Crispin asked curiously.

"Waste of time," Willie said, "what with footmen and butlers and all asking questions till you're dizzy and not letting you go a step till they got permission. Why wait when there's windows everywhere? Anyway, guess what?"

"Oh, wonderful—games. Just when things were getting boring," Crispin said, sounding so much like his friend the earl that Dulcie giggled. She was sorry the news wasn't about her father, and yet enormously relieved, too. Now it would just be news—interesting, but not likely to shatter her life. Or more truthfully, she thought, suddenly sobering, not likely to shatter her dream.

Crispin saw her smile falter, and took her dismay for fear. He spoke quickly, "Who is it, Willie? We haven't time for games."

"I'll say," Willie said. "It's Snode!"

For a moment neither Crispin nor Dulcie, preoccupied with their own fears, could remember who or what "Itsnode" was.

"He's here. In town. Or what passes for town around

here," Willie said. "Jerome Snode himself. Nosing about out in the open, giving his right name and all, bold as you please. Talking to everyone in the tavern, and half of them he meets in the street. 'And how is the new viscountess? Does she seem happy? Is the viscount happy with her?' he asks. Going 'um-hmm' and 'aha,' like he has a right to know. Pure brass," he said with a certain admiration.

"Why, I wonder?" Crispin mused.

"Trying to see if he can drive in a wedge," Willie said knowingly.

When they both stared at him, he said, "He's wishful of knowing how you two are doing. Harry sent him—had to have. See," he said with impatience when they both continued to look at him, uncomprehending, "if he can't get his hands on the lady, or her da, he's wondering how to make some kind of money out of it, anyway. So he's asking how the newlyweds is doing, 'cause he's wanting to know how anxious the viscount is to be rid of you, lady. That's 'cause he does disposal work, too, you know."

It took a moment for Dulcie to understand what Willie meant, and then she went pale.

Crispin's jaw clenched hard, and he swore beneath his breath. "Well, if that's it," he said, his anger held deep and hard, "we'll just give Snode something to see, won't we? If the only way he can gain anything from us now is to sense an opening for mischief, let's close that opening. There's no money to be made from a loving couple, is there?

"Dulcie," he said, turning his back on Willie and speaking in a voice for her ears only as he took her hand, "can you pretend to love me, just for a little while? Can you come to the village with me now and play the doting bride? Can you pretend to be absolutely besotted with me? I'm not asking you to fall all over me; people wouldn't expect that. But can you gaze at me lovingly, treat me to little whispers, knowing glances, tolerate my advances—a hand held here, a small caress there? Can you do it, for Jerome Snode's sake, if not for mine?"

But that was exactly what they'd been doing until Willie came in, she thought. She ducked her head to hide the confusion she felt. "Yes, of course I can," she said. And then she raised her head and grinned. "For Jerome's sake, of course."

It was in the vicarage garden that the viscount planted a light kiss on his lady's blushing cheek, when she wasn't looking and everyone else was. She gave him such a look of coy reproach that all the women sighed, and the men tried to remember when, or if, they'd ever felt that way.

The viscountess was given a hug by her husband, along with a rose, when the pair stopped at the farrier's cottage and she admired the climbing roses there. She tucked the bud in his buttonhole and bent her head of curls beneath his chin as she did. The way he lowered that proud head of his so that his chin grazed her shining hair, stroking it as a great sleek cat might do, was seen by everyone and sighed over for hours after.

They had a pint of ale, and one of cider, at the tavern. When they exchanged glasses the viscount took care to place his lips where hers had been. And then the smile he gave her was so warm, the tavern wench reported later, that she was surprised the cider didn't bubble over.

They walked close together and spoke to each other in murmurous whispers, and their hands, everyone noted, were always clasped. When they left the village, they could be seen sitting close together in the coach. That left everyone wondering just how long it would take them to get even closer. The most popular wager was: as soon as the coach turned the corner and went out of sight.

But when that happened, Dulcie moved away from Crispin. His breath had been soft on her cheek, his hand hard on her waist, and the combination made her yearn to burrow into his arms and find whatever else was waiting for her there. She tingled in places she hadn't known existed, but when he tried to draw her closer, she moved as far away as she could with his arm still around her shoulders. She was self-conscious at last—too conscious of how much she had enjoyed the deception they'd staged, too fearful that he knew it. She looked down to avoid his knowing gaze.

"Another kiss wouldn't be amiss," Crispin said softly, as his fingers toyed with a stray curl of hair at the nape of her neck.

"Or necessary, now that there's no one to see it," she said, hoping he'd deny it. When he didn't speak, she did, too brightly. "I didn't see Jerome, did you?"

"He knew," he said dismissively, and sighed. "Dulcie," he said, giving the wayward curl a little tug to get her attention. "We'll have to do this again and again until we're sure Jerome and Harry get the idea firmly fixed in their little criminal minds. You didn't mind my kisses in public, so why balk at them now? I didn't attempt anything else, did I?"

"We've had such a good day," she said, staring down at her twisting fingers in her lap, trying to ignore the delicious chills his light touch on her neck caused her to feel. "Don't ruin it now, please. You know why." She paused and swallowed hard. "I like your kisses, my lord," she finally said, looking up at him, "but I can't afford to submit to them. I must not, and so I shall not."

He removed his hand from her hair and his arm from her shoulders. He had touched her and held her and breathed in her scent all day, and she'd responded to him. Now she was seated just inches away and he felt incomplete and alone. He ached to have her near again, and nearer still than that.

He gazed at her and saw a young woman, moderately lovely, prettily dressed, yet with nothing so extravagantly beautiful about her as to account for how much he loved to look at her. As his eyes roved over her, his need to hold her close, her bare skin to his, almost overwhelmed him. He spoke for himself then.

"It's not a question of what you can afford or think wise, or even of what *I* think," he said. "It's a question of time. A day in April may be just as cold as one in November, but flowers will emerge from the earth on such a day and not in November, because it's time. Things bloom at the right time, no matter the weather. This is our time, Dulcie. You feel it, as I do. So it's not a matter of what we wish, but what we must. You'll see."

"No. That's so for flowers," she said, "and maybe for those who don't have to live another season. But not me. I shall have a life, I hope, beyond this time. I know what I can and cannot do, whatever the season, my lord."

He sat still, and then took her hands in his. "Please don't call me that. I am Crispin," he said softly. "At least call me Crispin, please."

The viscount and viscountess paid two more visits to the village—once to buy ribbon; a second time to call on Granny Higgins, the oldest woman in the district. Each time, their loving behavior caused all observers to sigh with pleasure.

The viscount, however, was as taut as a string, and found himself wandering his acres each afternoon, on or off his horse, trying to walk his frustration out. He decided he'd need an estate the size of all England to do that.

The viscountess sat awake each night alone and lost, thinking that all she needed to do was wander next door to find a way to sleep easily again. Or perhaps she would never sleep easily again.

They didn't know what Jerome Snode thought, because they didn't see him.

"We have to beard him in his den," Crispin said at breakfast, putting down a fork he'd been using to push his bacon around the plate.

"Do you think that would be wise? Dulcie asked as she continued to draw little circles in her oatmeal with a spoon.

He looked up to see her dressed in a new amber gown, and looked down at his plate again, as if the sight of the way the silk matched her eyes and enhanced her creamy skin had hurt his eyes. He addressed his egg instead, tapping it open.

"Would you rather keep visiting the village, having me paw you and nibble you, touch you and fondle you on every visible bit of your skin, until he shows his nose?" he asked.

She caught her breath at the thought.

"No," she lied in a small voice. She wouldn't have argued with him whatever he'd said. His mood was increasingly bleak. There were no more cozy chats at night before the fire, no more long, meandering walks. As his public intimacies had grown warmer, Crispin himself had grown colder to her. She missed him.

"Willie says that Snode is staying at the Hound and Hare, right in the heart of town," Crispin said. "He stays in his room when we appear and comes out after we've gone. We'll pay a call on him. It's time. But I remind you," he said, and looked up and, having met her eyes, was unable to look away again, "that we . . . that we must keep pretending to be lovers. Most especially now."

She nodded. And managed to look away from him, at last. They said no more then, or later, when a footman came to clear the table of two uneaten breakfasts.

Jerome Snode answered the tap on his door at once.

"My dear Dulcie!" he said, bowing as though she were an empress, sweeping his outstretched arms down to either side of him, "or I should say, Viscountess. And your lordship. You do me great honor."

"I remind you we can do you a great deal more," Crispin snapped as he studied the room. It was a low-ceilinged, tilt-floored inn room, bare except for bed and chest. Jerome's few belongings were stuffed into an open bag on the floor.

"Please," Jerome said humbly, "won't you come in?"

The three of them crowded into the little room, with Dulcie's skirts taking up half the space. Crispin had to lower his head, which instead of making him appear smaller made him seem to loom even more menacingly over Jerome.

"What are you doing here, Snode?" Crispin demanded. "Don't say you came for the country air, because there's plenty of country between here and London to breathe in. You're a long way from the Fleet, and there's nothing of interest here but the old church. And us. That being so, why haven't you been sketching the churchyard—or visiting us?"

"I wouldn't presume!" Jerome said with horror.

"Then why are you here?"

Jerome looked abashed, which immediately made Dulcie suspicious. Men like Jerome, she'd learned from long years with her father, were never ashamed of anything they did.

"I thought I would . . . that is to say . . . now that Dulcie, ah, the viscountess, is in such good hands, and I have so little—it took every last penny to get me out of the Fleet—I wondered if . . ."

"That won't wash!" Dulcie snapped. "If you were going to ask me for money, you'd have done it right away. You wouldn't have been one bit embarrassed about it either. You're spying for Harry, aren't you? Don't bother to deny it."

"That Willie . . ." Jerome growled, his eyes narrowing.

"We did not learn about you from Willie," Crispin said quickly.

Jerome looked skeptical, but then his padded shoulders drooped. "It hardly matters," he said. "I'm leaving. There's nothing here for me—or for Harry. You're right. Harry thought there'd be something for him in this, but you two are like April and May now, aren't you? This is all a result of Harry's efforts, and yet he can't make a penny from it," Jerome said more cheerfully, picking up his bag.

"Wait," Dulcie said suddenly, laying a hand on his sleeve. "What of my father? You were his friend—or said you were. Do you know where he is?"

"Oh," Jerome said, straightening, looking doubtful, "well, as to that, he hasn't written to me, but I've heard . . . Still, I have an obligation to Harry, you see. Much as I admire you, my lady, I have some fears for my own safety. I can hardly . . ."

Crispin reached into his pocket and pulled out his purse. Jerome's voice dwindled as he saw the coins Crispin was taking out. When five lay on Crispin's palm, he offered them to Jerome, who looked at them uneasily. But he seemed to grow more uncomfortable as each new coin was added to the heap. When Crispin stopped adding coins, and Jerome still didn't answer, Crispin began to close his hand.

Jerome grabbed the coins. "Philip is not in Europe—he's nowhere on the Continent," he said briskly, "Harry knows that for a certainty. The word is that he's shipped for the Colonies, with a new name. Harry knows that too, but it hardly matters. He can't reach him there anyway."

"*Where* in the Colonies?" Dulcie asked.

"North America. The Bay Colony, likely," Jerome said, as he gazed lovingly at the coins in his hand.

"No, never. That can't be my father," Dulcie told Crispin, caught between disappointment and relief. "Father would never go to a savage place. He likes civilized company."

"He likes life," Jerome said, "and they say some of the American colonies are not so primitive anymore. Moreover there's the chance for a new life there. A new married life, even. It's done often enough. Because, you know, my dear lady, your father can never wed here or on the Continent. But who is to say that a man in a new land, far over the seas, with a new name to call his own, can't take a new wife?"

"But that's bigamy," Dulcie gasped.

"He could even have children," Jerome added. "Philip isn't an old man, you know. He often told me of his disappointment with his life, how he yearned for a wife, and sons—"

"That's enough," Crispin said as he saw Dulcie grow pale. "We'll leave you now, Snode, for good, we hope—for your own good, at least. Tell Harry we agree: there's nothing for him here."

Seeing Crispin's concern, how he put his arm around Dulcie to hold her tenderly as he led her from the room, Jerome didn't doubt him for a moment.

Crispin helped Dulcie into the coach, where she moved to the far end of the seat and gathered herself into a little knot. When he reached for her, she curled herself into a tighter ball, so he sat back. He didn't press her to talk because he saw that the life had gone from her face when she heard what Jerome said. It was as though a light had been blown out. He didn't dare touch her now. She seemed fragile, as though she was desperately holding herself together.

He waited for her to speak, and after a while, she said, "You would have thought he'd write to me, wouldn't you?"

"Maybe he will," Crispin said.

"Oh, *really*," she said, and he had to smile at the wry wisdom in her voice, with all her sorrow.

"I knew he wanted sons," she said in falsely bright tones. "He mentioned it whenever he had too much to drink. And of course he detested Mama. I tried to be enough, but a daughter can't make up for the lack of sons. That's true, that's entirely true."

"Marriage is a serious thing, Dulcie," Crispin said carefully. "Unless his wife dies, a man gets only one try at it. Jerome's right. If your father wants a new life, he has to leave this one, one way or another. I don't say your father was right. In fact, we both know he was wrong. But he's fortunate, in a way, that this is a widening world. Now he can make himself a new life, although it will mean he can never return to the old.

"Don't forget how this all began. Whatever new reasons Philip has now, he originally left for your sake. He loved you enough to disappear, taking your wedding papers with him for what he believed to be your own good. Try to see his side of it. He's only trying to make something good from something wholly bad. Marriage is forever, Dulcie. It doesn't matter if a man is happy or unhappy in it, it is a life sentence. And a hard one if a man is wretched in it. Your father knew that, too well."

And then she wept. Although she tried to cry silently, Crispin could see her shoulders shaking. He took her in his arms, holding her close and whispering words of comfort and consolation.

"I'm so sorry, Dulcie love," he said as he stroked the hair back from her damp and heated face. "He loves you. Truly he does. He did it all for you. Don't weep. Hush, please don't cry."

"Oh, Crispin," she sobbed, "what have I done to you? I'm so sorry. Forgive me, please."

His hand paused, his breath arrested. "What?" he asked dumbly.

"Look what I've done to you," she wept, her fingers convulsing on his coat. "I've taken away your life, haven't I? Crispin," she said suddenly, pulling back, holding him at arm's length, "I have an idea: I'll go too! I'll go to the Colonies. I shall book passage at once. I can't join Father— that would jeopardize his new name and position, even if I could find him.

"But I can go under any name I choose," she said, "and then you'll be free. You'll never see me again, I promise. I'll be a world away, and no one will ever have to know. Don't you see?" she asked, her eyes searching his. "It's the only answer. You'll be free." She ran the back of her hand under her nose and sniffled defiantly. Her eyes were red, her face was streaming with tears, and the fragile skin beneath her eyes was puffy. Her lower lip trembled, and so did her chin, but she tried to smile. She looked terrible.

He gently shook her until her hair tumbled from its pins. "Idiot," he said. "Idiot, fool, mine."

And kissed her until she could only breathe his name, and not to beg him to let her go.

They didn't speak when they left the coach. Dulcie hurried up to her room and Crispin followed her.

"First," he said, when he entered her room, and she spun around, surprised to see him there, "some water, for your face."

Her maid rushed to do his bidding. When she returned with a basin and towel, Crispin dismissed her. Then as Dulcie sat in a chair near the window, he held her face up in one hand and washed it with the cloth. She giggled. He stopped and looked at her intently, wondering if hysterics were coming.

"You're like a mama cat, cleaning my face," she explained. "Haven't you seen the way they do it? Seriously and with concentration. You're holding me down firmly with one paw while you do it. I expect to feel your rough tongue any minute."

"Not so rough," he said, dropping the cloth in the basin and bringing his lips to hers.

It was what she'd wanted, through all her pain, though she hadn't known it. She'd thought kisses were only for pleasure or thrills; she hadn't known they could ease pain. His mouth was comforting. Even the touch of his tongue was solace in a deeper way than she'd ever known. His shoulders were hard and strong, and she clung to them. They were her anchor in a lonely, painful world. They helped her keep her head high in the darkness that seemed to be swirling around her.

And yet, when he groaned in his throat and lifted her from the chair to swing her up to her high bed, she felt suddenly light, and frightened, as though he had plucked her from safety to danger again.

He knew it. He paused, one knee on the bed, and looked at her. "Is a kiss in a bed so much worse than one in a chair?" he asked. He was short of breath.

"Yes," she said, wide-eyed. "You know it is."

He drew himself up to sit beside her. He sat for a moment looking at her, his hand going to her hair to brush back a dislodged curl. His fine-featured face was intent as he studied her, and then he suddenly came to a decision.

"Dulcie," he said, drawing her to his chest so that she

could hear his heart beating. "We are wed. That is so. Your father is gone and has taken our wedding papers with him. I lamented it at first. But now I see that that was foolish. We are married, Dulcie. It's time you were my wife."

There was no getting around it, Crispin thought, reveling in how good she felt in his arms. They were married and would remain so, barring an act of God, or of Parliament. He could rail against his fate, but was powerless to change it. He couldn't imagine being without her. How could he ignore her for a lifetime, when he couldn't keep his hands off her for one day?

He wanted her badly, she was adorable, and she belonged to him. If a thing couldn't be changed, it had to be accepted. He would acknowledge Dulcie and make her his wife.

"But, your lady . . ." she said, and buried her face in his shirt, so she wouldn't have to see the quick hurt that always sprang to his eyes when she mentioned Lady Charlotte.

"She will be someone else's wife," he said after a pause. "You and I are married in the eyes of God and man, Dulcie. That is so, and we would be fools to deny it any longer."

"If you mean to . . ." Dulcie said, looking anxiously at the bed.

"I mean to," he said.

"Well, that's not a simple thing," she said nervously. "There could be a child from such a thing. And then there'd be no going back, even if my father appears and gives up the papers."

"It is a beautiful thing," he said, his mouth on the back of her neck, his tongue tracing it.

"I don't know how," Dulcie whispered with a shiver.

"You don't want me?" he asked.

"I didn't say that," she said. The late afternoon light showed a fine new growth of beard on his lean cheeks, outlining them like the strokes of an artist's pencil. He looked weary and hungry and more handsome than she'd ever seen him. It distracted her for a moment, but only for a moment, for she knew what she had to tell him.

"I cannot be a London lady, Crispin."

"You can't spend my gold, order servants about, talk through the music at concerts, and dance all night?" he asked with a quizzical smile, holding the side of her face in one long hand as he gazed down at her.

"I can't flirt with other men or take lovers, and—and I won't stand by and watch you take lovers!" she blurted. "No, I can't do that," she insisted bravely. "I just won't, Crispin. So if you want a complacent wife, shear off now and we'll work for a miracle, because I won't share you, I won't. Not ever. I couldn't bear it. I'd make scenes and make your life miserable if I heard of any such thing, even though I know fine ladies don't mind that sort of arrangement," she added conscientiously.

He remembered all too well a lady who didn't mind it. "All right," he said quietly, realizing it was time to tell Dulcie exactly what he would ask of her, or of any woman he took as his wife. "You'll not have to share me, I promise you. Now. Let's work for that miracle, shall we?" And kissed her long and hard, and earnestly.

But she pulled back and looked at him gravely and fearfully. "Truly, Crispin?" she asked, unable and afraid to believe in such an ending to her sorrow and loneliness. "Truly?" she asked, touching his lips with trembling fingertips, as though she might only be sure of finding the truth that way. He kissed her fingers and then found her lips again, and kissed her until she no longer cared about anything else.

His kisses were sweet but urgent—harder and softer, longer and deeper than they'd ever been. And his hands roved everywhere. When he opened his shirt to get closer to her, she was so entranced by the soft curling hair on his hard-muscled chest that she couldn't stop touching and petting it. He lifted his head from her breast, and laughed low in his throat.

"Now who's the little cat?" he said.

She didn't know exactly how they got her out of all her

clothing. It required effort and cooperation and haste, she knew that. She remembered how they tore her hoop away and how he slipped off her garters and rolled down her stockings, following the slide of the silk with his hands, and the look in his eyes as he did it. She would never forget that. But she recalled little else besides his kisses and caresses and the scent and feel of him.

And so she only realized she had completely undressed when she discovered herself sitting in her bed watching Crispin extract himself entirely from his shirt—the last thing he wore. But she had no time to think, and when he turned toward her, she gasped.

This thing they were about to do was real, and she had real fears about it. But not about him. She'd never seen anything like him. He was lean and muscled, his chest wide, his stomach flat, his limbs long and graceful. He was as beautiful as he was unexpected. That part of him rose up to her gaze, long and supple, an ivory and coral column.

"What is it?" he asked gently, pausing, seeing her sudden doubt.

"I was about to ask *you* that," she said with a nervous laugh, hiding her face in his chest. He smelled like herbs and soap, and himself, and she shuddered with expectation as much as fear.

He smiled at her shyness and lifted her head in both his hands, tilting it so he could see her expression clearly. "Are you sure this is what you want, Dulcie? Because I am telling you now that if we go any further, I won't be able to stop . . . I want you so much."

She nodded. He drew the bed curtains halfway closed, but they could still see well enough. He came to her, and she wished she had something equally beautiful as his body to show him. But he gazed at her tilted breasts and then followed the arc of her ribs down to her gently rounded stomach, and his eyes glowed. Her hand went to the thatch of curls at the apex of her thighs, to conceal it. It was too private, too vulgar, she thought. But he picked up her hand

and smiled, and replaced it with his own. She lay back as he nudged her down onto the bed, and she shivered in his arms.

She was beautiful everywhere, just as he'd known she would be. Her breasts, high and shapely, were infinitely sweet to his taste. Her legs were slender and curved and smooth to his touch. Her grace and delicate shyness enthralled him. She was elegant in her response, eager but gentle. She charmed him, even in the tumult of his need, and though he knew he should go slowly, he couldn't think anymore; he could only feel, and he tried to make her feel the same way.

He was successful, for she thought of nothing but sensations. She was very cold, and his mouth was a fire at which she warmed herself. Then she was hot, but when he lifted his body from hers for a moment to adjust their position, she felt chilled without him. She wished she could touch him as he touched her, but a flood of sensations overwhelmed her, and she could only lie back, amazed at his knowledge, yearning to know more. Sometimes she shrank away because his touch was too new, and when his hand moved between her thighs and then inside her, she drew back.

"No," he said, breathlessly, "you'll like this, I promise."

She was unable to protest because she hadn't the breath or the sense left to do it.

When she felt she could bear no more, and wanted to bear more, and all her thoughts were a jumble, he kissed her and moved over her. She felt the wonderful strength of him against every inch of her. When she felt unexpected pain, she gasped and tried to draw back. But before she could move, he had his arms tightly around her and was whispering comforting words to her.

He paused. "Oh, Dulcie," he sighed, his damp forehead against her own. "I'm sorry. I know it hurts, but it will pass, please trust me. Let me show you," he said, as he began moving again, bringing jolts of fire as he probed deeper, losing all control. He was one with his pleasure now and couldn't stop. He was driven, his body a hammer, until he was gripped by an ecstasy so keen it looked to her as if he was in pain. She felt his pleasure and yet she felt regret when he groaned and slumped against her, exhausted.

He was instantly contrite. "Dulcie," he said, gathering her in his arms. "I wanted so much for this to be perfect for you, but I felt so overwhelmed. It gets better, I promise. You'll see."

"It wasn't awful," she said, but so doubtfully that he winced.

"You are a terrible liar," he sighed, holding her close.

"Is that sort of talk your idea of making love to me?" she asked.

She felt his body shake with laughter. "Oh, Dulcie," he said as his hands caressed her, "how is it that you bring me as much laughter as pleasure?"

"Did I bring you pleasure?" she asked, eager for his approval.

"Entirely, Dulcie," he whispered into her hair. "Sweetly, and generously, and completely. Thank you, my lady." His arms went around her again and did not loosen, even in sleep.

Dulcie was too pleased to sleep, so she curled up against him instead, and sighed at how right it felt—as though she had come home at last.

"I don't care," the lady said, turning away and fanning herself. "He is married. I am not. As far as I am concerned, he is dead."

"He still lives. He was married under false pretenses. The point, my dear," the lanky gentleman told the lady, "is that we have little time and much to do. Granted, you detest me. Given, I dislike you. But we both wish to save Crispin from the clutches of the little jailbird. So, then, I ask you, will you cooperate with me, or will you not?"

"How do you know it isn't already too late?" Lady Charlotte asked.

"Because," the earl of Wrede said, "it is never too late to

redress a wrong. We have the means and the power, and she is nobody."

"Why should he repudiate her?" she asked with a show of disbelief, but with hope that he had an answer. "She is young and passing fair, and not without wit."

"Yes, but I know Crispin. He is sensual, but his passions are fleeting."

"He is honorable," she argued.

"She is not. Is it dishonorable for him to admit that he made a mistake?"

"You interest me," the lady said, turning to face him at last. "Go on."

CHAPTER

14

The maid sat at the far end of the long gallery, close enough to see what her lady and the tall gentlemen were doing but too far away to hear what they said. It was a very long hall in a fine house, and the two gentlepersons in it suited its grandeur as much as the portraits that frowned down from the high walls. The lady wore a voluminous sack gown of ivory with yards of precious blond lace at its waist and sleeves.

The two drifted through the hall, still talking, while the maid dozed with her eyes open, as she'd learned to do. She was there for propriety's sake, after all, only to be seen, not to hear or be heard.

Charlotte looked at the earl of Wrede with equal parts suspicion and distaste. That was how she had always looked at him. He was oddly attractive in his saturnine way, and he was very wealthy and wise, but he left her unmoved. Still, he was Crispin's friend, and so she had to be civil to him. Perhaps, she thought now, eyeing him over her fan, they didn't get on because they were too much alike.

"But of course," Wrede said silkily now, "if you prefer to forget the matter and wed Prendergast after all, there's nothing for me to do but wish you joy. You *will* invite me to the wedding, will you not?"

He looked at her shrewdly, and she damned his eyes. He knew that Prendergast was much less attractive to her now that she could no longer use him to make Crispin jealous. She had always wanted Crispin. She had led him a merry dance, but that was just her way. Things fell flat when there was no friction, and life was too short to be dull.

She'd accepted that she had to give Crispin up when he lost his money. It was unfortunate, but she was a mistress of reality. Her options were very simple, her life lay clear ahead of her. There was no way she could share his poverty, but she had consoled herself by thinking how she would share herself and some of her money with him after she'd married the way society and her upbringing demanded. Of course she had expected to get him back again when she heard he'd recovered his fortune.

It was unthinkable that she should not, and wrong that the little adventuress had caught him first. More than wrong, it was criminal, and painful, because she had no way to fight back. Until now. Perhaps.

"No, I've no immediate plans to wed Prendergast," she said, and turned aside so she wouldn't see Wrede's mocking smile.

"Ah," he said, and strolled on with her, his hands locked behind his back.

"What have you in mind?" she was forced to ask when he said nothing more.

"A great many things," he answered with that same smile.

"If you want to fight with me, I'll oblige you," she said, "but I thought you came for my cooperation. I assume you'll need it. I know you're all-powerful, Wrede, but it does appear that you'll need me—as bait for a trap perhaps?"

"If it was Crispin I wished to trap—perhaps. Just *perhaps,* of course," he added to make her fume and stir the air angrily with her fan, "but I don't think you would appeal to her."

"Cut line," she snapped. "What *does* appeal to her? Money? I have that, but so do you. You didn't come to me for that. What is it you want of me?"

"Just your awareness of my game. And your word that you won't plunge headlong into marriage with anyone else just yet."

"I see. Do you want me to become a nun? Or merely take a vow of celibacy? For how long? Twenty years? Done. Anything for love." She laughed without humor.

"Don't be absurd," he said with a withering glance that silenced her. "Listen. I cannot tell you all, but I can tell you something: the marriage may not be permanent. There may be a way out of it."

"Does Crispin *want* a way out of it?" she asked bitterly.

Wrede stared down at her from his great height. "You are jesting, surely," was all he said, but it made her smile, and her spirits rose.

"Why can't you tell me more?" she asked, as wary of him as ever. Her doubt was clear in every line of her posture and expression.

He sighed. "Because you are a woman, and women love gossip. Men do too, but we are cumbered with a code of honor. I have not noticed such a code among members of your sex. This information isn't for others' ears, no matter how delicious the gossip would be. And ladies of fashion, I fear, have long tongues."

"I see," she said, as slow rage burned in her. But she was a woman in a man's world and had learned to control her rage long years before. The earl might be feared for his rapier wit, but hers was no less deadly. Nonetheless, she was a lady. She couldn't use aggression as openly as he, and so she had other weapons at her disposal. Silence was the last and most effective refuge of the weak as well as the strong. "Very well," she said and began to walk away from him, down the long hall. "If you cannot talk, I cannot listen. Good afternoon, my lord."

His long legs took him to her side in seconds. "Do you

promise to keep silent, then?" he asked. "Swear it on your honor, if you have it. Or on your life, if you don't believe me when I say this goes no further. I am quite serious."

She stared up at him, her anger warring with her curiosity.

"This is very important, Charlotte," he said. "I do not jest now. I haven't been sworn to silence myself, only because I suppose Crispin has known me long enough to trust me. Ordinarily I would tell no one and he knows that. But these are not ordinary times. I have to help him, and only you can help me. Your spreading the tale would only make matters worse for him—and for whatever ambitions for him you might still cherish. So, before I say another word, I need your vow of silence."

"You have it," she said at once. She would have sworn to anything to hear what Wrede had to say.

"Now," he said quickly and quietly, "listen. It was a Fleet wedding—"

She gasped and he shot her a furious look. "Are you going to keep interrupting?" he said savagely. She fell still, but her round blue eyes were wide with shock, and her hand remained over her mouth.

He went on, glaring at her to warn her against interrupting. "I'll spare you the details. The prison wench trapped him in bizarre fashion. You may let your imagination run rampant; I assure you that you'll not be far off the mark, whatever you conclude. He did not truly intend to marry her; that I *will* tell you. And he's been racking his brain for a way to free himself of her—until recently. Recently I fear he has begun to accept the situation. Worse, I fear he may yet come to accept her as his wife.

"But there is a chance . . . for now, however, we must keep the hope of freedom alive in him. This is where you are important. So long as you remain unwed, his hope of reclaiming you will remain alive. The thought of being wed to you may help him keep her at arm's length. Failing that, it may overcome any qualms he might feel if we are successful in freeing him from the wench. He has a conscience, does our Crispin. I lament it, but it's why we're friends, I suppose. I find him unique. I know his history, and history sheds light on a man's character.

"He's easily bored," the earl went on pensively. "He may hope to make the best of it now, but there's nothing but lust and pity in this union for him. When the lust fades, so will the pity, I think. Men have wed beneath themselves, for money or for love—look at Trencher and that actress, or Bradford and his wife, who was once his mistress. Those women came from nowhere and are recognized everywhere now. Those marriages were shocking at first, but we are an enlightened society, after all. Noblemen have married merchants' daughters, millers' daughters, even actors' daughters. But *not* felons' daughters. At least, not convicted felons. That, never.

"It's more than her not being his kind. Where is the love? Where is the passion? Where is the meeting of minds? This union was only the result of a passion for money; it was the work of crafty minds. No. This marriage is outrageous. Even if Crispin thinks to accept it now, why should he have to endure a lifetime of misery because of a fleeting fancy? Crispin's passions have always been short-lived. She won't enchant him for long—no female ever has, except you, and I assume that's because he hasn't had you."

She glowered at him. It would have been useless to play an outraged innocent maiden with Wrede. She might remain chaste until she was wed, but there was nothing she didn't know and little she hadn't said, for a jest, or for the sake of good gossip, and Wrede knew it.

"Yes," he said, unmoved by her silent fury, "that's precisely why I believe Crispin hasn't gotten over you. Your aloofness would explain his sustained interest. He never finds the prey as interesting as the chase, or satisfaction as glorious as anticipation. He may deny it, but I know him well—better than he knows himself."

"Which is how you think you know everyone," she muttered, unable to stop herself.

He either didn't hear her or didn't bother to answer, but went on, "He may not have cluttered up his estate with Gothic ruins, as is the current craze, but Crispin *is* a Romantic, and this girl won't keep him fascinated for very long. But if you were to wed . . . Men do strange things for revenge. He may decide to remain in that foul marriage no matter how many avenues of escape are open to him, just to show you how content he is—*if* you marry another."

"And if I do not?"

"Ah, then there are possibilities. No one approves of these sordid Fleet marriages. There is proposed legislation afoot. These things move slowly, I grant, but it will happen. Too much money is being lost when pauper brides hand over their debts to nonexistent husbands. The situation can't last long. Money likes to remain at home, and wherever there's a leak, you may be sure the government will plug it up—when it notices. It's like pricking an elephant: it takes a long time for the beast to realize that it's bleeding. There are, however, other things we might do—like separate Crispin from the girl, for a start."

"I see. You want to send in some of her naughty friends from the Fleet to throw a sack over her and carry her off?" she said, only half joking.

"Alas, abduction has already been tried by lower minds than ours. No. Absolutely not," he said. "Not only would that be difficult, but it would run counter to our cause. Crispin would grieve. Nothing fosters love like forcible separation. Haven't your novels taught you that? No, not abduction. But comparison might do what separation can't."

"Very well, I'll go there," Charlotte agreed eagerly. It was a confrontation she was sure she couldn't lose.

"No, no," Wrede said wearily. "That would frighten the girl, rouse Crispin's protective instincts, and end badly, I assure you. But I do think that if he could see you again, in a different setting, it would help. If he could be away from her for a while and see what he's missing. If we could arrange for him to see her in his natural element, after they'd been parted for a while. That might do it. And that might buy me time to push and wheedle and pay in the right quarters, to get the carcass of government to sit up and take notice.

"He took the wench to Darnley Hall to prevent her from running away and ruining his name and to protect her from those who might ruin her. From what I've seen, I think he knows she won't leave him now. And from what I've heard from a source of mine at the hall, he no longer worries about threats to her either. There was a time when he thought you might cause a scandal—don't scowl, you were obviously bent on mischief when you last saw him—but I think I can talk him around that now.

"And so what we need," Wrede said, stopping and looking down at Charlotte, "is a flood of invitations. Many invitations to fascinating entertainments. Crispin has a lively mind; he says he loves the countryside, but it will bore him soon enough. I doubt he'll accept any invitations from you, but if you cooperate with me, perhaps the deed can be done."

"But even if he leaves Darnley Hall, won't he take her with him?" she asked.

"It hardly matters. Once they are in our bailiwick, we can separate them easily enough, using a dozen ruses, reasons, and excuses—pleasant ones that won't alarm either of them. And then? London's filled with reasons why a man can't see his wife for days—weeks—on end. There are homes so vast that a man can get lost in them, and where his mistress, his wife, *and* his mother-in-law will never meet in the halls. It doesn't matter where we lure him, so long as we get him away from Darnley Hall and her private attentions. But we must hurry. She's clever, and while he is alone with her in the countryside, he'll be susceptible to her charms. We must move faster than nature."

She frowned at him in puzzlement.

"Shall I discourse about the birds first, or the bees?" he asked.

She flushed and looked at Wrede from the corner of her eye. "What is she like?" she asked as casually as she could. Jealousy was new to her. She'd felt anger and even pity for the girl before jealousy crept in. She had never felt such an emotion before and didn't know what to do with it—so she hid it.

But nothing remained hidden from Wrede for long.

He looked down at her. Gold and pink and white, she was a justly famous beauty. He admired her mind as well as her beauty, and wanted neither. She was too tart for his taste. He appreciated wit, which she had in plenty, but he liked more heart with it. He knew his own lack and sought it in others. It was why he valued Crispin, did not desire Charlotte, and found himself increasingly uneasy with the woman Charlotte was asking about.

"She's very beautiful now that she's dressed properly. No—rather say she's lovely," he said thoughtfully. "You are more beautiful, I think. Yes. But she has a certain charm, a grace that borders on elegance: a refreshing quality that is lacking, perhaps, in society's jaded beauties. A coltish quality. A newness, a freshness, a certain gift of laughter. Most unexpected, very novel. That's what I fear in her. Crispin may not have met her like before."

"*You* certainly haven't," Charlotte snapped, and then grew quiet beneath his icy, quelling stare.

"All right," she said, turning aside, "let me see. . . . there is the Coopers' ball on Wednesday next."

"Crispin never cared for the Coopers," Wrede said, all business now. "Next?"

Dulcie was shy in the morning. And tired, because she'd kept waking up to reassure herself that he was really there. She'd look at him until her eyelids drooped, or until the force of her stare woke him. Then he would chuckle and murmur something sleepily and draw her back against his warm hard body and hold her close as he slipped back into sleep. She would feel the delicious warmth and nearness of him and revel in it, unable to sleep because of the wonder and joy of it.

He was so handsome, so gentle. And he was truly her husband now. She'd given him all: her heart, her hand, her body. She had nothing more to offer him. But he had given her love. Hadn't he? She had to try to stay awake to believe it. So she was tired when she woke to find him gazing at her. And shy because she'd never woken with a man before. She couldn't think of what to say.

She didn't have to say a thing. His eyes held the answers to any questions she might have asked and then his lips told her the rest, although he didn't say a word.

"I shouldn't," he finally muttered as he drew her down beside him again and buried his face in her neck.

She squirmed against him, free at last to run her hands up and down his hard frame. She'd longed to do that all night but had been afraid of waking him. She didn't know whether he wanted her to be bold or shy, nor did she know if he would prefer to sleep or to kiss and cuddle, as she wanted to do. After all, he'd already done what men were supposed to be primarily interested in.

"What shouldn't you do?" she whispered.

"Make love to you again," he said, tasting the skin stretched tight across her collarbone.

"Oh. Yes, oh, please," she said, "It's what I wanted last night. But I was afraid to wake you."

"Afraid?" he asked, stopping to lean on his elbows and look down at her. His hair fell free, and as he held himself above her, it fell like a blunt curtain over their faces.

"Well, you'd already done what you wanted. I didn't know if you wanted me to bother you anymore," she said, glad of the shadowy drape of his hair, hoping it would cover her blushes.

"Dulcie," he said fervently, "you may bother me that way any time you wish. Any time, you hear? It's just that I don't think we ought to make love again so soon. And I don't think I'll be able to stop myself from doing it if I touch you. I've always had such control," he said with wonder, his lips against her cheek, "but not with you, sorceress."

"Why don't you want to?" she asked in a fearful voice, wondering if the light of a new day had made him see his mistake in taking her as his wife.

"Because you must be sore." He smiled, kissing the tip of her nose.

"Oh," she said, taking inventory of her sensations. She felt only a little ache, but that was drowned in the surge of need she felt for him. "Well, yes, a little," she reported, "but I don't mind."

"I do," he said ruefully, moving away from her. "You didn't feel what I wanted you to because it was your first time, and I was overeager. I want it to be perfect the next time."

"I don't mind, truly," she said, putting her arms around his neck to draw him back.

And she really didn't mind. She needed his hands on her, she needed his approval, she required his absolute attention now. The intimacy of the act was more important to her than any pleasure she might feel. She hadn't felt the ecstasy he was talking about, but that didn't matter. She had almost died of the sheer happiness of having him so close, having him need her so much, provide him so much pleasure.

"Oh, Dulcie," he sighed, moving in her arms again, "I want more than that for you."

"I have more than I could ever want," she whispered, "much, much more." She could never tell him how much, though, for he had only said that he needed her and wanted to bring her to joy. She wanted so much more from him, but how could she ever tell him?

His touch set off sensations that alarmed her and thrilled her at the same time. It was a long time before he came to her, and he made her ache with desire for the ecstasy he had promised. This time Crispin went slowly, and she delighted in his strong, caressing touch. He devoted his strong, hard body to her, and she rejoiced in his sweet deliverance, taking his final groan as a tribute to her.

He lay propped up on one elbow beside her, stroking the damp body that had given him such pleasure. His face was grave and rueful when he kissed her lips again.

"I'm a greedy man, and you're too sweet, too good to resist. But you shall know what I want for you, I promise you that, Dulcie. I know you don't understand," he said, before she could protest. "Be patient with me, I've never been with an inexperienced woman before. Damnation!" he groaned, and rolled over on his back, away from her.

She sat up, wide-eyed and still, the bedcovers clutched to her breast in tight fists. Seeing her distress, he rose with swift grace, took one of her hands, uncurled it, and pressed a kiss to it.

"I'm sorry. That was insensitive of me," he said. "Forgive me, please."

"For what?" she asked, puzzled. "Those other women were all in the past."

"Dulcie, Dulcie," he said, his expression tender, as it had been when they'd made love. He gazed at her where she sat in a pool of morning light, pink and white and tousled, her mouth stung to ruddiness from his kisses, her breasts half exposed. He swiftly rose and clambered down from the bed while he still could.

"A bath. Then breakfast. I'm ravenous," he muttered.

"Oh, good, so am I," she said. She wrapped herself in the sheet for modesty and climbed down from the high bed. But she winced as she did so, for her inner thighs suddenly ached with each step she took.

"Still so forgiving?" he asked wryly, watching her.

She came to him and leaned against him, her head on his chest. "Not forgiving," she said fervently. "Grateful. Now we are truly wed."

"So we are," he said quietly, looking over the top of her

head to the window and the new day that stretched before them. "So we are."

"I haven't done much but plant here," Crispin explained as they strolled over the grounds.

He was taking Dulcie on a long walking tour of his land. It was a very warm day, but after a week of rain—a week passed in delicious intimacy—they both relished the chance to walk. All of the flowering trees and shrubs were blooming, and the heavy air was filled with sweet aromas. Dulcie felt as though she was walking in a scent bottle.

"*Only* plant? But you've put in such beautiful trees and shrubbery. Why should you sound apologetic?" Dulcie asked. "What else would you do here?"

"Gentlemen of property are erecting things these days," he said, and grinned like a boy as he added, "aside from what I've been treating you to." She ducked her head, and he was half sorry that he'd teased her. He continued, "Gentlemen of fashion are erecting follies and ruins and such," he explained. "It's the latest craze.

"Horrie Walpole started it with his house, Strawberry Hill," Crispin went on, stripping the bark from a willow twig between his long fingers as they strolled. "It's a marvel of gloom and dark corners for evil deeds to be done in. Everyone went to see it. Envy started a trend, and now they all want a medieval romantic legend of their own. It's not enough to have temples to Pan, Chinese gardens, or mazes on one's grounds anymore. 'Happy is the man who has a decaying abbey or a ruined castle on his land,' as Wrede says. Those who don't already have them are building them. Yes, really. They're actually building things that are half destroyed, that look better in moonlight than in sunlight: wrecked towers and crumbling walls that look haunted or eerie or melancholy. We've nothing like that here at Darnley Hall. My ancestors didn't know it would become fashionable to be too poverty-stricken to rebuild. Too bad. It would have saved my poor father a lot of worry.

"It's damp at the bottom of this hillside, and there are marshy places. See all the marsh orchids in the hollow? Those are the purple flowers—and there—the flags, the yellow ones. They thrive on damp land. That's how you can tell. Maybe I'll put in a grotto here and get a hermit to live in it. Truth," he said, laughing at her expression. "Some gentlemen hire old men to live in their grottoes, to give visitors a thrill. I imagine it's a soft enough life, aside from having to wear a thin brown robe and sandals during the cold English spring. That, and the danger of ague and rheumatism. What say you, Willie? Want a job lurking in a grotto instead of a hedgerow?"

Willie stepped out from behind a towering old willow, looking grieved. "Damned if I know how you knew this time," he said sulkily.

" 'Dratted,' if you please; there's a lady present," Crispin corrected him immediately, "and it's simple, little clodpole —shadows. I doubt there's room for them on the streets in London, but here they don't appear for no reason."

"Shadows," Willie grumbled in disgust, kicking a stone, "leaves and pebbles and wet grass. No wonder there's no crime here—there's no way to get away if you do pull off a good dip. Though what you'd find in a cow's pocket beats me."

"Want to go back to London?" Crispin asked.

"In a minute!" Willie said, but then his face fell. "But you're staying on here, ain't you?"

"I don't know," Crispin said, though he felt Dulcie's hand suddenly tense on his arm. "We've been invited everywhere. More invitations arrive each day. What do you think, my lady? It seems the social world wants a better look at you. I don't know that they deserve one, but maybe you would enjoy yourself."

She remembered that terrible night when he'd dragged her through the crowd of guests at his ball, declaring that she was his wife. "Perhaps," she said gravely. "I would like them to think you have a better bride than the one you showed them that night."

He put his hand on hers and held it tight. "I'm sorry I did that, Dulcie. I've apologized and I meant it. Gossip doesn't bother me. I didn't want to remind you of that night either. But why should there be any gossip at all? Hiding here will serve no further purpose; Harry doesn't care about us anymore and I begin to think you care enough about me not to flee."

She smiled, and he pressed her hand and said, "Yes, I begin to think it would be better for you in the future if we let people see you. They'll have to meet you sooner or later. Why not now? It's time. Once they see us together, all rumors will end. A look at you would show them that what they saw was a lovers' quarrel, no more. We routed Jerome Snode by acting, but we don't even have to pretend now.

"We'll have to go to London, I think. We can't invite people to come here without having to put them up to eat and sleep and bore us out of our minds for weeks. Travel is difficult, summer approaches, they'd have a right to expect that. I hate the thought of giving a house party for weeks . . . especially these days—and nights."

When he smiled at her like that, as if remembering exactly what they'd done last night and again at dawn, she could forgive him anything and face anything with him—even her fear of entering his world.

"But if we do go to London," he mused, "we will have to leave soon, before summer sets in. I don't care what you think, Willie; London's no place to be in the summertime."

"Aye, well, that's so," Willie said grudgingly. "The water gets very nasty in the summertime. Dogs go mad, and so do lots of people. And folks die of flux almost as often as they do from the cold in the winter. Dropped like flies last summer, leastways."

"It's somewhat cleaner where I live in London," Crispin commented, but his smile faded as he added, "but the air can't be scrubbed. The miasmas of summer infect everyone in London, which is why those who can, leave—in less final ways than Willie's neighbors. So, Dulcie, shall we go to town? We can leave tomorrow."

She nodded, but she was afraid—and not of unhealthy miasmas.

"I'll send word ahead to have the house prepared. We'll take the journey in easy stages; there's no need for hours of steady riding. Oh, and yes," he said, patting his coat pocket and pulling a letter from it. "We'll stop off in High Wycombe on our way. I was trying to decide if, and how, I could get there. Now it's simple. It's on our way to London, or only a little off it. There's a friend of Wrede's there who says he has an offer for me—how did he put it? Oh, yes, an offer that is"—he scanned the letter—"much to my advantage, but not one he can commit to paper. But knowing my ways and means, he writes that he thinks I'll want to join him in 'a delicious venture' of his devising that is sure to give me the satisfaction I seek. He urges that I come to his 'humble home' to see for myself."

He folded the letter. "Flowery, but that's Wrede's friends for you. The man's a literary type. He founded one of Wrede's favorite clubs: the Dilettanti. Very high-minded, though Walpole says their erudite opinions come from too much wine. Still, notable men from town and court are members. The duke of Dorset and the earl of Sandwich belong, along with many others of rank and fortune. I don't think I can afford to pass up an offer so intriguing.

"Oh, don't worry. I've plenty of money now," he assured Dulcie, "but I've learned the hard way that more is better. I'm always on the lookout for new investments. Good ones, sure ones, even if they are slow ones. I won't leap into anything anymore. Everyone knows that. Wrede must have told his friend about me—he sounds like a man with a good financial prospect on his mind."

"I wasn't worried about money," she said. "I may have married you for money, but I remind you that it wasn't *your* money I married you for. It was only your name, 'Mr. Black.'"

"I know, I know. If your nose goes up any higher you'll hurt your neck." He laughed. "Don't get angry, I know it wasn't the money."

His answer seemed to please her.

"So we're going?" Willie yelped in delight.

"So we are," Crispin said.

CHAPTER
15

She stopped laughing abruptly when he asked her. When she spoke again, her voice quavered. Although he couldn't see her face distinctly in the growing twilight, he heard her fear clearly enough.

"No," Dulcie said, "I can't. I'd be too ashamed. I know you think I'd enjoy it, if I just tried it once, but I know I wouldn't. It's too soon, we've only been married a little while, really. Don't be angry with me for it, please. Ask it of me some other night and I'll try, but not tonight, Crispin. I can't do it. I can't even try."

"Dulcie," he said patiently, watching her in the fading light that managed to sift in through the dusty coach windows, "you're ready, whether you know it or not. You were born ready for it. You're a born lady. All a lady needs do when she meets a gentleman is to blush at his praise, which he will give her if she's rich and highly placed, no matter what she looks like—never mind being such a beauty as you. All she has to do after that is look interested in what he's saying to her—but not too interested," he cautioned, "because she has a jealous husband, remember. She can talk if she wants to. If not, all she has to do is continue to look interested, or at least not look as though she's ready to fall asleep. You can do that, can't you?"

"No," she said stubbornly, "not yet. Maybe when we get to London. But we've been traveling all day, and I'm dusty and travel-weary. And I look it. Even if Annie gets a flatiron for my gown when we get to the inn, my hair is all disarranged from . . . you," she said with a little giggle, "and from falling asleep with my head on your shoulder. It's all lopsided," she wailed. "I'd have to wash it again to get it looking right, and it's such a chilly night that even if I sit in front of the fire it won't be dry until dawn."

"I, too, am weary and travel-stained," he said. "I'd thought to go tomorrow."

"Ah, Crispin, please," Dulcie said, "I'm not ready. Meet with your Sir Francis tonight or tomorrow, but leave me at the inn, please. I promise you that when I do meet him in London, I'll try to dazzle him. Don't be angry with me or disappointed in me. I'd disappoint you more if he saw me looking and feeling this way. Oh, Crispin, I will meet him if I must, but please, not now."

It was odd to hear brave Dulcie so defeated, and by such a small thing. But it was as painful to him as it was odd.

"I'm not disappointed," he said, hugging her. "How could I be, for such a little thing? At any rate, it will be better for me if you stay at the inn," he said and then added, when he felt her tense in his arms, "because if he saw you looking this way he might try to keep you with him forever."

She threw her arms around his neck and kissed him, and he tasted tears.

"Such a fuss for nothing," he said on a smile. "Very well. You stay at the inn; I'll go to see him and return as soon as I can," he promised, his lips to hers. And then proceeded to *completely* dishevel her hair.

"Oh, excellent," Sir Francis said. "Not that the lady is indisposed, of course—we regret that and hope she recovers quickly—but that you had the foresight to come alone this time. Otherwise we'd have to have invited you back again, alone. This business, as you must understand, my dear sir, is for gentlemen alone."

"Such business usually is," Crispin commented. "I've known talented and clever ladies, but even they don't usually care to involve themselves in these affairs."

"Precisely," Sir Francis said with glee. "Well said! That is *exactly* why we asked you here. Wrede spoke highly of you. You're a man of mystery, you know. One never sees you anywhere a fellow ought to be, at clubs or coffeehouses," he chided playfully. "You're elusive, wealthy and wise, and newly wed in such secrecy. How you intrigue us! A fellow who dares much, we hear. Oh, you are in the right place, sir. We believe you'll find satisfaction in our little venture, we really do!" Sir Francis Dashwood rubbed his plump hands together as he spoke.

His overeagerness made Crispin wonder if he actually wanted to do business with this odd man after all. One might be excused for being excited about a good financial prospect—Crispin himself was—and he realized it wasn't fair to judge the man for not being able to conceal his excitement. In every other way he was a gentleman. Sir Francis was a short thickset man who wore subdued clothing and whose heavy face was framed by his own dark ringlets. He had a large nose and a double chin, but it wasn't his features that made him unattractive to Crispin. It was the way he wore them. His thick lips were wet, and his eyes held too much excitement and dark laughter.

"Ah, here is Montagu!" Sir Francis cried as a tall gentleman joined them. "Montagu, we are pleased to make you known to our new guest: Crispin Knightly, Viscount West. Crispin, if we may call you that, sir? We give you John Montagu, earl of Sandwich, one of the members of our little cabal."

Crispin bowed. He didn't like the look of the earl any more than he liked his reputation. Sandwich was gangling and sly looking, his thin lips always quirked with private amusement, his pale eyes seeming to glint with pleasure at secret thoughts. He was known to be brilliant, and whispered to be other things not generally spoken aloud. And he was known for his many mistresses as well as for his intelligence. His work at the Admiralty was still spoken of with as much astonishment as his visits to the lowest brothels in London. The earl's appetite for work, and for women, was notorious. Men could be admired for either, but there was something extraordinary and feverish about Sandwich's pursuit of both.

It was a fair, mild day, just drawing into evening. Crispin had left Dulcie at the inn and had been driven to this meeting. The carriage had let him off by a gate to one side of a country road. He'd been invited not to Sir Francis's manor house but to his retreat nearby. He was told it was his lordship's folly, where he met with gentlemen friends from London—many men secluded their families from their friends and business acquaintances. That way they spared them the smoke of their pipes, and spared themselves the trouble of entertaining them. Every gentleman had his own study or library for such meetings. Crispin supposed a rich and eccentric man could move his retreat as far from his house as he liked.

"Come, come," Sir Francis said merrily. "Older gentlemen arrive by boat on the Thames. But 'tis only a short walk, no trouble at all for such a fit-looking young buck as yourself. He's a fine specimen, is he not, Montagu? Speaking of specimens, we hear you're a horticulturalist. We're sure you'll love the specimens you will find here. Come along, we've a fine ruin to show you, too," he said as he led Crispin down a path of crushed white shells. "An abbey—ruined but newly refurbished for comfort. Gothic is fine, but comfort is our byword. No need for a ruin to be ruined, is there?" he tittered at his own weak jest.

"This evening is just a trial for both of us," Sir Francis quickly cautioned Crispin, "although in no way will it be a trial, we do sincerely hope. Quite the contrary. But we must have twelve members in our little group in addition to myself. One has left, and now there's room for another, which is why we asked you here. We are a close and secret order: gentlemen of note who need more than the workaday world can offer us. Daring men who are not afraid of risk in pursuit of our goals. Men who know the joys of life, who are used to them, and who seek more. Indeed, we believe men of such inclination and education can appreciate more than others can and deserve more! You're said to be such a man. Being newly wedded, you most especially need what we can offer." He laughed, then added, more seriously, "But you will see, and we shall see. If you don't care for us, or we for you, this will be merely an enjoyable evening. But if we suit, it will be a wonderful thing for us all."

Money was always a wonderful thing to Crispin, who had spent his adult life building up his fortune. He nodded, hoping they would suit. The men Sir Francis and the earl associated with were rich and powerful. Such men had opportunities that others lacked. Opportunity given to a clever man meant money, and although Sir Francis had enough money for any man now, he could always use more.

The grounds over which they walked were covered with neatly shorn grass. Young trees lined a silver brook that coursed beside the meandering path. As they walked down a hill and up to the crest of another, Sir Francis stopped and waited for Crispin to comment on the scene that lay below.

An ardent gardener, Crispin noticed the trees and shrubs first. He wondered what Sir Francis expected him to comment on. The man was clearly waiting for him to say something about the vista before him, but Crispin was disappointed. The lawns were edged by common hedges of privet and boxwood. The trees he quickly identified as willow, larch, oak, and alder. It was a pleasant vista, but there was nothing to account for the sudden silence and obvious anticipation of the men with him.

And then Crispin saw what they were looking at. It was the paths, not the greenery, that he was supposed to be impressed with. From this higher vantage point he saw that the path he had walked diverged to become two paths. Cut deep into the turf and covered with crushed shell, they shone brilliantly white in the ruddy light. Now he saw that each was shaped oddly, in long and sinuous lines. Each was, in fact, contoured to look exactly like a shapely female leg. The limblike paths bent wide apart before they finally met up again. At their apex was a dense bushy green hedge with a tunnel cut into it. The whole scene was crafted so that a man watching another walking the path from either side would see him seem to enter a woman's sex at its end.

It was childish and vulgar. Obscene, certainly. But it *was* funny. Crispin laughed.

Then he noticed what he had missed before when he was trying to identify the many shrubs. This time he looked at their shape and saw what they'd been clipped and grown to represent. The organs he was familiar with; they merely amused him. Others astonished him, because even with all his experience, he'd never known people could do what some of those bushes were shaped into doing to each other.

"Extraordinary," he said.

"Just so!" Sir Francis giggled, delighted. "And that is just the beginning, we promise you, sir. Oh, what a night awaits you!"

Dulcie sat and stared into the fire, hating herself. A *lady* would have gone with her husband. A *lady* wouldn't be sitting by the fireside filled with regret, her hair as dismally damp as her mood. He had asked her to go, but she had feared the unknown more than his disappointment. Now she sat by the fire combing out her hair and counting all the ways that she didn't deserve Crispin as her husband.

She scowled into the fire, not noticing that the serving girl had brought her a pot of coffee and a tray of cakes, until the girl cleared her throat after she'd set them down near Dulcie.

"Ma'am," the girl said, and then her broad face, already

ruddy from the heat of the cooking fires, turned redder as she said, "My lady, your maid's gone and got herself something to eat, so the missus, she said I was to bring you something, in case you was feeling peckish. There's strawberries and mulberries, wine jelly, and some pastries and clotted cream, if it please you," she added, bobbing a quick curtsy.

Since Dulcie had eaten dinner, she didn't so much as lift her aching head.

"Thank you," she said in a pinched voice. She sat before the fire in a fine silk robe patterned with flowers as blue as her mood. She hung her head down, her hair hanging in front of her eyes so that the fire would dry it faster. She didn't know she looked like a picture of sorrow.

The girl nodded her lacy cap, and then hesitated. "Ain't there nothing I can get you, your ladyship?" she asked. "Food or wine, or nothing?"

"Nothing that will help," Dulcie thought, and then realized she'd said it aloud. When she looked up through the screen of her hair, she saw the girls' round blue eyes register sudden concern. "Nothing, really, thank you," Dulcie said. "I've been traveling long and hard today. I just need to sit in the quiet and rest, thank you."

"He'll be back," the girl blurted. "They goes, but they comes back every time. And they only meets once this time of year."

"They do?" Dulcie asked, with a feeling of dread. The girl was as nervous as she was forward, but she seemed to be trying to give comfort, although she couldn't possibly know why Dulcie needed it.

"Lor', I shouldn'ta said nothing. The missus will skin me. But you was looking so forlorn. Listen, lady," the girl said, bending near, her eyes darting to the door as she whispered hoarsely. "Most of them, they comes down alone, but seeing as to how your man came with you, he prolly won't even stay out there overnight. Even them that do is gone by Monday. They have their"—she hesitated—"their *rites* on Saturday midnight and lay about all day the Sabbath after. Then they're gone. You'll see."

"No. I won't," Dulcie said, sitting up abruptly, swinging her hair back so that it hit the back of her neck with a cold, wet slap. "How can I? I'm not there, so I can't know. You do. Tell me."

It took coaxing and bribery, sweet reasoning, and then outright bullying, to get the girl to agree to talk.

"Bolt the door. I'll tell my maid to wait if she comes back before you're done. But tell me you will," Dulcie ordered, "if I have to keep you here all night. And then what will the missus say?"

"The gentlemen have a club, like, at the old abbey. Sir Francis runs it," the girl said fearfully, sitting in the chair, as Dulcie commanded her to do, and twisting her apron string around her work-worn fingers as she talked. "Medmenham Abbey. It was ruint, till he had it fixed up. It's far from his house, and that's where the gentlemen go. They got the place fixed up as fine as fivepence, painted and primed, with furniture fit for a palace. The devil's palace it is. The paintings and statues they got would make your eyes bug out and stay there."

"Go on," Dulcie said.

"I'm sure I can't say any more," the girl said, with a stab at being demure, "you being a lady and all."

"I'm sure you can," Dulcie said implacably, and folded her arms across her breast.

"Well, maybe I can. But as for what they do there! I can't even talk about it 'cause I'm a good girl. It's a sin and a profanation, turning the abbey of the good brothers into a place of the devil, and that's sure. Still, nobody's powerful as the Dashwoods hereabouts, and money talks, so nobody does nothing but shake their heads. Not even the vicar, and there's a shame."

"If nobody goes there except the gentlemen, how does everyone know what the abbey looks like?" Dulcie asked, fascinated.

"Well, but who do you think cleans it?" the girl asked, amazed enough to forget her place entirely. She remembered in time to duck her head and add, "They live like pigs, not to mention what they do. Someone's got to clean up after them. They say it's not for no one else's eyes, but I guess they think we ain't no one. I seen it!" she said in a burst of bravado, "and I ain't never likely to forget."

"If you don't go on, I'll wring it out of you!" Dulcie cried, looking every inch a outraged lady. The girl quailed. She hesitated and then looked up, her cheeks red, clearly excited. "They got pictures of people doing it," she said in awed tones. "Naked and dressed, going at it every which way, doing it to each other and to themselves and to goats and swans, and what all! Swiving, rutting, rogering each other—you know. And doing other things with their privates and such like, too. All being done by such handsome people, too. Real as life, in beautiful colors—even on the ceilings! And they got statues big as life, of men with their things out to here! Struth! Standing up like soldiers, bold as brass, and true to nature. They got hedges clipped to look like your, you know, top and bottom parts and even more shrubs shaped like gents' particulars. You don't know what a turn it can give you to turn around and see a man's particular that's as big as you are, my lady, and I hope you never do," she added fervently.

"Go on," Dulcie croaked. "What else?" Either the girl was mad, she thought, or she herself was—to think she'd ever understand the workings of the noble mind. If this incredible thing was true, how could Crispin go to such a place? Worse, how could he have asked her to go there with him? Worse yet, she thought again, how could he have gone there without her?

"They worship the devil!" the girl said.

Bad as that was, it wasn't as shocking to Dulcie as the other things.

"It's the Hell-fire Club. They don't care for God's punishment or nothing. They dress like monks, all in brown, and hold blasphemous services." As if realizing how weak that sounded after her previous lurid detail, the girl added defensively, "I ain't seen the rituals, though. Nobody from 'round here is ever allowed in the chapel, so I ain't seen exactly what they do. But I seen the women they get to come down and pretend to be nuns, dressed up like them and all, only doing things no nun ever heard of—with the gentlemen, after the services, all together, on the floor and on the altar, too! 'Services,' they call them—orgies is what they is.

"I ain't seen the orgies neither," the girl admitted, "but I seen the women. Some stayed here after. They was laughing and joking about it, and I heard them saying what they do. Common whores playing at being whoring nuns for the gentlemen of the Society of Saint Francis—that's what they call themselves. That or the Mad Monks of Medmenham Abbey! Struth! Their motto's carved on the abbey in Latin or French or one of them jawbreakers. I can't read it. But the whores, they said it means 'Do what you will.'"

"I see . . ." Dulcie said, although she didn't see, and only wanted to say something to fill up the silence and stop her from thinking about what she'd heard. And then she noticed how the girl was watching her. "I see," Dulcie said again, coldly this time, drawing herself up, "and I begin to wonder why you told me all this."

"I only told you 'cause I din't want you to worry none if the gentleman comes back late. I—only wanted you to know he would—he will come back," the girl stammered.

But Dulcie looked her steadily in the eye and knew the truth. She saw it before the girl averted her face. She too had once been poor and poorly dressed, and she had envied fine ladies. But she would never have hurt them in the guise of helping them, just to get even with them for their fine clothes and their easy life.

Dulcie gave her such a look of cold contempt that the girl stopped sniveling and drew in a quick breath of fear.

"Thank you for your concern," Dulcie said silkily, unknowingly imitating the earl of Wrede, down to his least inflection, "but I should be more concerned about myself if I were you, not just because the missus might find out but also because Sir Francis wouldn't be pleased to know his doings were common gossip for the visitors to this inn. I should think a man who worshiped the devil could think of some fiendish things to do to someone who gossiped about him, if he did find out. Don't you? Go," she said, sickened by what she'd heard, tired of the girl's face, and afraid of whatever else she might say. "Take your money and go now. And be quiet about this if you know what's good for you!"

The girl bobbed her head and scurried out. Dulcie wished she could do the same, but there was nothing for her to do but wait for Crispin to return. She could hardly dress and join him—he'd think she distrusted him.

She did.

He'd said it was a meeting to do with finances. Why should she doubt him? There had been nothing in his behavior in the past few days to hint at anything so awful. She'd talked with him; she'd lain in his arms, completely at his mercy, and he'd been far more than merciful. He'd been tender and gentle, and impassioned. But she hadn't matched his passion, not really, she thought dismally. She always obliged him, but she knew he wanted more from her. She just didn't know how to give it.

Maybe he was weary of her. He was always carried away at the end of their lovemaking and, after it, always disappointed because she hadn't been transported to rapture. He blamed himself, and the newness of it. But maybe, she thought, he also blamed her. And who could blame him if he did? She no more knew what he wanted of her than she really understood the ecstasy he obviously found.

But he had asked her to come along with him tonight. Would he have done that if he was going to an orgy? Would he go to an orgy after promising her that she would never have to share his attentions? But what if all he meant by that was that he was willing to let *her* share, too? What did she know of orgies? Or noblemen? What had her rash act in the Fleet chapel led her to? And why, she asked herself briskly, as she paced the room waiting for him to return, should she believe a sly, gossipy serving wench and not believe Crispin, her husband? Her immaculate, handsome, gentle, and beautiful lover. The man who had never wanted her, but was making the best of the marriage, as best he knew how.

Dulcie had to wait a long while for Crispin.

The clock downstairs in the common room had chimed well into a new morning when she heard him open the door. She leaped to her feet and rose to face him. When she saw him she caught her breath. All her worst imaginings seemed not too foolish now, but too true.

The fire had died long since, and the candles were burning low. She saw in their guttering light that he looked weary unto death, and disheveled. Strands of hair drifted around his face; his coat was half open, his shirt half out, his stockings smudged, rumpled, and uneven. And worst of all, the harsh light and shadow showed a look on his face that she'd never seen before.

"I see you thought fit to return," she said haughtily. "I wonder why you didn't spend the night."

He stopped in the doorway. "I thought you'd be asleep by now," he said.

"Ah. Is that what I am supposed to be doing?" she asked defiantly.

He closed the door carefully. "Dulcie," he said very quietly, "I've had a long night. I'm very glad to be here at last. If I'm late, and if I kept you waiting up for me, I'm sorry. I never intended that to happen. I'd have told you to go to bed without me if I'd known how long it would take."

"How long *does* an orgy take?" she asked angrily. "Not this long, I should think, if there was only one woman for you. Unless you were supposed to watch first. But two or more—why, then, I'd think—"

He reached her in a few long steps and took her by the

shoulders. His grip was so firm that the rest of the hateful words she was going to say died in her throat. The fury in his eyes was clear even in the flickering light.

"Who told you?" he asked quietly.

That broke her spirit.

"Oh, Crispin!" she cried, her hand going to her mouth. "Oh, Crispin," she whispered, her eyes wide, her rage turned to grief, "how could you?"

He stood looking down at her and at her tears, and then he sighed. He drew her close and held her against him in spite of her struggles to be free. "Dulcie," he said into her hair as he buried his face in her disordered curls, "what mischief is afoot? Who has spoken to you? Someone grossly misled me tonight. And now here you are, all upset—and this I cannot bear, dearling," he said.

She stopped weeping, because she loved it when he called her that, but she had never heard that soft, despairing tone of voice from him before.

"I was sent on a wild-goose chase—say, rather, a wild-gander chase," he said. "No new investment was offered to me tonight—only a chance for some vulgar sport. Had I known, I would not have gone. Now, who told you what I would find there? I wish they'd told me before I left.

"Look at me," he said with rueful laughter in his voice, as he stepped back from her. "I look as if I'd been dragged through a hedge backwards, don't I? I have been, or at least I stumbled into enough of them. I left Sir Francis's folly— was ever a place so well named!—and since it was the middle of the night and everyone else was too occupied to find me transportation, I had to walk miles in the dark till I reached the road. There I found Willie, bless his crafty soul, waiting with an ancient farm horse. God knows what lies he told in order to borrow it. God, I hope he only borrowed it! But it was for a good cause. We rode home double, and I stink of the stable because of that. But at least it's better than the stink of the incense that Dashwood uses in his damned chapel. To say nothing," he muttered, "of the cheaper perfume of some of his guests. And how could you have believed ill of me?" he added, with no laughter at all in his voice.

She touched his hair and his shirt, trying to neaten them, before her hand fell to her side in a hopeless gesture. "I tried not to, Crispin, honestly, I did. But you were gone so long. Here, get out of those clothes," she said more briskly. "The water in the pitcher's not hot anymore, but at least it's not icy cold. I'll get some soap. My towels are dry now . . ."

He took her hand and held it before she could leave. "Now," he said, "tell me, Dulcie. Who told you? And what did they say?"

"The serving wench. She came up to bring me some pastries and fruit after dinner. She started talking, and then hinting. I forced it from her. She told me about the so-called Society of Saint Francis and all about the abbey, the pictures, the sculptures, the bushes and . . . and the nuns. I think she did it was because she was jealous of me, Crispin."

"Ah," he said, "I see. That remains to be seen, but you believed her." It wasn't a question.

"I didn't know what to believe," she confessed, "and so I suppose I believed it—yes. Because she talked about all the gentlemen and the women from London and all the fun they had. I'm not as . . . tutored as they are, Crispin. I could understand you wanting someone more . . . adept. I'm not very good at what they do, I know that," she said as she brushed a leaf from his coat, not meeting his eyes.

"Dulcie?" he said, and something in his voice made her look up. "Dulcie," he said very earnestly, "did I ever say that? Did I ever make you think you weren't good enough for me? After we came to terms with our marriage, I mean."

"Well, no, but—" she said.

"But you thought I would want a whore from London instead of you?" he asked, running a hand through his hair in exasperation.

"Well, you were in such a fine place, with all those exotic things in it for men of experience, and women from London were there," Dulcie said, each word paining her.

"You think I am eager to copulate on the floor of a drafty chapel with a painted, worn-out London whore?" he asked in wonder. "You think I'm so jaded, so coarse, that I'd become aroused by rooms filled with badly painted erotic pictures?" he asked with a little more anger. "You think I'd find sport in climbing into fusty monks' robes with a clutch of fools pretending to be schoolboys? Or that I enjoy the idea of public fornication? Do you think what we have means nothing to me?" he thundered. "That I would leave you to sport with drabs? And, God in heaven, whatever you imagine I think of you, do you really believe I find a garden full of bushes shaped like breasts and ballocks appealing? God help you, Dulcie, but you are a silly fool!"

He stood, hands on his hips, staring down at her. He was rumpled and smudged, dirty and tired, and absolutely furious with her.

She giggled. She tried to stifle the sound, but she was tired and relieved and delighted with his anger. No excuse could ring so fine upon her ear as his fury did. She'd lived with a father who, when he was guilty, met every accusation with a pretty story and reassurance. Crispin did neither. He looked ready to kill her, and she believed him entirely. She could almost imagine that he loved her. At least, he'd as much as said he loved making love to her. That was good enough for her, for she loved him very much.

He was beginning to smile sheepishly himself when she stopped giggling.

"I'm sorry if I made you mad," she said, "but you really frightened me tonight."

"Oh, Dulcie," he sighed, pulling her into his arms, "I'm sorry. That was the last thing I thought would happen."

He'd first stayed at the abbey because he couldn't believe he really understood what they were about. Then he lingered because he didn't quite believe what they were doing. When he did leave, it was without a word, in disgust. The men were jaded fools. He had only been angry at the inconvenience until he saw how unhappy Dulcie was. Her sadness was more than he could bear.

"Forgive me, Dulcie. I didn't want you to have to know," he said. "I thought I might wander those lawns forever, or fall into the river in the dark. But I never thought you'd be hurt in any way. I'm glad I didn't know how upset you were, for that would have made me—What's that scent in your hair?" he asked, drawing in a deep breath.

"I washed it," she said, "so it's soap, or vinegar, I imagine."

He breathed in the fresh, clean scent of her, and his arms tightened around her. The chapel had smelled of the heavy perfume of the whores and the gentlemen; the room itself had reeked of narcotic incense. When Sir Francis had done with his stupid ceremony, the whores had been brought out, and the stink of sweaty excitement had hung heavy in the thick air. The scent of the cool spring gardens to which he'd escaped had been like a deliverance, but nothing smelled as sweet and pure as his wife's clean hair did now.

And her mouth was sweet and fresh, and her skin was scented with soap and tasted of lemon and roses and salt.

"I'll wash," he muttered, pulling off his neckcloth. "I must smell like the old horse."

He was a riot of scents, she thought—horse, yes, but incense and strange perfumes, too, the perfumes of the spring night, and a unique scent that was only him: tangy and complicated by shaving soap.

"No," she murmured, pulling him back, "stay here with me."

She might not have known what she'd asked of him, but he did. He drew her to the bed with him, struggling out of his coat and shirt as he did. She was so anxious to have him whole and naked against her that she helped him from his breeches and hose. She had only the silken gown to remove. And that was removed in the space of a sigh.

They didn't bother with much play. She was too impatient to have him, too eager to reassure herself that he desired her, to convince herself that she was good enough for him. And he was too overcome by her desire for him to temper his yearning to have her. The eroticism he'd seen earlier hadn't left him entirely untouched, but the unaccustomed eagerness of her touch almost undid him. He was as avid as a boy, with just enough control to remember some of the refinements of a man. They met in mutual passion.

She forgot her fears of inadequacy and simply rejoiced in his return, feeling the blessed need and heat and touch of him. And then she felt something more. A stirring, a gathering, a tingling sense of something that was neither him nor her but the two of them together as he rocked against her and caressed her. Before she could think about the feeling and what it meant, it overcame her. She rode with it, and with him. She followed where it led, though it led her far away from herself. It made her shiver and gasp and finally emit little sobs that might have embarrassed her if she'd been aware of them or of anything but the pulsing surge of devastating feeling that followed.

He paused above her, and she felt his chuckle deep in his chest. "Yes," he said with enormous pride and satisfaction, his voice low and rich against her ear, "yes, Dulcie. There you are." And while she still shuddered and wondered, he took his own pleasure, made exquisite now because of hers.

"Is it always like that for you?" she asked when he lay beside her again, their heartbeats slowing as he held her and soothed her.

"Always, with you," he said dreamily, as he stroked her.

"Then I can understand why men buy women," she said in a brave voice. "If it always feels like that for them, who can blame them?"

"It doesn't," he said, on the edge of sleep, scarcely knowing what he'd said. "It's not anything like this, I promise you." Then he said no more, because he slept.

She did too, after she'd thought about what he'd said and

stored it in her memory for comfort during whatever lay ahead.

The serving girl was gone in the morning.

"She's feeling poorly, sir," the innkeeper said.

"Good," Crispin said. "I'd have made her feel worse," he muttered as he helped Dulcie into the coach. "We'll be in London by this afternoon," he told her. "Willie will be ecstatic."

"You're keeping him on?" she asked, "I had hoped so, because he did help you last night."

"More likely he was spying on me and just happened to be there when I needed help," he answered, smiling. "Willie is like a force of nature. One doesn't keep him on any more than one keeps it raining. He stays because it suits him. I think I know some of his reasons, but probably not all. That wise, I am not. Silly wench, why are you looking at me like that? So doting? Just because I pleased you once? Why, then," he said, when she giggled and nodded, "we must see what two nights will do, mustn't we? Or one morning," he said, advancing on her, in spite of her screeches.

"Oh, no!" she cried, not joking anymore. "Crispin! No! Someone might look in!"

"We're traveling in a carriage, Dulcie," Crispin said in a silky undervoice. But then he raised his head, sighed, and sat up again. "But you're right. I know who might look in."

"Willie?" she asked, grinning so merrily he tweaked her nose for her.

He nodded. "He's riding with the baggage. I've assigned him a room in my house this time. He'll go where he pleases—I might as well pretend it pleases me to have him there all the time."

She kissed him without caring who might be looking in.

After the coach arrived in London, Willie stowed his belongings in his new room, admired it for a half second, and then went out again. He sidled past the footmen and slipped out the door. Then he squared his shoulders and made straight for his meeting. But he stopped in the alley behind the viscount's town house and looked back for a moment, his small face grim in its stark longing before he remembered to erase all expression from it. He had a report to make and didn't know how it would be taken, or if he could ever come back.

CHAPTER
16

There was no moon, but Willie Grab never needed light. He'd grown up in the dark, and he found his way to the appointed spot at the exact hour he was expected. He had no clock, but didn't need one. He'd learned to count the hours from his heartbeat, mark the day by the rising of the moon and sun, and he measured out his days in breaths. He wanted to keep counting them, so he decided he would speak as little as possible at this meeting, for he didn't trust his voice. It was weaker than his will and might betray him. And he was frightened, though no one watching him walk down the street would have guessed it.

He went on his way undisturbed, for those who knew how to look also knew what they were looking at. Willie Grab was many things, but he did not look like a victim.

He swaggered, for one thing. Small as he was, he walked like a man with a weapon, though his only weapons were speed and guile and a certain furtive grace. He was also armed with experience far beyond his years. Most of all, he possessed intelligence, which was why he was so frightened tonight.

He stopped at a tavern with the sign of a hissing cat

hanging over its door. He drew in a deep breath and went inside. The room was hot and damp, in marked contrast to the cool night. No fire burned in the hearth; the heat was provided by the people packed inside—too many people, too much smoke and noise. The smell of ale and gin wafted in the stale air, and everyone seemed to be talking or laughing. There was even some raucous singing going on. The laughter was very loud, considering no one could hear a word that was spoken unless he put his ear to the speaker's mouth. But it wasn't necessary to hear, not with so much gin available for a halfpenny, not with the ale flowing so lavish and cheap.

Willie went straight to the barkeep and got a wink and a quick nod to indicate a table in the back. He turned and made his way through the crowd to it. He wasn't the only boy there and not the youngest, either, but he was the only sober one. Twelve glasses of gin wouldn't have gotten him high tonight. He'd already had two at his last meeting, and they might as well have been water. He was used to drinking. But even so, he was too nervous to allow anything as simple as alcohol to muddle his wits. He needed them too badly. He had another report to make, and a handsome payment to get for it. Still, he thought he'd be lucky to escape with his wits when he was done tonight.

The man he'd come to see sat in the shadows with his back to the wall. He wore a black cloak, and a black tricorne was tipped forward to hide his face, but Willie knew him immediately.

"I'm not late," Willie said defensively, sliding into a chair beside the man. "You must have got here early. I just came back today, and I come soon as I could, like I said I would."

"Nice place you have here," the man observed.

"Well, I couldn't come to you, could I?" Willie said in grieved tones, "and I didn't know where else we could meet. No one would expect to see you here, even if they could recognize you in all that black. And everybody would expect me. So I reckoned it was best."

"Oh, it is, it is," the earl of Wrede said. "I was only making an observation. Well, then, my child, what news?"

Willie swallowed and then cursed himself for it, because he knew the earl had noted it. An honest man speaks right up, a liar swallows first, he reminded himself savagely, and spoke up quickly. "Not much. They're April and May, more so than ever. They're here for the last of the season, or till London gets too hot for them. That's all."

"Is it?" the earl asked languidly.

"What else do you want to know?"

"A little bit about their stopover in High Wycombe would not be amiss."

"Oh. Well," Willie said, "he got asked to Sir Francis's place, and he went, and came back mad as thunder. You never seen such a taking! He's usually such a mannerly gent. He didn't like the orgies, nor the fact that nobody had told him about them, nor that he had to wander around half the night to get back when he wanted to leave."

"Indeed? Ah, well. It was a small chance," the earl murmured to himself, and then asked, "And the girl, how did she take his absence? She was told of what went on there, was she not? I do hope so, since I spent enough coin to ensure it."

"She was told," Willie said gruffly.

"And?"

"And she cried her eyes out. He came back, and the next morning they never let go of each other's hands until they had to eat breakfast, but they took them up again right after that. Like a pair of simpletons. Couldn't keep their eyes or their hands off each other after that. He rode in the coach all the way back to London with her. Didn't leave it to sit his horse once—not once," Willie marveled.

The earl fell still. He sat back and observed the doings of the couple at the next table for a few minutes while Willie fidgeted. Willie found he was the one to break the silence.

"That's all," he said abruptly. "There's no more to say about them. I didn't tell Harry nothing I didn't tell you. My word on it. But listen, my lord, I got something else to say: I can't work for you no more."

"Indeed?" Wrede said with interest. "And why not? Is Harry paying you more? Or threatening you? I wouldn't let that bother me, were I you. I have power as well as money, you know."

"No. I'm not working for Harry no more, neither. Thing is"—Willie took in a deep breath—"I don't want to be a rat no more. For anybody. Thing is, the viscount treats me good, and so does she. He done me a favor once, and I reckon I ain't been too much of a friend to him lately. See, at first I thought, What's the harm? Then there was all that at High Wycombe. That Sir Francis and his friends are real perverted, you know. It ain't like I never seen such stuff before. What else do poor folk got here? Gin and maybe a grab at a thrill before God or the hangman gets them. But gents that's got all that those lords got, doing the same and worse? It's crazy. And it ain't nice," he said primly.

"It was fixed so the viscount would do what Sir Francis and his lot was doing and break her heart. Or at least go to the abbey, so she'd think he was doing it even if he wasn't. Either way, he'd look bad. Still, it turned out good for them. But I don't like it, I really don't. I'm not much, but I know what I owe. You paid me, my lord, I delivered, and now I'm saying, thanks, but no more.

"If you push me, I'll disappear," he warned the earl. "There's truth. Even Harry knows that. I got a talent for making myself scarce. But I don't like to go to ground. So I'd like to just go now and stay friends, like. Maybe you'll need me again sometime for something else. Something I can do. I'm good. I can spy and fetch and keep my trap shut. I'm fast, I think on my feet, and I got connections. Not like yours, but at the Fleet. Sometimes that's just as good—for some things. And I don't hold grudges. I'll work for you anytime. But not at this. I can't do this no more."

The earl regarded Willie from his heavy-lidded eyes. His face was so white and still that Willie shifted in his seat, ready to take flight at any motion more threatening than a blink. He didn't expect a long gusty sigh.

"Well!" the earl said. "To think I'd finally be put in my place by a boy! . . . So be it. Be easy, lad. I've no further use for you. Now that they are in London, I can see to the matter myself. Believe it or not, the viscount is a friend of mine. I mean him no harm, I promise you. What I do, I do for his sake. Yes, that's so, and I won't go into it now, so spare me that look of utter disbelief. But tell me, are you going to stay on in my friend Crispin's employ and Harry's as well? Or were you braver with me than with Harry?"

"I didn't need to be brave with Harry," Willie said, amazed at the thought. "Why should I? He's all business, so he don't care much about the viscount now that he don't think there's any money to be made from him. But yeah, I'm staying on with the viscount, for now. The pay's real good," he said, and added with an attempt at nonchalance to cover the enormous pride in his voice, "They lets me stay in the house now, too."

"Ah. So. I see," the earl said with a smile.

"No," Willie said abruptly, "that ain't it. I slept in a real house before—lots of times, lots of places. Listen, my lord," he said, jumping to his feet and drawing himself up to his not very impressive height, his thin hands holding the edge of the table hard, "a bed ain't my price. And all the money in the world ain't, neither. I got no price, you hear? I can't be bought. I do what I do 'cause I want to. I ain't got much, but I got myself. Now you could collar me—if you're quicker than a snake, maybe—and call the watch down on me. You could have me in jail quick as a wink for anything you say I done. You could maybe even get me to swing for something you want to make up. You're a nobleman, and I ain't nothing at all. I know that. But I'm telling you the truth anyway, because I want you to know Willie Grab is his own man, or he's nothing. And there it is."

"I see," the earl said quietly, studying him. "Our business is done, then, but our acquaintance, I hope, is not. Listen, lad. I don't encounter many in my usual rounds, but I *do* enjoy meeting men of honor. Will you stay and have a drink with me now, Willie Grab?"

"Oh. Well. Don't mind if I do," Willie said graciously.

"This is nothing, of course, to the Vauxhall Gardens," Crispin said, and when Dulcie gazed up at him with a disbelieving stare, he touched the tip of her nose with one long finger. "I had to say that," he whispered, "just the way I'll have to say that Vauxhall is nothing to Ranelagh Gardens when we're there instead of here. A gentleman never admires any place where he is, as much as the place he is not. It's just not done."

She giggled. She'd been laughing all day, and now, at twilight, all she could manage was a contented giggle. They'd been together all day, and because it was such a beautiful evening, he'd brought her to a pleasure garden.

They'd come by the Thames on a barge decorated with flowers. The bargeman had bellowed bawdy songs, between riper curses at any fellow bargeman who got in his way. Crispin had made her laugh, comparing him to the gondoliers in Venice. Now they were strolling the long walks of Ranelagh Gardens, hearing music being played from out of the green and growing dusk. While all of it was wonderful, she knew none of it would be as wonderful as the night to come, for each night in their bed he showed her even more wonders. She'd never been happier; she hoped it was the same with him—and so it seemed to be.

"Tonight is fine, but how many nights can we go to the gardens?" he mused. "Now, tomorrow night we've been invited to a ball. A very grand affair."

She grew wary because there was something in his voice that hadn't been there a moment before. "Oh. Do you think I'm ready for a ball?" she asked, meaning she wondered if he was ready to take her.

"Of course. You were born ready."

They paused. The fireworks had begun. They stood silent,

arm in arm, and watched as a streaming golden star rose from the earth to shatter in the dusky sky above them.

"Whose ball is it?" she asked as they began to stroll again, toward the source of the light.

"Lady Charlotte's," he said.

She was very glad that a bombshell burst just then, fracturing the growing night with red and gold. She waited until the last glowing spark had left the sky before she spoke again.

"No," she said. "I can't. There are some things I can't do yet, or maybe ever. I can't, Crispin. Lady Charlotte was supposed to have been your wife."

"What better way to show that I have made my choice, that it is you I want and need, than to take you to her ball?" he asked reasonably. But he didn't look at her, and looking up at him, she saw only the reflections of the fireworks in his eyes.

"That's true," she said, "but please don't ask this of me. How can I go, when I'm not yet sure enough myself that that's true?"

Now he did look at her. "How can I make you see that it *is* true?" he asked.

"I don't know," she said miserably.

"Like this?" he asked, bemused, as he lowered his mouth to hers.

When he raised his head again, both their hearts were beating hard. But she still didn't answer, and only rested her head against his chest.

"Not through pleasure, then?" he mused. "Nor my constant company? Nor my flattery and encouragement? Then what do you want of me, Dulcie? Tell me, and I'll try to do it."

"I want only you," she said.

"You have me."

Do I? she thought, and answered. "Then I need time. Only time. Please, Crispin."

"It will be a very grand ball," he said hopefully.

"Yes? Well, then, it will just have to be less grand—without me!" she said with a burst of bravado, and he laughed. Then they strolled on in silence, she grateful, and he very thoughtful.

He didn't mention the ball again, but she knew he was thinking of it. The next night before they dressed for dinner he specifically requested she put on her new gown.

"The yellow? Certainly," she said, deliberately misunderstanding him. "I love the bright color of it."

"No, the new rose-colored one. I've a special reason. Please oblige me in this, Dulcie," he said before she could protest.

Of course she could not refuse such a simple request, but she *would not* go to Lady Charlotte's ball, she vowed as she went upstairs to her room. She would go through the mouth of hell itself for him, but not there, for if she did, she was afraid she would lose him forever.

In all fairness, she knew she *should* go with him. He'd been patient with her. They'd been invited everywhere, but he hadn't looked up any old friends, or even told Wrede he was back yet. He'd taken her out alone instead. She'd had a wonderful time, but of course she knew she must do more than be entertained by him. She would. But not at Lady Charlotte's ball. Not for her first foray into his world.

The lady was everything she was not. Dulcie knew she looked good now, but she could never look like Lady Charlotte Barrington. Charlotte was tiny and golden and perfect. She was also born to privilege, not just getting used to it. And Crispin had once loved her. If Dulcie went to the ball, he would see them together, and the comparison would make him regret having married her. That would be too much for her to bear.

Sometimes she wondered if he'd been so patient with her, keeping her to himself, because of his own fears, too.

Dulcie paced her room. The new gown was brocaded rose-colored silk, the hue deep and rich, the fabric embroidered with floral sprays. It was low in front, with a long train in the back. She had a matching fan and slippers to go with it. The high color brought her own color up, and when she had tried it on she'd thought she'd never looked so pretty in all her life. But she couldn't go to the ball tonight even though she knew he would ask it of her and it wouldn't be right to refuse him.

Every instinct she possessed warned her away from Lady Charlotte's ball. She was not a coward. In fact, what she found herself planning would take great courage. She shivered at the thought of the possible results of her impudence: she might be embarrassed, rebuffed, even laughed at. But she would dare anything if it kept her away from Charlotte Barrington tonight. She dismissed her maid and waited for Crispin.

Evening was drawing in when he came up to the bedroom they had shared since the night they'd returned to London. He dressed in his father's old room and kept his clothes there. But, town or country, he remained in her bed.

"Dulcie," he called as he entered the room, "come, let me see you. Let me see anything. The curtains were drawn, and there was only a small lamp glowing. Are you feeling all right?" he asked in sudden alarm.

"I'm fine," she said quietly.

"Dulcie," he said with heavy patience, "hiding in the dark won't answer, you know. I'm not asking you to attend a cockfight or a bullbaiting. This ball should be sheer pleasure for you, and for me. You look so wonderful in that gown that I want to show you to the world. And I want to dance with you—we've never done that, you know. A minuet, a country dance—any or all will do. Where the devil are you?" he asked as he stumbled over a chair.

"Here," she said simply, drawing the bed curtains back.

She'd kept a lamp burning, and so he saw her suddenly, in the rosy glow of its light. She lay back against the high pillows and smiled at him, hoping he was far enough away not to see how her lips were trembling, hoping he would see only the rosy length of silk she lay upon. That and nothing else, which was all she wore. No petticoat, no corset, no chemise. Only her own hair and a tremulous smile.

She'd never been so bold. Always before, no matter how impassioned their lovemaking, it had been done after he'd disrobed her. She'd never come to him naked as she was now. She scarcely knew herself. But she knew what she had to do.

He stared down at her and then came and sat gingerly on the side of the bed, next to her. He touched her hair and then her cheek. He smiled. But she saw, even in the dim light, that there was something other than tender humor there. His face was still, his eyes serious.

"Not just because you haven't had time to dress?" he asked.

She shook her head.

"I see. Not because you have a headache? Or a pain in the stomach—is it time for that?" he asked, remembering another night.

She grinned and shook her head in denial.

"Ah," he said, considering this, and her. "Then, because you do not want to go to the ball?"

"Oh, Crispin," she wailed. She drew her knees up and covered her face with her hands, because she knew she couldn't cover the rest of herself fast enough. But he didn't let her try.

He gathered her up in his arms and laughed, rocking her as she babbled in her consternation. "I thought you might enjoy seeing me like this," she said. "I didn't think you'd know what I was up to. This seemed like a good idea, even though it frightened me. I thought maybe you'd laugh at me, or even be bored with me by now, but I never thought . . . Oh, Crispin!"

He wasn't listening anymore. One minute he'd been holding her and touching her, and then he abruptly let her go. And then he was struggling out of his own clothes.

He'd never seen her so blatantly naked, and his instant

arousal had shamed him when he'd thought she was ill. He'd been relieved that she was not, and then amused at her idea of seduction. He was less amused, though, when he looked at her high firm breasts and the sweet swelling curves of her, all stretched out on bold display for him. But finally, with the warm, sweet weight of her in his arms, her smooth bare body sliding against his, her arms around his neck, his arousal overwhelmed him. He let it.

He tried to tell her not to worry, he was going to say she shouldn't be embarrassed, but, "Dulcie, Dulcie," was all he could whisper against her breast when he'd finally freed himself of all his clothes.

"I thought I'd say something provocative when you saw me. I was going to ask you if you thought the silk suited me . . . oh! Crispin," Dulcie said.

"You suit me. Good God, Dulcie, just look how you suit me!" he groaned.

Shedding her clothing had made her free. Now, for the first time, she told him just what she thought of his lovemaking. "Crispin," she whispered, "how I do love it when you do that to me."

It wasn't much, but it was more than she'd ever said when she was in his arms. He sighed with the pleasure of it, then found more to take his breath away. Soon their lovemaking was too overwhelming for words, too intense for thought, and she was with him every moment of the way.

When he could finally speak again, all he could do was praise her. It was a while before he could think of anything other than their lovemaking. It was a time before she could think to worry again, too. Until he spoke.

"The silk does suit you," he said with a smile, as he covered his hand with the silk and stroked it against her skin and wondered where the one left off and the other began. "Dulcie," he said, rising to one elbow, looking down at her, "as much as I loved this little surprise, was it only to avoid the ball?"

She knew just what he meant, and answered from her heart. "At first. Now I think I'll do it every night."

He fell back to the pillows and laughed with her. "This sort of intimacy instead of social intimacy? It's a fair trade. But I was going to give you pearls to wear with your new gown tonight. They're in my pocket." He stretched one long arm out toward the floor, but since he refused to take the other from around her, he couldn't lean down far enough to fish up his coat from among his discarded clothes. "No matter," he said, giving up, "there will be another time— but only if you'll come to a ball with me. Lovely pearls, they are, really. Don't you want to see them? How about now? It's early yet," he teased. "Want to get dressed now? We still have time to go to the ball."

"No more time for loving?" she pouted, linking her arms around his neck and pressing against him, greatly brave, entirely brazen now, secure in her achievement.

"A lifetime for this," he said fervently, turning her over atop him, pulling her close.

When she finally rested against his chest, he lay back and stared into the darkness. Now he could think clearly again, and what he thought made him smile. He hadn't taken her to meet society tonight, as he'd planned. But there would be other nights. A lifetime of nights: enough for both ecstasy and conviviality. And maybe, he thought, running his hand along her back as she stretched and made a small sound of contentment, even something else from this night's work. Maybe even a child. It was possible. From such ecstasy, a child? His eyes flew open wide. Then he closed them and grinned. Why not? Tonight every miracle seemed possible.

After all, he had already plucked triumph from the ashes of his dreams. A bad bargain was turning out better than he could ever have anticipated. She was beautiful and had been innocent, was charming and bright and a sheer delight in his bed. If he had to bear with an unwanted wife, he could have done much worse. Tonight, he knew that he could not have done much better. Sated and sleepy, he slept.

She burrowed into his arms and smiled, smug and sleepy, thinking of her great triumph on the night of the grand ball.

The house blazed with lights, a hundred candles on each chandelier. The guests looked like a company of angels. The ladies' gowns were made of silks and brocades. Their fans and slippers twinkled with myriad jewels. The men were dressed as fine and colorfully, with as many gems at their throats and toes. They danced in careful measures to delicate music, creating intricate patterns as they threaded their way through the grand ballroom. Everyone of note in London was there—except the two who were the hostess's reason for giving the ball.

And so she told the earl of Wrede when he finally arrived.

"They are not here!" Lady Charlotte snapped, looking up at the earl. He'd arrived at midnight. But although her ball would go on until dawn, no one of importance ever arrived after midnight.

"Behold me unsurprised," he said. But if he wasn't surprised, he was certainly excited. She could see it. There was only a faint flush on his high cheekbones, a certain glitter in his bright eyes, an impatience in his stance. But he looked ready for something, ripe for mischief and entirely full of himself. Something had happened. But nothing she could see. That added to her anger.

"Three hundred people eating everything in sight and boring me to death," she whispered harshly, as she flashed a bright smile at a passing couple. "Not a sign of them. And for this, I gave a ball? A splendid plan, your grace. Everyone seems to believe I planned this gala in order to announce my engagement to Prendergast. He's strutting around like the cock of the walk, not knowing that all I shall do is bid him good night. Not only is there to be no announcement tonight, but there will be no scandal to overshadow that fact. Everyone will think I have lost my wits, instead. Next time, *you* give a ball on some absurd pretext, and I shall arrive late, glittering and vastly amused."

"Oh, more than amused, my dear," he said.

"If I were a man I would call you out!" she said through gritted teeth.

"You would kiss me when you heard my news, even if you were a man," he assured her. "I've heard a wonderful thing. No, I have *done* a wonderful thing, which has led to wonderful news."

"And will I live long enough to hear it?"

"Softly, softly," he said with great amusement. "Let me relish the moment. Great news should be told at great leisure, rare vintages should be sipped, delicious dishes tasted, not bolted, beautiful women—"

"If you do not tell me now, you may leave!" she cried, cutting him off. "Don't play with me, Wrede. I won't have it."

He moved away from her, strolling to one side of the room, nodding at passing acquaintances, and she thought he was leaving. But then he stopped and looked back at her expectantly. She snapped her fan closed, pasted a smile on her lips, and followed him. It wasn't until they stood in a window embrasure, nearly out of sight of her other guests, that he spoke again.

"We have triumphed," he said. "It is done! Or rather, it is undone. Come, my lady, rejoice with me. Crispin is unwed!"

"You are mad," she said in disgust, "or disguised. Come to me sober, if you dare come to me again."

"I tell you I have not drunk anything tonight, only deeply from the cup of exultation," he said. "I come from a special meeting of some friends of mine who are members of Parliament, my dear, not from a tavern—although I grant you there is not much difference."

He became serious, his eyes bright. "Charlotte, I am the first to know. You, the second. Not even Crispin knows as yet. But I tell you, it is *done,* or as near as done. They're going to end Fleet marriages. Lord Hardwicke has pushed through his act. There are enough votes. There are to be no more Fleet weddings."

"Wonderful," she said bitterly, "but I remind you that Crispin is already married. You may as well tell me they've done away with hangings at Newgate. What good does that do a man after he's been hanged?"

"All the good in the world. That poor demented vicar is now out of the way. He performed many of those damned marriages. The bishop was told of this, and he was appalled. And so the old fool was examined and was of course unfrocked. He's been committed to a place where he finally makes sense to everyone. He's in Bedlam, my dear. And all of his marriages have been declared illegal.

"It took money and time, but I had both. And wit and great powers of persuasion, which I, of course, have in plenty. But it is finally done. The ceremony is invalidated, the marriage register erased, the vicar vanished. It is done and Crispin is . . ."

"Free?" she breathed.

"Entirely," he said with a huge smile. "Free as a newborn babe."

CHAPTER
17

"Good afternoon, West," the old duke said, pausing in the street. Then he added, with twinkling eyes, "and heartfelt congratulations. I heard all about it. You're a very lucky fellow, you know. Just ask any of us old married chaps. What you've done is enviable. My sincerest congratulations!"

"Thank you," Crispin said calmly, although he was puzzled. He scarcely knew the old duke. "I didn't know you knew the lady. But thank you."

"Hardly have to know her, my dear fellow. Heard of her, you see. Best of luck, although you hardly need it now, you lucky dog," the duke said, before he sauntered away.

Crispin wondered why the duke had stopped him. Tonight was the night he expected to take the polite world's congratulations. Tonight he was going to launch Dulcie into society at three different affairs. The duke hadn't seen her yet—at least not amid the splendor in which she was going to be presented. They hadn't gone to Charlotte's ball, and she had hardly shown her nose outside her bedcovers since then. He grinned to himself, remembering why.

But it was possible the duke had noted Dulcie's beauty on that terrible first night when Crispin had introduced her. This time he was going to do it right. Crispin smiled at the thought of the stir she would make in her new gown, on his arm willingly now, radiant in her obvious content. He sauntered on down Bond Street. But he didn't go far before he was stopped again.

"My dear Lord West," Lady Exeter said, stopping and giving him her hand. She turned to her companion. "Elizabeth, here is the Viscount West, the gentleman we were just speaking of. Crispin, this is my bosom companion, Elizabeth, Lady Dace."

Lady Dace's blue eyes grew wide as she curtsied to Crispin. "Congratulationth, my lord." she lisped. "We are all tho happy for you."

"Yes, a happy day, is it not? We hope to see more of you now, my dear sir," Lady Exeter said.

"And my wife, of course," Crispin said, bowing.

He was surprised when both ladies went into gales of laughter. Lady Exeter smacked him with her fan. "Oh, you!" she said. "Yes, it will be delightful seeing you. What a humorist! Good luck and congratulations, my dear," she said, and went off down the street arm in arm with her friend, their heads close as they whispered together.

Lady Exeter was a silly little woman who had more ancestors than sense. Crispin had never paid much attention to her or she to him. He was bemused by her sudden friendliness. But not for long.

"Oh, I say, Crispin, Crispin West! The very chap!" a gorgeously dressed gentleman called. Crispin stopped and bowed. He knew the fellow, but not his name. He'd seen him at Wrede's club.

"Just had to stop and wish you well. Well done! *Stunningly* done. *So* pleased for you, my dear fellow. Words cannot say. Congratulations."

Crispin thanked him, but was more puzzled than grateful,

and his befuddlement continued: by the time he got to the end of the street, he had been stopped several more times by bare acquaintances, all of whom were pleased to shake his hand and offer hearty congratulations. But they were *too* happy for a stranger's luck, too full of mirth even for congratulating a new groom. They mouthed pleasantries, but there was something unpleasant in their smiles. Something that bothered him.

Crispin turned on his heel and changed direction. He'd been on his way to the tailor, but he decided to go to Wrede's house instead; he needed to find out what was going on.

He was accosted every step of the way by people who wanted to offer him congratulations. He accepted them with increasingly gruffness. He walked faster, head down. He wished he could just relax and enjoy the day without hurrying, without this new niggling discomfort he felt. He wanted to saunter along the streets of London, enjoying the rare fine weather. He especially wanted to think about the night to come. He'd persuaded Dulcie to agree to wear her finest gown, an amazing thing made of silk and pearls, as white and pink as her own sweet body. He thought of that body, and a slow sensuous smile grew on his face.

"Thinking of me, are you?" said a sweet voice filled with mirth.

"Charlotte!" Crispin said, stopping abruptly.

She smiled at him radiantly, but all he could do was stare blankly down at her. She'd looked beautiful, of course: she wore butterscotch silk trimmed with fabulous lace, and her unpowdered hair gleamed like gold in the sunlight. But he noted her beauty as he would a work of art, as something lovely and well executed that had nothing to do with him or with his life. He felt absolutely no tenderness for her, he realized. In fact, he resented the way her presence suddenly shadowed his joy. He heaved an inward sigh. He dreaded what he had to do now, but knew he had to do it as soon as he could. Telling her the truth would be hard; that was why he'd avoided thinking about it. But now that they'd met, he couldn't put it off any longer. His task was made harder because she was looking at him with such a fond, glowing smile.

"Naughty," she purred, shaking her finger at him. "I expected you on my doorstep at dawn, not with pistols drawn, but with flowers. But you're going to make this reunion difficult, aren't you? We're going to begin again, are we? Ah, well, I suppose I deserve it. But wait!" she said gaily. "I think you're right. To redeem the future, we must recapture the past. Yes. I think it's incredibly romantic. Where did we go that first time?"

He stared at her blankly.

"Never mind all those stolen moments at balls and musicales," she said teasingly. "I mean, *after* you were given permission to pay your addresses. When was the first time we were permitted to be alone together?" She folded her arms and waited for him to answer, looking up at him with a pretense of impatience. It was hard to maintain, because she looked radiant and very merry. Even her dour faced old aunt stood by her side treating him to a rare vinegary smile.

"Charlotte," he said, "Whatever are you talking about?"

"Oh. This is going to be *very* difficult, I see. Come, Crispin. The jest is over. You missed my ball. Will you take me to the Burtons' tonight? It's as good a place as any to begin."

There were a dozen questions to ask, but all he could do was stand rooted to the spot and say dumbly, "What?"

"Your wedding," she said gaily, "has been invalidated. The marriage," she said triumphantly, "is over. Over! First the House of Commons, then the House of Lords forbade them. There are to be no more Fleet weddings. And Wrede and his friends have seen to the rest of it. Crispin, your marriage has been annulled—as though it never happened. You are rid of her. You're free."

He had lost both of his parents. He had lost his entire

fortune. Yet he'd never felt such sudden, cold, and numbing horror at a loss before. But how had Charlotte found out about the Fleet wedding? he wondered. Wrede! Of course, he thought with growing fury. And then he froze as another thought occurred to him.

"Oh, my dear . . ." She laughed, and then paused when she saw his expression. "Oh, my dear," she finally went on, observing his sudden pallor and feeling a chill along her spine, "can you say nothing?"

"Dulcie," he said numbly.

"His lordship is still abed," the butler said.

"His lordship will see me now," Crispin snarled.

The earl's butler wasn't supposed to admit visitors before noon, but there was no way he was going to refuse the viscount. Besides, the butler told himself as the tall nobleman shouldered him aside and strode into the house, there was no danger to his employer. Whatever murderous expressions they wore, gentlemen didn't slay each other at dawn, except with pistols or swords on a grassy field somewhere, not in each other's bedchambers. Or so he hoped as he saw Crispin charge up the stairs to the earl's bedroom.

"Wrede!" Crispin shouted as he burst into the room.

The earl's valet put down his razor, looking outraged. But his master took one look at his visitor and picked up the towel to remove the rest of the lather from his face. He waved a hand to dismiss his valet, but didn't look at him as he scurried out. He was staring at his unexpected guest.

Crispin's face was tight and set, his blue eyes blazing. His hands were in fists at his sides, and his whole lean body seemed to vibrate with tension.

"And a good morning to you, too," Wrede said calmly, but he wore a watchful frown.

"I met Charlotte, and half London as well, on the way here. She told me that *you* invalidated my marriage."

"Damn the woman!" Wrede said, flinging his towel down in disgust. "Never confide in a female; that has always been my rule. Still, yes, my friend, simply put, after all my travail on your behalf: yes. You are a single man again."

Crispin stood still and stared at him. For once, his friend couldn't read his expression.

"Hardwicke finally pushed through his Marriage Act," Wrede continued. "It needs only that the king sign it and a date of enactment be set. It will be more difficult to wed in England in the future. That means no more spontaneous weddings. No more mad elopements. More to the point, no more pledges made in drink and rued in the morning. The banns must be posted first. There will be a wait of weeks . . . unless one is a nobleman with friends in the right places, of course. But that's always the way, isn't it? At least the drunken nobility will be protected from the depredations of commoners. And the merchants will be saved, too. Paupers will have to find other ways to escape debt. There's more to it, but what's the point of laboring over the details? I'm no politician and neither are you.

"But as for you, my good fellow! I found one crack in the wall and pushed until it all came tumbling down. Only see what I have done: Harry Meech has already closed his marriage shop. Dear Dr. Featherstone has a congregation in Bedlam now. The marriage register he scrawled in has been . . . misplaced. In the Thames, I believe, or so Harry said. And so any paper the girl's father has is only that now—*paper,* nothing more. Give her a sum of money for old time's sake and for any services rendered. Then send her on her merry way. The farce of a marriage is over, my friend. Entirely. Come, what have you to say to that?"

Crispin said nothing. He tightened his fist and sent it crashing into Wrede's face. The earl stumbled and fell. He lay on the floor, staggered by more than the blow.

"Damn you for a fool!" Crispin snarled. "Get up so I can kill you."

"You wanted to be free," Wrede said in amazement.

"Once, yes—but now . . . My God, this will kill Dulcie," Crispin muttered, his eyes wild. "Why didn't you ask me—tell me, first?" he raged at the earl. "Why was I the last to know? My God, Wrede, why did you have to tell all London? Are you a washerwoman now, so full of gossip that you tell the world and its uncle all your personal business?"

Wrede struggled to his feet, touched his lip, and found blood on his hand. He drew himself up to his full height. "I did what I promised, Crispin—no more, no less, whatever you think now, after she's spent time in your arms," he said coldly. "How was I to know she had beguiled you? You were on fire to be rid of her. How did she put out that fire—by starting another in your bed?"

"Enough!" Crispin said tersely. "Don't say another word about Dulcie. You're not worthy to discuss her. What you've done is bad enough. Don't make it worse. Let me remember you for better things and better days. Because I *will* have satisfaction, Wrede."

"I see," Wrede said with glacial calm. "I take it, then, that the blow you delivered was in lieu of slapping me with a glove?"

Crispin nodded. He was beyond furious and seemed to see Wrede's cold, contemptuous expression through a fine red mist. What Wrede had done was too terrible for him to fully comprehend yet. Only years of training kept him from hitting the earl again.

"I suppose your second will contact mine?" Wrede drawled. "I use Bledsoe. He's a fool, but he's honest. The usual then? Swords at dawn? Tomorrow, I suppose?"

"I don't need a second," Crispin said. "I want satisfaction. You have the choice, of course, but I would prefer pistols. And not at dawn," he said, trying to free his mind of fury so he could plan. "I'd prefer to meet at dusk tomorrow. I have things that need to be done—or rather, undone. It will take me at least until dusk to fix what you've done. But you're the challenged, so it's your choice."

"Pistols, then," Wrede said with nonchalance, but his eyes were troubled. "Dusk. Tomorrow. At the dueling oaks?"

"Done," Crispin said, turned on his heel, and was gone.

Crispin strode home. He refused to meet the eyes of passersby. But his expression was so thunderous no one stopped him this time. He thought furiously. He had a dozen things to do. One thing was foremost: he had to get home and be sure Dulcie didn't go out. She must not know of this until he undid it.

He picked up his pace until he was almost running, impelled by his surging thoughts. She was his wife. There was no going back now. She'd given herself and her love. He'd given his word; it was his bond. There was even a possibility they might have forged another bond between them by now. She had already suffered too much because of this odd marriage; he would not expose her to the gleeful spite of his world. When she met them again, he was determined that she would be his wife in every way—or his widow, he thought, remembering his appointment with Wrede.

She wasn't in the parlor or the sitting room. When he found her in their bedroom, he was filled with wild relief. And then great sorrow. He leaned against the doorjamb, catching his breath, watching her.

"Look! Isn't it perfect? Oh, Crispin, just see!" Dulcie turned for him, a perfect pirouette. "Have you ever seen such a gown? I know it's petty and doubtless vain and very foolish, but, oh, Crispin, I shall look so fine tonight. And you'll have to hand over those pearls now. But you won't be ashamed of me, I promise!"

He wasn't, but he closed his eyes as though he were in pain.

She was spectacularly lovely. Her new gown was a confection; he was half convinced it was made of spun sugar and sparkling sugar dust. It was white shot with pink flowers and tiny sparkling gems. Wide in the skirt, low at the breast, it made her skin pink and her eyes bright. She looked as dainty as a pampered girl-child and as wildly tempting as a woman. He'd never seen anything like her in it.

"Crispin? Crispin?" she asked, as she stopped dancing in place. "Don't you like it? Oh, what's the matter?"

He couldn't tell her. Not now. Not yet. Their marriage was too newly settled for him to tell her that she was, as of this moment, no longer his wife. When he'd remedied that, he'd tell her. *If* he was there to tell her, he thought, closing his eyes again as he was struck by the enormity of the folly of letting his rage rule him. But what Wrede had done—especially what he'd said about Dulcie—had hit Crispin like lightning, blasting away his good sense. Now he had to live with it, or find a way to die with it.

But, most important, he had to keep her safe from his folly as well as Wrede's. He knew, from his own experience, that a disaster in retrospect was only an interesting memory if it was set right again. It wasn't lying to keep her ignorant of danger. Not if it protected her from pain. No, he was decided. Whatever else happened, she wouldn't know about any of this until she could no longer be hurt by it.

In the matter of his duel . . . He wouldn't think of that. He had too much living to do in too little time to dwell on the possibility of death.

"Crispin, what's wrong?" Dulcie asked again.

He took her hand and kissed it. One lie, then, he thought. Surely she could someday forgive him one lie.

"I have a headache," he said. "I get them sometimes."

True enough, and untrue enough to buy him time. Hadn't she seduced him once in order to avoid a reality she wasn't ready for? Turnabout was fair play. But it was only noon now. With all his best efforts, and even with best results, it would only be evening when they were done. And once pleasured and sated—especially once sated—she would be ready for a night on his arm on the town. As he'd promised. She wouldn't be ready to lie in his arms, safe and away from the world in his bed, as he needed her to be.

"An indisposition," he said, "only that, but it aches like the devil."

"Mint tea," she said with determination. "Willow bark. Not Dr. Hart's powders. They'll upset your stomach, no matter what his medicine show says. Then you must lie down in a darkened room. We'll draw the curtains . . ."

"Play ministering angel later," he said gently. "I have things I must do now. I just wondered what your plans were for the day."

"Oh. Well, I certainly won't wear this gown all day. I just had to see what it looked like when I was alone, without Annie telling me I look like an angel, and that sort of rot. But I do, don't I?" she asked, giggling. "Heavens, what a gown!"

"Pulling compliments out of me, are you? You don't have to. I've never seen anything to equal you. And it's not just the gown. But you're not going out today, are you?"

"No," she said, puzzled. "Do you want me to?"

"No, actually I want you to stay home," he said with relief. "I want you to burst on the scene like a comet tonight. Surprise them all. Dazzle them. I've been thinking about it. If you go out today, you'll take some of the surprise from it. Please do this for me, Dulcie. Remain unseen until this evening."

First, Crispin scrawled some hasty notes and dispatched them. Then, after ordering his butler to admit no one until he returned, he went looking for Willie. He found him moping around the stable, looking disconsolate, kicking the ground as though he himself were a testy colt. When he saw Crispin, he didn't look much happier.

"Willie," Crispin said, calling him aside as his horse was being saddled, "here's a chore for you: keep an eye on my lady. I don't want her leaving the house today. If you see that she's about to, for any reason, remind her of my wishes, will you?"

"Yeah," Willie said, looking moodier than ever.

"The devil," Crispin said, and bit off another curse when he saw the boy's face. "Look you, lad, I haven't time to chat. Is there a problem? Something I can tend to immediately? Otherwise, we'll speak later. I've got to be halfway cross London and back by evening."

"Nah. Nothing you could do nothing for, leastways," Willie said with barest civility.

"So be it," Crispin muttered. He mounted his horse and rode off, leaving Willie to stare after him, frowning.

Crispin rode until he saw the high gates to the massive building ahead of him. Then he swung down from his horse, tossed a waiting boy a penny, and strode up to the gate. His title was his admittance fee.

He was sorry to leave the sunshine and enter the building. The furnishings were old and good, but the huge entry hall was dark and malodorous, and the noise was indescribable. Crispin had heard something like it once, when he'd toured the exotic menagerie at the Tower. But there had been more light there, and confined and cramped as the animals had been, they'd smelled fresher. The noise they'd made had sounded better, too. He wondered, not for the first time, why this place was so popular with the upper classes.

It wasn't long before a thin, pock-faced man in a yellowed wig joined him, bowing and rubbing his hands together, the picture of a concerned host.

"My lord," the man said, bowing low. "Welcome. Come right in. How can we at His Majesty's Royal Bethlehem Hospital assist you today? We've a group visiting even now. You may join them if you wish. Lord Stockwell and his party. No? Well, then, perhaps you'd care for a private viewing? Lord Stockwell's party has ladies in it, and so perhaps you'd care for a viewing of the sort not usually offered to them?" He winked, but a loud wail from nearby made his shoulders jerk, and the wink became more of a twitch.

"Mr. Greaves," Crispin said, "I'm here on business. I've

come to see a new inmate. His name is Dr. Featherstone. He's an elderly man, a vicar—or was, until recently."

"I know him," Mr. Greaves said, flapping his hands in dismay, "but surely you don't want to see him! A disagreeable old fellow. Moody and pathetic, really. No sport to him at all, my dear sir, I promise you."

"He's the man I've come to see," Crispin said, opening his purse.

"Ah! A relative?" Mr. Greaves said with interest, licking his thin lips as Crispin counted out coins for him. "I thought he had none. The party who brought him here said he was a charity case."

"Dr. Featherstone is—was—a friend," Crispin said.

"Ah. Well, then, my dear Lord West. Certain arrangements can be made. Our inmates can be made quite comfortable. Had I but known the vicar had such a friend, he would have had different accommodations, I assure you."

"Understood," Crispin said. "I wish to see him. Now."

"Certainly, certainly," Mr. Greaves said nervously, "but pray understand he is a new arrival. Such fellows are often moody. They complain a great deal. One mustn't take what they say too much to heart."

"Understood," Crispin said impatiently. "Now?"

He was led through the cavernous hall and down fetid corridors. The smell and the noises were worse here.

The old man was in a huge cell with dozens of other mad men and women. When they caught sight of Mr. Greaves the cell seemed to roil with their agitation. Some shook their fists, some shouted, some bowed and curtsied, and some began to sing.

"Dr. Featherstone," Mr. Greaves called. "A visitor, my dear sir. Is he aware of such things?" he asked a burly man who stood guard nearby.

"He don't say much, usually," the man replied. "Sometimes, when the spirit moves him, he preaches. They likes it," he added, jerking a thumb to the other inmates. "His sermons ain't bad, really."

"Doctor," Crispin said, as he saw the old man shuffle toward the bars and squint at him, "Dr. Featherstone. Do you remember me?"

The old man peered at him. His scant white hair stood on end, as if he'd just risen from his bed, although there was nothing but straw on the floor to sleep on. He moved like an ancient tortoise, and there was not much more reaction in his old, dimmed eyes. But then he began to grin.

"My boy! Fancy meeting you here," he said. "You bring such happy memories. I wonder, have you brought anything else? They don't allow me much gin here. I cannot afford it, you see. I, of all people, should have known better, but I began to drink because it helped me forget the loss of my memory." He chuckled. "Amusing, isn't it? In time, of course, it did the reverse. Or so I think. How am I to know? I am a madman, am I not? But I have my good and my bad days. Today is a good one, because I see you. How are you, my dear Lord West?" Dr. Featherstone asked. "And how is your lovely wife, Lady Dulcie?"

It was evening when Crispin finally returned to his own house. Half a battle won was still no victory. He had a great deal of work yet to do tomorrow. And tonight. He sighed and paused at the foot of the stair, looking like a man with a pack of woe. Then he tugged his coat down, smoothed a hand over his hair, and went upstairs to his wife.

His heart sank when he saw her. She had her fabulous gown on again. He'd never seen anything so lovely—white and pink and flowing like some exotic butterfly. She was a fabulously beautiful woman. He crossed the room slowly, took her hand in his, and bowed.

"My lady," he said, and kissed her hand.

And she *was* his lady, he thought with pride, as he stepped back and stared at her. "You are beyond beautiful," he said, and sighed again, because he couldn't show the world what she looked like tonight.

"Why so sad, then?" she asked. She was nervous, fragile in her delight. She was so pleased with how she looked that she was afraid to move, lest she destroy some of the wonder of it. She had the sense of being a spectator at the same time she was a vision, she was so unaccustomed to looking as she did. Every time she caught sight of herself in the glass she was astonished. But Crispin looked sad, and that caught at her heart.

"Is anything the matter?" she asked fearfully, wondering if she was entirely wrong about how she looked.

"Nothing—only that my head still aches. I was mad to ride out. I felt every step the horse took like a blow to my head. But you look lovely. Wait for me. I'll dress. I won't be long," he said, wincing as if he felt a spasm of pain as he stepped back.

"Oh, no!" she cried, as he knew she would. "Not if you're ill. There will be other nights," she said bravely.

Never such a night as this, he thought, as he devoured the sight of her. He didn't believe she could ever look so lovely again, because he'd never seen a woman look so beautiful. Now the pain on his face was real. He hated what he was doing, but he didn't know what else to do.

"No, Crispin, truly," she pleaded. "What pleasure would there be in it for me if you were sick? Go. Take off your clothes and then come back and lie down. I'll take this dress off and order dinner for us. I'll fix a posset too. It will make you better in no time."

"You'll do anything to get me out of my clothes," he said with a half laugh, "Are you sure? I know how much you wanted to go . . ."

"But I didn't," she said, smiling. "The ball was your idea. Remember? I'm relieved, actually. Truly." And since that was half true, she sounded sincere.

"I'll make it up to you," he promised. "Thank you," he

said, and hurried from the room before the truth showed on his face.

She fed him a light dinner and made so much of him that he felt worse than ever.

"Better?" she asked, hours later, when they sat in their high bed and the last of their dinner dishes had been taken out.

He closed the book he'd been pretending to read. "Much, actually," he said. "Very much." He laid the book down and looked at her. Her face was scrubbed clean and shiny, and she wore a night chemise, tied at her neck. He remembered how she'd looked earlier and how she looked without any gown at all. He nudged the ties apart with one finger. "Much, much better," he said, and kissed the rapidly beating pulse at the base of her throat.

He felt how her breath caught. He took her lips, and then her body into his arms. They made love slowly. She was careful with him because she wondered if his head still ached. He was exquisitely gentle with her because his heart ached each time he remembered how he was deceiving her. It seemed to him that he didn't deserve such pleasure. It seemed to her that he needed her desperately, and her pleasure knew no limits. They made love in total silence. He was afraid to speak his true mind, and she was silent because the pleasure she felt was too intense for words. She was afraid she might speak of love. She never forgot, even at the height of her pleasure, that he had never spoken a word of love to her, though she couldn't have wanted a better lover.

When they were done, they lay silent in each other's arms, listening to the fire grumble and sigh.

"Dulcie?" Crispin said quietly. "Thank you. I don't deserve you. I shall try to, though."

She smiled, and then, vastly content, she slept.

He waited until her breathing slowed and steadied. Then he tucked the coverlets around her, bulking them high at her side, where he had been. He rose from the bed, pulled on a nightshirt, and left her. He went down to his study and closed the door. He had many things to do before dusk tomorrow. But two things had to be done immediately. He wrote a long, detailed letter of instructions to his lawyers and passed hours composing a shorter one to Dulcie. Then he scrawled her another note—only one brief line. That was the one he took back upstairs with him.

He approached their bed just before dawn so he could see how she looked in the rising light, and so she couldn't see what showed plain in his eyes: it was nothing less than his heart.

She woke to find a note from him on his pillow.

"Wait for me," was all it said.

She rose and dressed, wondering what it meant and where he was. He didn't return all morning, and she fretted at being alone and uninformed. She paced, and kept peering out the window, and was pleased when she heard a commotion at the door. A visitor was arguing with the butler, obviously outraged at being turned away. By now Dulcie was so eager for distraction that she went straight to the door to oblige Lady Charlotte.

CHAPTER

18

"You? Still here?" the lady asked in astonishment.

Dulcie took a step back. She'd ordered an unhappy, reluctant Stroud to let the lady and her chaperon in. She'd been about to ask them into her sitting room, maybe even offer them some refreshment the way she was sure a real lady would. But now she could only stand at the door and stare—and try to defend herself in as ladylike a manner as she could. Not for the first time that day, she wished Crispin would come back quickly.

"Why, yes," she said as haughtily as she was able. "This is my home, after all."

"Oh, my," Lady Charlotte said, "oh, my, my. She doesn't know," she said to her stern-faced companion. "Or perhaps she does. Perhaps Crispin has decided to keep her on, in another position. Or she thinks he will. Oh, how I'll make merry with him about this—for *years.*"

"Are you sure you still want him?" the older woman asked with a sniff.

"No wonder you never wed," Charlotte told her. "I'm more realistic than you, dear aunt. No man is perfect.

Crispin is more nearly so than some others. I'll have him. And I'll keep him in line, too, see if I don't."

They spoke as if she weren't there at all, Dulcie thought in confusion. But she didn't try to understand more. She was afraid to because of her temper as well as because of what the lady was saying. She only knew that whatever they were up to, she had to get them out. And do it in a way that wouldn't anger or distress Crispin.

"My husband is not at home now. I don't know when he'll return," Dulcie said. "Would you like to leave a message for him?"

"Your husband is not at home or abroad," Lady Charlotte told Dulcie, looking her up and down. "Your husband is no more, in any case."

"Crispin's been hurt?" Dulcie gasped, growing white.

"No. The viscount is fine. But he is not your husband anymore—if he ever was," Charlotte said.

Dulcie stared at her.

"Watch yourself," Charlotte's aunt cautioned her niece, clutching her arm and dragging her back a step from Dulcie. "That sort go for your eyes with their fingernails."

"How can you say such things? What are you talking about?" Dulcie asked in bewilderment.

Charlotte studied her unblinkingly. The girl was young and lovely. Something twisted in Charlotte's own heart when she saw Dulcie's confusion and distress. The girl, however young, was an impediment to her desires. Crispin had left her standing in the street yesterday, stalking away from her without a backward look. She refused to believe now what she had thought then. Better to believe the girl a witch than even for a moment to consider that, given a free choice, Crispin had, all on his own, preferred her. That would be unendurable.

Charlotte had come like an avenging angel today. But now, oddly, she found no joy in her errand. Still, she would say what she must, and believe what she had to. She had one more card; she would play it. She had never lost any prize she'd set her heart on. She would not consider losing now.

"Don't you read the newspapers? Oh. I suppose you can't." Charlotte shrugged. "Well, if you could, you'd see that Lord Hardwicke's act has passed the House of Lords. That means nothing to you, I know. But there are to be no more Fleet weddings. You may still think it means nothing, because you've already snared Crispin. But you are wrong. Whatever form of marriage you entered into, it's not valid now. Records of the event have been destroyed, the wretched minister who did the deed is in a madhouse, and all his works have been repudiated. You are now exactly what you were before you met the viscount—only a bit richer for your labors in his bed, I see," she added, staring at Dulcie's gown.

"I don't believe you," Dulcie said, but she began to shake. "Crispin would have told me," she said, as if to herself.

"Would he have? I would not, were I he. The fighting, the reproaches, the threats. Gentlemen will do anything to avoid a scene," Lady Charlotte's aunt said wisely, nodding at her niece.

Dulcie was desperate to discount the wild story. They were only trying to hurt her, she knew that. She had to end this encounter. She thought feverishly, seeking a way out. "Ah!" she said suddenly. "But how could he have known?" she asked triumphantly. "We've only been in London two days!"

"He's known for exactly that long, at least, because I told him myself," Charlotte said, "just yesterday."

Dulcie tried to put her whirling thoughts in order. Something did not fit. When she realized what it was, she caught her breath. "But—but how did you know it was a . . . a Fleet wedding?" Dulcie asked in a shocked whisper.

Lady Charlotte forced a smile. This was the reason she had come. She would skirt the issue and hint at the truth, and if nothing else happened, at least maybe the girl would hurt as much as she did now. "How do you think I knew, my dear? Crispin told me he wanted me to wait for him, but couldn't ask it of me. He didn't know if he could win his freedom. But now he has. And so I am here. I only wonder," she said, her head to one side, "why *you* still are."

Dulcie didn't fly at her eyes or make a scene. She simply slammed the door shut in the lady's face.

Then she told an astounded Stroud not to admit any more visitors, and went to her room, holding her head high, but hardly aware of where she was going. It couldn't be true, she assured herself. But of course she knew it could be.

Who else could she ask if Charlotte's story was true? She knew no one of importance except Crispin and his friend Wrede. Crispin wasn't here. And she had never trusted the earl. Jerome Snode might know, and Harry Meech certainly would, but she didn't dare seek them out. She would wait for Crispin. He'd left a note asking her to do that, after all. But why had he left it, and where had he gone? She read the note over and over, as though there were some secret message in the three blunt words. She wouldn't leave until she spoke with him.

She wanted very badly to believe in him, to trust him. But trust had never been a successful course of action for her. Life had taught her how to deal with promises: she had to hope for the best and be prepared for the worst. She knew that Crispin would be hurt if he knew what she was thinking. She couldn't afford to beg or weep or argue if he admitted that what Lady Charlotte said was so. Even if she had lost everything else, she would at least have to maintain her pride, or she would have nothing at all. If it was true, she would leave. Instantly.

But where could she go? She reviewed her choices. She was a poor girl with few prospects—fewer, if Crispin had left her with child as well as a broken heart. She could go to her mother, she supposed. But she wouldn't. The thought of her rejection was almost as terrible as the one she faced now. And her father was gone . . .

Dulcie stopped wringing her hands. She snatched up a

chair and pushed it close to her tall wardrobe. She got up on the chair, reached back as far as she could into the top shelf of the wardrobe, and took her purse from its hiding place. Then she sat on the bed and carefully counted out her hoard of coins. When she'd married Crispin she'd thought it a considerable sum. Now she knew how little it was. Still, it was enough to buy her a room for a month with enough left over to buy food during that time. But she didn't know how she could get on beyond that month.

She was alone in a world that wasn't generous to women unless they had a family or a trade. She poured her coins back into the purse and drew in a deep breath. She needed more money—enough to journey to the New World, just as her father had done.

She knew who she had to speak with. She sent word for him.

"You wanted me?" Willie asked when she opened her door to him. His eyes roved her room, assessing everything in it.

"Come in, close the door," Dulcie said. "I need a favor of you, Willie, for old times' sake."

"Yeah?" the boy asked casually, hands in his pockets as he leaned against the back of her door. But his indigo eyes were intent.

"I need money," she said. "I need it kept secret, and I need it today. I've these things," she said, waving a hand toward the articles she'd placed on a small table. "They're not much, but they should bring something. The watch was Father's. He left it for me, with his letter. The pin was his mother's. The cameo and necklace were given to me by my mother. And the ring," she said, after she swallowed hard, "was given to me when I reached sixteen. I know you have connections; I'd like you to use them for me. I'll pay your usual percentage. But I need this done quickly. Get me the best price, will you?"

"Oh, Lor'. You know, then, do you?" he said sadly.

She froze. *"You* knew?" she managed to say.

He nodded as he fingered the jewelry. He kept his head down as though he were evaluating it as he spoke. But he only pushed the pieces around aimlessly as he did. "Yeah. Well," he said, "it's all everyone's talking about. When I heard, I wondered about you and the viscount right off. So I listened here and there and asked around a bit. Harry's plain wild. Had to shut down his wedding game. That ain't bad—fact is, it's kind of funny. But it's too bad about poor old Featherhead. He was as crazy as a loon, but he didn't hurt nobody, did he? Bedlam's a hard place—worse'n the Fleet, believe me. Even Newgate's better. They top you there, sure: drop you into air and let you kick to glory, but then you're done with it. Bedlam's forever."

"And me?" Dulcie asked, holding her breath.

"Well," Willie said, keeping his eyes averted as he began stuffing the jewelry into his pocket, "this lot ain't much, considering the dirt they done you. I say we go into his lordship's rooms and get some real jewelry. He won't miss it, and you're sure going to need it."

She never knew a breath could hurt, but it seemed as though the air was on fire and she couldn't draw enough into her lungs. When she did, she shook her head and blinked back tears. No time for that, she told herself harshly, no time right now.

"No," she told Willie, "what is his is his. I want none of it. Just get me as much as you can for that lot, please."

He nodded. His thin shoulders drooped, but he knew the way of the world. "So. What are you going to do?" he asked.

"Go to the Colonies. There's a need for women there. I can start anew."

"Lor'," Willie said, "you'll need more money than this for your passage!"

"Get as much as you can," she said again. "I'll find a way to get more. But hurry. I want to leave here by nightfall."

"If you wasn't so honest, I'd try to talk you into staying

here and getting the money out of him," Willie said. "Gents pay up handsome for their pleasure, y'know. But it wouldn't do any good to ask you, would it?"

"No," she said simply.

"Yeah, thought not. Good for you," Willie said suddenly. "Listen. I got some money put aside. I know you're good for it . . . Nah, don't argue with me yet. We'll see what I get for these. But don't you worry none: one way or another, we'll get you on that ship soon as you want. But it's funny," he said wistfully, pausing at the door, all the sadness of the world on his young face, "I wouldn't have thought it of him, would you?"

"No," she said quietly, "no."

When Willie left, she packed her few things. Just to be sure—in case—she told herself. It might not be true. But it sounded possible enough. In any case, it wouldn't hurt to be prepared. If she was wrong, she would rejoice, and he would never need to know about her fears. If she was right . . . She packed her old things, from her life before Crispin: one gown, a cloak, and a few trinkets. She left the rest, everything he'd bought for her. She didn't want to feel like a thief. If he'd deceived her, she had to show herself she was better than he was. But she'd never met anyone better than he was. She fought back tears and waited for him.

Dulcie paced the afternoon away, but Crispin didn't return, and neither did Willie. She was alone with her doubt and fear. She went over every syllable she'd ever heard Crispin utter, wondering if she had missed something. She couldn't believe he would deceive her, and yet she'd never really believed he could love her. He'd never said he did: with all they'd done, he had never said a word of love to her. He'd married her for money and had stayed married because he saw no way out. He had never lied about that. Now he was apparently free of the marriage, but he hadn't told her about it. Perhaps this was his revenge for the way she had been forced upon him.

That possibility was too monstrous to contemplate. Instead she thought about him, his smile, his eyes, his beautiful starry eyelashes. She remembered his touch, the ways he loved to have her to touch him, the strength in his shoulders, the long, clean-limbed grace of his powerful body. She remembered the exact timbre of his voice. It was as if she grieved for him. She hadn't lost him yet, but she was preparing herself for that loss. And through it all she realized that if he had lied to her, the worst part was not that she would lose him, it was that she would lose the love she had for him, which was the best thing she'd ever had. Finally, then, she wept.

"My lady," Stroud said as he came into the sitting room, "beg pardon."

She dashed away her tears with one hand and pretended she was just shading her eyes, as though the late afternoon light bothered her. Stroud's voice had sounded gentle and concerned. That alarmed her.

"The servants wish a word with you in the kitchens, my lady," he said, "but if you'd rather attend to it later . . . ?"

Dulcie hesitated. The servants *never* wanted a word with her in the kitchens, or anywhere else. Crispin's household ran like clockwork. Something was afoot. Maybe they planned to put a bag over her head and carry her away so as to save Crispin the trouble, she thought wearily. If so, so be it. She was sick of inactivity.

"I'll go now," she said.

A babble of voices stopped abruptly when she stepped into the hot, crowded kitchen. Three grooms, all the housemaids, two footmen, and the housekeeper gazed at her hopefully. They looked anxious. Dulcie braced herself.

"It's our Willie," the cook said grimly. "He needs help."

Then they all began talking at once.

"Please," Dulcie said, beginning to understand.

"One at a time. Here," she told the head groom, "you tell me again, and this time speak slowly, please."

"Certainly, mum. See, I got the word from a man who knew the lad when he was in the Fleet. Seems our Willie was trying to flog—that is, sell—some jewelry. He said Harry Meech—him who Willie used to work for—closed all doors to the lad. So Willie had to go far afield to be rid of the jewels. Don't know how he got them, and it may be that it wasn't entire the right way, my lady, I ain't going to lie about that. But Willie ain't no common thief. I'd stake my name on that."

There was a murmur of agreement among the servants as the groom went on. "The trouble's in it that someone peached on the boy. He was nabbed toot sweet, with the goods hot in his hands. That's done it for him."

"Oh, but Willie knows the Fleet like the back of his hand," Dulcie said, feeling relieved. "He may be uncomfortable there, but when his lordship returns, I'm sure he can set things right again."

"No one can find his lordship," the groom persisted, "and Willie ain't in the Fleet, mum. He's in Newgate, and that's a whole different kettle of fish. He's there because the goods was worth more than thirty shillings. So now it's the drop for the lad—I mean theft is a hanging offense. Begging your pardon, but there's more. See, someone there recognized Willie and got word out. Seems Willie ain't himself since he got took there."

Dulcie wrinkled her brow.

"His brother was in Newgate, my lady," the groom explained urgently. "Last place he ever was, in fact. Y'see?"

She did, all too well.

"Well, and so we thought if you could give Winston here"—he pointed to the tallest footman—"some money, he could get it to a jailer and we could at least make the poor lad more comfortable until his lordship returns. Give him some hope, like. If there is any," he said sadly.

"There is," Dulcie said decisively. "There's more than hope. Come with me, Winston. Stroud, fetch me a carriage."

"Oh, no, my lady!" Stroud said in horror, as they all gaped at her. "A lady shouldn't go near Newgate!"

"Thank you for your concern, but get me a carriage," Dulcie said. "Annie, fetch my cloak, you're coming with me."

Her mind was made up, and her topaz eyes blazed with resolution. There was a limit to her patience; she was willing to wait forever to learn her own fate, but she would not let Willie wait another minute.

She had little money, and she had no name, if Lady Charlotte was to be believed, and Willie was being held at the king's convenience, preparatory to being hanged for trying to sell her jewelry. Crispin would know what to do, but Crispin wasn't there. He owed her nothing now, anyway. She had her own debts; she would try to pay them. This was probably the last thing she would ever do as a viscountess, but she *would* save Willie. If her father had left her nothing else when he'd deserted her, he'd at least bequeathed her a quick wit and a sharp tongue. At least she hoped he had. She would soon find out.

The Fleet prison had been a lively place. It was a small walled city within the city, squalid and noisy but always bustling. It was even possible sometimes to forget it was a prison—if you could forget the simple fact that some of the people within were not allowed to go out. Newgate Prison was, as the groom had said, a different kettle of fish. She could feel it in the air as she approached the place. The Fleet was for debtors. While debt was a shameful thing, and shameful things could be done to those who incurred it, still there was always a way out of debt for those clever enough to find it. The only way out for many in Newgate was death.

Death came as a result of the prisoners' crimes: murder, arson, treason, or any one of two hundred different degrees of theft and forgery, from counterfeiting a bank check to stealing a shoe buckle. The Fleet prison bustled with a parade of prisoners and visitors going about their daily lives. The condemned at Newgate were paraded across London to Tyburn to be hanged in groups of two to two dozen at a time, according to their crime or occupation. There was commerce in the yards at the Fleet, but there was a press yard at Newgate, where the condemned could have their lives squeezed out of them. Sometimes death came as a result of Newgate itself: jail fever was common and often cheated the hangman. Weddings had been performed at the Fleet, but Newgate was the place for funerals. Dulcie shivered as she stepped out of the carriage.

She raised her chin, put a handkerchief to her nose, and with her maid at her side and her footman to knock at the door, Dulcie prepared to enter Newgate as the haughty Viscountess West before they could discover she was only what she'd always been: poor Dulcie Blessing, pauper and pawn.

"You can't see the judge now!" the jailer said. "Old Bailey don't sit till tomorrow. Not for the king 'isself, my lady. Don't matter if you claim the lad ain't done it. That's for the judge to say, and 'e don't sit till tomorrow."

"Then tell the warden I wish to speak with him," Dulcie said.

"I can't just up and see the warden, beggin' your pardon, my lady. 'E don't chat wi' the likes of me," the jailer said with a smile that showed each missing tooth. "Nah. I sees 'im at Tyburn Fair when I brings the unfortunate there to be topped. That's it. Fancy me, goin' for a chat wi' 'im," he said. "No, sorry. Ain't possible, my lady. But that's not saying other things ain't," he added hopefully. "The lad could be moved to a nicer cell. I could get 'im good grub, a fine mattress, fresh straw. 'E can be made comfortable as pie—for a consideration, understand. But that's all. Fancy me chatting wi' 'is 'onor," he marveled again.

She supposed she had enough money to make Willie more comfortable for the night. But that wasn't what she'd come for. She glanced around and then down at her trembling hands. There was no way anyone could be comfortable here, especially not Willie. There had to be something she could do, and she wouldn't leave until she'd done it. She tightened her hands to fists around her handkerchief and steadied herself as she concentrated.

She remembered how Crispin sounded when he was mad at her. She pictured Wrede when he was annoyed with her. She remembered exactly how Lady Charlotte had looked at her.

"I should like to see Willie Grab—*now*," she commanded.

"Oh. Certainly, my lady," the jailer said, flinching, then bowing low.

He led her down reeking corridors. After one glance to the side to see who had called out in such despair, she looked nowhere but in front of her. That was just as well, because she had to watch her step carefully as he led her down what seemed like an endless flight of stairs.

The jailer kept talking as he went. "Well, but if 'e'd said a word, we'da kept 'im 'igher," he grumbled. "For two shillings 'e coulda had a fine bed. But not 'im. Din't say nothin', not a word. Just shaking like a leaf, 'e was. Them that brought 'im in knew 'is name. The lad never said a word. Is 'e a dummy, my lady? A mute?"

"No," Dulcie said in sorrow, taking her handkerchief from over her nose and mouth so he could hear her. "No, he is not."

The cell was huge, but there were too many prisoners in it to single out just one of them. Still, she was grateful that the few torches didn't lighten the gloom enough for her to see them more clearly. The floor was base stone. There was nothing for the prisoners' comfort on it except some rotting straw. The stench of humanity, human waste, and gin, the omnipresent solace of the poor, was powerful. But not so strong as the stink of fear. The place was as dank as a cave, because they were far beneath London now, and these poor creatures, Dulcie realized, were not far from being put beneath the ground permanently.

"Willie! 'Ere, where's the lad called Willie Grab?" the jailer called.

He and another jailer waded into the cell, pushing prisoners aside, swinging clubs to clear a path through them. Dulcie stood back with her footman by her side; her maid had been too overcome with fear to make this final journey. Dulcie didn't blame her and was only grateful that the footman's sense of duty had won over his obvious reluctance to come. They watched as the jailer picked some tattered thing up from the floor.

"This 'im?" the jailer asked. He left the cell and thrust a little boy at her.

"No," Dulcie said, eyeing the small, shivering boy with pity. "No, it is not— Wait! Willie?" she asked, fearfully. "Willie?"

She saw his thin shoulders hunch at hearing his name. She knelt and looked at the boy's averted head. There was no recognition in those indigo eyes. He was scrawny, white-faced, shuddering, but yes, this was Willie. Willie, with his swagger and bravado stripped from him. Willie, without his guile and wit. Willie, who was just, after all, a very little boy. She was the one who was kneeling. But it was Willie who had been brought to his knees.

"Oh, Willie," she said, and took him in her arms.

The footman moved to stop her, because the boy was filthy. But then he saw Willie's body convulse and Dulcie hug him tighter. He stepped back again.

"They're going to top me," Willie whispered, burrowing into the warmth of her embrace, his thin arms wrapped around her as though he were drowning. Her warmth delivered him from the terror that had gripped him, to a horror he could speak of at last. "They're going to take me to Tyburn and dangle me there. Oh, lady," he said, his voice shaking, "please don't let the surgeons get me. Please don't. I ain't got the money to pay for my burying. And them that don't are given to the doctors to be cut up. I'll go to the topping like a gent. I swear. But don't let them cut me up after, like they done to my poor Luke."

So now the poor ghost had a name. Dulcie drew the small

shuddering body closer. Crispin would know what to do, she thought, but Crispin had left her. She would do anything to save this boy. She tightened her grip on Willie and firmed her resolve. No matter what Crispin thought, she was not nothing.

"No," Dulcie promised fervently, "The surgeons won't touch you. I won't let that happen. You're coming home with me now, Willie. And so I vow."

The Fleet prison was a much gloomier place than Crispin remembered. The last time he was here he'd had Willie swaggering at his side, and the Fleet had seemed like a rollicking street fair. And when he'd seen Dulcie, it had become a magical place. Now that he was desperately racing against time, he saw that the Fleet, even with all its tumult and activity, was a dismal place where a man's time was never his own. And all the colorful people within it were only poor wretches trying to win their freedom. As he was.

He was told to wait in the room where he'd been married. The irony didn't escape him. He peered out the small window at the dying day, and murmured a curse as he paced. He had done much in a short time, but he had more to do, and there was little time left.

"He won't come, you know," a voice said.

Crispin's head snapped up.

Jerome Snode bowed. "Harry's terrified you'll kill him," he said calmly, "so he won't show his nose."

"Odd. There's money in it for him," Crispin said.

Jerome shrugged. "Well, but it's hardly worth his life."

"True, I threatened to kill him if I saw him again, and I am as good as my word . . . usually. But this time I need to buy something from him. Are you his emissary?"

"I could be," Jerome said.

"I want that marriage paper and the register it came from."

"Oh? Harry said the papers were at the bottom of the Thames," Jerome said with interest.

"So I heard. Then I remembered who I was dealing with," Crispin said wryly. "Meech wouldn't throw away the bones from his dinner plate if he thought he might find a use for them someday. He would never destroy that register or those papers. I know that. I want them. And I'll pay well."

"How well?" Jerome asked calmly, but his pale eyes glittered.

Crispin named a price.

Snode's eyebrows shot up, but he shook his head.

"I haven't time to haggle," Crispin said impatiently. "A hundred more, then, and that's my final price. It may be the best he'll ever get. I am to meet the earl of Wrede in an hour on a grassy field outside of London, with pistols drawn. You've heard of Wrede's prowess with pistols?"

"Done. The amount will do," Jerome said quickly. Crispin thought he heard a hastily suppressed gasp from somewhere in the gloom behind Snode.

"Done, then," Crispin said, pulling notes from his wallet and throwing them on a table. "The paper? The register?" he asked, reaching out a hand.

Jerome turned and disappeared into the gloom he'd come from. He returned in minutes, carrying the tattered register. He gave it to Crispin. Then he handed him a torn-out page.

And watched in astonishment as Crispin put the page back in its proper place and snapped the book closed over it.

"Done!" Crispin said with relief. A small smile lit his sternly handsome face. "I've undone all the mischief at last. Featherstone is free, you see. Who can say what drives a man mad? Whatever it is, influence can declare him sane, and so it has. He is again an ordained minister of God. That's only fair. He may be closer to God than the rest of us, anyway," he muttered. "He won't preach again, but at least he no longer resides in Bedlam. The bishop has found a retreat for him. And all his previous work is again made valid.

"Tell Harry I wouldn't have killed him this time," Crispin said with a wintery smile, "because he was innocent in this, at least. Dulcie Blessing is my wife, and so she will remain—

God willing—for as long as I continue to breathe. An unlikely Cupid, our Harry. But a very good one. You might suggest matchmaking to him as a new line of work, now that Parliament's closed down his old one. Tell him that instead of killing him for squirreling away this proof of my wedding, I'm tempted to shake his hand."

"Ah, but you see," Jerome said with a smile as he pocketed the money, "there's more. Harry thought you might be angry with him for something else. You know the lad that both you and he employed? Willie Grab? Well, he's in Newgate, awaiting the hangman. He's small, but he'll hang high enough. Harry peached on the lad, you see. Informed on him, for the theft of over thirty shillings' worth of jewelry, if you please, and you know what that means. He'll dangle—"

Jerome gasped as Crispin's hand shot out. Crispin grabbed him by the front of his coat and hauled him up so that he could glare into his terrified face.

"No, no," Jerome panted. "I had no part in it," he whined.

Crispin slowly released him.

"And Harry didn't invent the theft," Jerome babbled. "He just made sure the authorities knew of it."

"Well, then," Crispin said, staring at the shaking man, "you tell Harry he's lucky I haven't got the time to seek him out today, and that he had better pray that I don't have a tomorrow."

And tucking the book under his arm, he strode out. It seemed he had more work to do, but not the time to do it in, for he had an appointment at dusk, and the night was coming on fast.

CHAPTER
19

The mists of evening looked like those of morning to Crispin as the carriage halted beneath familiar tall oaks. The light was dying in the west, not rising in the east. It was an unusual time for a duel, but perhaps it was more fitting to face death as the day ended, he thought. He had met a man on this field once before, long ago, at the proper time, in the mists of dawn. Afterward, the sun had mounted in the sky, and he had been glad his foe would live to see the day. He had had his revenge: his enemy might never fence again, but he would live to regret his error. Crispin had been on fire for revenge then. Now he only wanted this to be over. And he didn't want to kill or hurt the man he'd called out.

He regretted having arranged the meeting, but he could not avoid it. He was a man of his word. The fact that the man was his best friend made no difference. Wrede had made no apology, and no mutual friend had tried to negotiate a peaceful solution. No. Crispin had issued the challenge and his honor had to be satisfied.

When he had dueled before, he hadn't thought much about the outcome; he'd been in too great a fury to prove himself. Besides, he'd been very young and had thought he would live forever. He wanted desperately to survive this meeting, but he didn't know if he would. He wasn't anxious now—he was numb with despair.

He could face his own death without flinching, but thinking of Dulcie made that prospect unendurable. He was being selfish, for he wasn't worried about her. She would do very well by herself. He had left explicit instructions with his lawyers to ensure her prosperity, in case his efforts today hadn't been successful. But they had been. He had reaffirmed the legality of the marriage. She was still his wife, and she would be his widow, if it came to that. As his sole heir she would be wealthy and titled, with all the influence and honor that came with it. He had seen to that. She was young and beautiful, and clever, too. His lawyers would advise her. And she would not be lonely for very long.

But she would never have his children. And he would miss her through eternity. That grieved him more than the thought of his death. That was why he'd raced through the day, never allowing himself to think beyond the urgency of his errands.

Worst of all was the thought that he had not allowed himself to consider until now: Dulcie would never know how much he loved her. At first he hadn't known it himself, and then he had denied it. And later he'd stupidly believed he had all the time in the world to tell her how he felt. "Wait for me"—those were the last words she'd heard from him. He had not even offered her a fitting farewell. He forced himself to stop thinking about her, so he could try to return to her.

As Crispin approached Wrede, he could see that the earl's long face was expressionless. He inclined his head to acknowledge Crispin's approach. He stood very still in his shirtsleeves. Crispin sketched a bow and removed his coat. A foppish fellow presented a case of matched dueling pistols. Wrede nodded to Crispin, who picked one. It felt right to his touch. But then, any of Wrede's pistols would; he had a magnificent collection of them. Crispin wasn't a bad shot, but the sword was his weapon. He stood, arms crossed, waiting for instructions.

"Let's get on with it," Wrede said impassively.

Strange, Crispin thought sadly as he took his place. It felt so odd to stand back to back with his friend, preparing to duel with him after they'd walked side by side all through their lives. And yet now he would not only walk away from his friend but maybe also from his life, and his love. He would *not* think of Dulcie, he told himself sternly as he stepped forward to count out his ten paces. He must think only of the moment, and not the whole bungle of his life.

At the count of ten, he turned. He saw that he was the one with his back to the setting sun. Wrede had to squint into the light to see him, the fool. Not that it made any difference. Crispin's finger curled on the trigger. He braced himself. There was only one thing he could do.

"Fire!" Wrede's second called, his voice cracking with excitement.

And two shots rang out.

When the smoke drifted clear, Crispin saw Wrede still standing tall. This was no surprise to him, since he'd fired his own pistol into the sky. He looked down at himself. He'd heard that men with mortal wounds sometimes felt nothing but shock at first. But his heart thundered on, and his shirt remained spotless.

"I imagine," Wrede commented as he strolled toward him, "that with a little better aim we might have brought down a pheasant apiece."

Wrede smiled as he took his pistol back from Crispin. He sighted down the barrel and weighed the weapon in his hand. Then he looked at Crispin. "Why?" he asked simply.

"Because you were right," Crispin said. "At least you thought you were. You believed you were doing me a favor. I never gave you any reason not to, damn my eyes. But I love her, Drum," he said, using his friend's old school name for the first time in years. "I really do. More than I thought possible. What I felt for Charlotte was nothing, compared to what I have with Dulcie. I realize that now. She's everything I need. She is so innocent in everything, and she's good to the bone, and good for me. When you destroyed my marriage to her, the hurt I felt for what she'd think unhinged me. For that I apologize. How could I have wanted to kill you for trying to be a friend? That's why I fired into the air. But why did *you* fire at the rising moon? I insulted you."

"Ah, well, I have a thick skin. And when you hit me, I realized that I had done you no favor. You're a temperate man, Crispin, whose rage is so much more violent because of it. I've never known you to be angry for no good reason. Then, too, I remembered that you always get what you want, and yet you were still very much married. I realized I'd botched it. How could I kill my friend for an injury I'd done to him? I never realized how deeply you cared for her.

"So, are you off to render your abject apologies to your wife?" Wrede asked, as he put on his coat.

"No. No need to. I never told her any of it."

"Really?" Wrede said, genuinely surprised. "What did you do? Lock her in the cellar? Drug her?"

"Neither," Crispin said with a reminiscent smile. "At any rate," he said quickly, as he saw Wrede grin too, "I can't go home just yet. Before I came here I had word that young Willie's been clapped up in Newgate. They want to pose him in the sheriff's picture frame. They say he stole some jewelry—enough to earn a hanging. His brother died of the same complaint at about Willie's age. I'd like to rush home to Dulcie now, but I know I couldn't rest easy with the boy in prison. He played Cupid for me, after all. I owe him something—a life, in fact. I'll have a word with the warden, lighten my purse, and take the rascal home. Why don't you come along?"

"You think she'll never know?" Wrede asked incredulously.

"Oh, she will. Tonight, in fact. I'll tell her. But a wrong that has already been righted is easy to tell, and easier to take."

"You're a wise man, Crispin," Wrede said as they walked back to the carriage together.

"The Fleet was a pleasure garden compared to this," Crispin said grimly as he paced the entry hall at Newgate Prison. "Poor lad. I'll have him out, but God help Harry when I have time to sort him out!"

"Doubtless Harry deserves your wrath for many reasons," Wrede agreed, "but aren't you forgetting something? Dreadful as the circumstances are, it is entirely possible that the boy stole the jewelry. It's probable, actually. After all, although he's young and possesses a bizarre charm, there *is* the little matter of his being a thief."

"A vice he may forgo, but not if he stays here," Crispin muttered.

"Well, yes, there is that," Wrede agreed, as he began to fidget. "What's keeping the man? He's politically ambitious enough to know better than to keep us waiting."

"My lords—" a portly man in a full wig exclaimed as he puffed into the room and dropped into a low bow. "Honored to have you here this evening. Most unexpected, though. We seldom get callers this late. Still, we are at your service. How may we help you?"

"As I told your man, we're here about the prisoner Willie Grab," Crispin said. "He's a foolish boy, but no thief, as I understand has been claimed. He's in my employ. We've come to see if we can secure his release. I'm sure if we discuss the matter," Crispin said as he extracted his wallet, "we can convince you that a mistake has been made. The case need never go to trial. We're prepared to make full restitution for the amount the boy is said to have stolen— along with adequate payment for the Crown's trouble in the matter, of course."

"Oh, my dear lords," the man said in consternation, "I should be only too happy to oblige you, but, you see, the lad is no longer with us."

"Released, already?" Crispin asked, grinning at Wrede.

"Ah. No, I am sorry to say," the man said, taking out his handkerchief and wiping his forehead, though the dank room was cool.

"Then where is he?" Crispin demanded.

"Alas," the man said hollowly, avoiding Crispin's eye, "he is . . . gone."

"Gone?" Crispin asked. "Gone?" he said as a meaning for the man's gloom occurred to him. "No," he said firmly, "not possible. I saw him this morning and heard of his arrest only this afternoon. Tyburn Fair was held three days ago. It will be at least another week until the next hangings. I doubt he's even seen the judge yet."

"I did not say he was hanged, though that is the law of the land for his offense. But the truth is that he is simply gone. I don't know how. None of the jailers know, they say. I wasn't here at the time. But there are fevers that kill swiftly, my lords," the man said with desperation, seeing the look in their eyes. "Difficulties with other prisoners can sometimes bring sudden death, as can injuries resulting from capture. And he was rather young and small. I don't even know if the lad's remains can be found now—so many prisoners, so little room, and such a demand from the good doctors. Crime is a great boon to education. The surgeons are busy with us here even when the hangman rests, you understand.

"If you wish, I'll conduct a thorough investigation, but I've little hope of finding an answer soon. I'm sorry, my lords. Had I but known . . . perhaps something might have been done—before, that is to say. But it is the Lord's will," he said piously.

The coach left Newgate and moved toward Crispin's house as slowly as a funeral carriage.

"A hundred boys are hanged every month, and though I often regretted that fact, I always did so over my coffee or after reading news of it," Wrede said, his usual humor gone from his voice. "And even then, I regretted the *need* for it, not the way of it. I never knew one of them before, you see."

"Damn, damn, damn," Crispin said, and put his head in his hands. "I don't know how Dulcie will take this news. She complained about Willie all the time, but she treated him like a younger brother. So did I, come to think of it. We made an odd little family. But so we were," he said softly.

When the carriage stopped, Wrede got out and hesitated. "Do you want me to come in?" he asked, unsure of himself for the first time since Crispin had known him.

"Now more than ever," Crispin said. "Dulcie will need company. Lord, *I* need company."

They mounted the steps to Crispin's house as though they were going to the scaffold themselves.

"Where is my lady?" Crispin asked the butler as he came into the hall.

"Oh, my lord, we'd hoped she was with you," Stroud said.

That was when Crispin noticed that the front hall was filled with staff. Footmen and maids peered at him from the corners of the great hall. Even the cook and his helpers stood by the stairs.

"What's happened?" Crispin asked, wondering if the servants had somehow discovered what had happened to Willie. It was a hard thing, and he had wanted to cushion the terrible news for Dulcie.

"Well, the mistress, she heard young Willie had been apprehended by the law for a crime he hadn't done," Stroud said, as Crispin grimaced. "She went tearing out of here to right the wrong. The lad's a lively one and no mistake, my lord, but he's not evil," the butler explained, "and so say all of us."

"I know, I know," Crispin said impatiently. "Go on."

"Well, there it is, my lord. She went out, and she hasn't returned. It's been hours, my lord," he said anxiously, and Crispin looked around to see fright and worry on the many faces peering at him.

"She went alone?"

"Oh, never, my lord," the butler said in horror. "Young

Winston, he went with her, and so did her maid. When she didn't come back straightaway, I sent Trickle and Capstone running after. But they didn't find her."

"And where did she go?" Crispin asked, fearful of hearing the answer.

"To Newgate Prison, my lord," the butler said unhappily.

"But we just came from there." Crispin's face was ashen as he turned away blindly. "I'll find her," he told Wrede, "if I have to search all of London."

"Where could she have gone?" his friend asked.

"I don't know," Crispin muttered as he strode out the door again. "She must be grieving over Willie. She'll need someone to talk with. She hasn't heard from her damned father. She has only me." On the front step he turned and stared at Wrede, his eyes lucent and glowing with pain, "But I'm afraid she doesn't even know that *I* am her friend! Damn my black soul, Wrede, if she doesn't know that! But how could she know?" he asked furiously. "Even now, how could she know, when I never told her? I *have* to find her."

"Wait!" Wrede said, holding him by his arm. "Where will you go?"

Crispin shook him off impatiently. "I'll go to Harry and hold him up by his heels and shake the information out of him if I must. I'll scour her old haunts . . . Ah, God in heaven, I'll go to the docks first, and have them watch for her. I will find her. Maybe she's gone to seek her father. Maybe she's gone to seek something else . . . The news of Willie may have hurt her more than she could bear. Oh, my God," he looked at Wrede in sudden shock, his pale face haggard. "The news *you* spread . . . what if she heard *that?* I have to find her now. I must! Wrede," he continued wildly, "you don't understand. Till now, I don't think I did, either. When I lost my fortune, I thought I'd lost everything. But I didn't know what loss was then. You see, if I lose Dulcie, I shall have no need of a fortune, or even of life itself, because she has my heart. I love her."

And turning on his heel he strode off into the growing darkness, followed by his friend.

They returned in the dark, without speaking. And without Dulcie. Wrede knew his friend was returning home only because he had no place left to search.

"There's nothing else you can do," Wrede said, continuing to argue. "You've told everyone to send word of her to you. How can you get the news if you're not at home? You must stay here now—it's the only choice left to you."

Crispin nodded, but didn't speak. He was too exhausted and sick at heart to try. His face was drawn and shadowed. He had searched London from top to bottom, and had never before realized how low the bottom was, nor how near it was to the top. He'd been among the dead and dying, in soul and body. He'd hung between hope and despair too many times this night in places where he had hoped to find her—and prayed he would not. No one had seen the beautiful lady; he was sure of that. He would have seen it in their eyes even if their lips lied, they were that much afraid of the lean nobleman with murder in his eyes. And no one knew where Willie was, either.

Despite his weariness, Crispin walked with tense wariness. Wrede, worried beyond jest, kept stride behind him. Crispin's fists were clenched to white knuckles. Waiting wasn't a thing he did well. But he couldn't see an alternative.

The two men climbed the steps to the house in silence—and were shocked to find the door ajar. Crispen cautiously pushed it all the way open, his breath stoppered, afraid of what he might find inside.

He only breathed again when he saw the footman's happy grin. And let out all his pent-up breath at once when he saw Stroud's wide and slightly drunken smile as he greeted them.

"Here. She's here. Our lady's in the parlor, my lor', although she's not eating bread and honey, not she." Stroud's speech was slurred, and he kept giggling. "Forgive me, my lor', but we was—we were just havin' a toast to the happy day. Although 'tis night, to be sure." He giggled again.

Crispin strode into his parlor, but stopped in the doorway and stared. Wrede laughed, a full-bodied laugh such as Crispin hadn't heard from him in years. Willie Grab stood in a circle of admirers, talking and waving his glass of ale for emphasis as Dulcie smiled down at him. But she stopped laughing when she looked up and saw them.

"Crispin!" she said, growing pale.

He said nothing. He went straight to her, opened his arms, and closed her tightly inside them. She felt his heart racing against hers as he hugged her hard, rocking her back and forth soundlessly.

Crispin's relief was so great that he couldn't speak; the words he had to say were so intimate that he dared not open his mouth for fear they might come tumbling out. He held her so close she found it hard to breathe, but it would have been hard for her to breathe anyway against the great flow of love she felt rising in her. He only let her go when he heard familiar laughter close by.

He released Dulcie and knelt down to face Willie squarely. "They told me at Newgate that you were gone," Crispin said.

"Yeah, well, *she* paid enough for my release," Willie said, looking up at Dulcie with pride. "She told the jailers it would be easy to lose a small boy in such a big place. She gave them all the money she had so they'd do it, and promised more to come later. But that ain't all she done. She got mad as thunder, but she stayed cool. You should have heard her!" he said with admiration, as he'd been saying to the household staff ever since he got back. "She even set *my* knees to knocking.

"'Release the boy or you will regret it, I assure you,' she says to them, grand as a duchess, cold as ice, and hot as hell. 'If you do not let him go, *you* will take his place on the morrow,' she says, cool as you please. Then, while they're thinking that out, she lowers the roof. She talks about every noble lady and gent in London town by their first names, like they took tea together every day, and every politician I ever heard of, too. The jailers get nervous, see. They talk about the warden, and so she asks why *he* has to know. Says if the warden knew, he'd want a share of their money, they knowed he would. Then she says it weren't like such things wasn't done all the time, which is true enough, too.

"Then she caps it by looking like she's lost her patience, and she says, '*I* am the Viscountess West. 'Twas *my* jewelry. He is *my* servant. And I shall have his release, or I vow you will live to regret this day!' And, I was out of there before they could stop shaking in their boots!" he crowed.

"And later, when I asked her how she done it so good, she said she was impersonating a nobleman. She said she thought of you, and it was easy," Willie said, looking at Wrede, mischief in his eyes. But Dulcie didn't smile, and neither did Crispin.

He straightened and looked at Dulcie. She wasn't celebrating. She was white-faced and still and stood with her head high, her back stiff, her hands clasped together in front of her.

"How did Harry trap you, child?" Wrede asked Willie, noting the tension between Dulcie and Crispin, his own eyes going from one to the other.

"Ah, well, Harry nosed on me," Willie said. "That is, he told on me."

"That was a fine way for you to repay the viscountess—by taking her gems," Wrede chided him. "I'm surprised at you."

Willie colored, but Dulcie spoke up quickly. "He didn't take them," she said quietly. "I gave them to him to sell for me."

"Ah," Wrede said, as Crispin winced.

"I needed money so I could leave, and they *were* my jewels, you see. Dulcie Blessing's jewelry and no one else's. I heard that I was no longer your viscountess, so Willie was right. What I did at Newgate *was* an impersonation. But

your name was all I had to keep Willie safe. I wouldn't leave
without him, and I used everything I had. Even something I
hadn't anymore. I'm sorry for my impudence," she told
Crispin, "but it was in a good cause, and don't worry, I
won't keep it up. I'll trouble you no more."

Crispin stepped toward her, but Wrede was there first.

"My dear lady, forgive me," Wrede said, taking her hand.
She bit her lip and looked away, but his voice was gentle and
sad.

"I almost got my foolish head blown off by your husband
this evening for my cruel meddling. And cruel it was,"
Wrede said. "I thought I was doing him a favor. I realize
now I was deluding myself. Loneliness loves company. I
think it was that which blinded me. I hope you will forgive
me. Crispin already has. He spared my life and took my
hand in friendship again. I hope you can be as merciful.

"Willie," Wrede said, turning to face the boy, "come with
me to the kitchens now, if you please, and leave these two
alone. I find myself devilish hungry after my exertions
today, and I reason that if anyone in this household knows
where the pies are when the cook is in bed, it is you."

The salon cleared in the blink of an eye, and Willie and
the earl ambled after the servants who were now returning
to their duties.

Dulcie turned as though to follow, but Crispin put a hand
on her shoulder and held her there.

"I didn't know," he said. "I swear on all that's holy I
didn't know until yesterday."

"Yes," she nodded, "but *I* didn't know until today."

"How could I tell you?" he asked in desperation. "I knew
what you'd think. I knew what I thought. Good God,
Dulcie! You knew what I wanted when we first made a
pretense of our marriage. But you must know what I feel for
you now. I didn't know that Wrede had been successful in
his attempt to have the marriage dissolved. When I found
out, I wanted to remedy the situation before you found out
about it. And I did so.

"Dulcie," he said, taking her by both shoulders and turning her to face him, "we *are* married. Now and forever. They had clapped poor old Featherstone up in Bedlam, but I had him reinstated and put in a home where he's safe—and likely cursing me, because no gin is allowed there. I bought the marriage register from Harry—well, from Jerome, actually, because Harry's afraid of me—with good reason," he added. "I have our wedding paper and the register. The vicar is as mad as a hatter, but the law says he's sane. There's no doubt of it: you are my wife again. I ran around town like a madman myself, but the deed is done. What more can I do?"

"Lady Charlotte knew that ours was a Fleet wedding. She said you told her," Dulcie said, her hurt still keen.

"I did not. I did a great many stupid things before I knew my heart, but not that. I am afraid that that was another indiscretion on the part of Wrede."

"But she is a lady," Dulcie persisted, her eyes searching his. "You could still have her."

He smiled, but his brilliant eyes were worried. "I have my lady," he said. "If you are not a lady, Dulcie Blessing West, I don't know what a lady is. And I don't care to know, either."

"I have no money," she said.

"Well, you did. And you would, if you didn't squander it on little boys."

Her smile was just a tiny, sad, and tentative lift of her lips, but it heartened him.

"Dulcie love," he said gently, "what shall I say? What would you have me do? I know!" he said with sudden inspiration. "Marry me. I mean marry me again—this time in a grand cathedral with everyone in London looking on. We'll never deny the truth about our first wedding. We couldn't. I suppose the news of that is as common in London as marmalade with morning toast by now. But we can celebrate it instead of ruing it. I certainly don't regret it. How could I? This marriage was the making of me."

He loosened his grip on her, but did not let her go. He cupped her shoulders gently, caressing her skin with his thumbs. He'd thought he'd lost everything once. Now he knew that wasn't true. With all he had, if she left him, he would have nothing at all. He chose his words with care.

"At first I thought our marriage was a bad bargain. Then I thought I'd make the best of it. Then I realized that the best was better than I'd ever known. Still, I didn't realize what I had until I lost it. I never want to go through that again. Never. I was half mad, I think, mostly because I was afraid of becoming sane again, without you. I didn't know where you'd got to, and I didn't want to think about the places you might have gone, although I searched everywhere for you. You are where you belong now: here. And here is where I want you to stay, Dulcie. Forever. With me.

"Maybe you think you don't need me," he said, his face grave. "After all, you're beautiful, bright, and strong. Look at today: I set out to slay a dragon—but found my lady had already done it. It's true. You would do well for yourself, by yourself. It's a hard world out there, but even so, you're capable of surviving in it. But there's so much more to life than surviving! Let me try to give you more. In a better world you might not need me at all. But I need you. Marry me again, Dulcie."

She looked deep into his eyes, resisting their lure, trying to get beyond their surface beauty so she could read his heart there. And then she risked hers.

"I'll always need you, Crispin," she blurted. "If you weren't here, this wouldn't be a better world for me. But you've never said you love me, and that drives me to distraction. I can't stop worrying about it. *Do* you love me? Or do you just like me and fear that I'll be hurt? Or maybe you're afraid that people will think badly of you if you leave me now. Or maybe you wonder if I'm going to have your baby. Or possibly you don't want to look foolish. Or . . ."

But now she could clearly read his mind. Joy was written

in every fine line of his face. His hands tightened on her shoulders. His eyes were tender. "I coursed over London today like a madman," he said. "I perjured myself and emptied my purse. I begged, threatened, and cajoled. I faced my best friend in a duel, prepared to die. Then when I didn't die, I wanted to, because I couldn't find you. I've been running since dawn and on into the night, and all for you. I turned my life inside out for you—and you're asking me if I love you? How could you not know?"

"Well," she said, raising her chin, "you never said it. Not ever. Not even once."

"Oh," he said, clearly ashamed of himself. "Well, that's because I'm a fool," he said quickly. "I love you, Dulcie. It's what I do best. Do you hear? I love your face, your body, and your mind. The day we met was the best day of my life. I don't want to think of another day without you. Or one more night. Now. Look you, wife: will you marry me?"

She didn't answer him immediately. But he was very pleased with her immediate response.

Eventually he raised his mouth from hers. When she had her breath back again, he caught his own long enough to insist on an answer. He held her tightly, tilted her head up so that she could meet his blazing eyes, and resisted her lips until he heard what she had to say.

"I have to hear your answer, Dulcie," he persisted. "Please!"

"Yes, I will marry you. Oh, yes, Crispin," she sighed against his mouth. "How I do love you!" And then he didn't let her say another thing.

They were on their way upstairs when they heard Wrede cough and Willie giggle, behind them. Only then did Crispin take his eyes off Dulcie.

"We're going to be married again. With all due pomp," he said, still not letting her go. "That ought to end the gossip, or at least make for some fresh romantic gossip. We don't have to say why we wed in the first place. Being carried away by passion is always a wonderful explanation for a wedding.

And it became true enough," he said more softly, meeting his wife's eyes and raising her hand to his lips.

"And as for you, bratkin," he told Willie, "we'll take responsibility for your upbringing. A guardianship, I think. We'll see to your education, send you to a proper school and make something of you."

"I don't think so," Wrede said.

They all stopped smiling and looked at him.

He clasped his hands behind his back and paced in front of them, his long nose in the air as he spoke. "You'll be burdened by a pack of your own brats before the lad's voice changes. He needs someone to be concerned solely with his affairs. I have no immediate plans to wed, and as they've discontinued Fleet weddings, I doubt I'll be able to find myself a bride as fine as Dulcie in the near future. Let me have the care of him.

"Then, too, we want to take full advantage of Willie's questionable gifts. If we send him to school now—as he is, as he speaks and acts—he'll have all the companionship that a leper might expect. That experience could turn him to a life of crime. Ah, but let me have the making of him for a year or so—say a grand tour of the Continent with me as his guide. I feel the need of travel now anyway. Yes, a tour would be the very thing. And then he can enter school already somewhat educated, and as a gentleman."

"*You*, Wrede?" Crispin asked doubtfully. Dulcie, too, looked worried.

"Who better?" Wrede asked, clearly affronted. "Who better to teach him fashion and the arts? Who else could expose the lad to the great minds and wonders of our world? What I don't know, after all, is not worth knowing. Whomever I do not know simply does not matter. I know men of wit and learning, title and achievement, everywhere in the civilized world. Let me take Willie in hand, introduce him to these men, and show him these wonders, and you will see what I make of him!

"The only reason I hesitate to do this—the *sole* reason,"

he told Willie seriously, "is that these two will be thrusting all their infants at me as they come of age, when they see what I have done with you."

"Wrede, your plan is fine with me," Crispin said, laughing. "Dulcie?"

"What do you say, Willie?" she asked.

"Fair enough," Willie said jauntily.

"Done! You'll have a new life, Willie," Crispin said with satisfaction.

At that, Willie stopped grinning for the first time. "Ah, as to that, my lord," he said, "if that's so, I'd like to have a new name, too. Yeah. I would."

Wrede's thin eyebrows went up. "But, my dear boy, I said nothing about adopting you," he said.

"No!" Willie said. "I don't wanna be your son! But I was thinking I'd need a new name, anyway. See, I don't got a real last name. They called me Willie Grab 'cause I was such a good dip—pickpocket, that is. Before that I was just Kid. I'd like something . . . finer."

"I see nothing wrong with Kidd," Wrede said thoughtfully, "William Kidd sounds very fine indeed."

"Nah. I was thinking I'd like a new first name, too. See, 'cause a new name is like another chance at life, ain't it? So I'd like to be Luke now, 'stead of Willie, if you please."

Dulcie drew in a sharp breath. Willie didn't hear her; he was too intent on watching Wrede's reaction. He looked very young and worried as he gazed up at the tall man who was going to be his guardian.

"Fine," Wrede said. "Very fine, in fact. Lucian Kidd it is, then."

Crispin looked questioningly at Wrede.

Wrede drew himself up. "Don't worry. I'll watch out for the lad," he said.

"Well, then, good night," Crispin said, and shook hands with him.

Willie said good night to Dulcie and added, for her ears

only, "Don't worry, my lady. I'll look out for my lord. You'll see."

"Well, then, Willie lad—ah, *Luke,*" Wrede said with pleasure as they left the hall together, "as for our itinerary— first, Italy, I think. Then we'll travel to Austria, Belgium, France . . . But Italy! Ah, what treasures I'll show you there."

"They'll suit," Crispin said with satisfaction, as he took Dulcie back into his arms. "Now let's see how we will," he whispered.

He led her to their room, and it took a very long time because of all the times they had to stop for kisses. He had even more for her when he kicked their door closed behind them. And she offered him more than that. Crispin forgot how weary he was, and Dulcie forgot how lonely she had been, and they both knew how fortunate they were.

"You still owe me the pearls," she said with drowsy content later, when they were finally drifting off to sleep.

"Yes. Wait!" he said, waking fully and rising from the bed. He padded over to his discarded clothes. "I've got something else for you."

She sat up in bed and watched as he took something from the breast pocket of his coat. He came back to the bed and laid it in her hands.

"Your gold piece?" she asked. "But I could never take that from you!"

"But you are the reason I earned it," he said, closing her hand over it. "It's what I was paid for marrying you. It was my luck, and now it's yours. I no longer need it, because you are my lucky piece."

"Thank you, I'm sure. Only you could pay me such a wonderful rude compliment," she said, and giggled.

But she fell asleep with the coin held tightly in her hand and with her husband's arms around her. They stayed that way all night and through all the nights of their long lives.